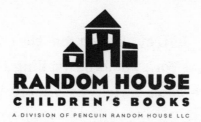

RANDOM HOUSE
CHILDREN'S BOOKS
A DIVISION OF PENGUIN RANDOM HOUSE LLC

TITLE:	Lucy & Andy Neanderthal
AUTHOR:	Jeffrey Brown
ILLUSTRATIONS:	B&W illustrations
IMPRINT:	Crown Books for Young Readers
PUBLICATION DATE:	August 2, 2016
ISBN:	978-0-385-38835-1
PRICE:	$12.99 U.S./$16.99 CAN.
GLB ISBN:	978-0-385-38837-5
GLB PRICE:	$15.99 U.S./$21.00 CAN.
EBOOK ISBN:	978-0-385-38836-8
PAGES:	224
AGES:	8–12

ATTENTION, READER: THESE ARE UNCORRECTED ADVANCE PROOFS BOUND FOR REVIEW PURPOSES. All trim sizes, page counts, months of publication, and prices should be considered tentative and subject to change without notice. Please check publication information and any quotations against the bound copy of the book. We urge this for the sake of editorial accuracy as well as for your legal protection and ours.

Please send any review or mention of this book to:
Random House Children's Books Publicity Department
1745 Broadway, Mail Drop 9-1
New York, NY 10019

rhkidspublicity@penguinrandomhouse.com

Dear Reader,

You already know Jeffrey Brown as the talented author/illustrator of the *New York Times* bestselling Jedi Academy and Darth Vader picture book series, with more than 1.4 million copies sold worldwide. But did you know that Jeffrey is also a fan of Neanderthals? After seeing a BBC series about them, he was hooked, and started reading and watching everything he could about them. Then he had a great idea. Wouldn't it be funny to write and illustrate a graphic novel series about two kids who lived 40,000 years ago?

Meet Lucy and Andy Neanderthal. They're just like you: They get into arguments. They have aches and pains. They don't always do their chores. They have to put up with bossy teens and clueless parents. They could be kids living today—except they make their own tools. And clothing (harder than it looks!). Lucy is an artist. Andy is longing to go on a mammoth hunt. But his first experience as a spectator is quite shocking (and hilarious).

We're delighted to welcome Jeffrey Brown to Crown Books for Young Readers/Random House with his fresh new send-up of the first cave dwellers. We promise, it's nothing like *The Flintstones*!

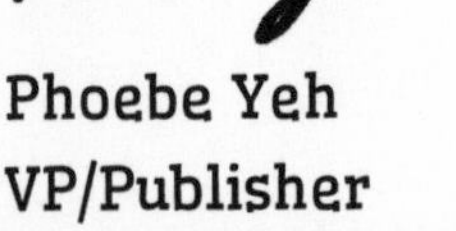

Phoebe Yeh
VP/Publisher
Crown Books for Young Readers

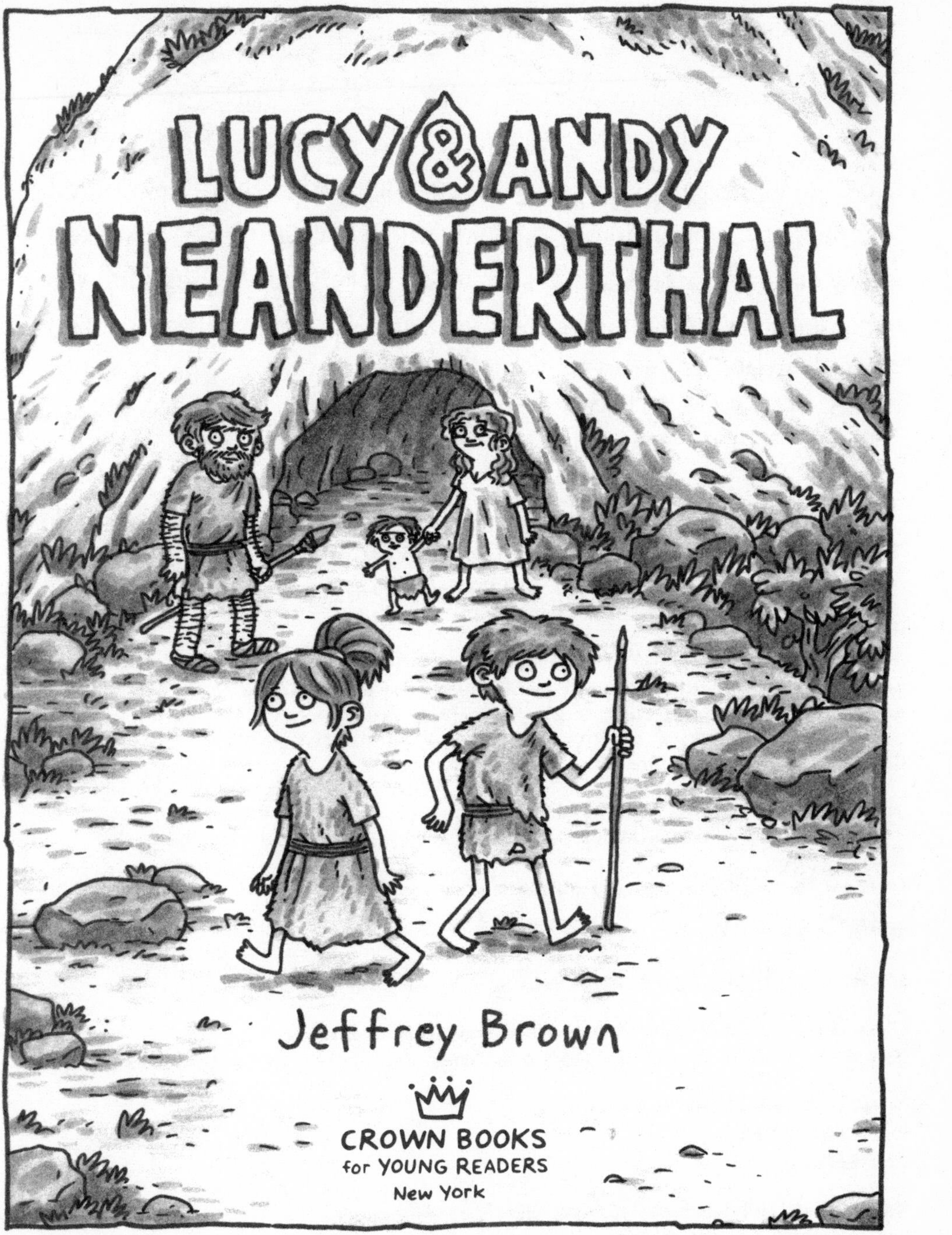
LUCY & ANDY
NEANDERTHAL
Jeffrey Brown
CROWN BOOKS
for YOUNG READERS
New York

What do you think all this writing is for, Eric?

Thank you to my family, friends, publishers, and readers for all of their supports. Thanks also to Marc, Phoebe, and everyone at RH for making this book happen. And special thanks to Kevin Lee for giving me the nudge that led to the idea for this book.

For his expert assistance, grateful acknowledgement to Jonathan S. Mitchell, PhD, Evolutionary Biology, and member of the Geological Society of America, Society of Vertebrate Paleontology, and Society for the Study of Evolution.

All rights reserved. Published in the United States by Crown Books for Young Readers, an imprint of Random House Children's Books, a division of Penguin Random House LLC, New York.

Crown and the colophon are registered trademarks of Penguin Random House LLC.

Visit us on the Web! randomhousekids.com

Educators and librarians, for a variety of teaching tools, visit us at RHTeachersLibrarians.com

Library of Congress Cataloging-in-Publication Data is available upon request.
ISBN 978-0-385-38835-1 (trade) — ISBN 978-0-385-38837-5 (lib. bdg.) — ISBN 978-0-385-38836-8 (ebook)

Printed in the United States of America
10 9 8 7 6 5 4 3 2 1
First Edition

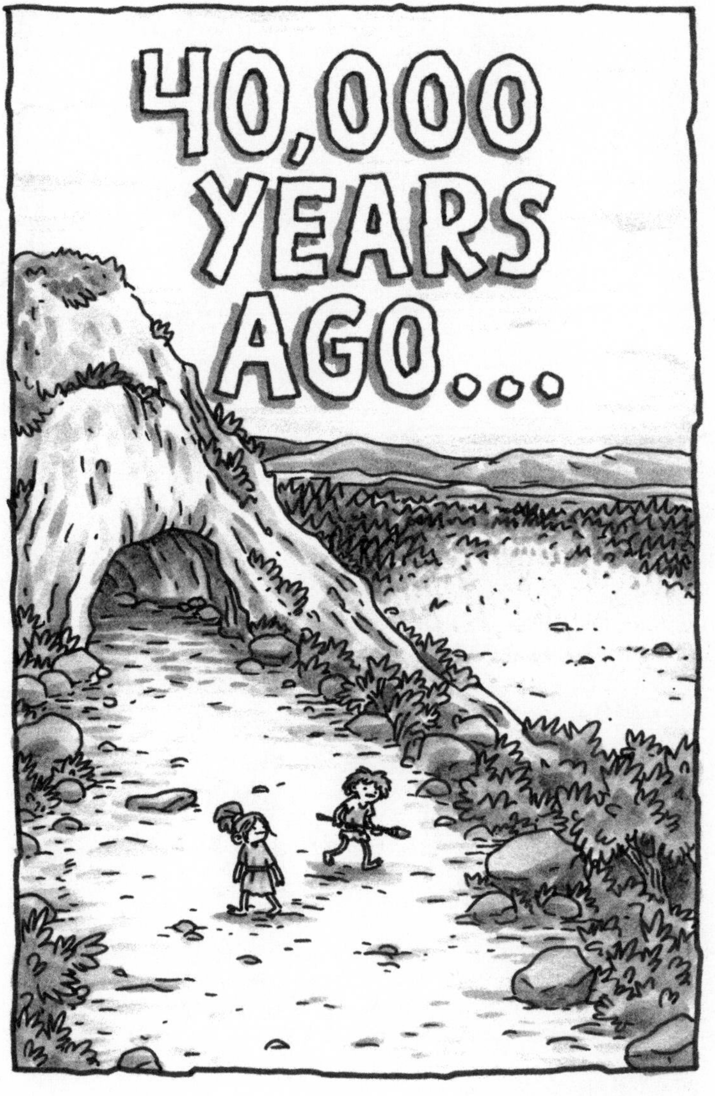
40,000 YEARS AGO...

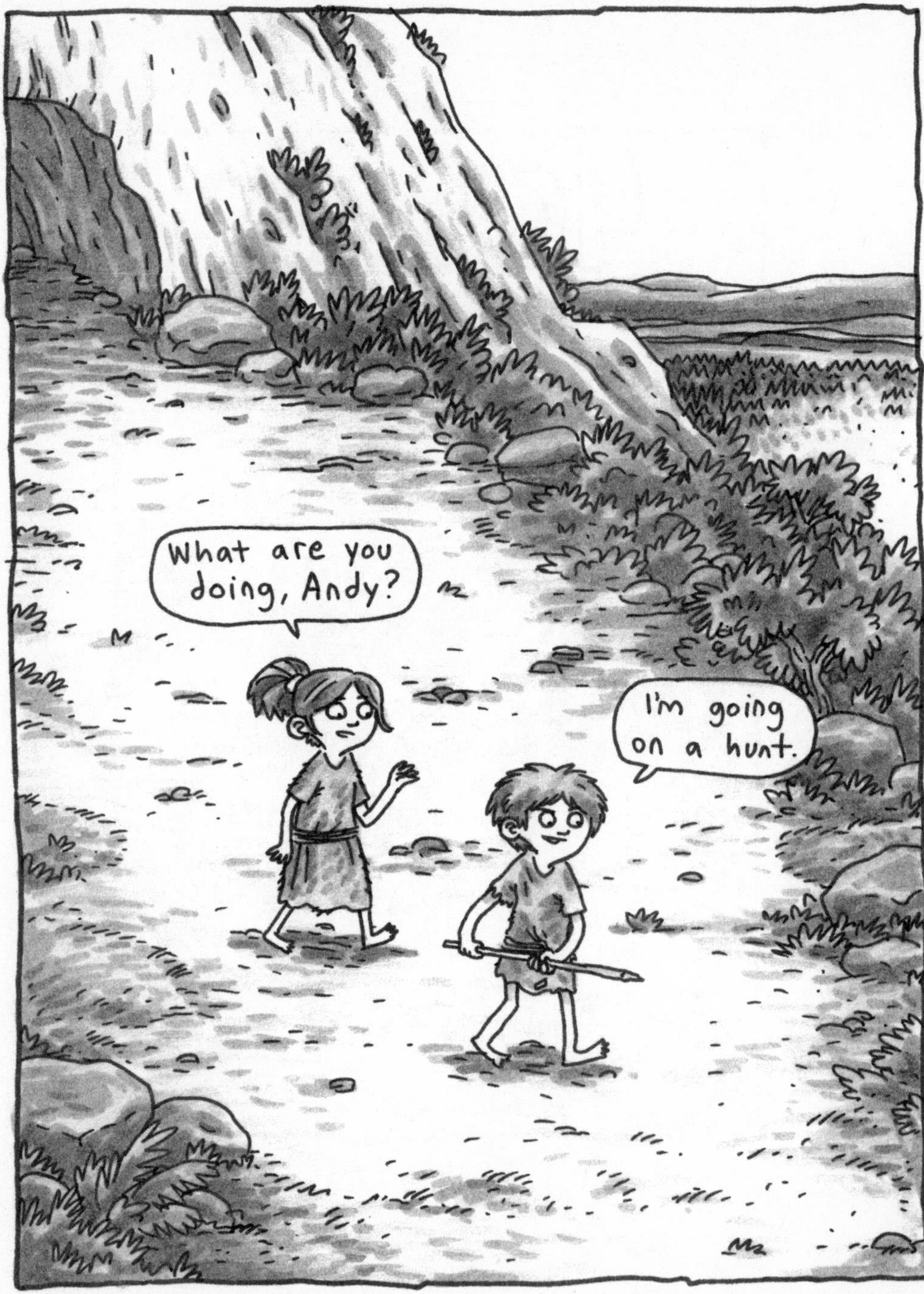
What are you doing, Andy?
I'm going on a hunt.

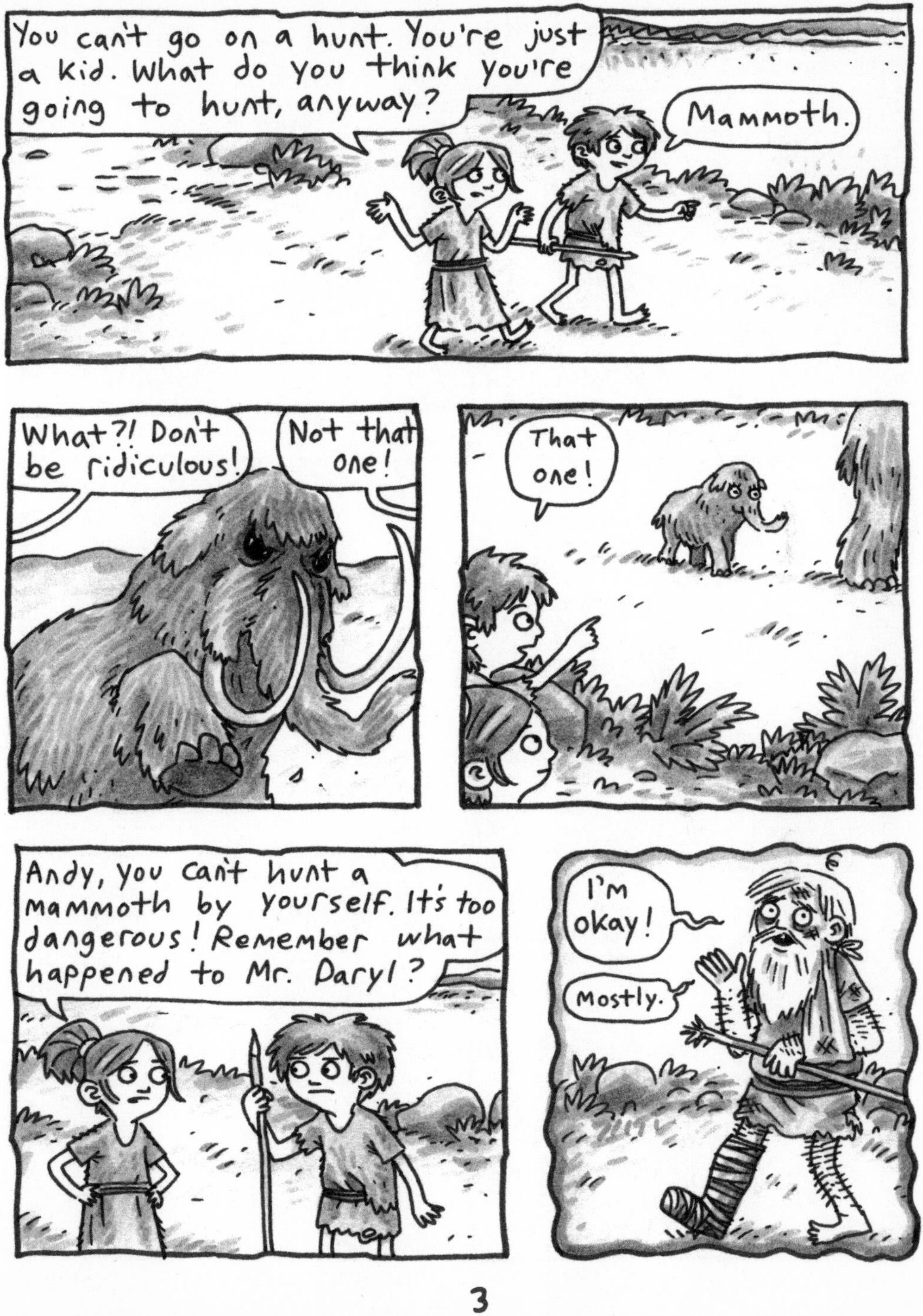
You can't go on a hunt. You're just a kid. What do you think you're going to hunt, anyway?
Mammoth.
What?! Don't be ridiculous!
Not that one!
That one!
Andy, you can't hunt a mammoth by yourself. It's too dangerous! Remember what happened to Mr. Daryl?
I'm okay!
Mostly.

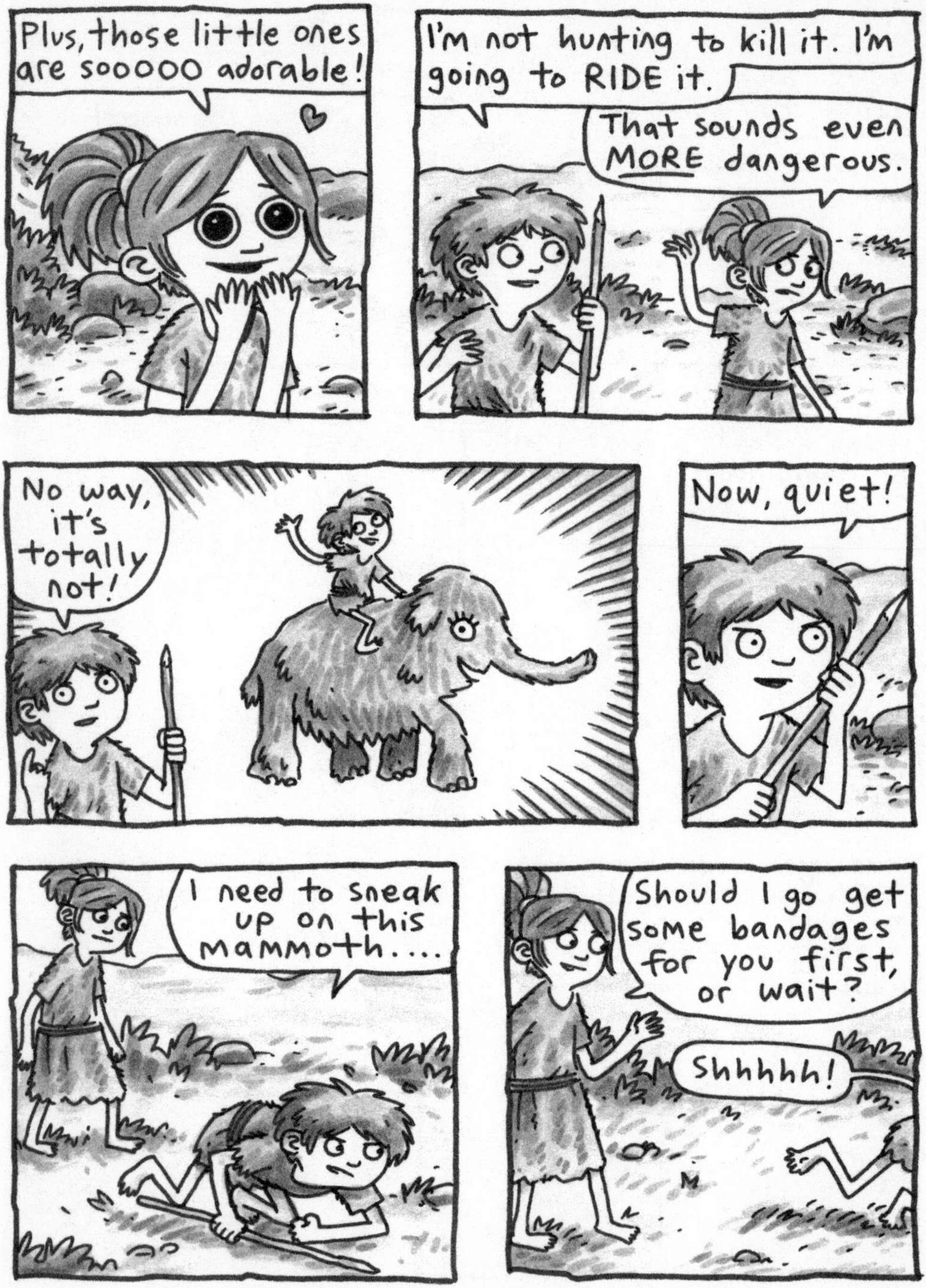
Plus, those little ones are sooooo adorable!
I'm not hunting to kill it. I'm going to RIDE it.
That sounds even MORE dangerous.
No way, it's totally not!
Now, quiet!
I need to sneak up on this mammoth....
Should I go get some bandages for you first, or wait?
Shhhhh!

After a brief interruption, the hunter once again identifies his prey....

Silently, he creeps closer....

Waiting for the perfect moment, he prepares to pounce on his unsuspecting quarry....

MREEEEOWWRRRRR!

YEOWCH!

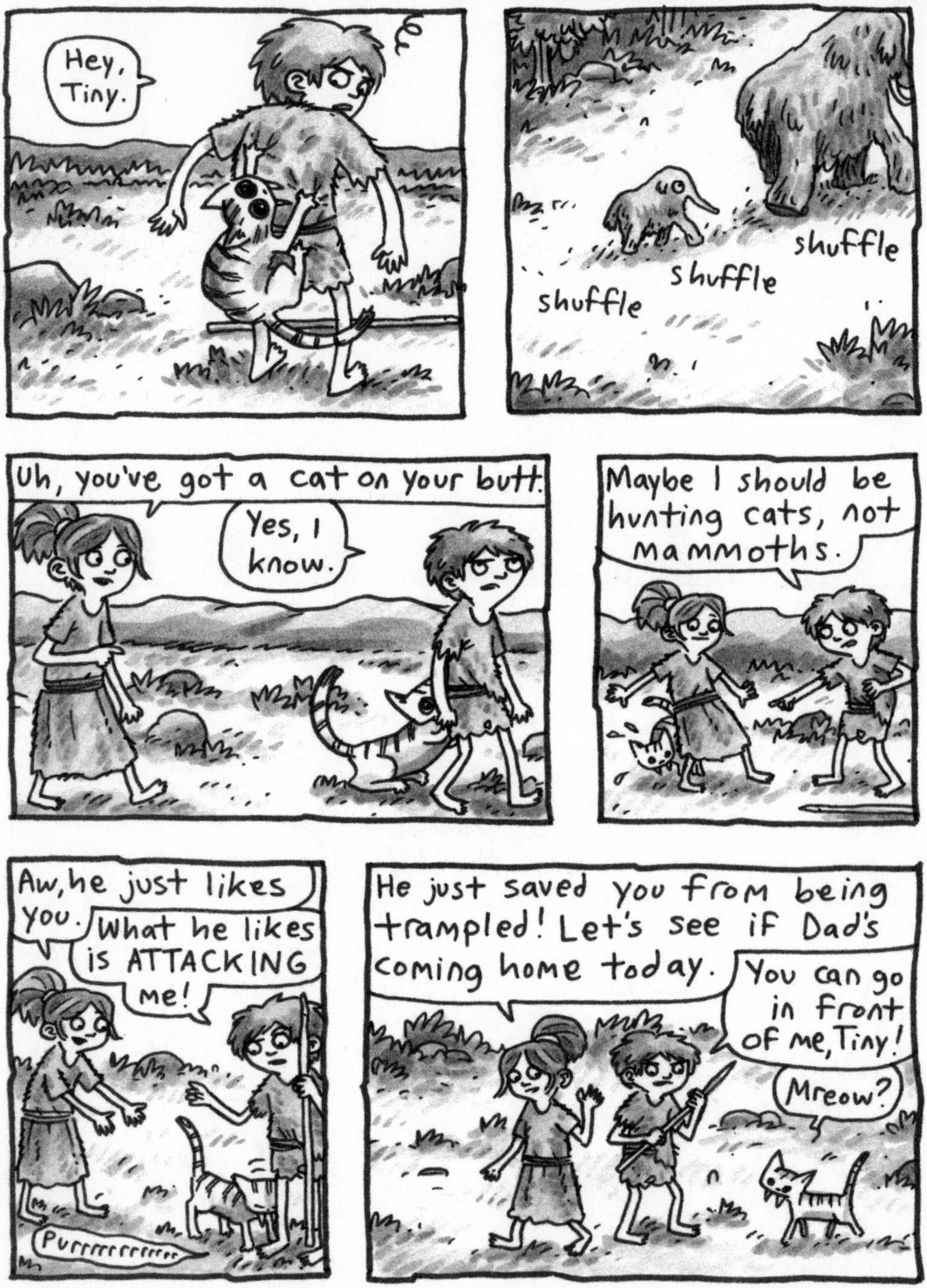
Hey, Tiny.
shuffle
shuffle
shuffle
Uh, you've got a cat on your butt.
Yes, I know.
Maybe I should be hunting cats, not mammoths.
Aw, he just likes you.
What he likes is ATTACKING me!
Purrrrrrrrrrr
He just saved you from being trampled! Let's see if Dad's coming home today.
You can go in front of me, Tiny!
Mreow?

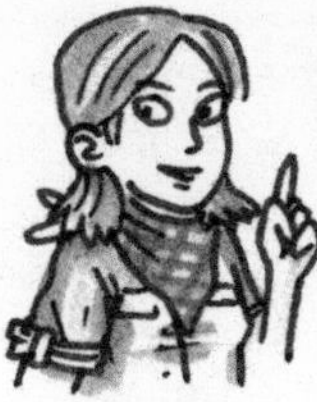

ACTUALLY, Neanderthals probably didn't have pet cats, because there were no house cats 40,000 years ago. The cats back then tended to be a lot bigger. Their pounces were much less friendly!

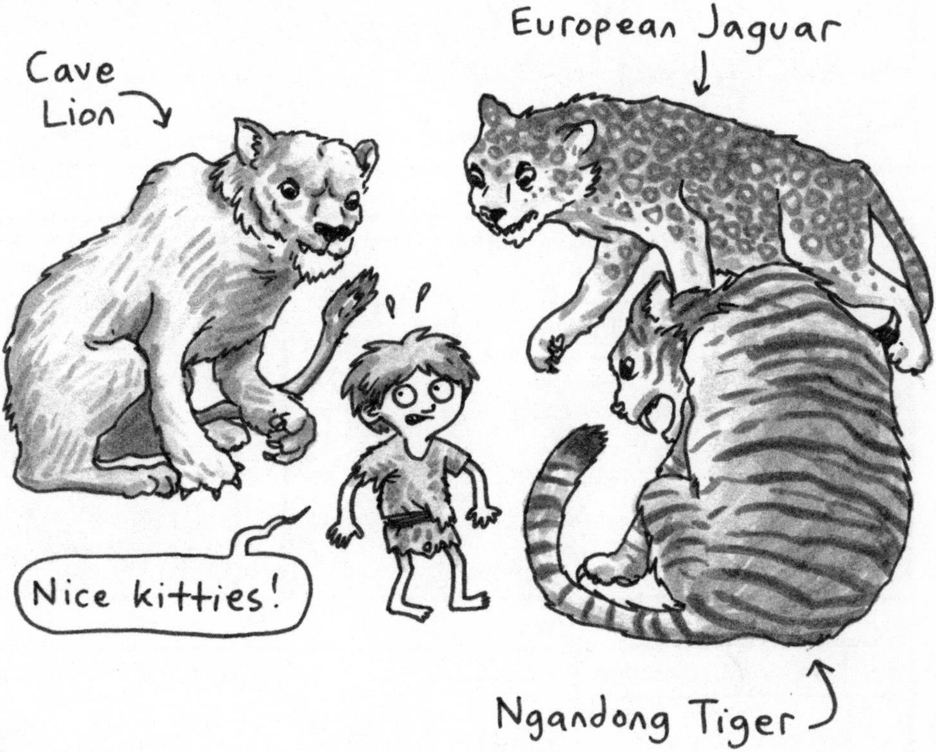

European Jaguar
Cave Lion
Nice kitties!
Ngandong Tiger

The sabertooth cat Smilodon didn't live in the same places as Neanderthals, but the smaller Homotherium—scimatar cat—did. It wasn't as tiny as a house cat in reality, though.

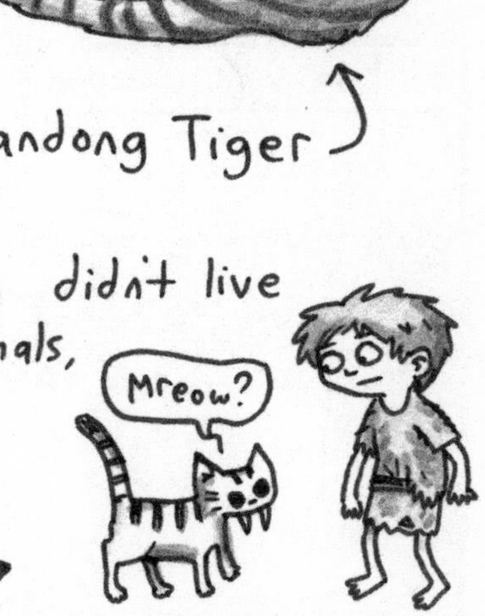

Mreow?

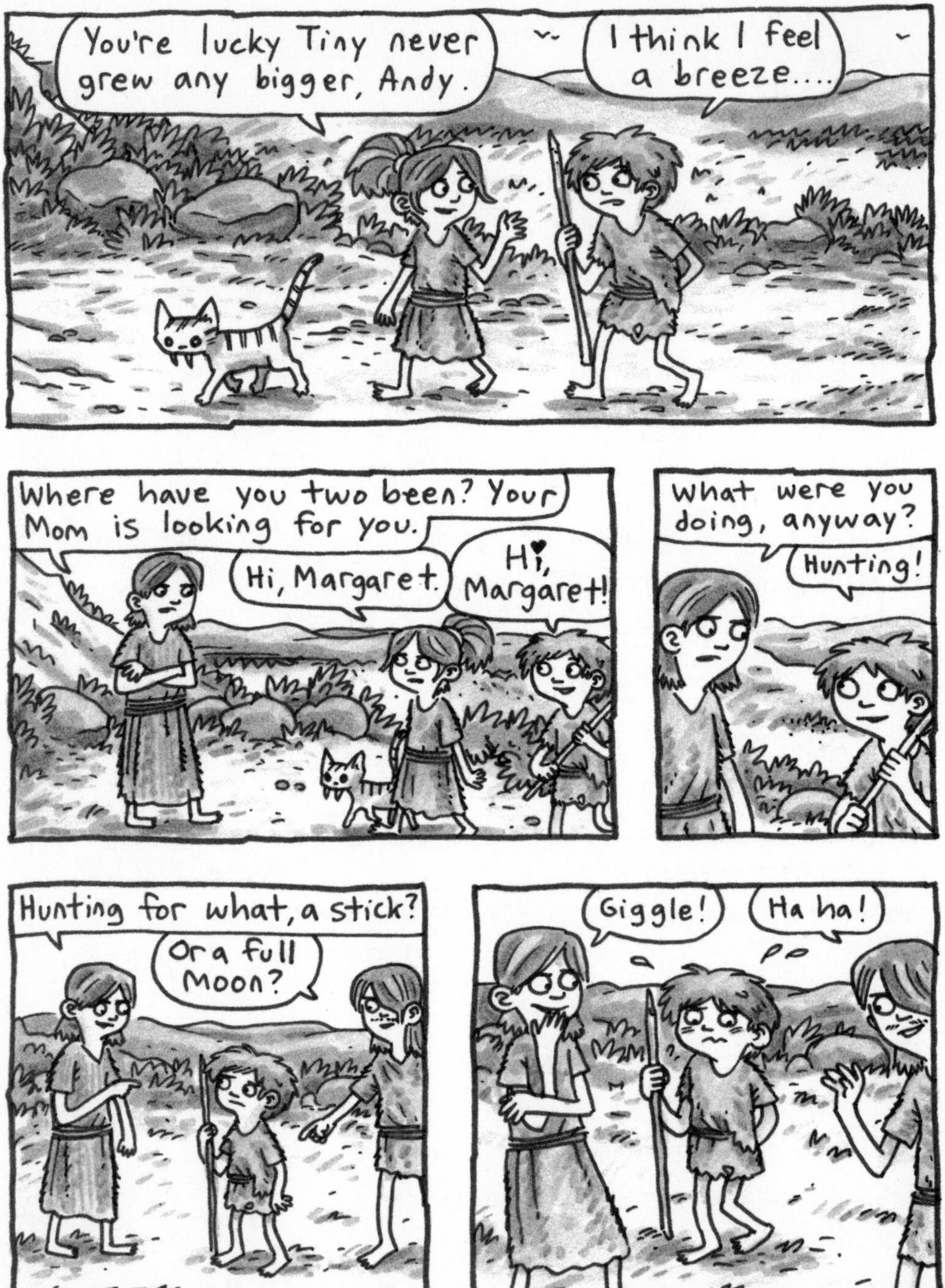
You're lucky Tiny never grew any bigger, Andy.
I think I feel a breeze....
Where have you two been? Your Mom is looking for you.
Hi, Margaret.
Hi, Margaret!
What were you doing, anyway?
Hunting!
Hunting for what, a stick?
Or a full Moon?
Giggle!
Ha ha!

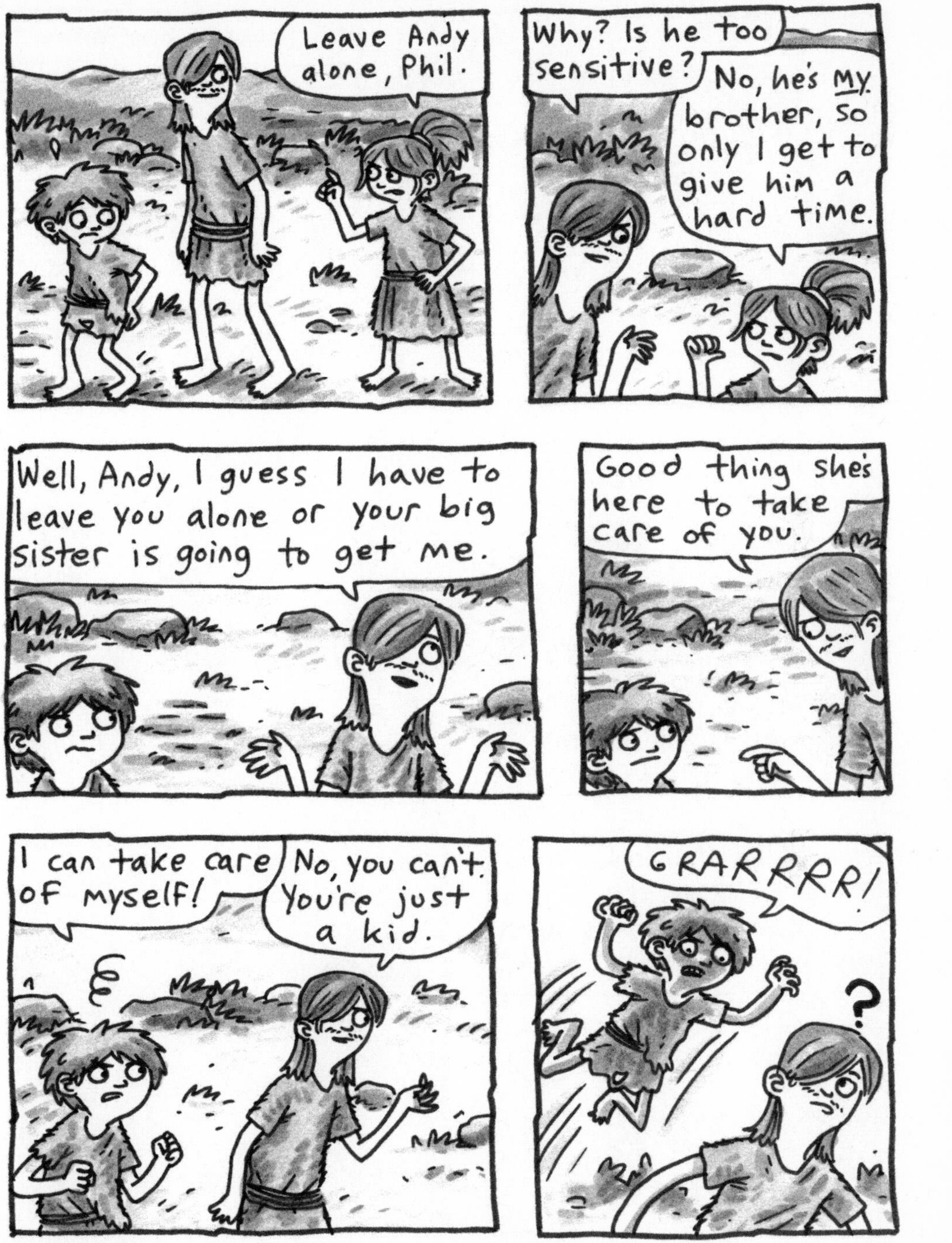
Leave Andy alone, Phil.
Why? Is he too sensitive?
No, he's MY brother, so only I get to give him a hard time.
Well, Andy, I guess I have to leave you alone or your big sister is going to get me.
Good thing she's here to take care of you.
I can take care of myself!
No, you can't. You're just a kid.
GRARRRR!
?

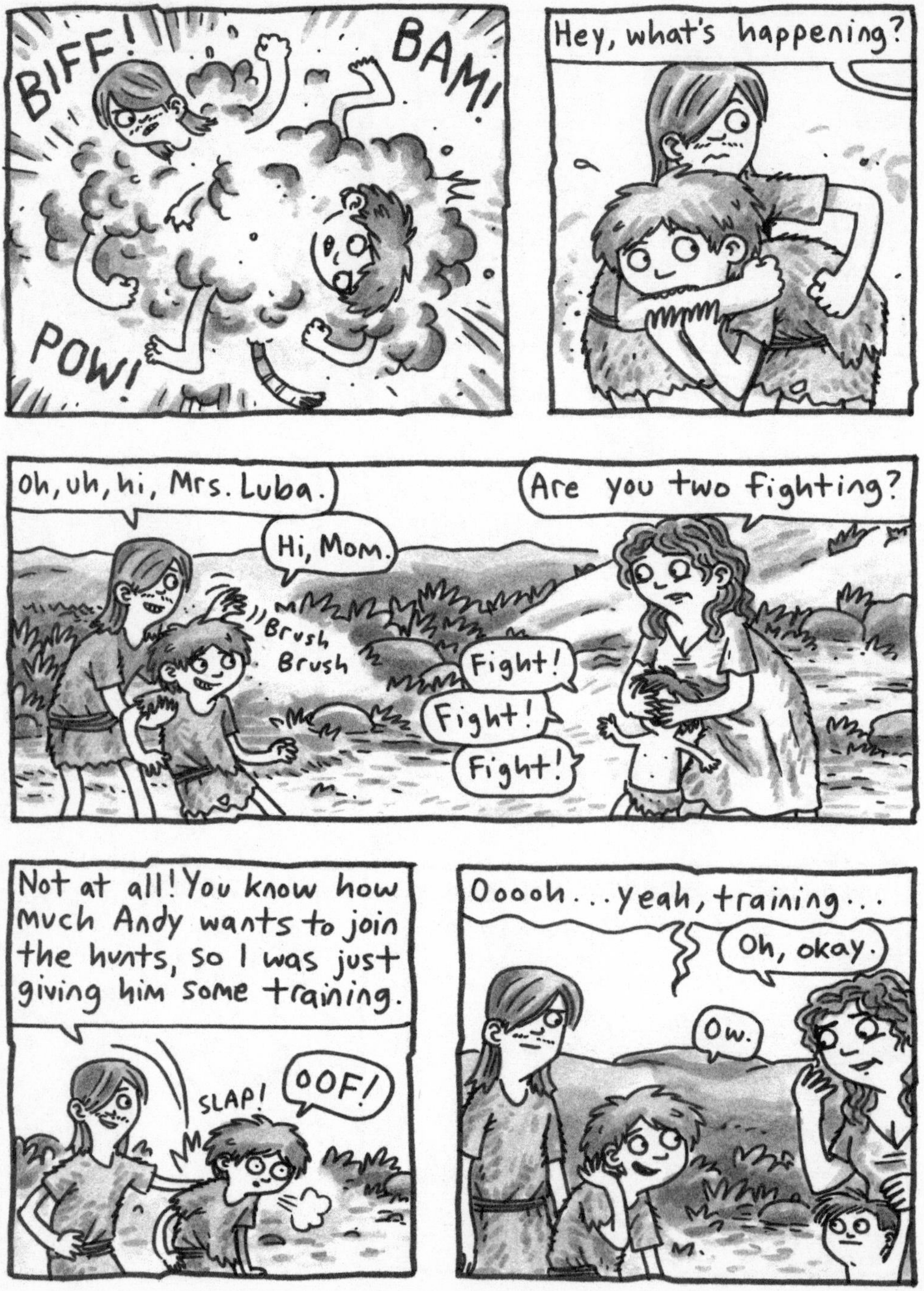
BIFF!
BAM!
POW!
Hey, what's happening?
Oh, uh, hi, Mrs. Luba.
Hi, Mom.
Brush
Brush
Are you two fighting?
Fight!
Fight!
Fight!
Not at all! You know how much Andy wants to join the hunts, so I was just giving him some training.
SLAP!
OOF!
Ooooh... yeah, training...
Oh, okay.
Ow.

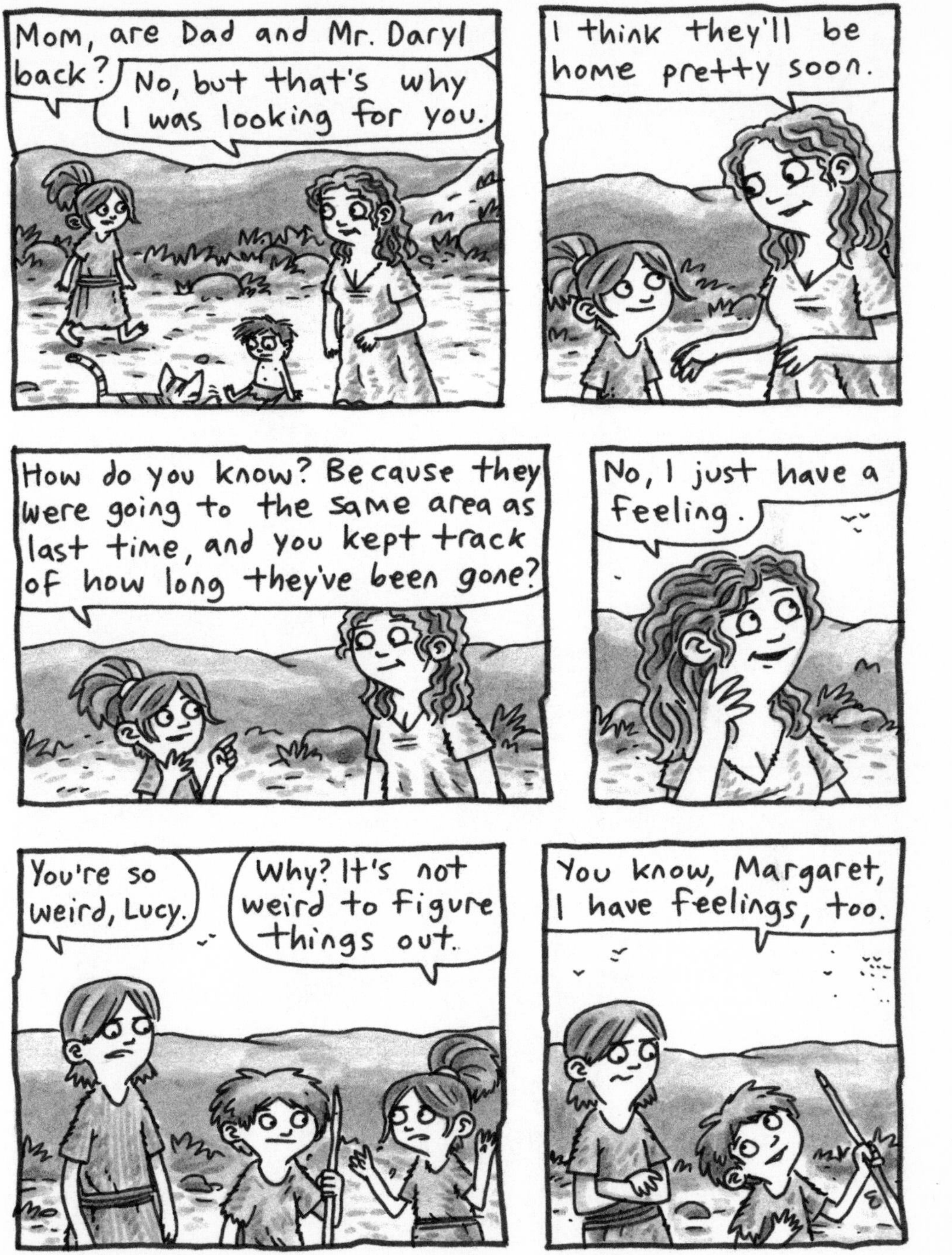
Mom, are Dad and Mr. Daryl back?
No, but that's why I was looking for you.
I think they'll be home pretty soon.
How do you know? Because they were going to the same area as last time, and you kept track of how long they've been gone?
No, I just have a feeling.
You're so weird, Lucy.
Why? It's not weird to figure things out.
You know, Margaret, I have feelings, too.

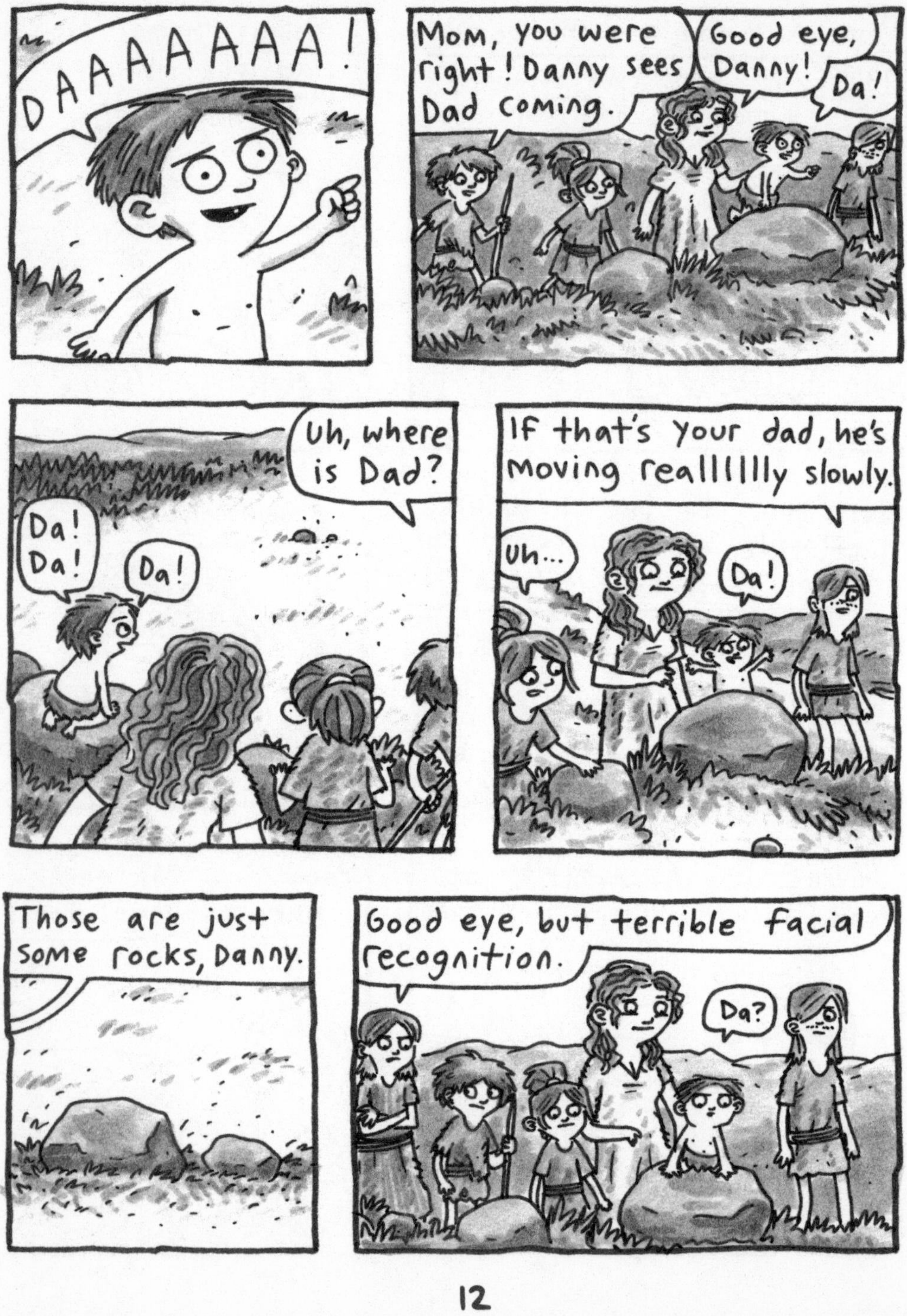
DAAAAAAA!
Mom, you were right! Danny sees Dad coming.
Good eye, Danny!
Da!
Uh, where is Dad?
Da! Da!
Da!
If that's your dad, he's moving realllllly slowly.
Uh...
Da!
Those are just some rocks, Danny.
Good eye, but terrible facial recognition.
Da?

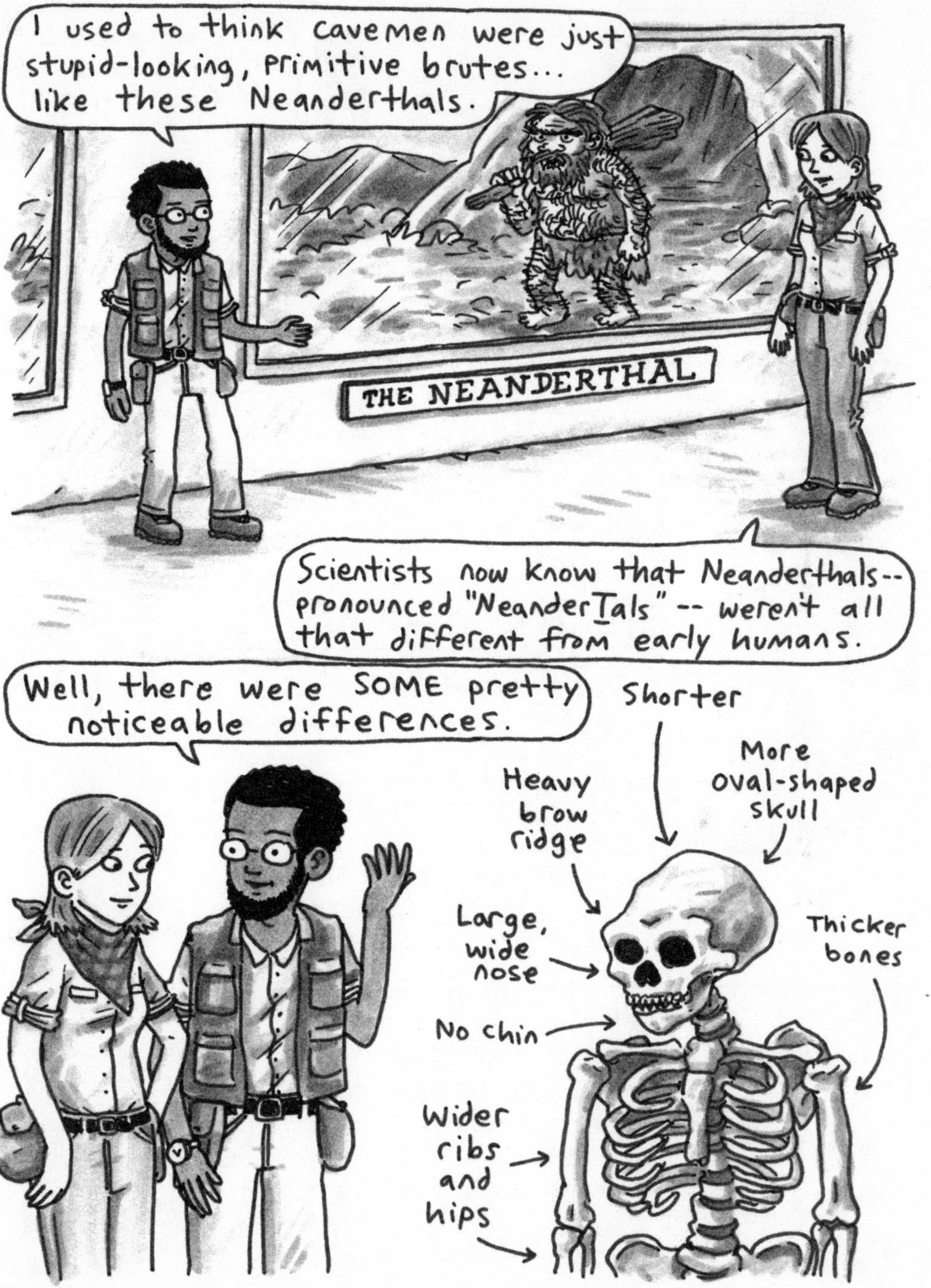

I used to think cavemen were just stupid-looking, primitive brutes... like these Neanderthals.
THE NEANDERTHAL
Scientists now know that Neanderthals-- pronounced "NeanderTals" -- weren't all that different from early humans.
Well, there were SOME pretty noticeable differences.
Shorter
More oval-shaped skull
Heavy brow ridge
Large, wide nose
Thicker bones
No chin
Wider ribs and hips

Scientists also thought Neanderthals only communicated by grunting. Now we know they could talk.

They were skilled hunters and cooked on fire hearths, just like early humans.

In fact, early humans and Neanderthals were alike enough that they even had kids together sometimes!

That would make Neanderthals our great, great, great, great, great, great, great...

You'll have to say "great" about 2,000 times.

LATER THAT DAY...

...great, great, great, great...

MUCH LATER THAT DAY...

...great, great, great, great grandparents!

Even if our research shows that the hairy, hunched-over, and dimwitted Neanderthal "caveman" is an inaccurate depiction...

We can still only imagine what life must have been like for them.

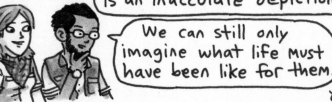

CAVE
SWEET
CAVE

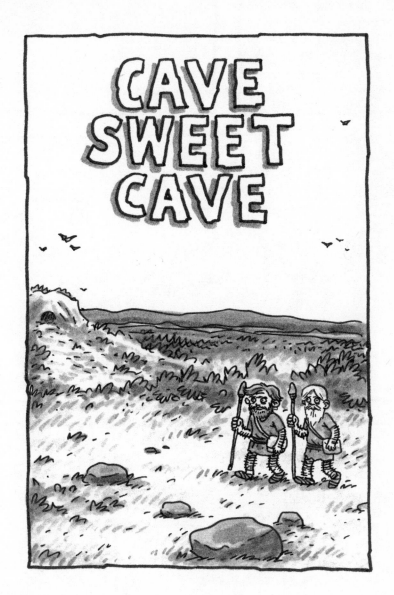

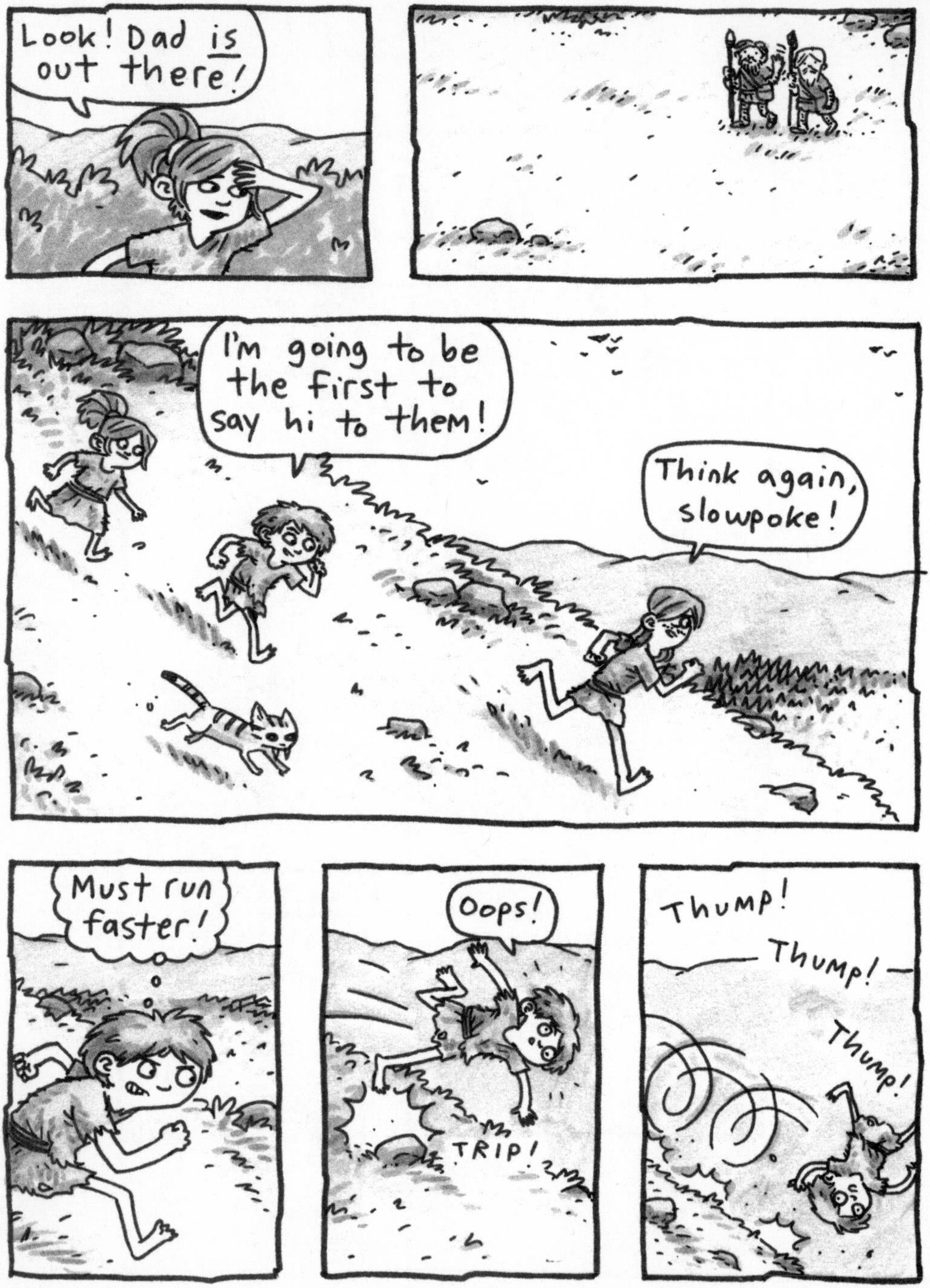
Look! Dad is out there!
I'm going to be the first to say hi to them!
Think again, slowpoke!
Must run faster!
Oops!
TRIP!
Thump!
Thump!
Thump!

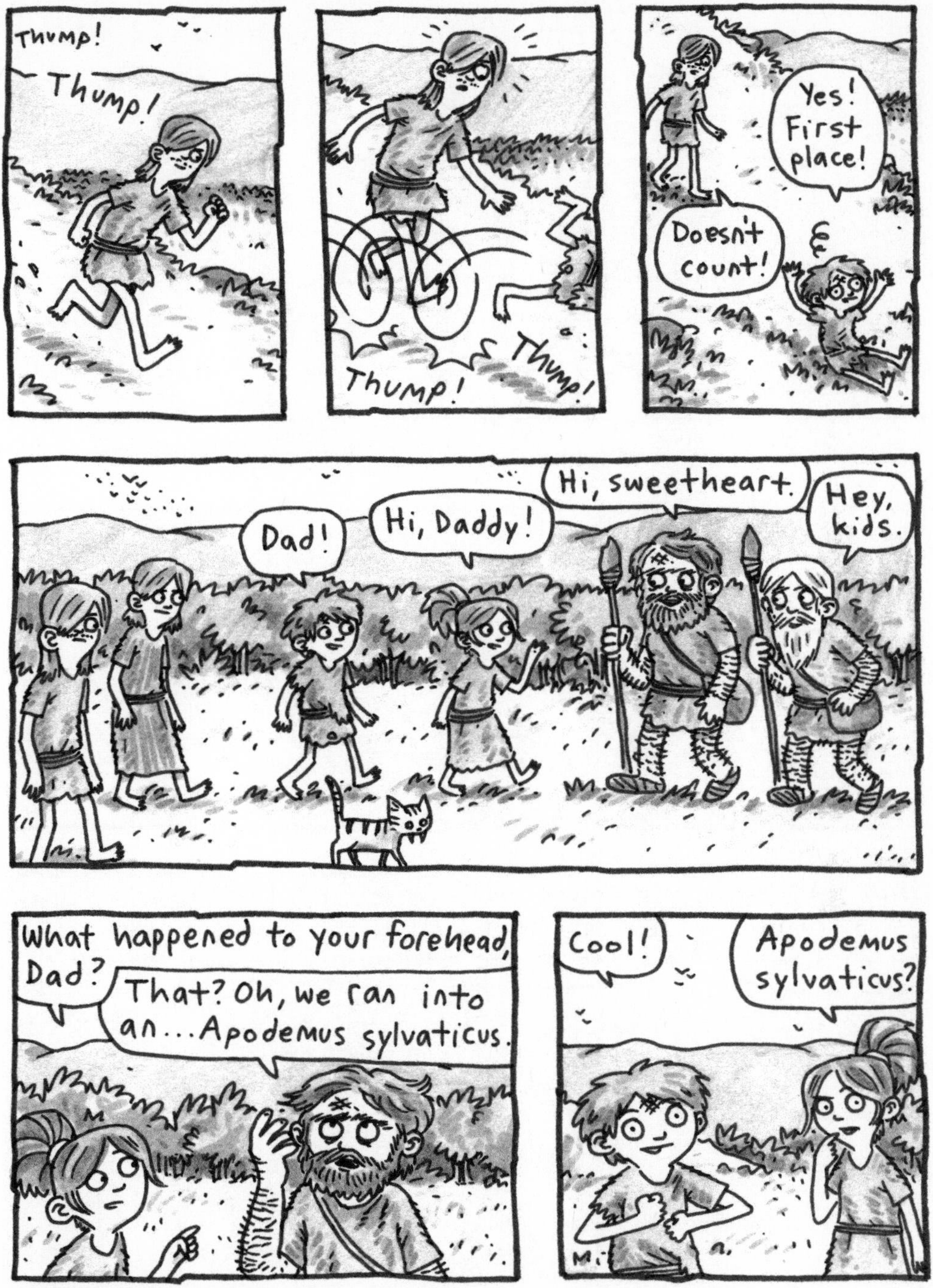
THUMP!
Thump!
THUMP!
Thump!
Yes! First place!
Doesn't count!
Dad!
Hi, Daddy!
Hi, sweetheart.
Hey, kids.
What happened to your forehead, Dad?
That? Oh, we ran into an... Apodemus sylvaticus.
Cool!
Apodemus sylvaticus?

Apodemus sylvaticus (common name: wood mouse)

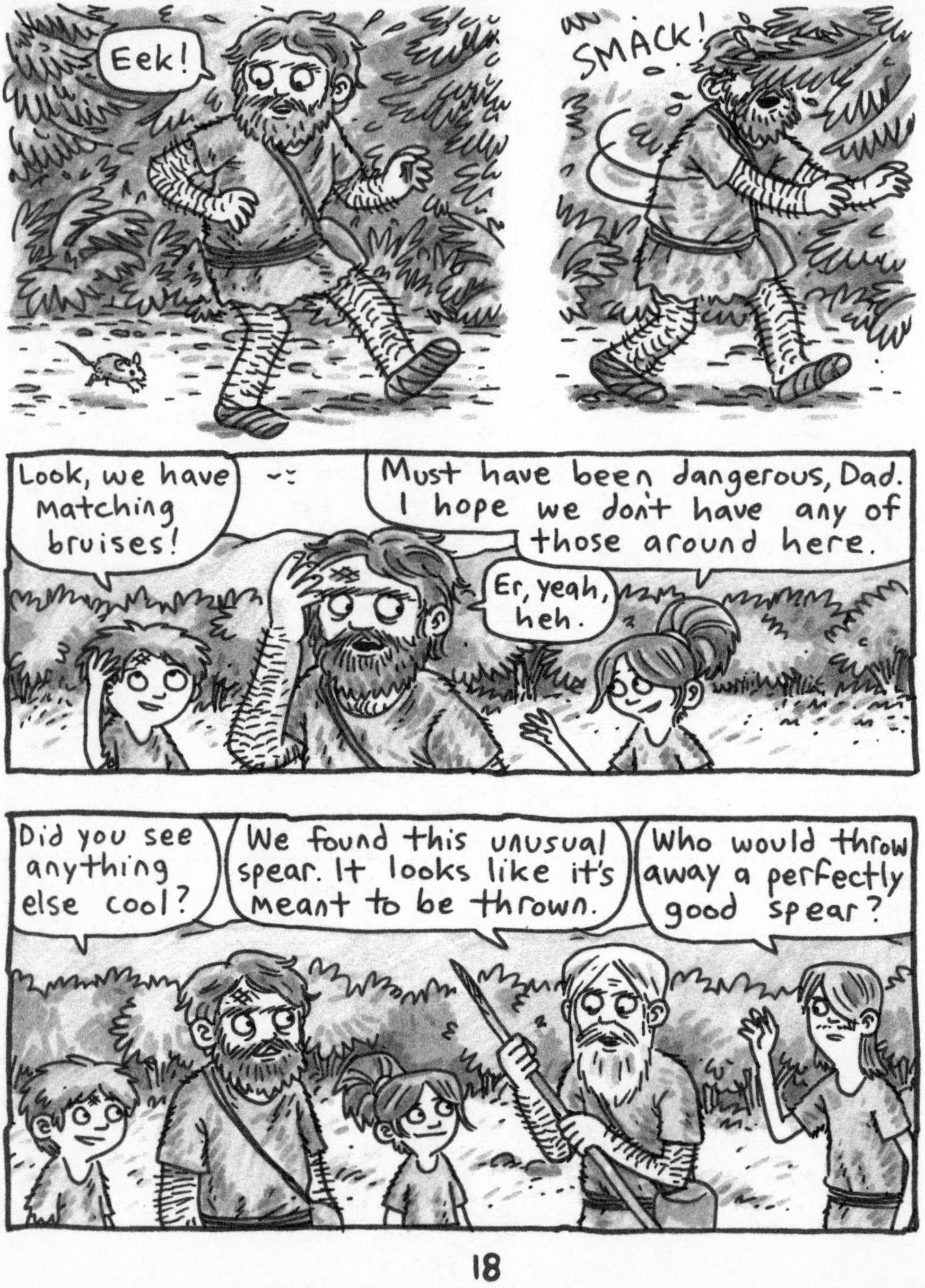
Eek!
SMACK!
Look, we have matching bruises!
Must have been dangerous, Dad. I hope we don't have any of those around here.
Er, yeah, heh.
Did you see anything else cool?
We found this unusual spear. It looks like it's meant to be thrown.
Who would throw away a perfectly good spear?

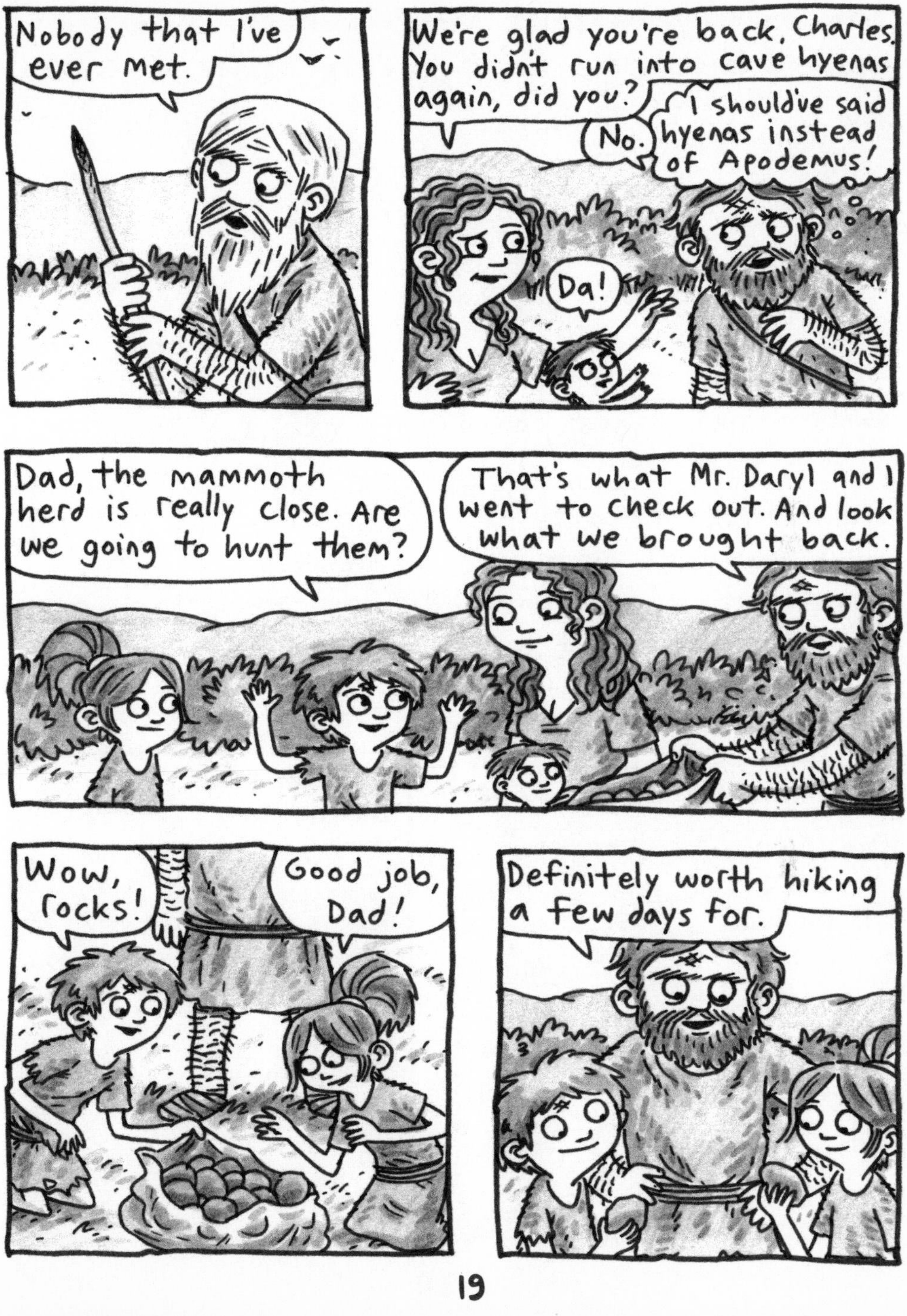
Nobody that I've ever met.
We're glad you're back, Charles. You didn't run into cave hyenas again, did you?
No.
I should've said hyenas instead of Apodemus!
Da!
Dad, the mammoth herd is really close. Are we going to hunt them?
That's what Mr. Daryl and I went to check out. And look what we brought back.
Wow, rocks!
Good job, Dad!
Definitely worth hiking a few days for.

The Stone Age gets its name from the material used at that time for toolmaking: Stone, of course!

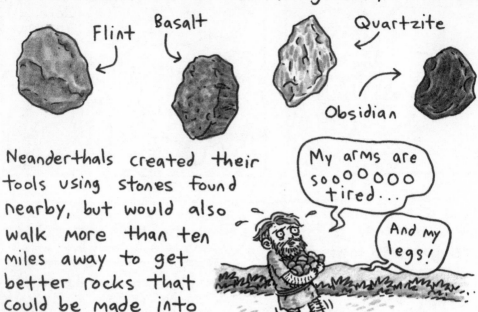

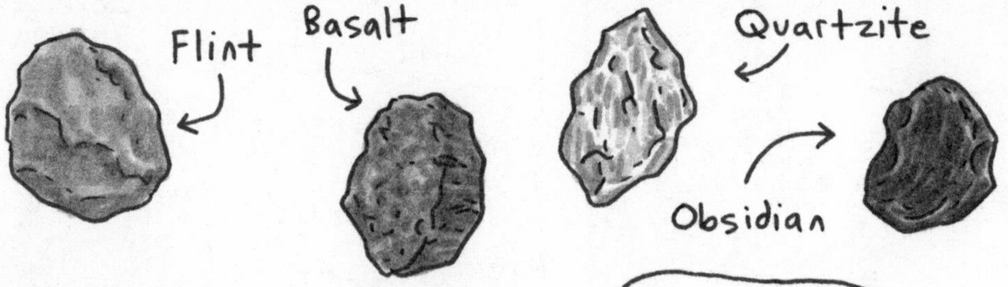
Flint
Basalt
Quartzite
Obsidian

Neanderthals created their tools using stones found nearby, but would also walk more than ten miles away to get better rocks that could be made into higher-quality tools.

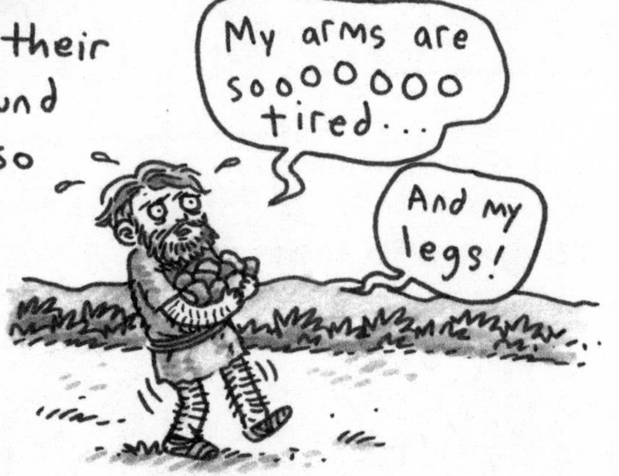
My arms are soooOOOOO tired...
And my legs!

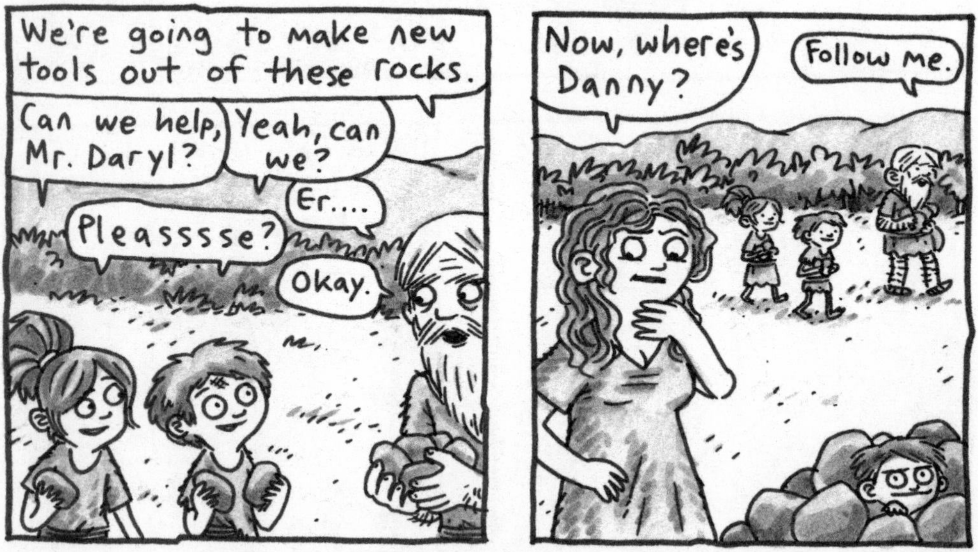
We're going to make new tools out of these rocks.
Can we help, Mr. Daryl?
Yeah, can we?
Er....
Pleasssse?
Okay.
Now, where's Danny?
Follow me.

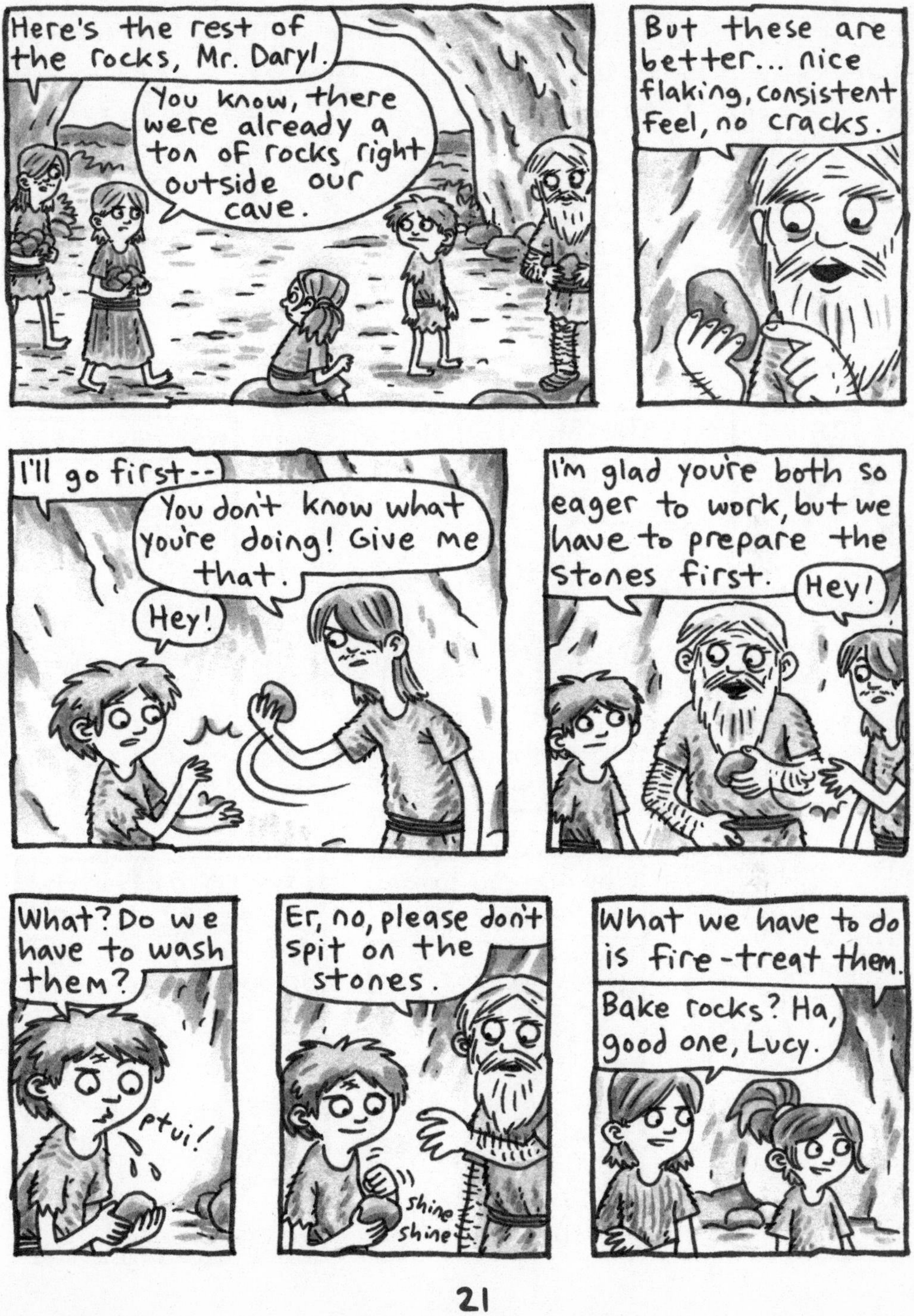
Here's the rest of the rocks, Mr. Daryl.
You know, there were already a ton of rocks right outside our cave.
But these are better... nice flaking, consistent feel, no cracks.
I'll go first--
You don't know what you're doing! Give me that.
Hey!
I'm glad you're both so eager to work, but we have to prepare the stones first.
Hey!
What? Do we have to wash them?
ptui!
Er, no, please don't spit on the stones.
shine shine
What we have to do is fire-treat them.
Bake rocks? Ha, good one, Lucy.

Lucy's right. We have to bury the stones under a fire, and afterward they'll be easier to work with.

Bury Bury

How long will this take?

Only a little while.

A LITTLE WHILE LATER...

Is it ready?

Not yet.

LATER THAN THAT...

Is it —

No.

STILL LATER...

Nope.

WAY, WAY LATER

Andy... ANDY! Wake up!

Zzzzz

The rocks are ready.

Huh? Oh, I was dreaming.

rub rub

Why are you looking at me like that?

I'm still dreaming.

You're definitely dreaming.

Are you dreaming, too?

Yes. I'm having a nightmare.

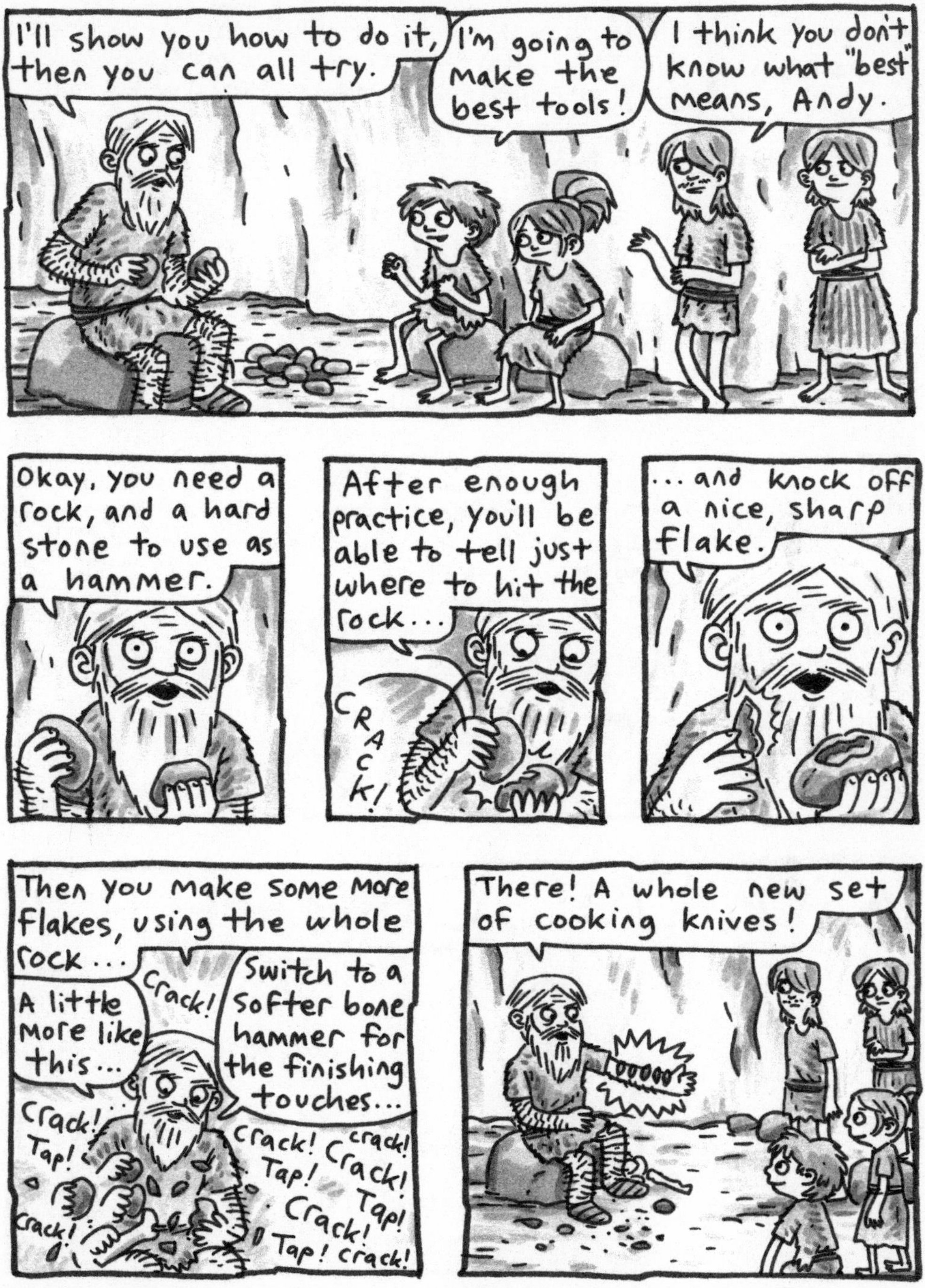
I'll show you how to do it, then you can all try.
I'm going to make the best tools!
I think you don't know what "best" means, Andy.
Okay, you need a rock, and a hard stone to use as a hammer.
After enough practice, you'll be able to tell just where to hit the rock...
CRACK!
...and knock off a nice, sharp flake.
Then you make some more flakes, using the whole rock...
Crack!
A little more like this...
Switch to a softer bone hammer for the finishing touches...
Crack! Tap! Crack!
Crack! crack! Crack! Tap! Tap! Crack! Tap! crack!
There! A whole new set of cooking knives!

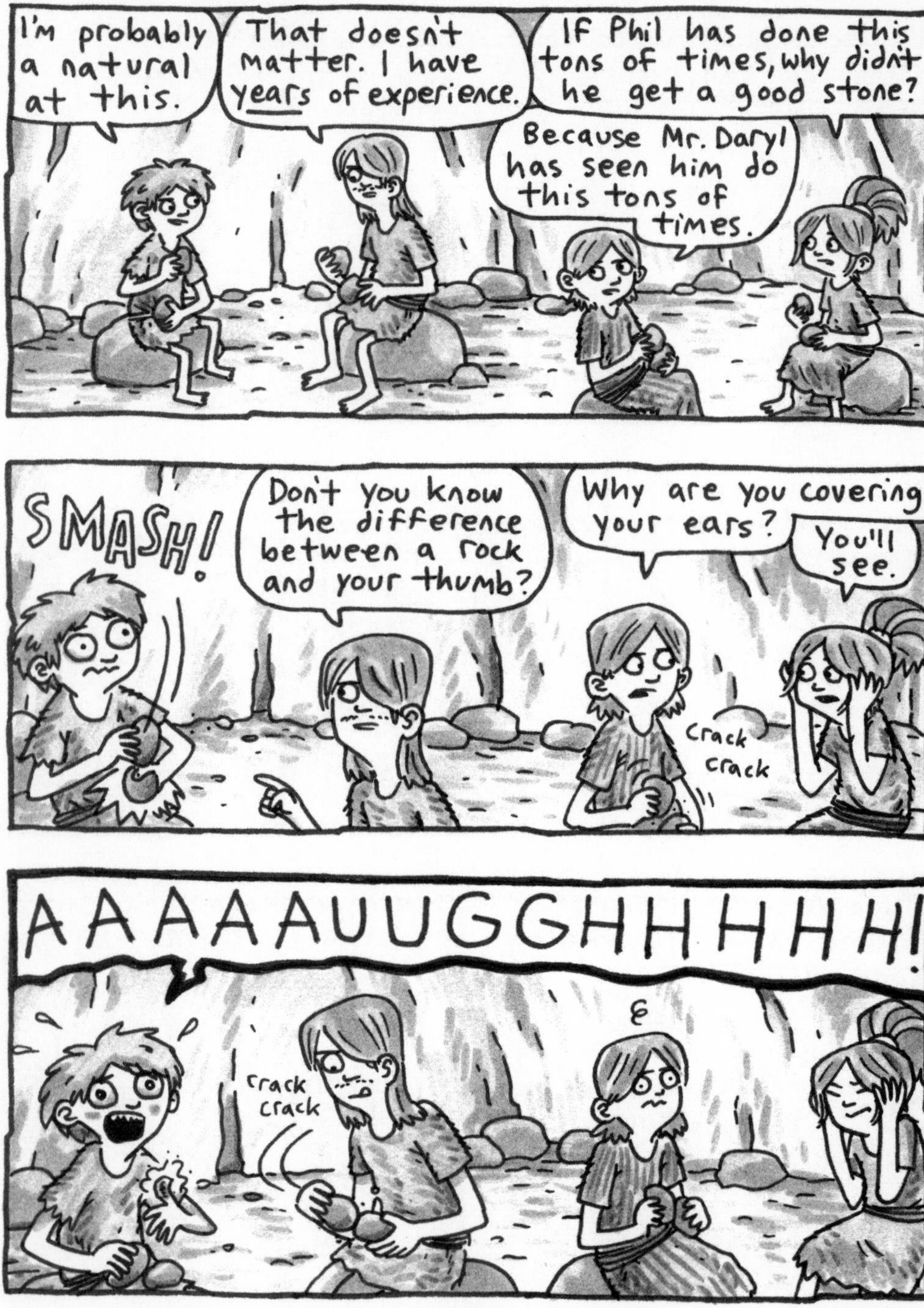

I'm probably a natural at this.
That doesn't matter. I have years of experience.
If Phil has done this tons of times, why didn't he get a good stone?
Because Mr. Daryl has seen him do this tons of times.
SMASH!
Don't you know the difference between a rock and your thumb?
Why are you covering your ears?
You'll see.
crack crack
AAAAAUUGGHHHHH!
crack crack

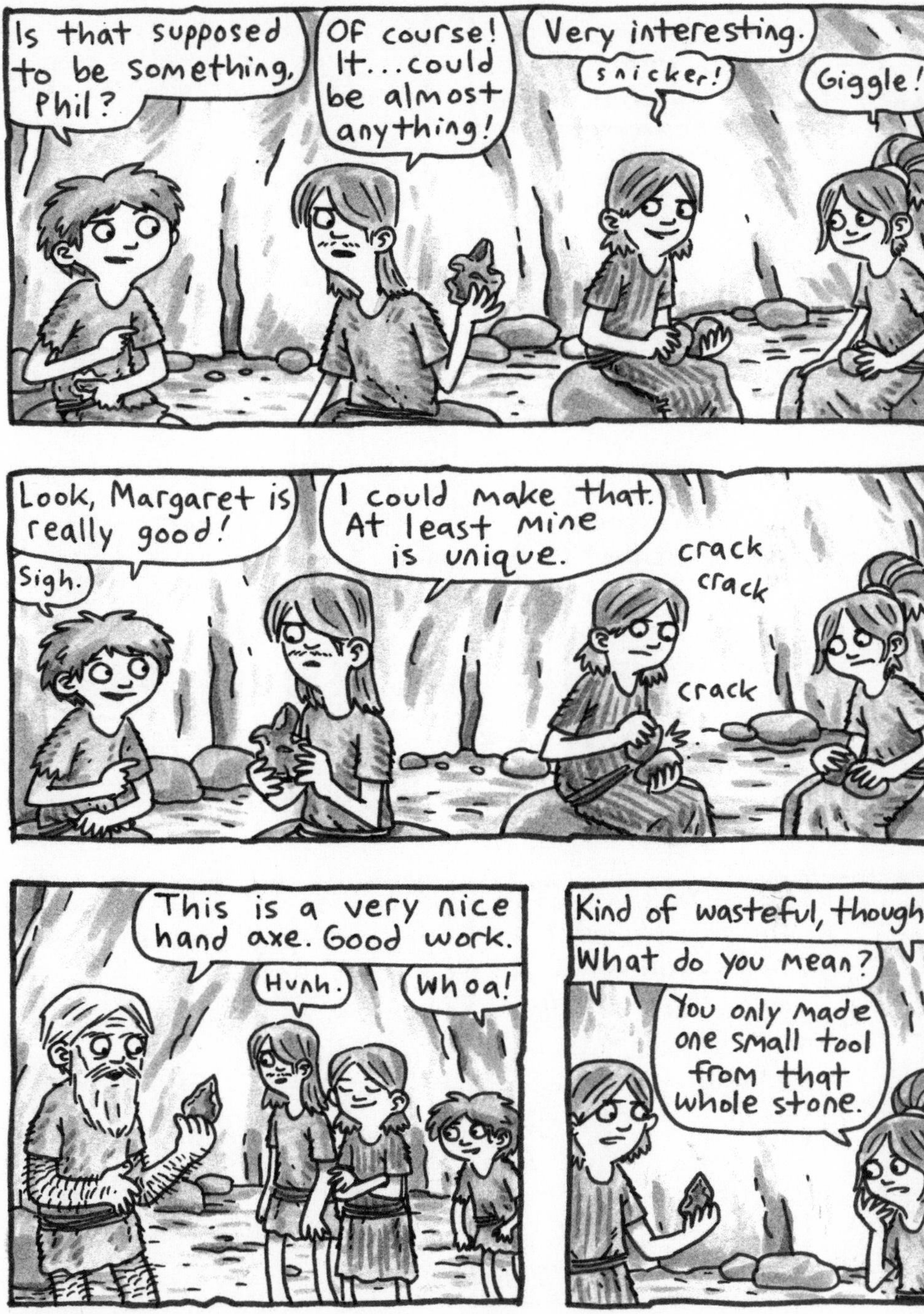
Is that supposed to be something, Phil?
Of course! It...could be almost anything!
Very interesting.
snicker!
Giggle!
Look, Margaret is really good!
Sigh.
I could make that. At least mine is unique.
crack
crack
crack
This is a very nice hand axe. Good work.
Hunh.
Whoa!
Kind of wasteful, though.
What do you mean?
You only made one small tool from that whole stone.

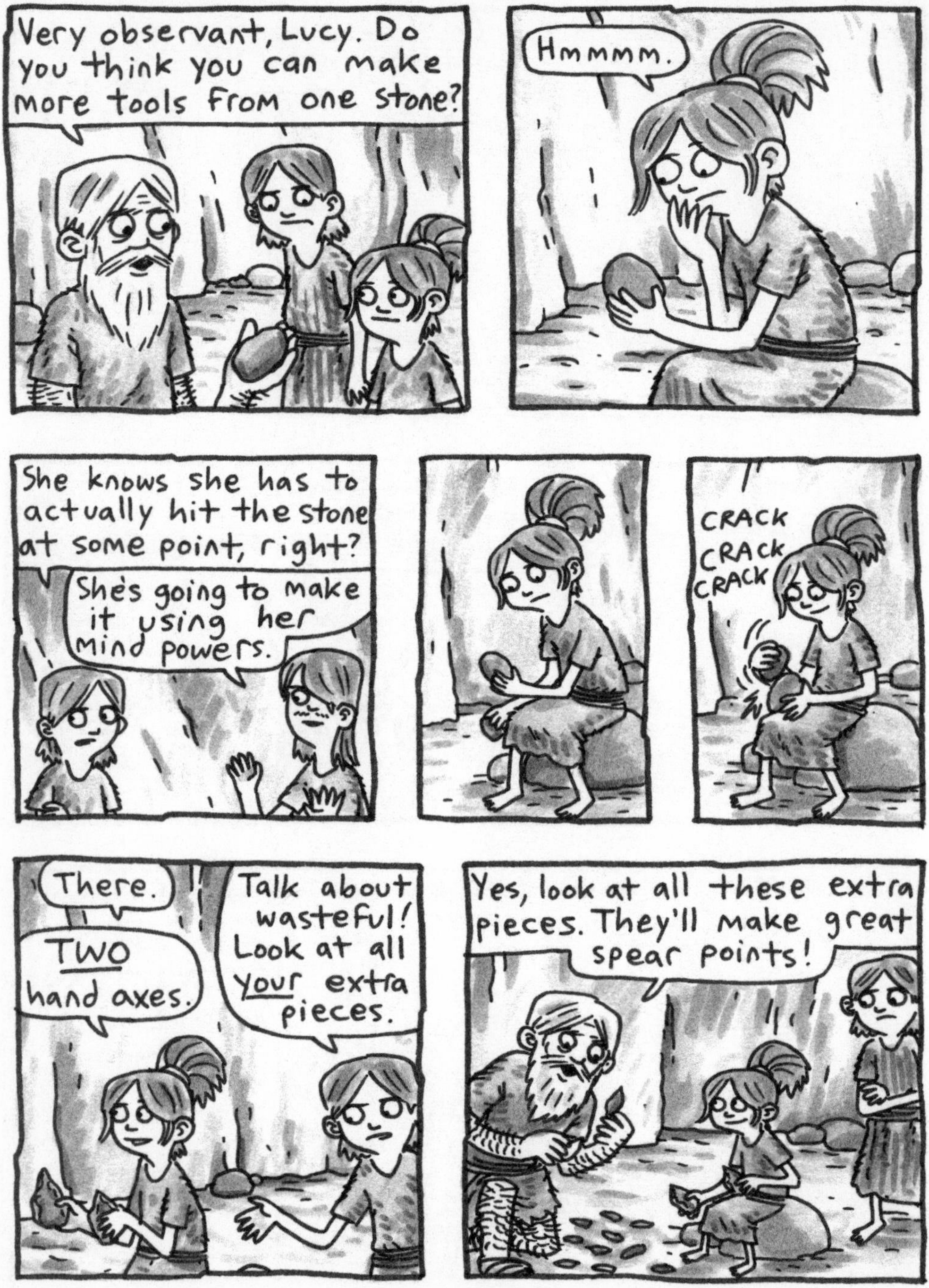
Very observant, Lucy. Do you think you can make more tools from one stone?
Hmmmm.
She knows she has to actually hit the stone at some point, right?
She's going to make it using her mind powers.
CRACK
CRACK
CRACK
There.
TWO hand axes.
Talk about wasteful! Look at all YOUR extra pieces.
Yes, look at all these extra pieces. They'll make great spear points!

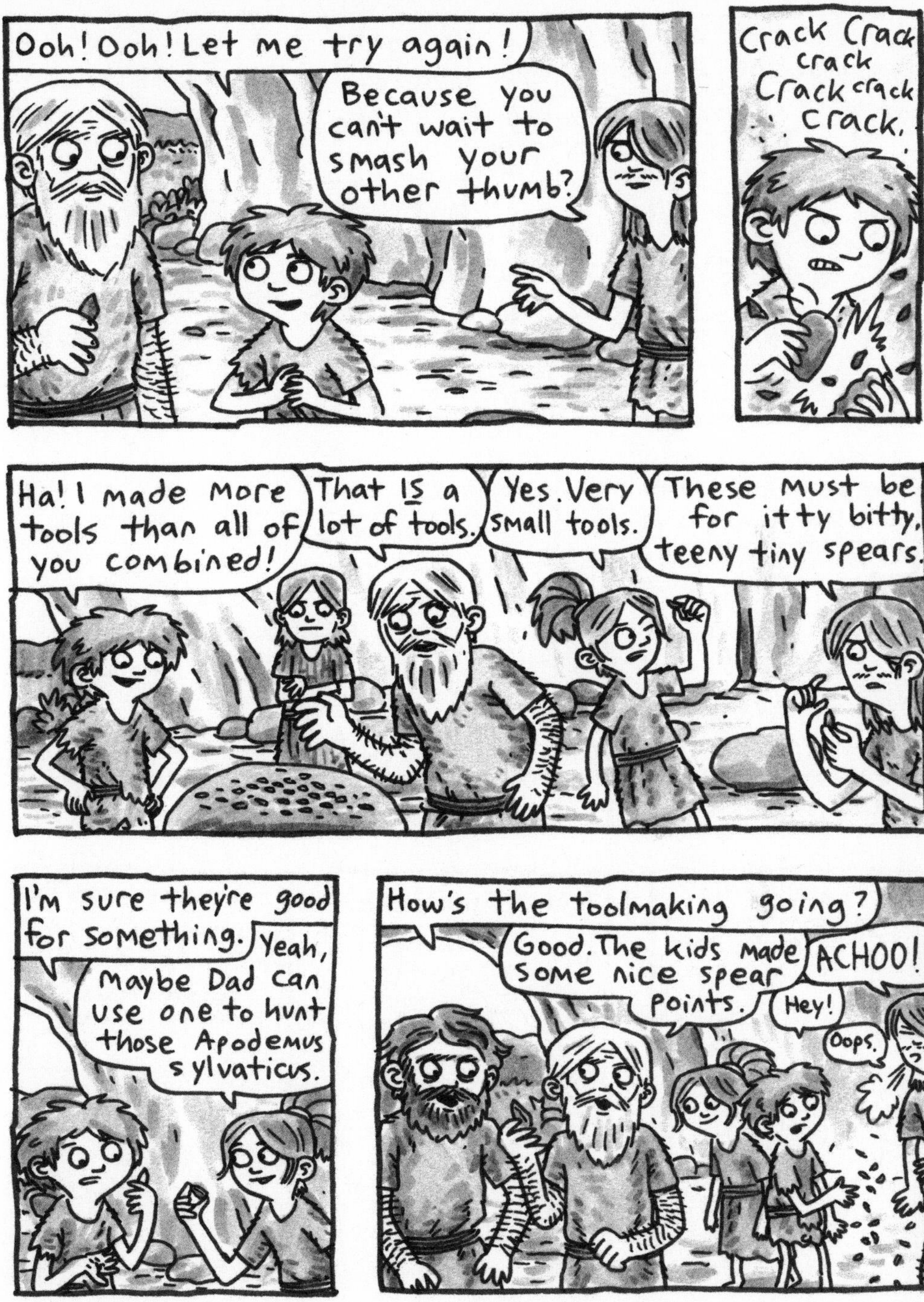
Ooh! Ooh! Let me try again!
Because you can't wait to smash your other thumb?
Crack Crack crack Crack crack Crack.
Ha! I made more tools than all of you combined!
That IS a lot of tools.
Yes. Very small tools.
These must be for itty bitty, teeny tiny spears.
I'm sure they're good for something.
Yeah, maybe Dad can use one to hunt those Apodemus sylvaticus.
How's the toolmaking going?
Good. The kids made some nice spear points.
ACHOO!
Hey!
Oops.

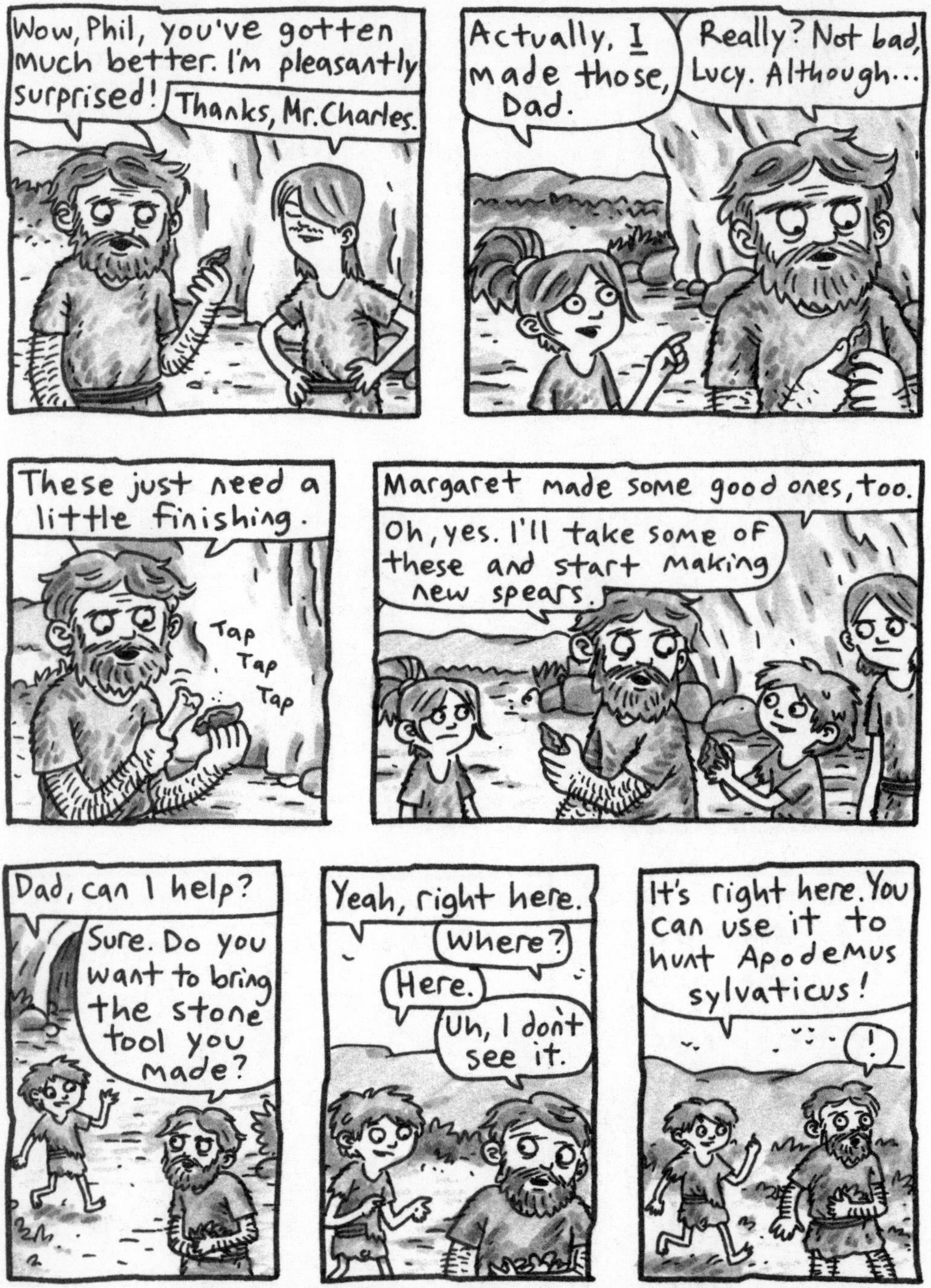

Wow, Phil, you've gotten much better. I'm pleasantly surprised!
Thanks, Mr. Charles.
Actually, I made those, Dad.
Really? Not bad, Lucy. Although...
These just need a little finishing.
Tap
Tap
Tap
Margaret made some good ones, too.
Oh, yes. I'll take some of these and start making new spears.
Dad, can I help?
Sure. Do you want to bring the stone tool you made?
Yeah, right here.
Where?
Here.
Uh, I don't see it.
It's right here. You can use it to hunt Apodemus sylvaticus!
!

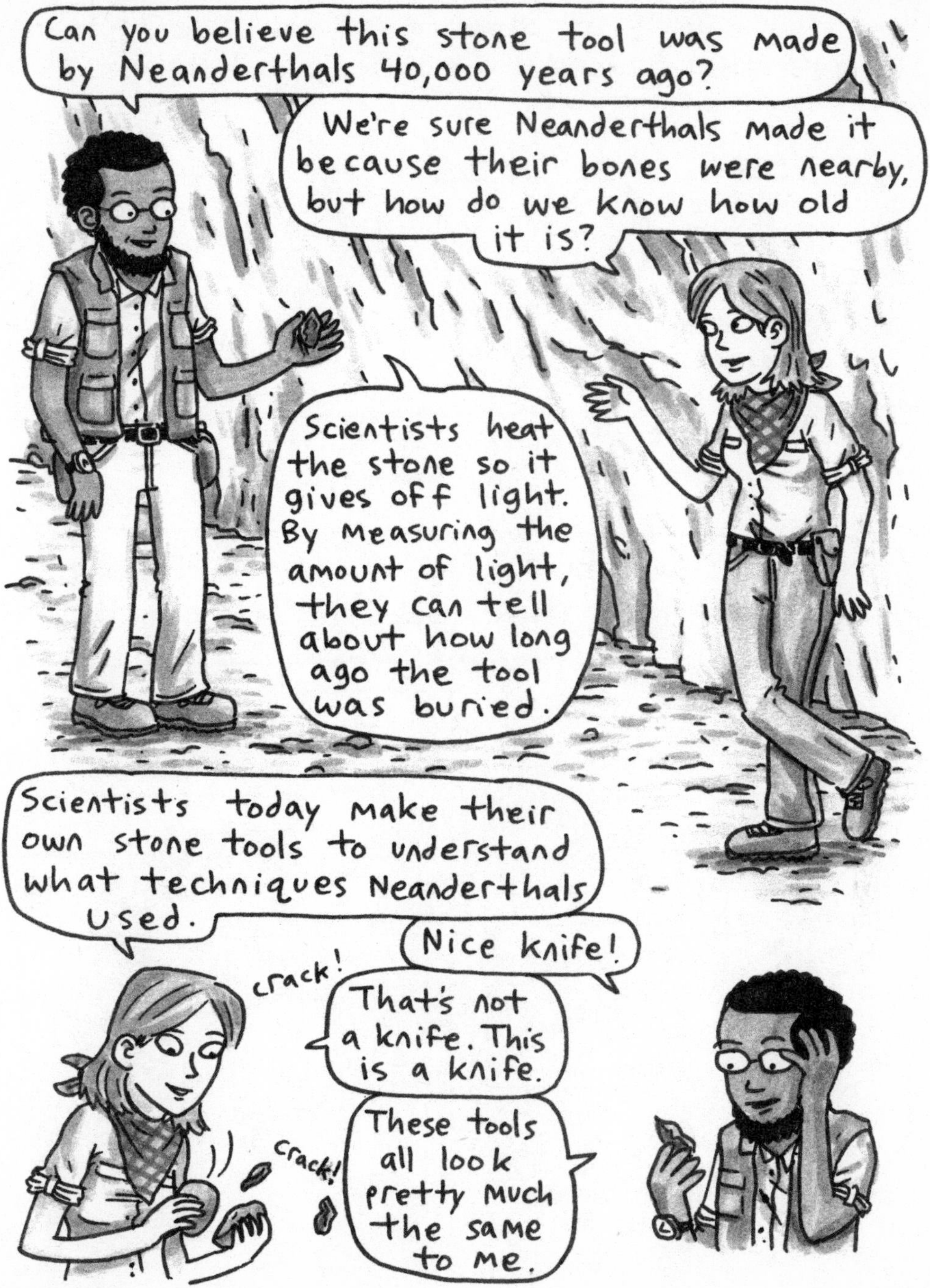
Can you believe this stone tool was made by Neanderthals 40,000 years ago?
We're sure Neanderthals made it because their bones were nearby, but how do we know how old it is?
Scientists heat the stone so it gives off light. By measuring the amount of light, they can tell about how long ago the tool was buried.
Scientists today make their own stone tools to understand what techniques Neanderthals used.
Nice knife!
crack!
That's not a knife. This is a knife.
crack!
These tools all look pretty much the same to me.

By looking closely at Stone Age tools, scientists realized there were a few different types:

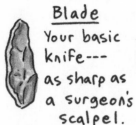

Blade
Your basic knife--- as sharp as a surgeon's scalpel.

Scraper
Used to clean off animal skins.

Hand Axe
Good for heavy-duty cutting. No handle, but Neanderthals had very strong grips.

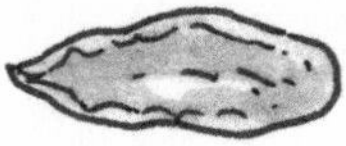

Point Attached to a spear using pitch, a sticky tar.

Sometimes we find stone flakes that came from the same original rock. We can put them together to see how different tools were made step by step.
I think I'm missing a piece.

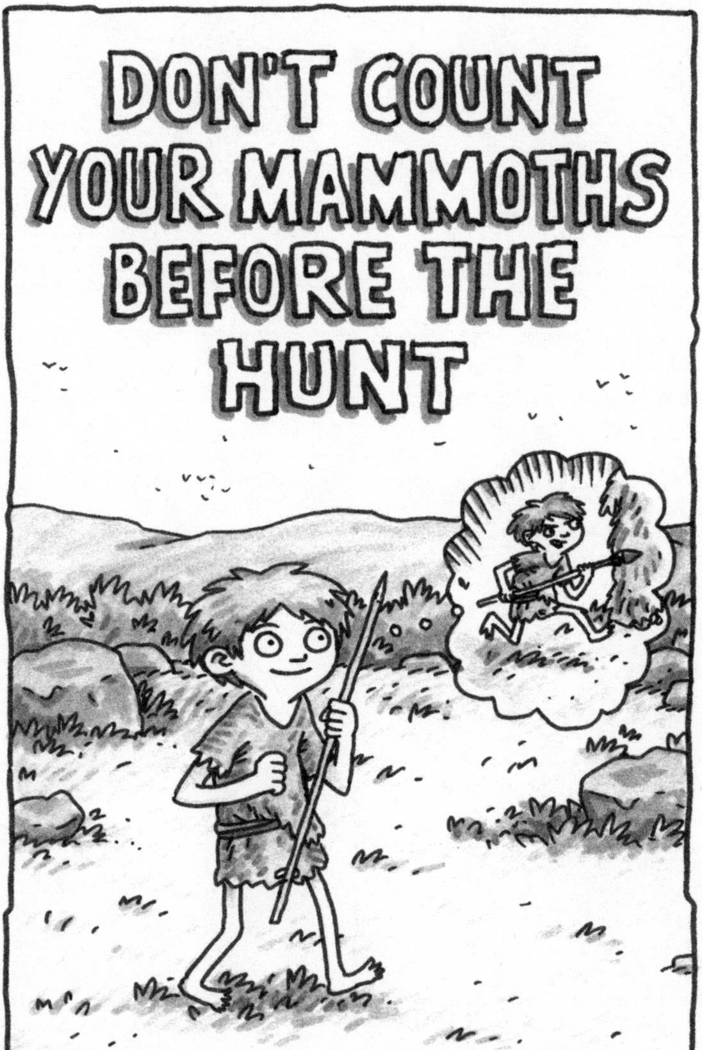
DON'T COUNT YOUR MAMMOTHS BEFORE THE HUNT

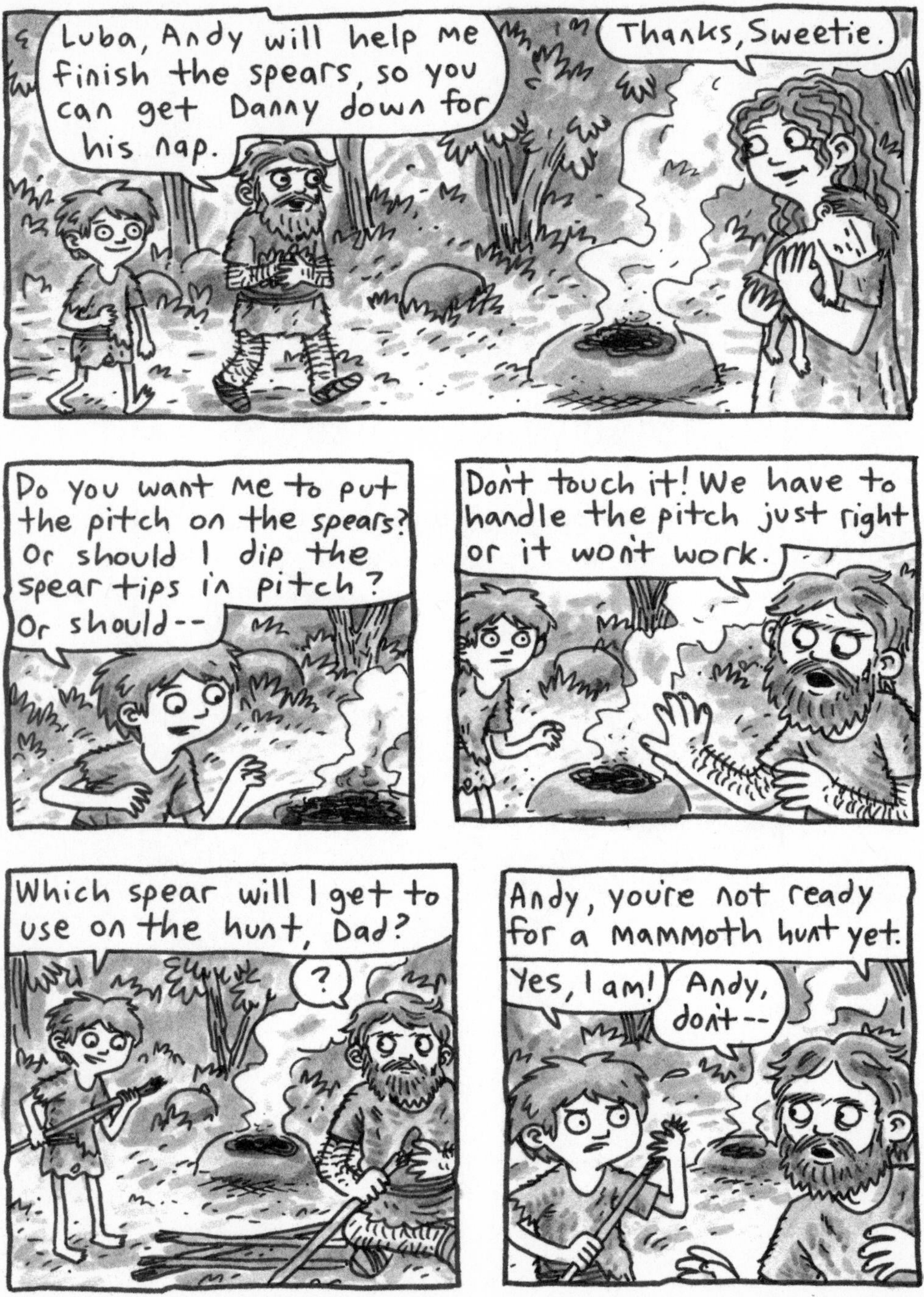
Luba, Andy will help me finish the spears, so you can get Danny down for his nap.
Thanks, Sweetie.
Do you want me to put the pitch on the spears? Or should I dip the spear tips in pitch? Or should--
Don't touch it! We have to handle the pitch just right or it won't work.
Which spear will I get to use on the hunt, Dad?
?
Andy, you're not ready for a mammoth hunt yet.
Yes, I am!
Andy, don't--

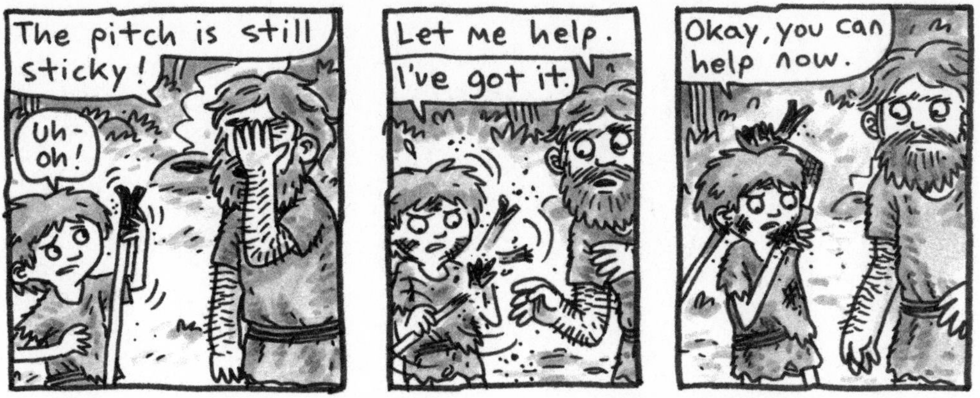
The pitch is still sticky!
Uh-oh!
Let me help.
I've got it.
Okay, you can help now.

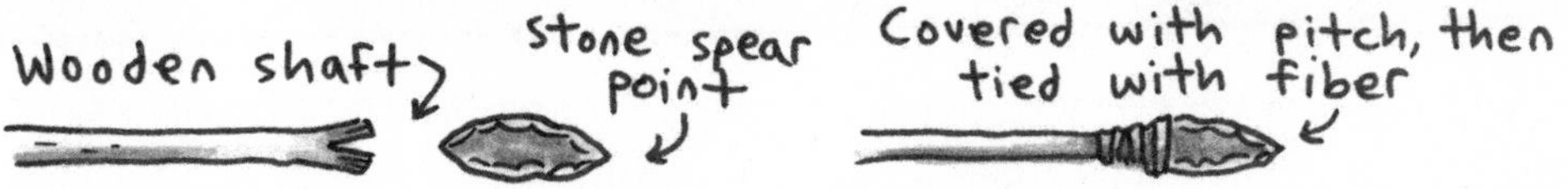
Wooden shaft
Stone spear point
Covered with pitch, then tied with fiber

Pitch is hard to make, so Neanderthals must have been smart and skilled to be able to make it!

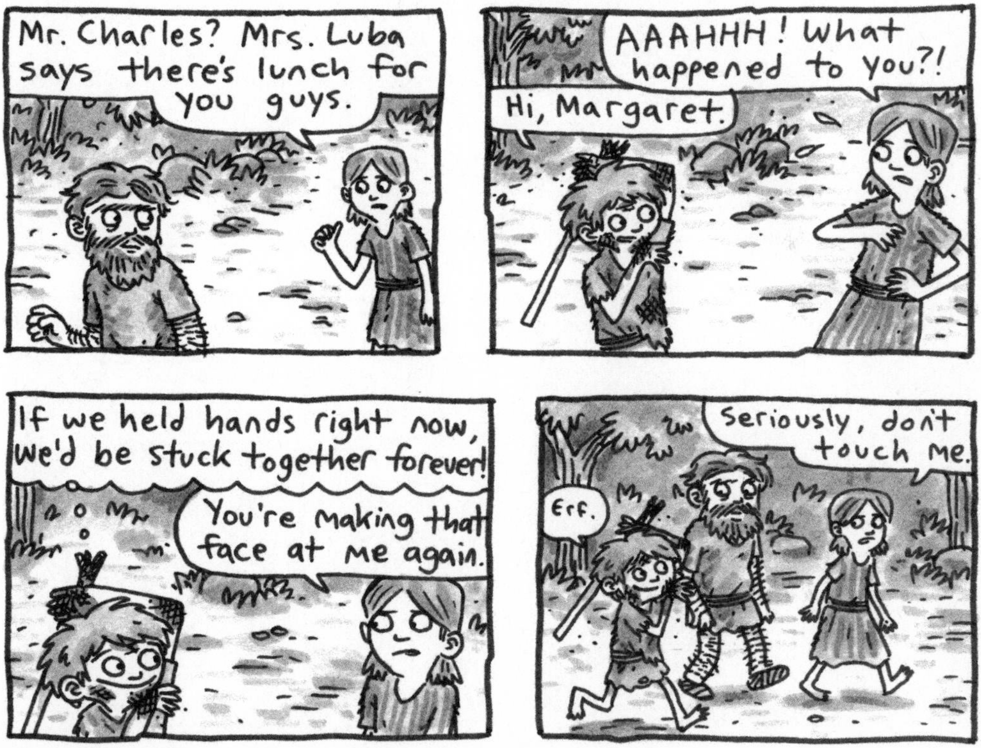
Mr. Charles? Mrs. Luba says there's lunch for you guys.
AAAHHH! What happened to you?!
Hi, Margaret.
If we held hands right now, we'd be stuck together forever!
You're making that face at me again.
Seriously, don't touch me.
Erf.

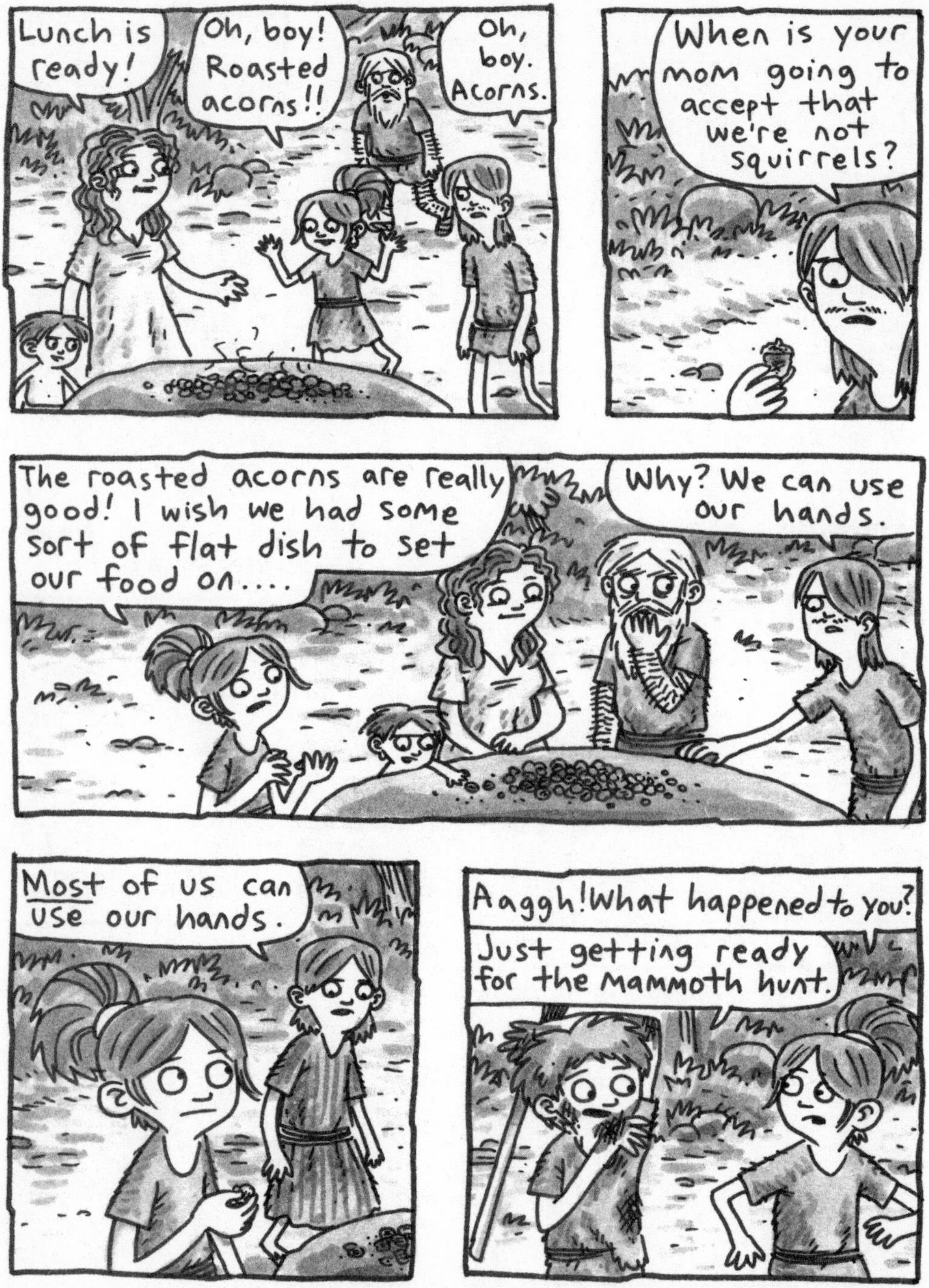
Lunch is ready!
Oh, boy! Roasted acorns!!
Oh, boy. Acorns.
When is your mom going to accept that we're not squirrels?
The roasted acorns are really good! I wish we had some sort of flat dish to set our food on....
Why? We can use our hands.
Most of us can use our hands.
Aaggh! What happened to you?
Just getting ready for the mammoth hunt.

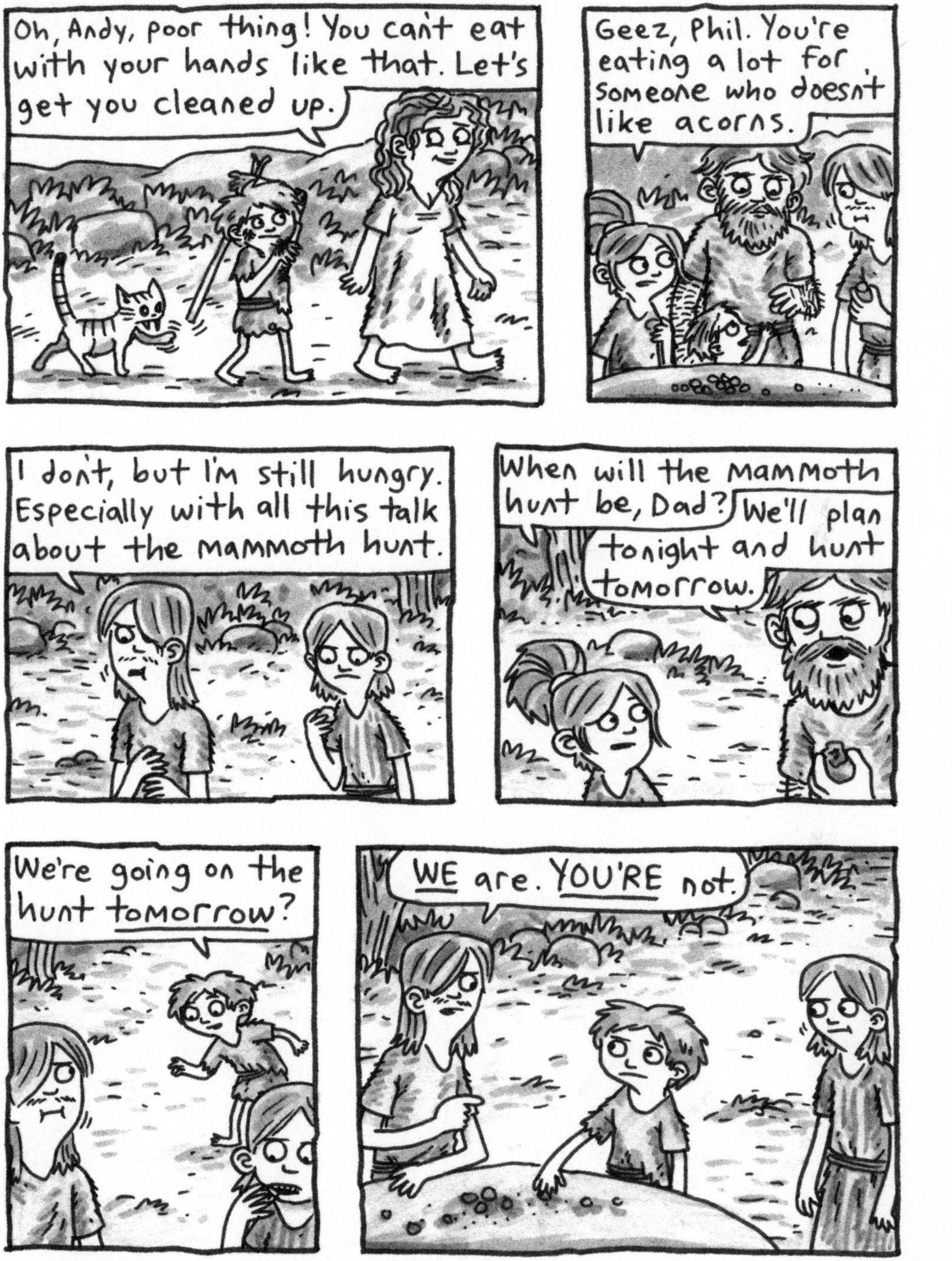
Oh, Andy, poor thing! You can't eat with your hands like that. Let's get you cleaned up.
Geez, Phil. You're eating a lot for someone who doesn't like acorns.
I don't, but I'm still hungry. Especially with all this talk about the mammoth hunt.
When will the mammoth hunt be, Dad?
We'll plan tonight and hunt tomorrow.
We're going on the hunt tomorrow?
WE are. YOU'RE not.

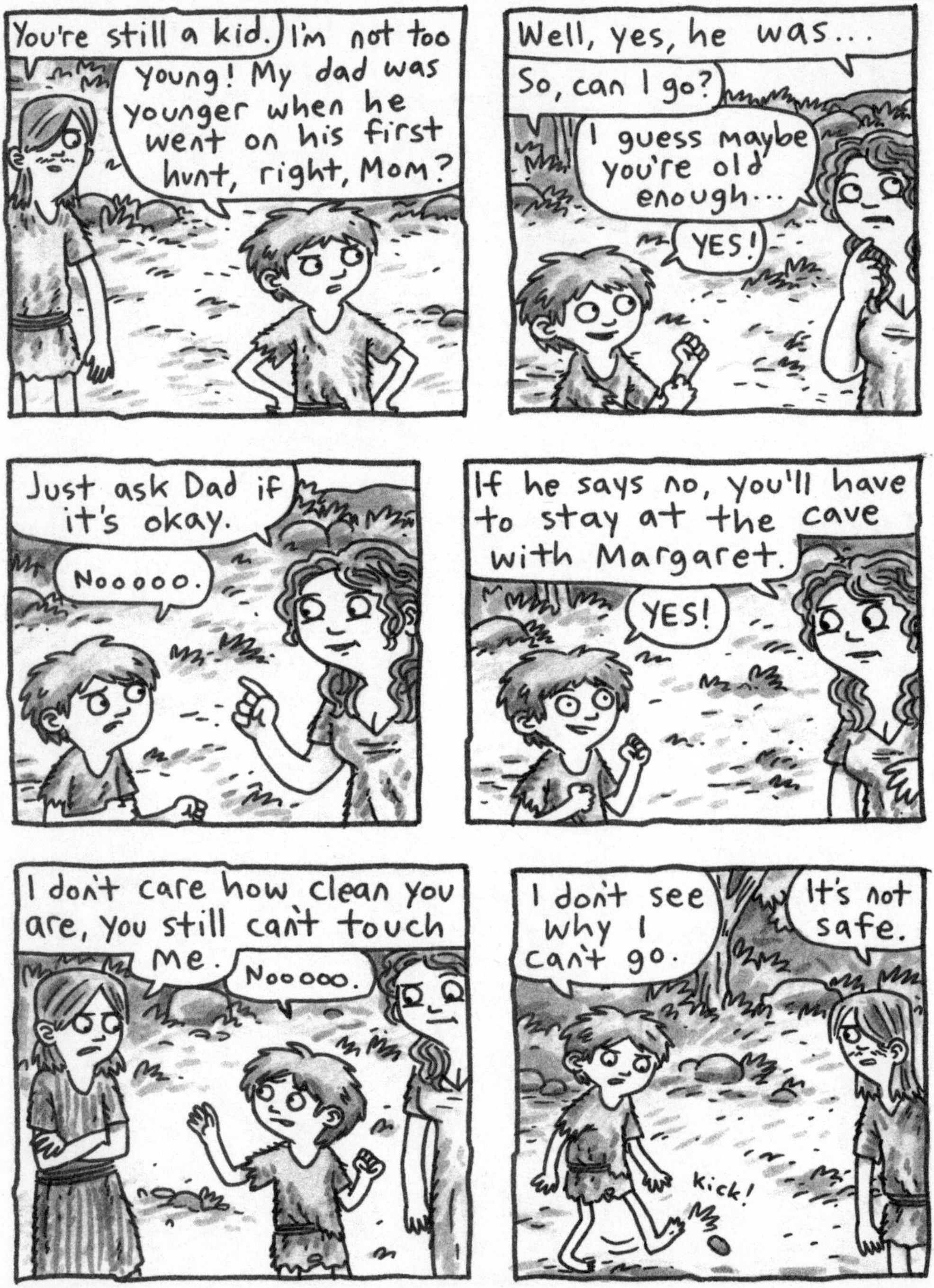
You're still a kid.
I'm not too young! My dad was younger when he went on his first hunt, right, Mom?
Well, yes, he was...
So, can I go?
I guess maybe you're old enough...
YES!
Just ask Dad if it's okay.
Nooooo.
If he says no, you'll have to stay at the cave with Margaret.
YES!
I don't care how clean you are, you still can't touch me.
Nooooo.
I don't see why I can't go.
It's not safe.
Kick!

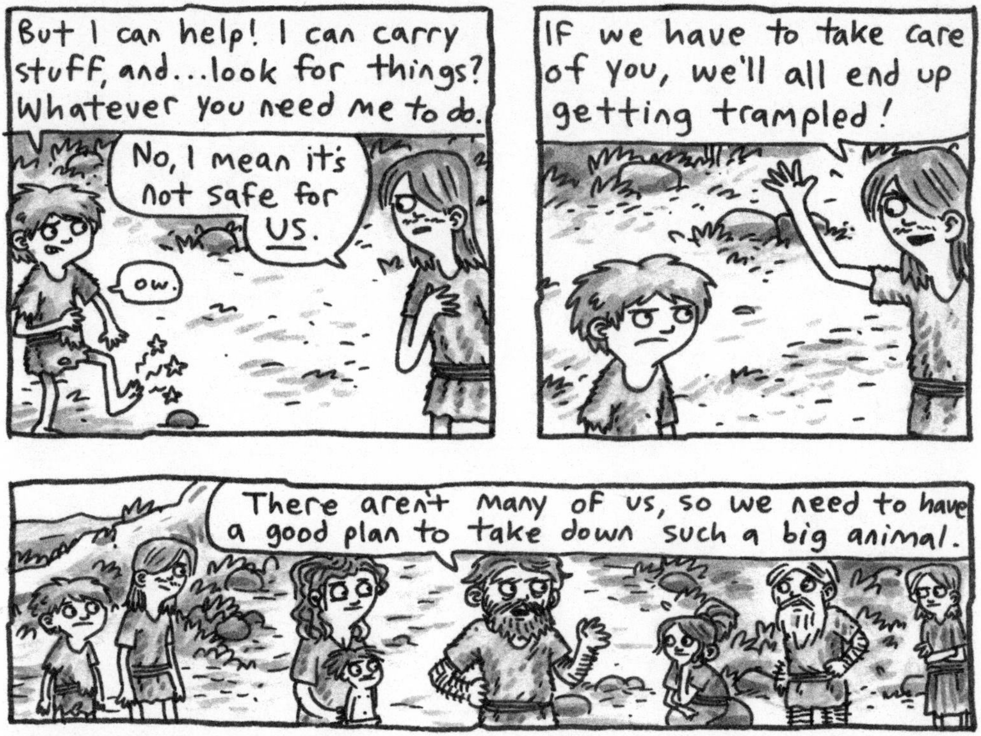
But I can help! I can carry stuff, and...look for things? Whatever you need me to do.
No, I mean it's not safe for US.
ow.
If we have to take care of you, we'll all end up getting trampled!
There aren't many of us, so we need to have a good plan to take down such a big animal.

The woolly mammoth lived in Europe and Asia until about 10,000 years ago.

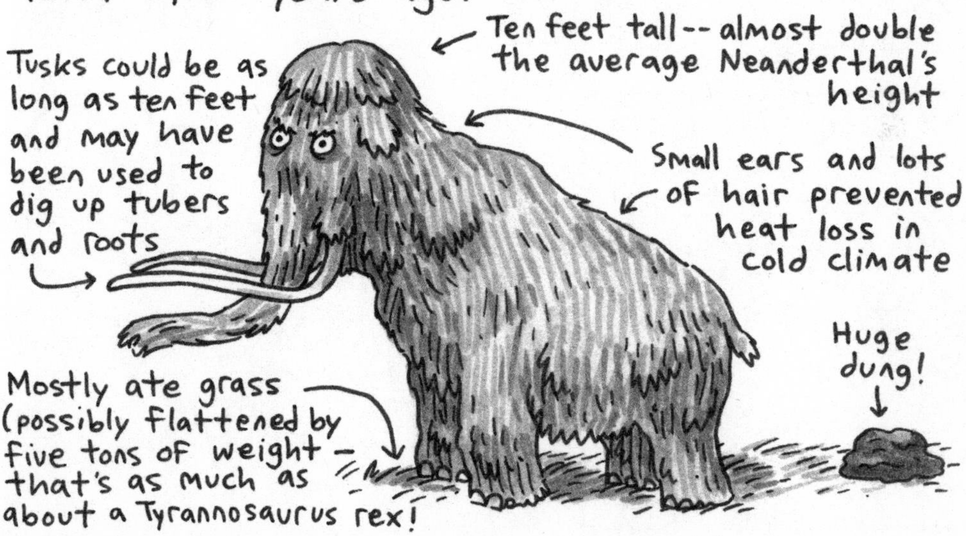
Ten feet tall -- almost double the average Neanderthal's height
Tusks could be as long as ten feet and may have been used to dig up tubers and roots
Small ears and lots of hair prevented heat loss in cold climate
Huge dung!
Mostly ate grass (possibly flattened by five tons of weight — that's as much as about a Tyrannosaurus rex!

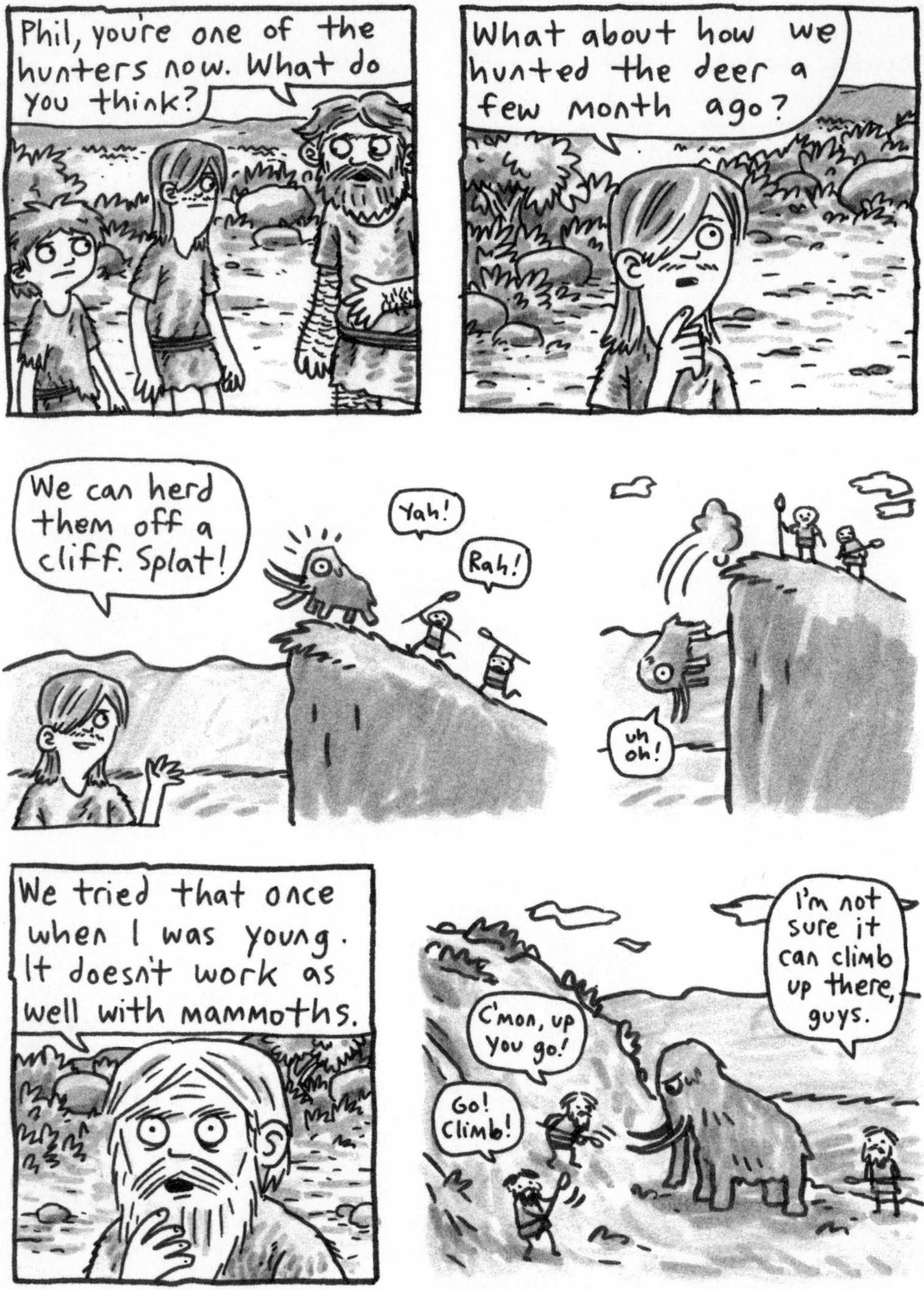

Phil, you're one of the hunters now. What do you think?
What about how we hunted the deer a few month ago?
We can herd them off a cliff. Splat!
Yah!
Rah!
uh oh!
We tried that once when I was young. It doesn't work as well with mammoths.
C'mon, up you go!
Go! Climb!
I'm not sure it can climb up there, guys.

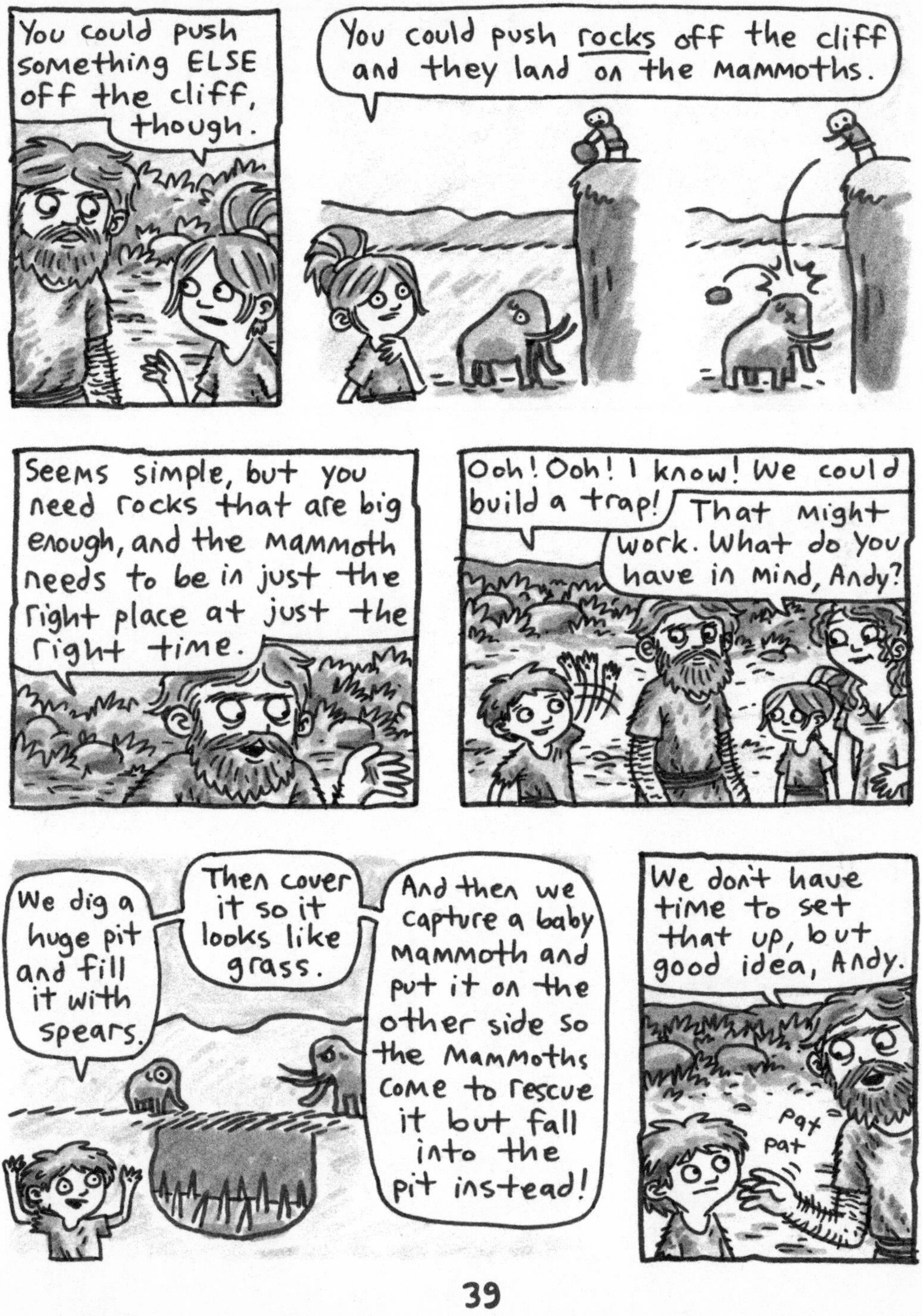
You could push something ELSE off the cliff, though.
You could push rocks off the cliff and they land on the mammoths.
Seems simple, but you need rocks that are big enough, and the mammoth needs to be in just the right place at just the right time.
Ooh! Ooh! I know! We could build a trap!
That might work. What do you have in mind, Andy?
We dig a huge pit and fill it with spears.
Then cover it so it looks like grass.
And then we capture a baby mammoth and put it on the other side so the mammoths come to rescue it but fall into the pit instead!
We don't have time to set that up, but good idea, Andy.
pat
pat

Why do you guys want to work so hard? Just wait for one to die.

That would be nicer to the poor mammoths.

Of course, we'd starve first.

So, the usual, then?

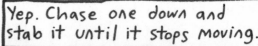

Yep. Chase one down and stab it until it stops moving.

We should scout the herd one last time and then get some rest.

Can I come?

It's not the hunt.

No, it's bedtime for you kids.

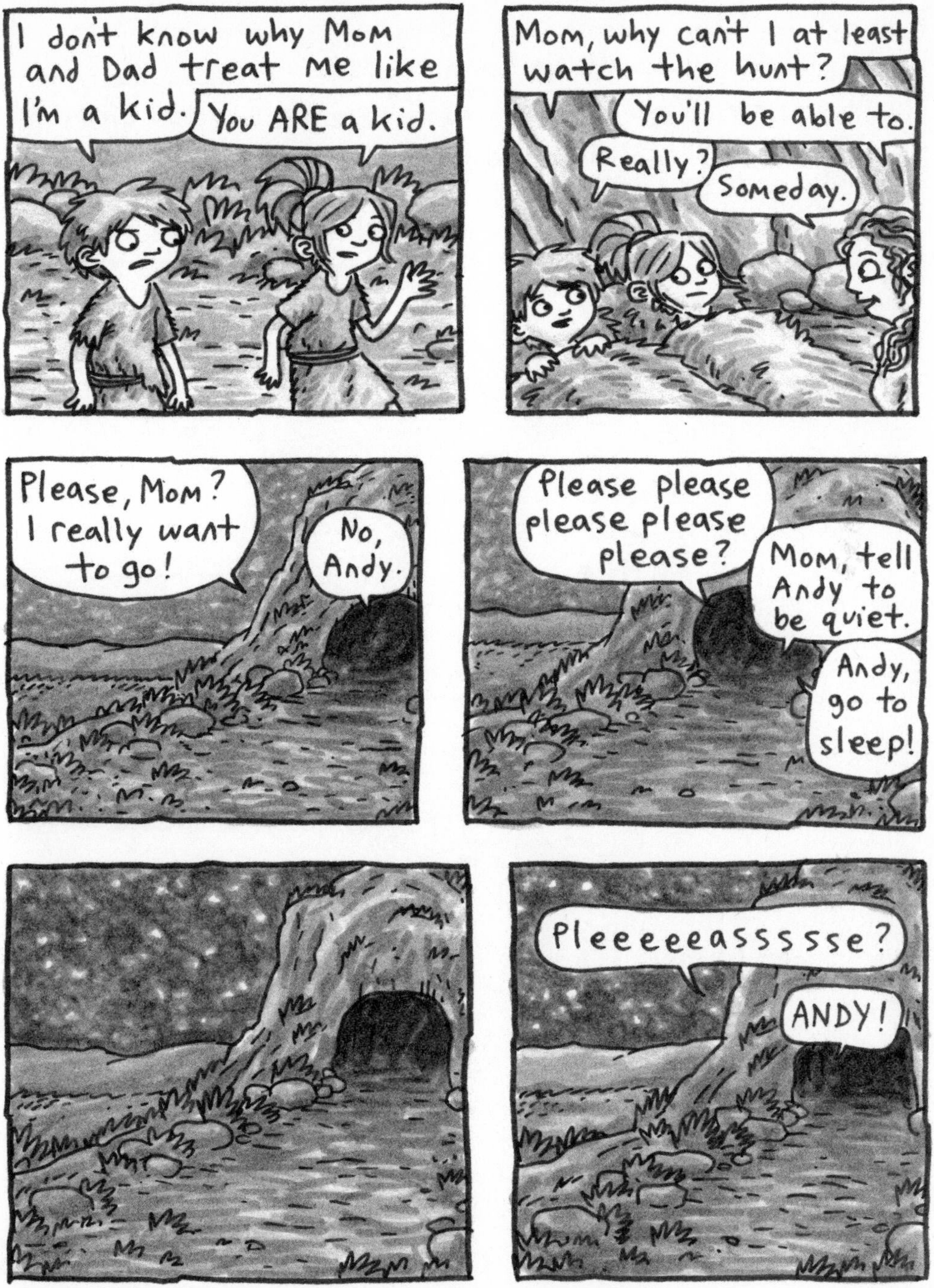
I don't know why Mom and Dad treat me like I'm a kid.
You ARE a kid.
Mom, why can't I at least watch the hunt?
You'll be able to.
Really?
Someday.
Please, Mom? I really want to go!
No, Andy.
Please please please please please?
Mom, tell Andy to be quiet.
Andy, go to sleep!
Pleeeeeeasssse?
ANDY!

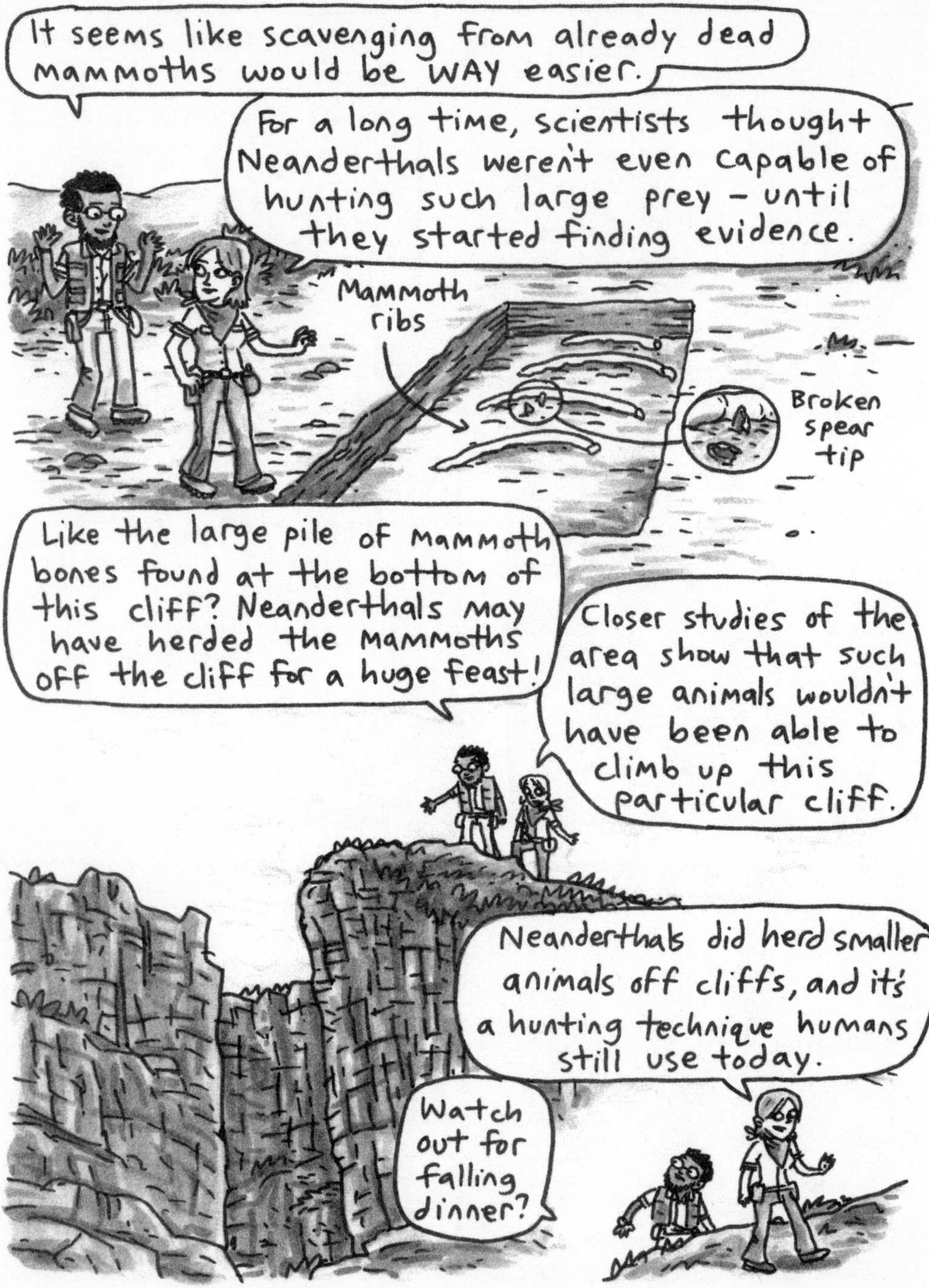
It seems like scavenging from already dead mammoths would be WAY easier.
For a long time, scientists thought Neanderthals weren't even capable of hunting such large prey - until they started finding evidence.
Mammoth ribs
Broken spear tip
Like the large pile of mammoth bones found at the bottom of this cliff? Neanderthals may have herded the mammoths off the cliff for a huge feast!
Closer studies of the area show that such large animals wouldn't have been able to climb up this particular cliff.
Neanderthals did herd smaller animals off cliffs, and it's a hunting technique humans still use today.
Watch out for falling dinner?

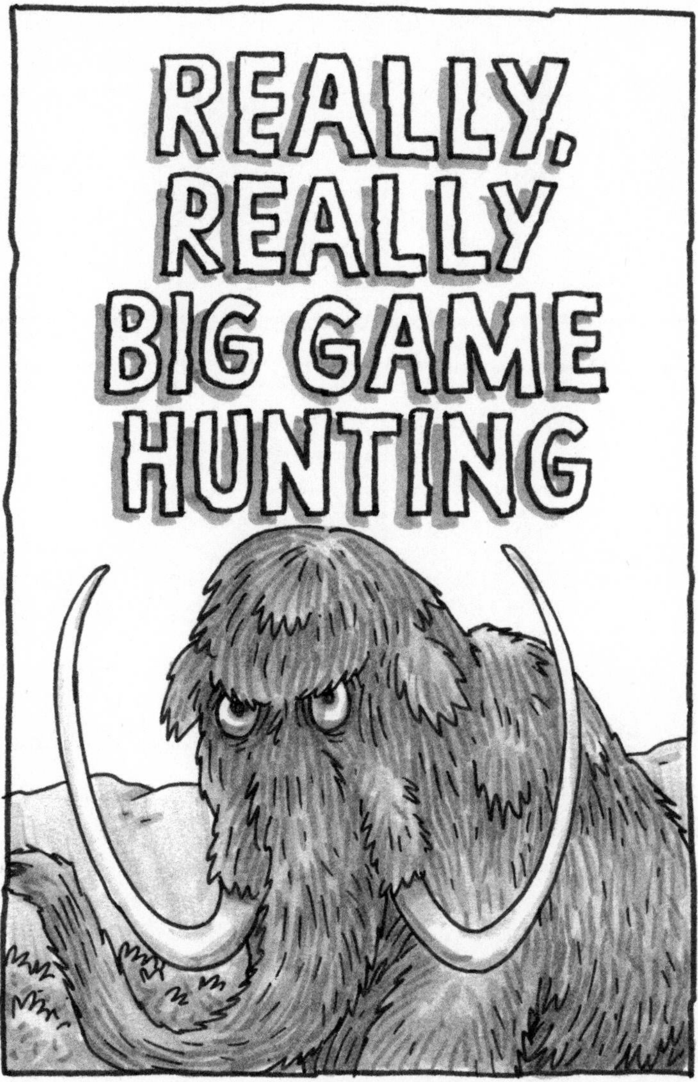
REALLY, REALLY BIG GAME HUNTING

Yawn.
Andy, what are you doing?
Shhhh! I'm going to sneak along on the hunt. This is my camouflage.
Poor Andy. He really wants to go on this hunt.
Maybe your dad won't notice the walking, talking bush that's following them.
Margaret, I'm surprised you offered to stay behind and watch us and Danny. You said toddlers are stinky.
They are, but have you ever smelled a mammoth? Yuck!

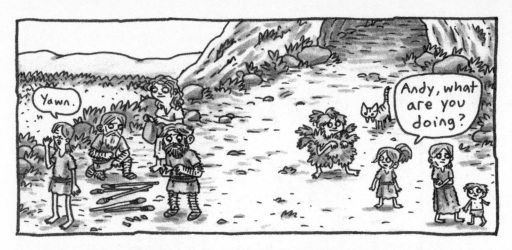

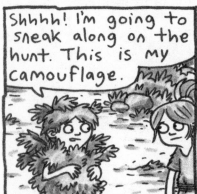

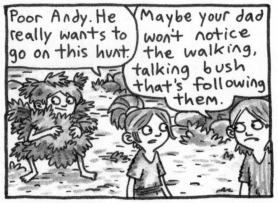

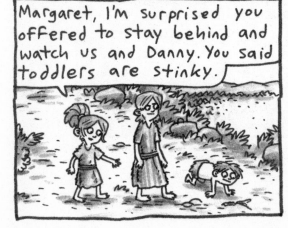

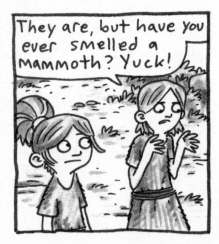

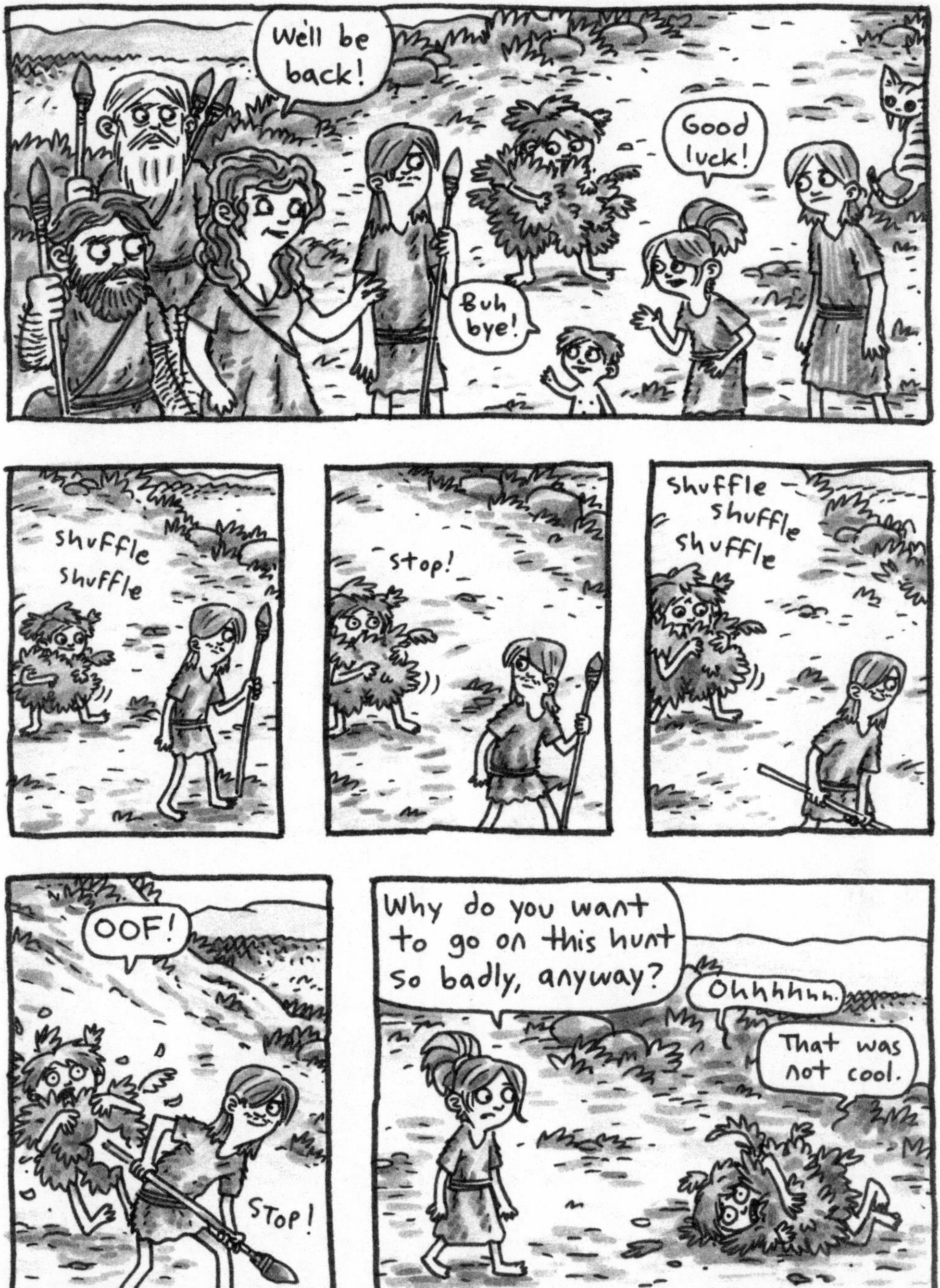
We'll be back!
Good luck!
Buh bye!
shuffle
shuffle
Stop!
shuffle
shuffle
shuffle
OOF!
STOP!
Why do you want to go on this hunt so badly, anyway?
Ohhhhhn.
That was not cool.

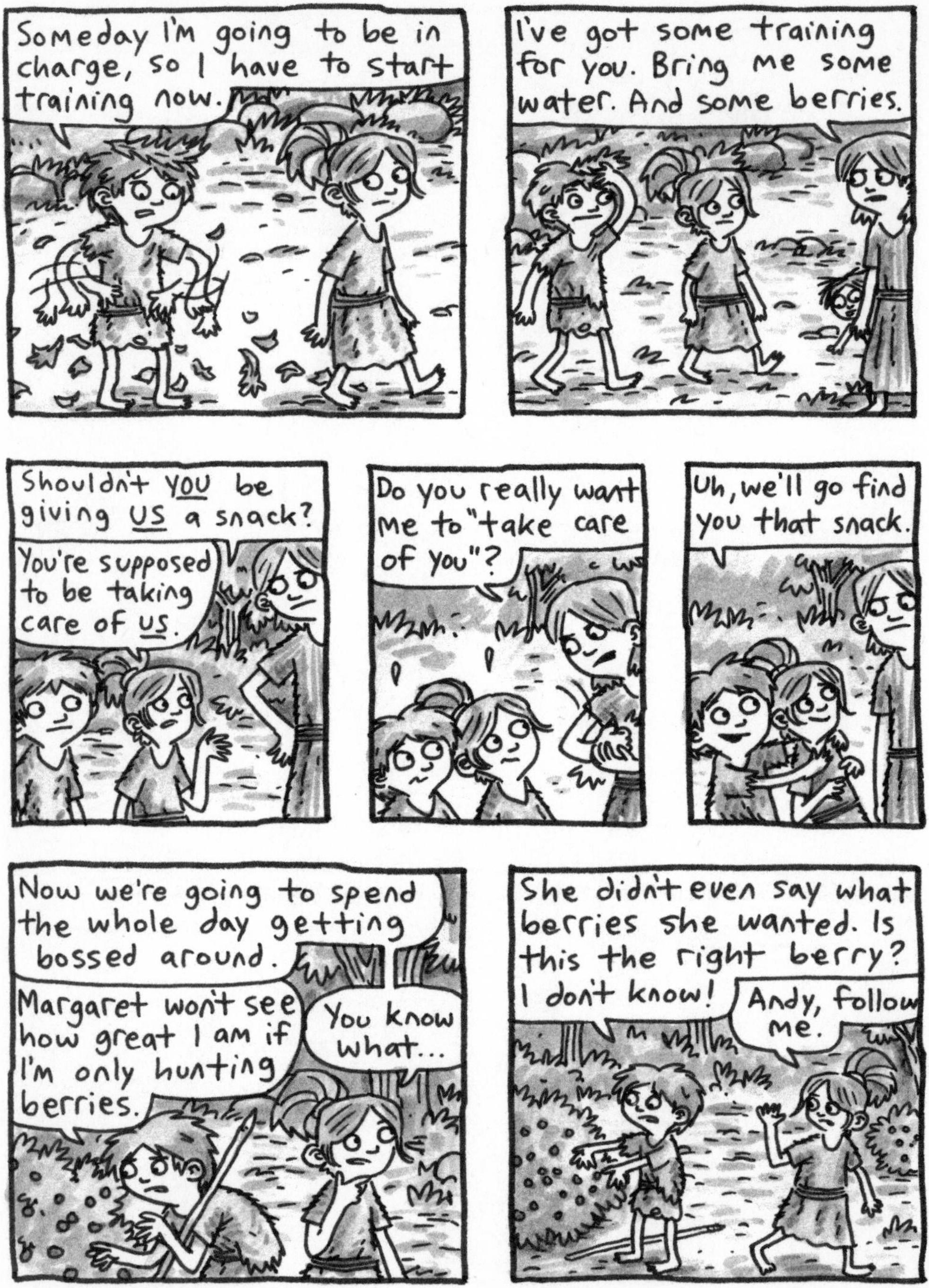
Someday I'm going to be in charge, so I have to start training now.
I've got some training for you. Bring me some water. And some berries.
Shouldn't YOU be giving US a snack?
You're supposed to be taking care of US.
Do you really want me to "take care of you"?
Uh, we'll go find you that snack.
Now we're going to spend the whole day getting bossed around.
Margaret won't see how great I am if I'm only hunting berries.
You know what...
She didn't even say what berries she wanted. Is this the right berry? I don't know!
Andy, follow me.

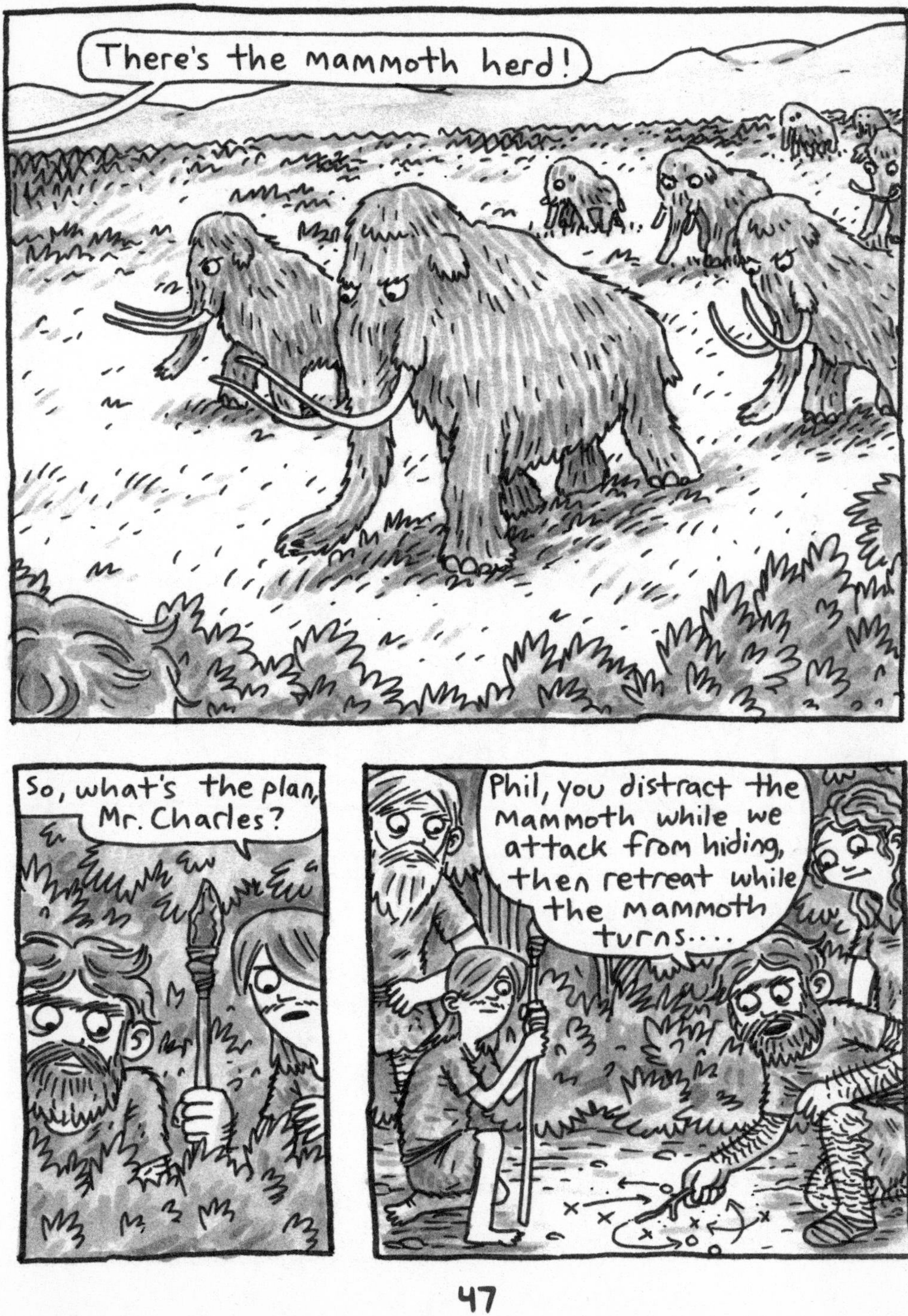
There's the mammoth herd!
So, what's the plan, Mr. Charles?
Phil, you distract the mammoth while we attack from hiding, then retreat while the mammoth turns....

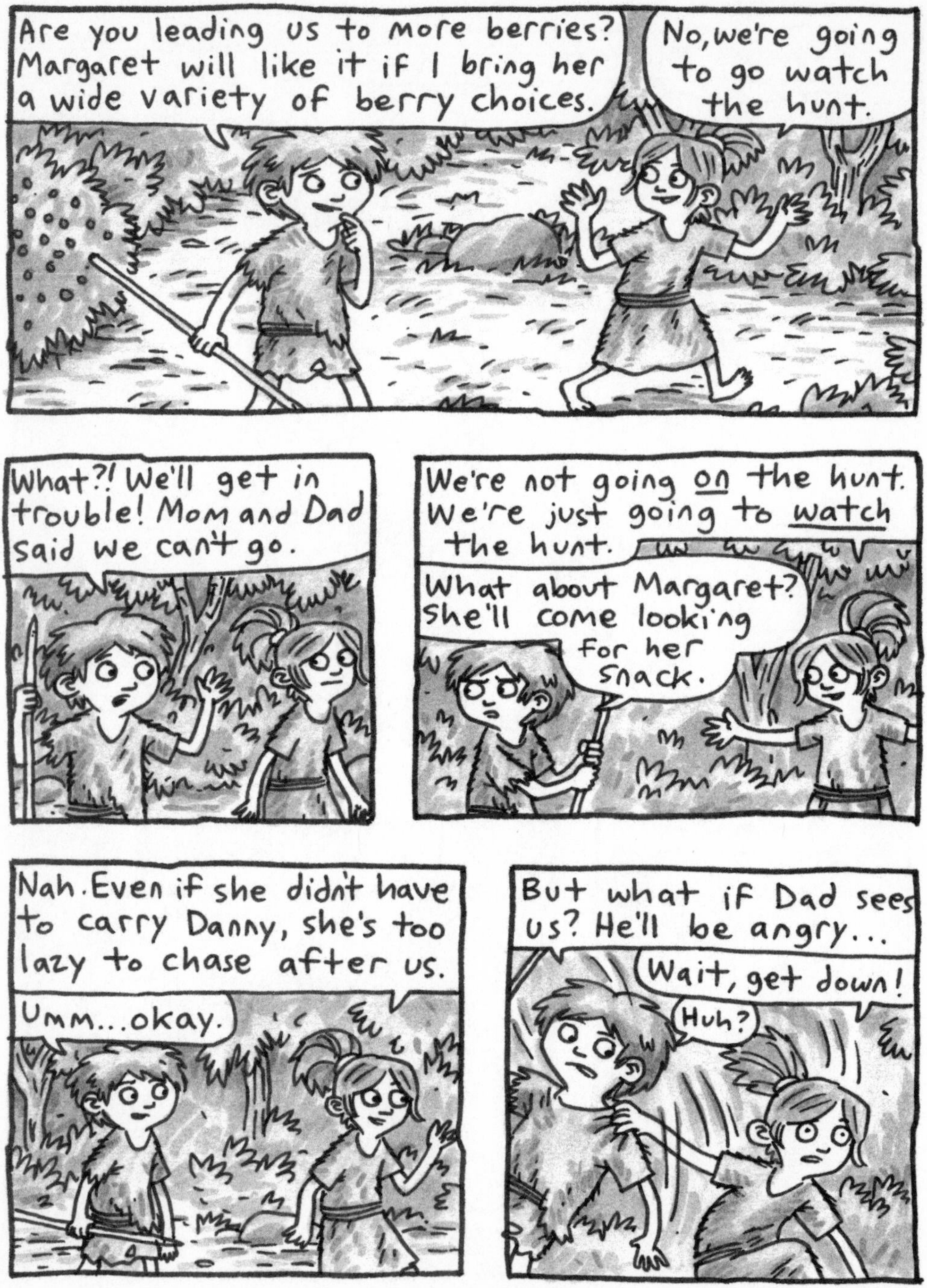
Are you leading us to more berries? Margaret will like it if I bring her a wide variety of berry choices.
No, we're going to go watch the hunt.
What?! We'll get in trouble! Mom and Dad said we can't go.
We're not going on the hunt. We're just going to watch the hunt.
What about Margaret? She'll come looking for her snack.
Nah. Even if she didn't have to carry Danny, she's too lazy to chase after us.
Umm...okay.
But what if Dad sees us? He'll be angry...
Wait, get down!
Huh?

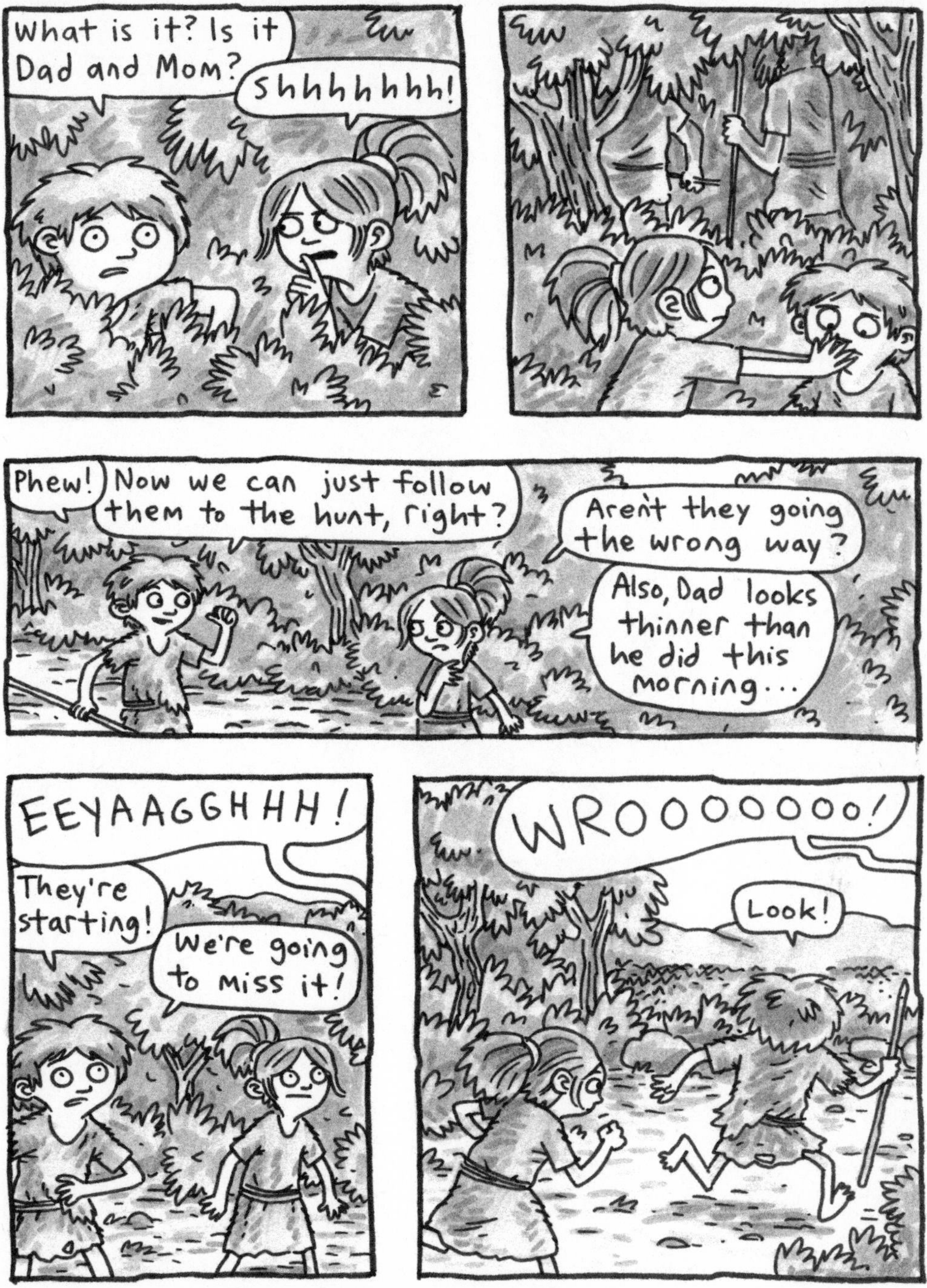

What is it? Is it Dad and Mom?
Shhhhhhhh!
Phew!
Now we can just follow them to the hunt, right?
Aren't they going the wrong way?
Also, Dad looks thinner than he did this morning...
EEYAAGGHHH!
They're starting!
We're going to miss it!
WROOOOOOO!
Look!

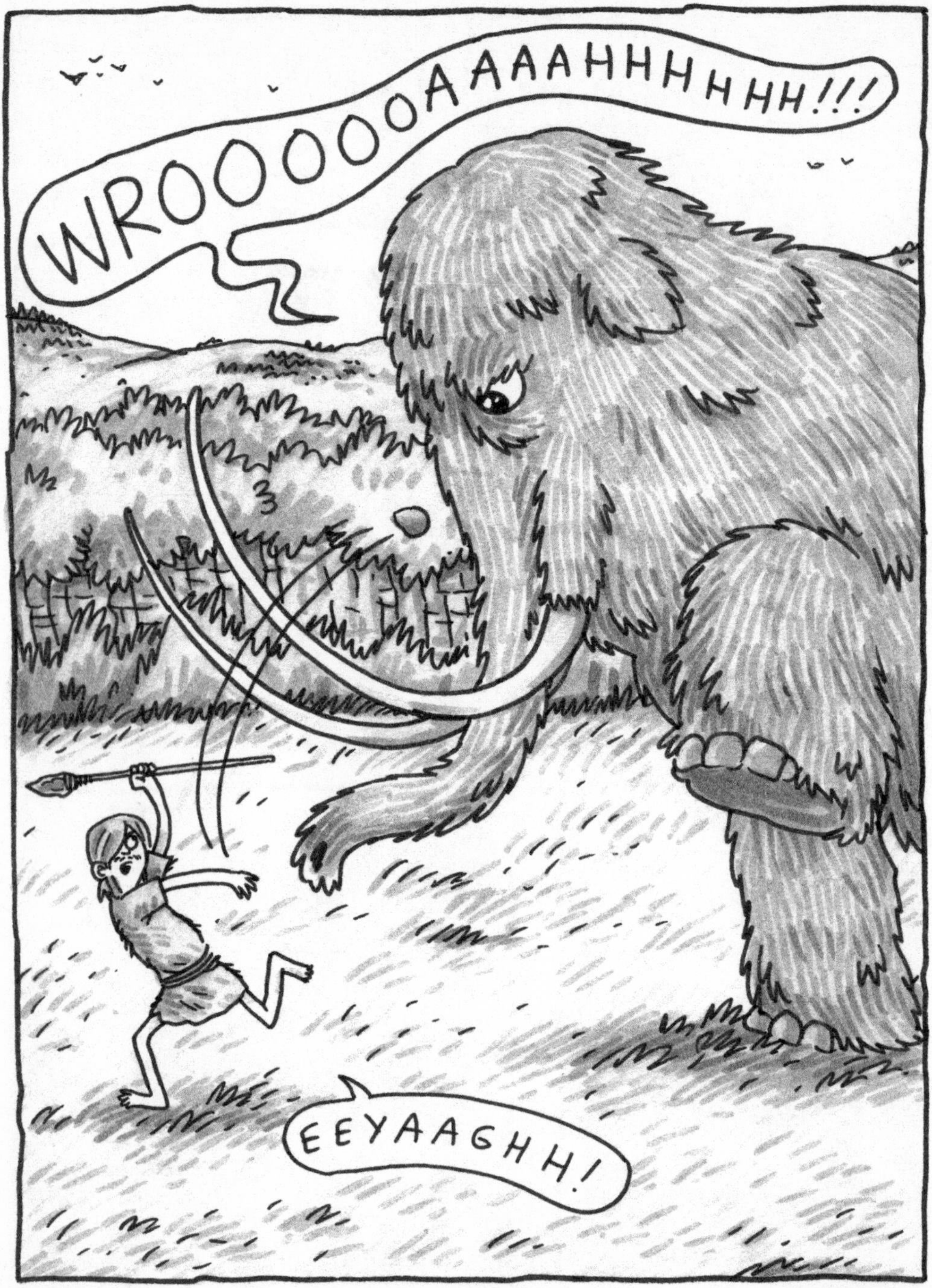
WROOOOOAAAAHHHHHH!!!
EEYAAGHH!

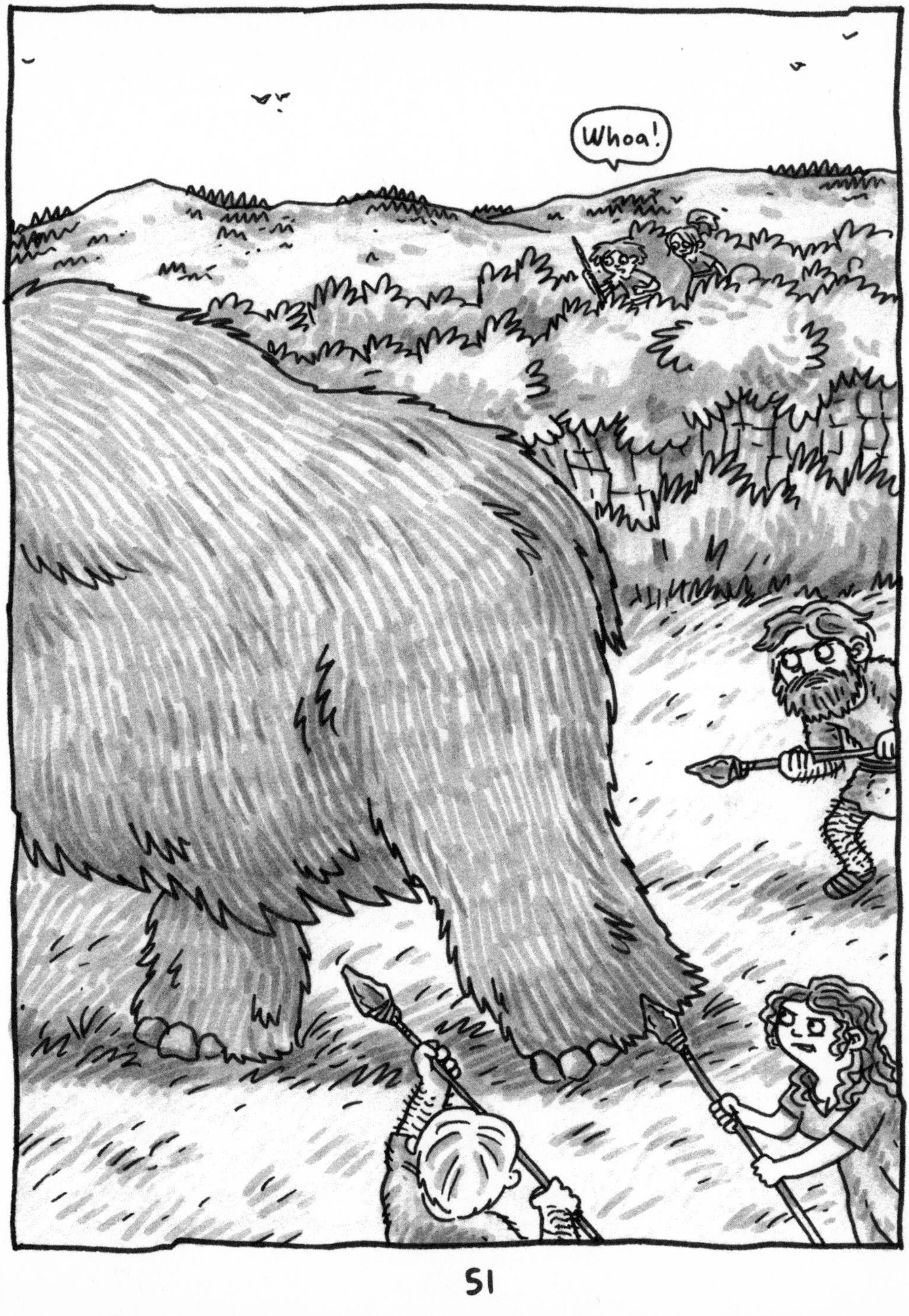
Whoa!

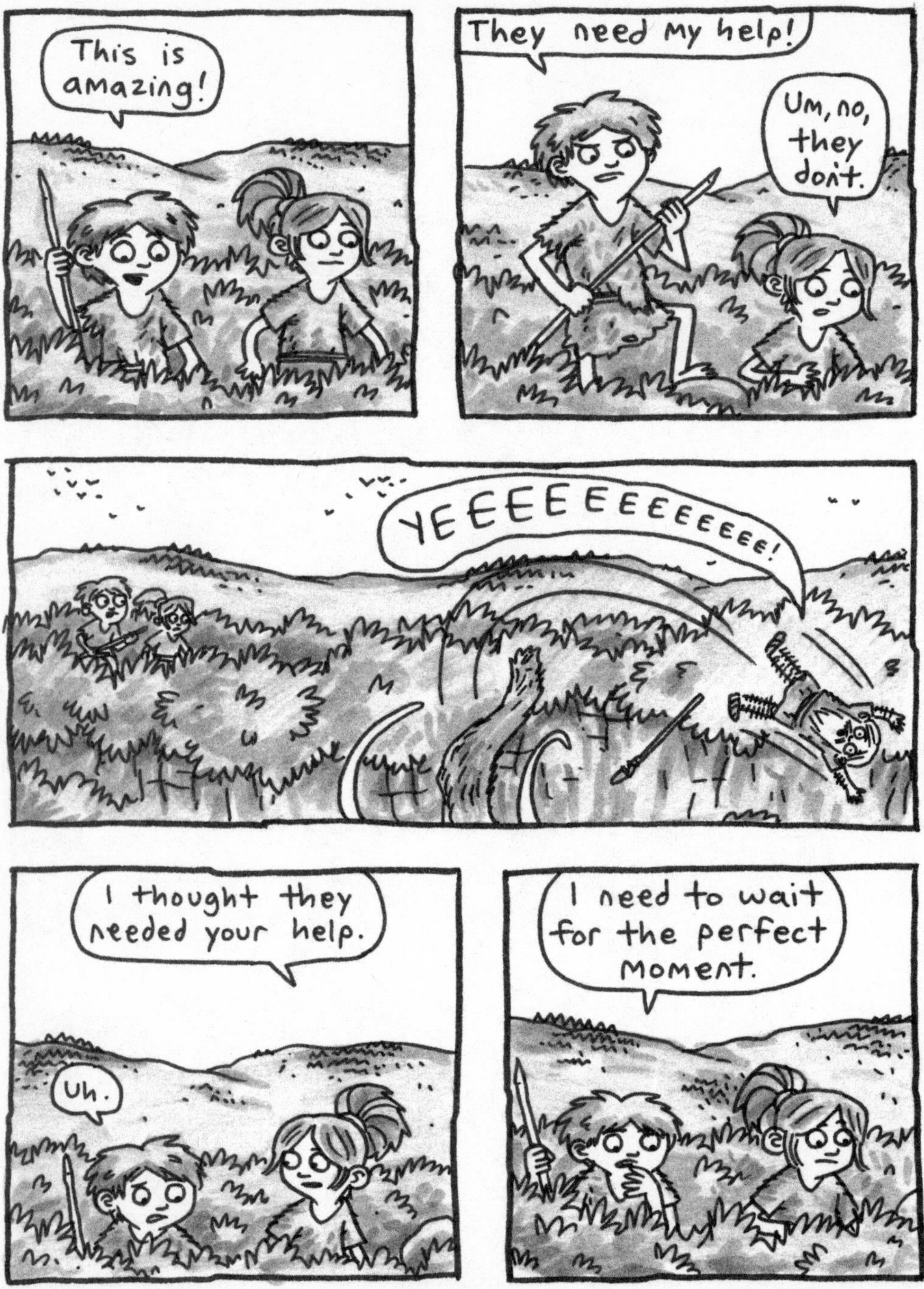
This is amazing!
They need my help!
Um, no, they don't.
YEEEEEEEEEEEEE!
I thought they needed your help.
Uh.
I need to wait for the perfect moment.

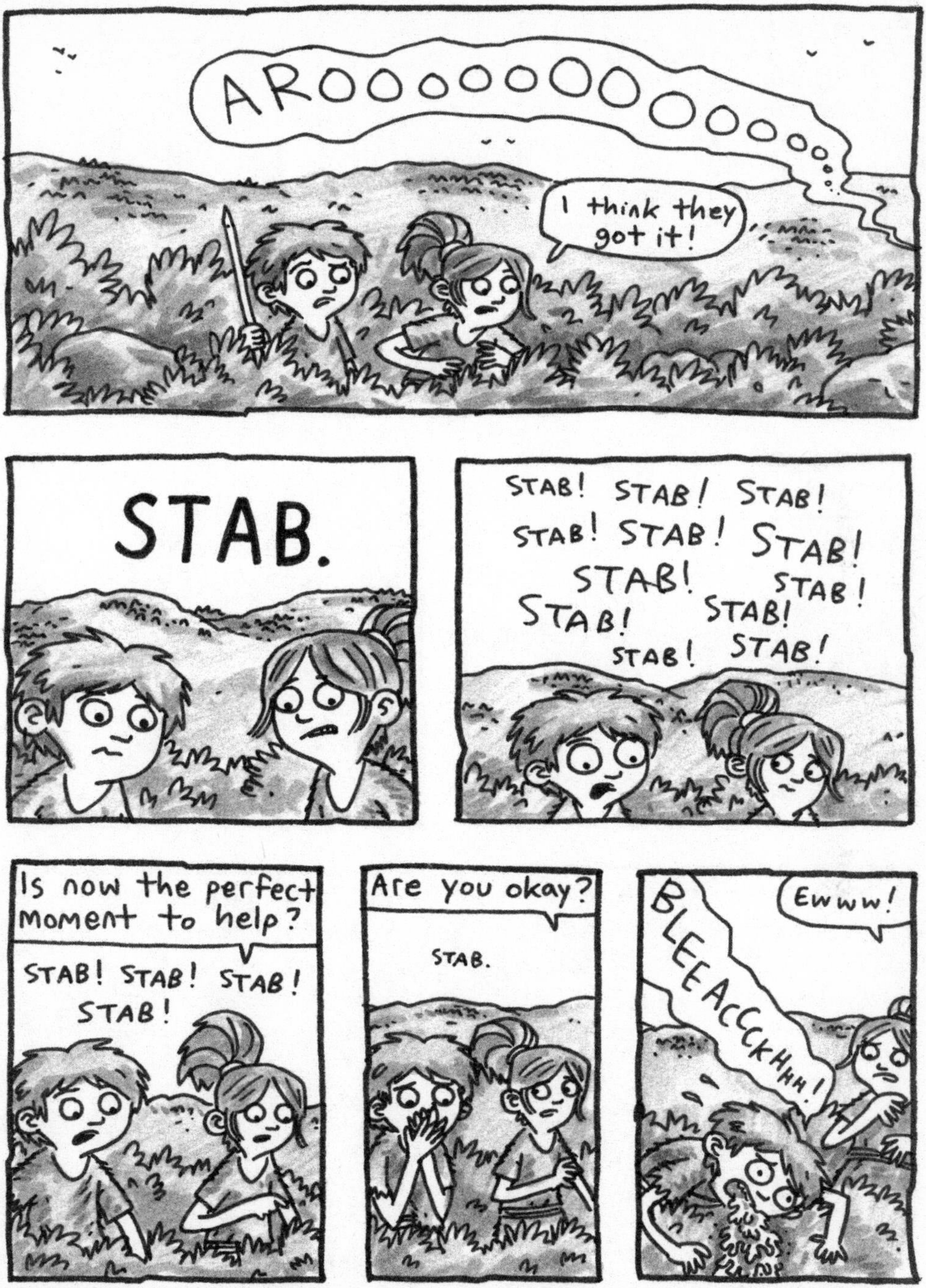
AROOOOOOOOOOOOOO...
I think they got it!
STAB.
STAB! STAB! STAB!
STAB! STAB! STAB!
STAB! STAB!
STAB! STAB!
STAB! STAB!
Is now the perfect moment to help?
STAB! STAB! STAB!
STAB!
Are you okay?
STAB.
BLEEACCCKHHH!
Ewww!

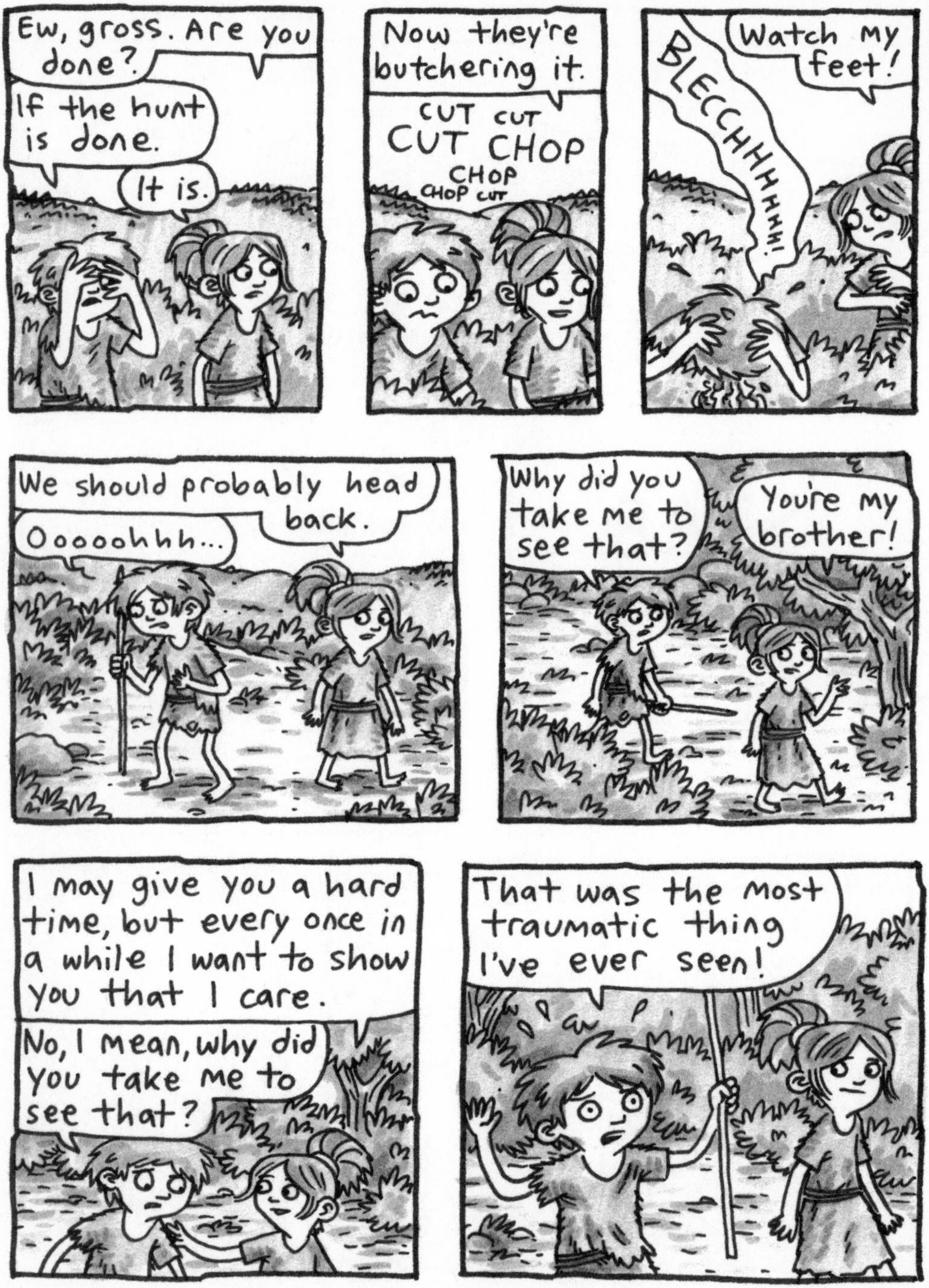
Ew, gross. Are you done?
If the hunt is done.
It is.
Now they're butchering it.
CUT CUT CUT CHOP CHOP CHOP CUT
Watch my feet!
BLECCHHHHHH!
We should probably head back.
Ooooohhh...
Why did you take me to see that?
You're my brother!
I may give you a hard time, but every once in a while I want to show you that I care.
No, I mean, why did you take me to see that?
That was the most traumatic thing I've ever seen!

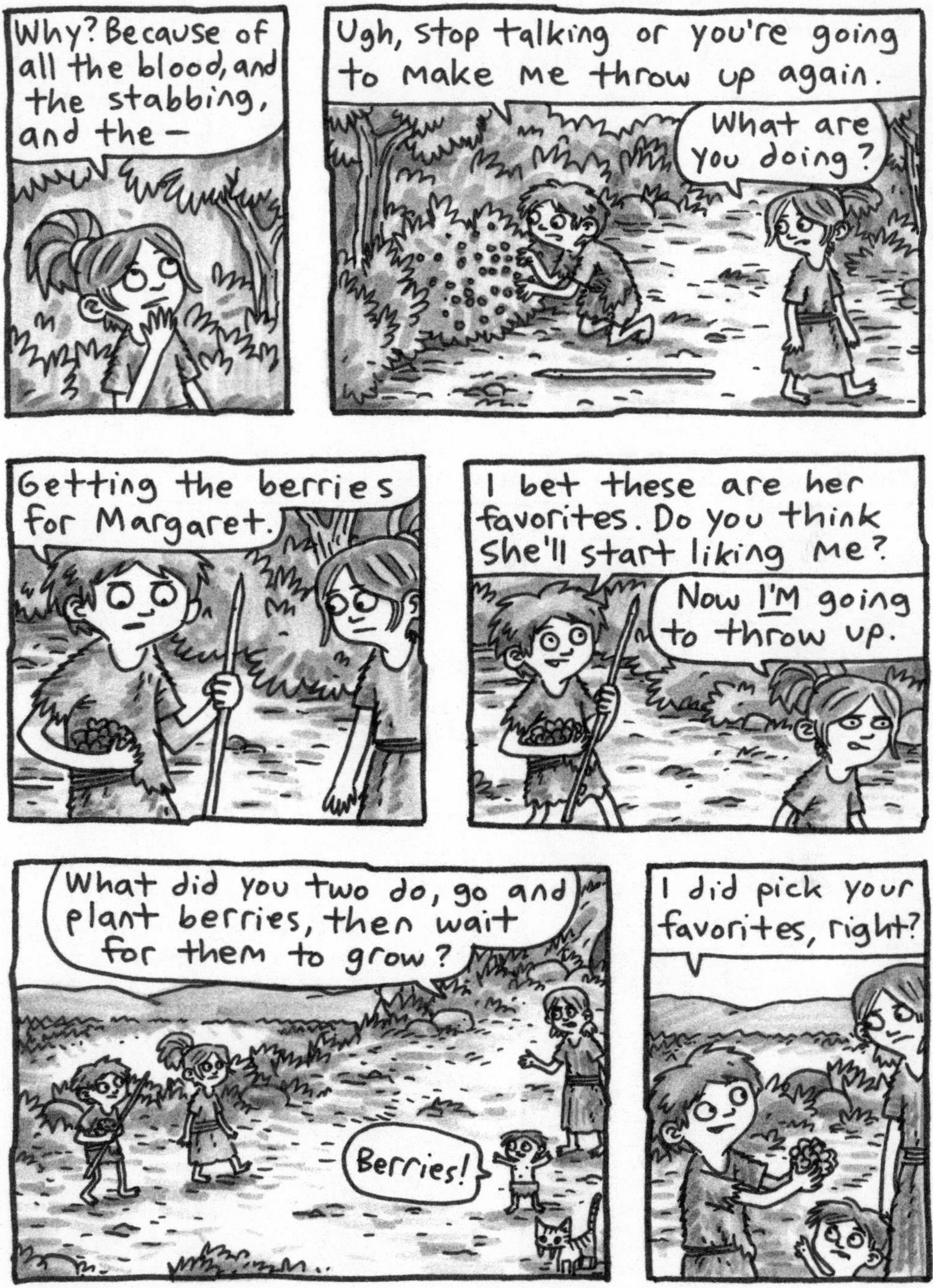
Why? Because of all the blood, and the stabbing, and the—
Ugh, stop talking or you're going to make me throw up again.
What are you doing?
Getting the berries for Margaret.
I bet these are her favorites. Do you think she'll start liking me?
Now I'M going to throw up.
What did you two do, go and plant berries, then wait for them to grow?
Berries!
I did pick your favorites, right?

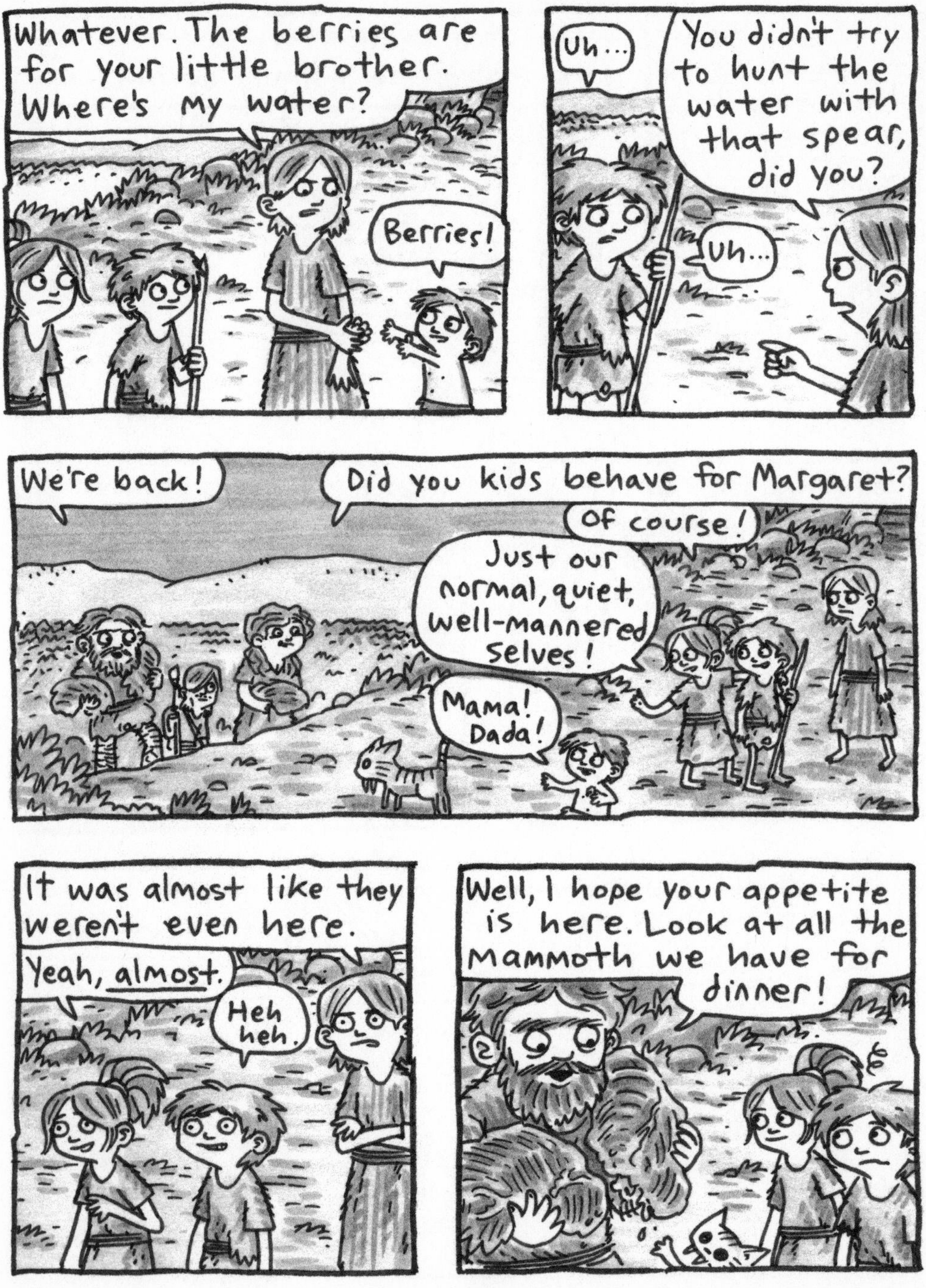
Whatever. The berries are for your little brother. Where's my water?
Berries!
Uh...
You didn't try to hunt the water with that spear, did you?
Uh...
We're back!
Did you kids behave for Margaret?
Of course!
Just our normal, quiet, well-mannered selves!
Mama! Dada!
It was almost like they weren't even here.
Yeah, almost.
Heh heh.
Well, I hope your appetite is here. Look at all the Mammoth we have for dinner!

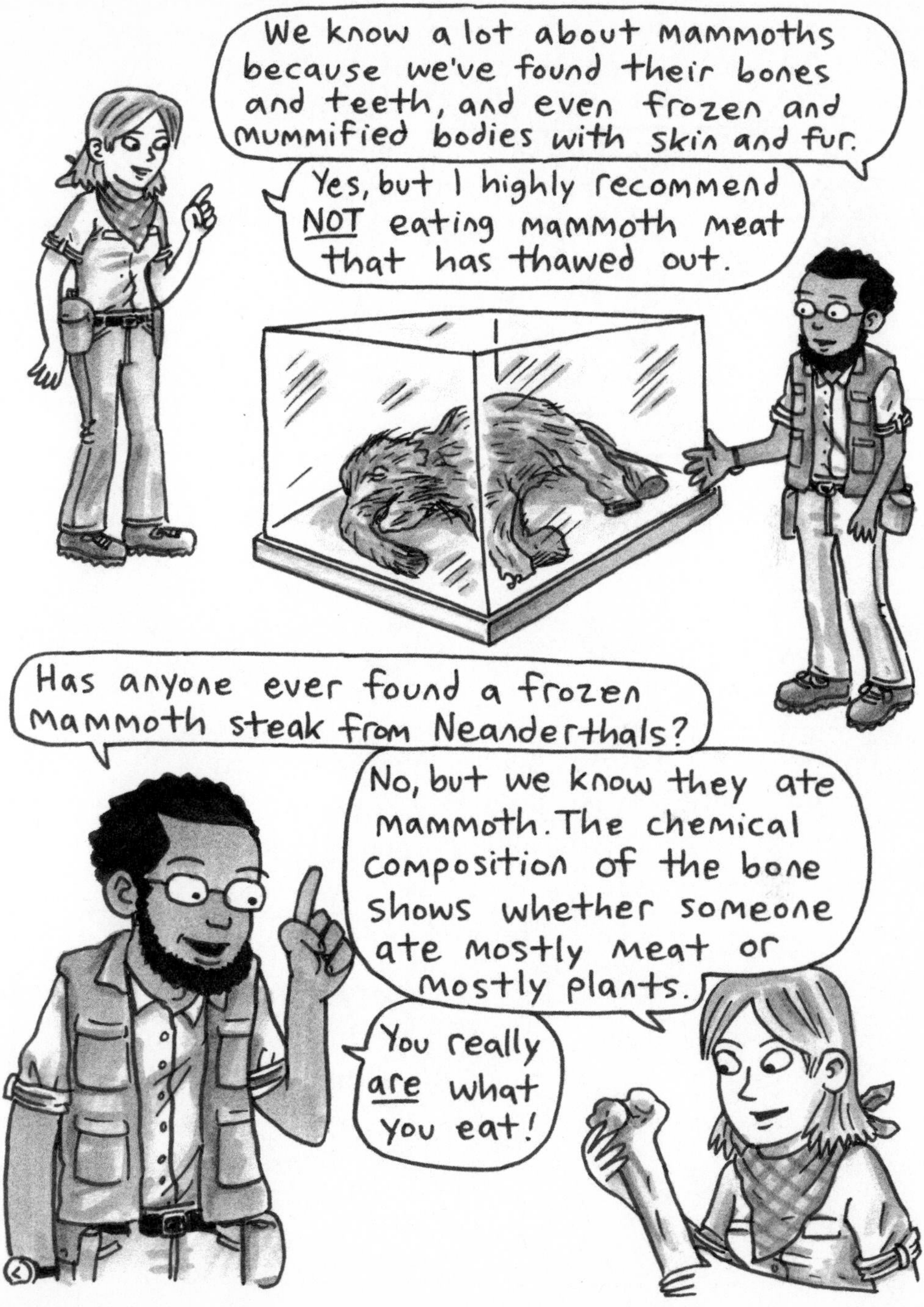
We know a lot about mammoths because we've found their bones and teeth, and even frozen and mummified bodies with skin and fur.
Yes, but I highly recommend NOT eating mammoth meat that has thawed out.
Has anyone ever found a frozen mammoth steak from Neanderthals?
No, but we know they ate mammoth. The chemical composition of the bone shows whether someone ate mostly meat or mostly plants.
You really are what you eat!

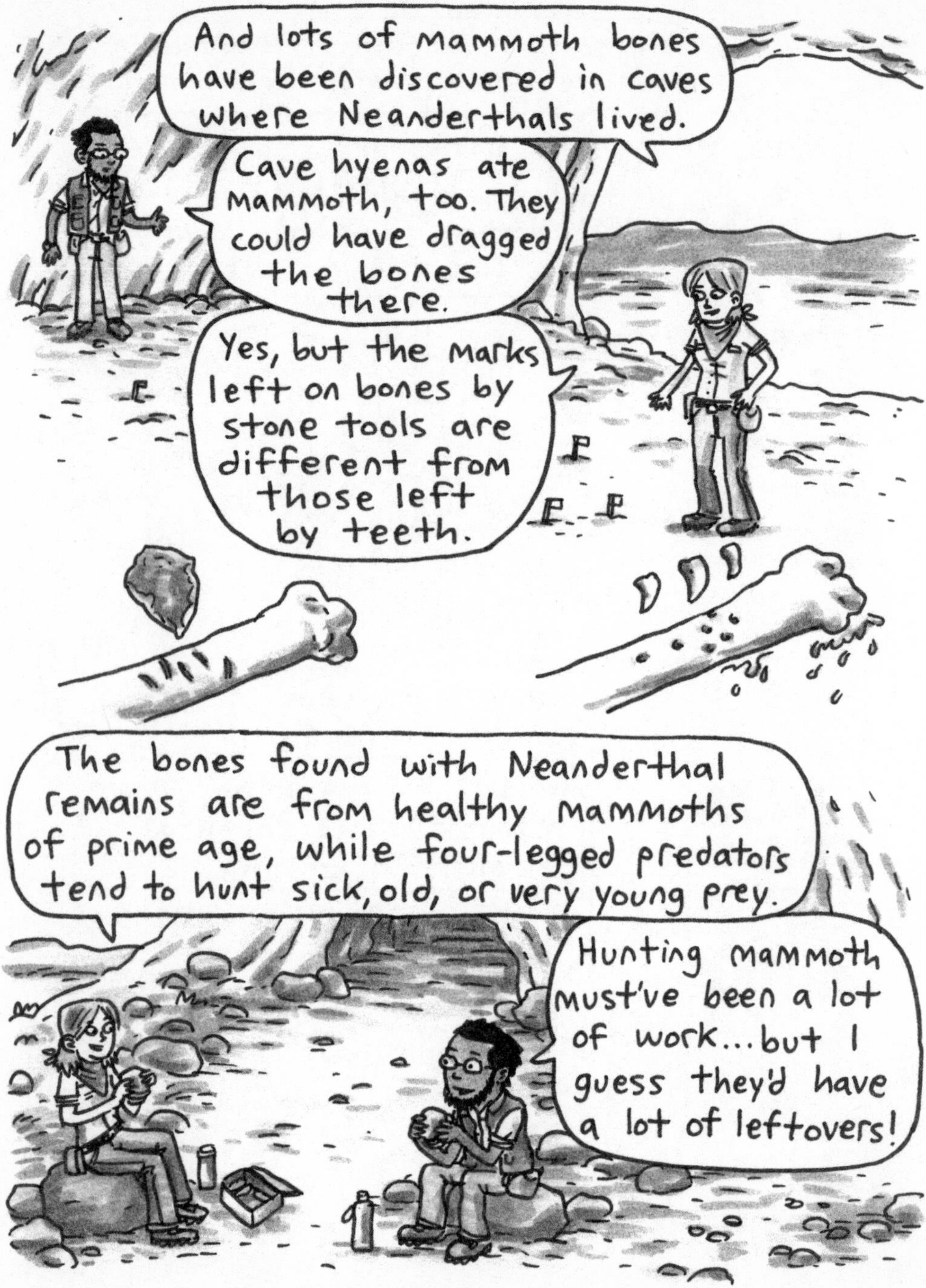
And lots of mammoth bones have been discovered in caves where Neanderthals lived.
Cave hyenas ate mammoth, too. They could have dragged the bones there.
Yes, but the marks left on bones by stone tools are different from those left by teeth.
The bones found with Neanderthal remains are from healthy mammoths of prime age, while four-legged predators tend to hunt sick, old, or very young prey.
Hunting mammoth must've been a lot of work... but I guess they'd have a lot of leftovers!

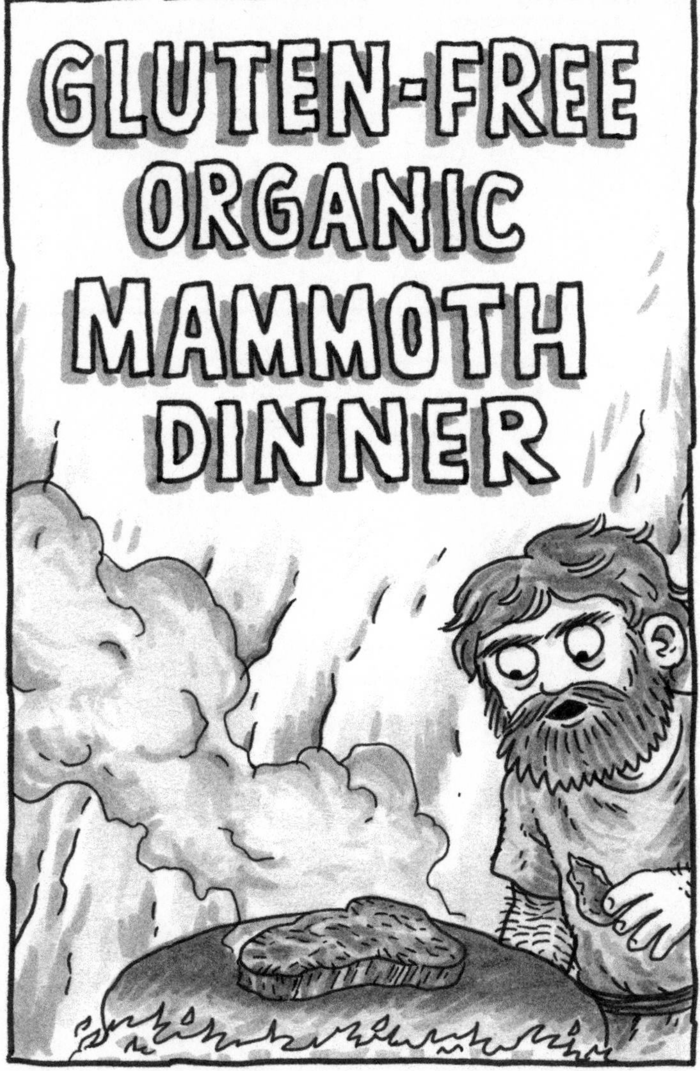
GLUTEN-FREE
ORGANIC
MAMMOTH
DINNER

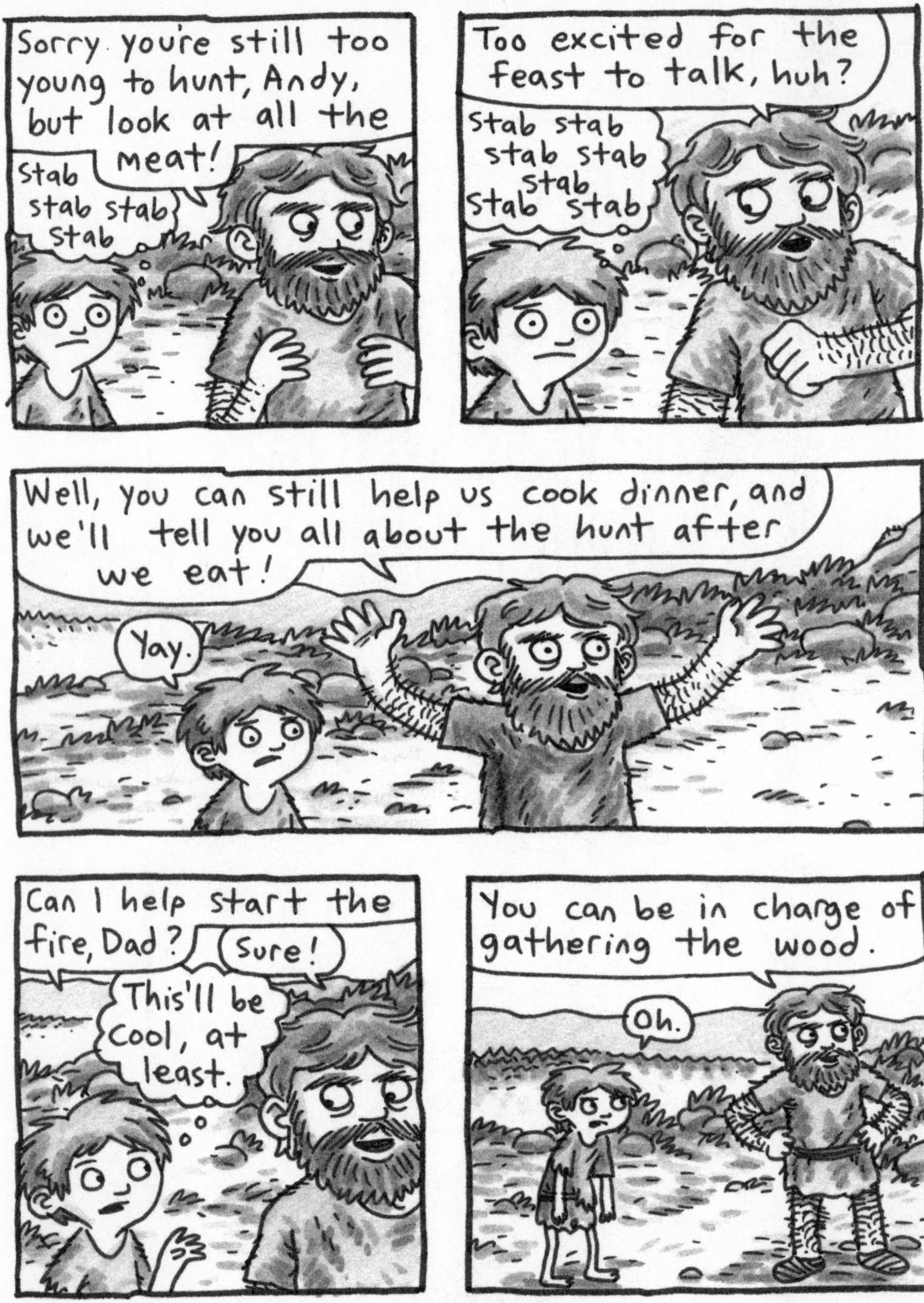

Sorry you're still too young to hunt, Andy, but look at all the meat!
Stab stab stab Stab
Too excited for the feast to talk, huh?
Stab stab stab stab stab Stab stab
Well, you can still help us cook dinner, and we'll tell you all about the hunt after we eat!
Yay.
Can I help start the fire, Dad?
Sure!
This'll be cool, at least.
You can be in charge of gathering the wood.
Oh.

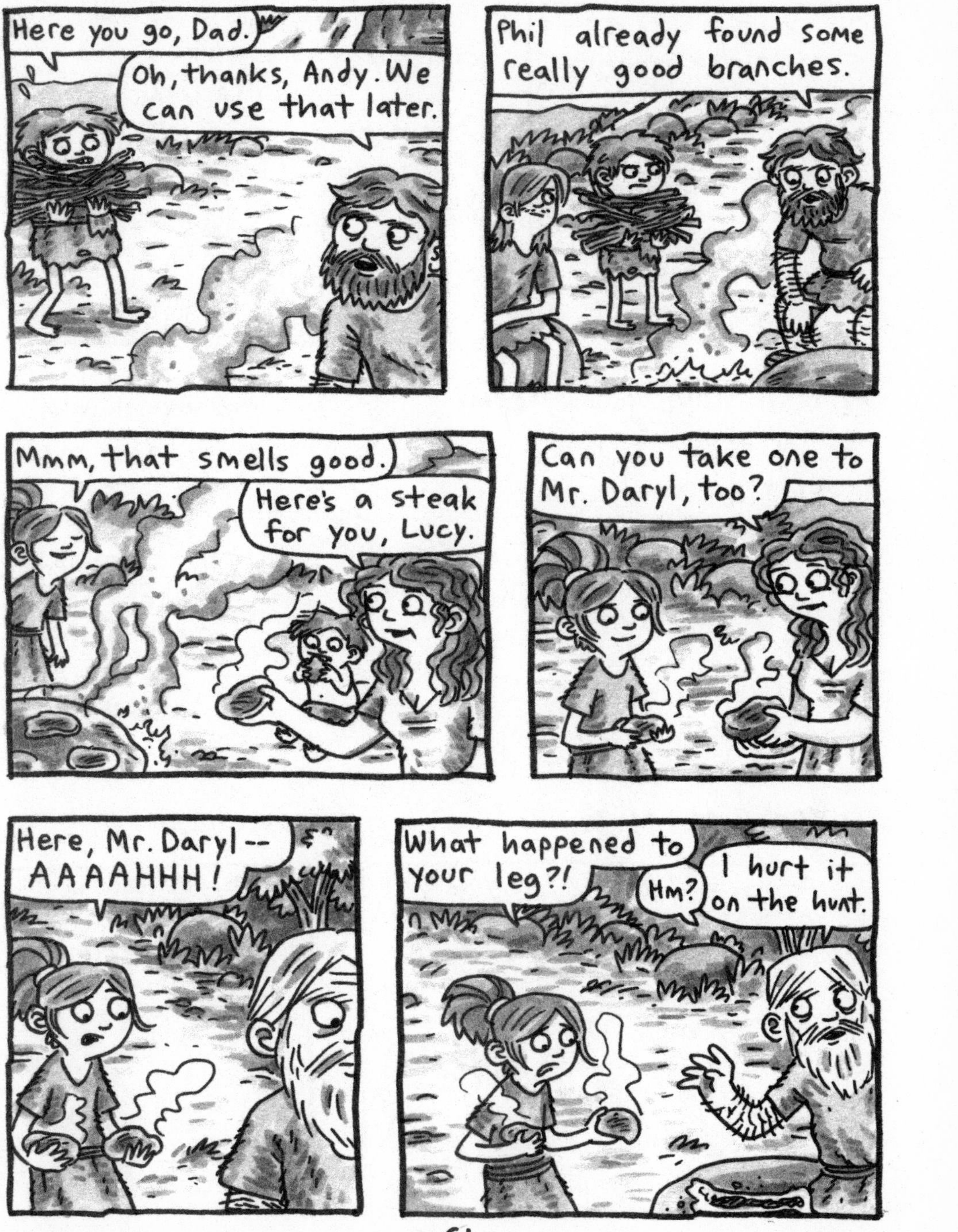
Here you go, Dad.
Oh, thanks, Andy. We can use that later.
Phil already found some really good branches.
Mmm, that smells good.
Here's a steak for you, Lucy.
Can you take one to Mr. Daryl, too?
Here, Mr. Daryl -- AAAAHHH!
What happened to your leg?!
Hm?
I hurt it on the hunt.

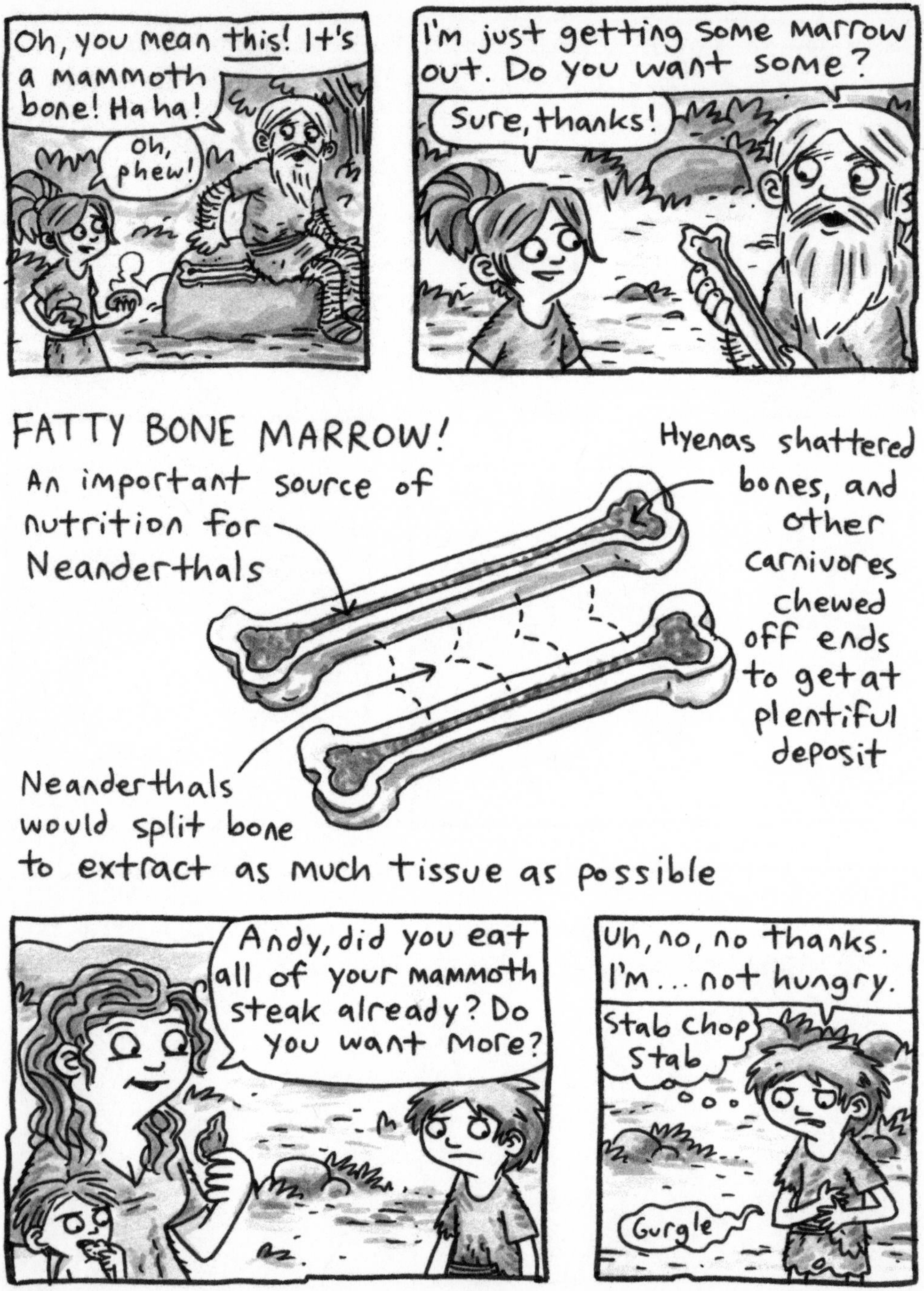
Oh, you mean this! It's a mammoth bone! Ha ha!
Oh, phew!
I'm just getting some marrow out. Do you want some?
Sure, thanks!
FATTY BONE MARROW!
An important source of nutrition for Neanderthals
Hyenas shattered bones, and other carnivores chewed off ends to get at plentiful deposit
Neanderthals would split bone to extract as much tissue as possible
Andy, did you eat all of your mammoth steak already? Do you want more?
Uh, no, no thanks. I'm... not hungry.
Stab Chop Stab
Gurgle

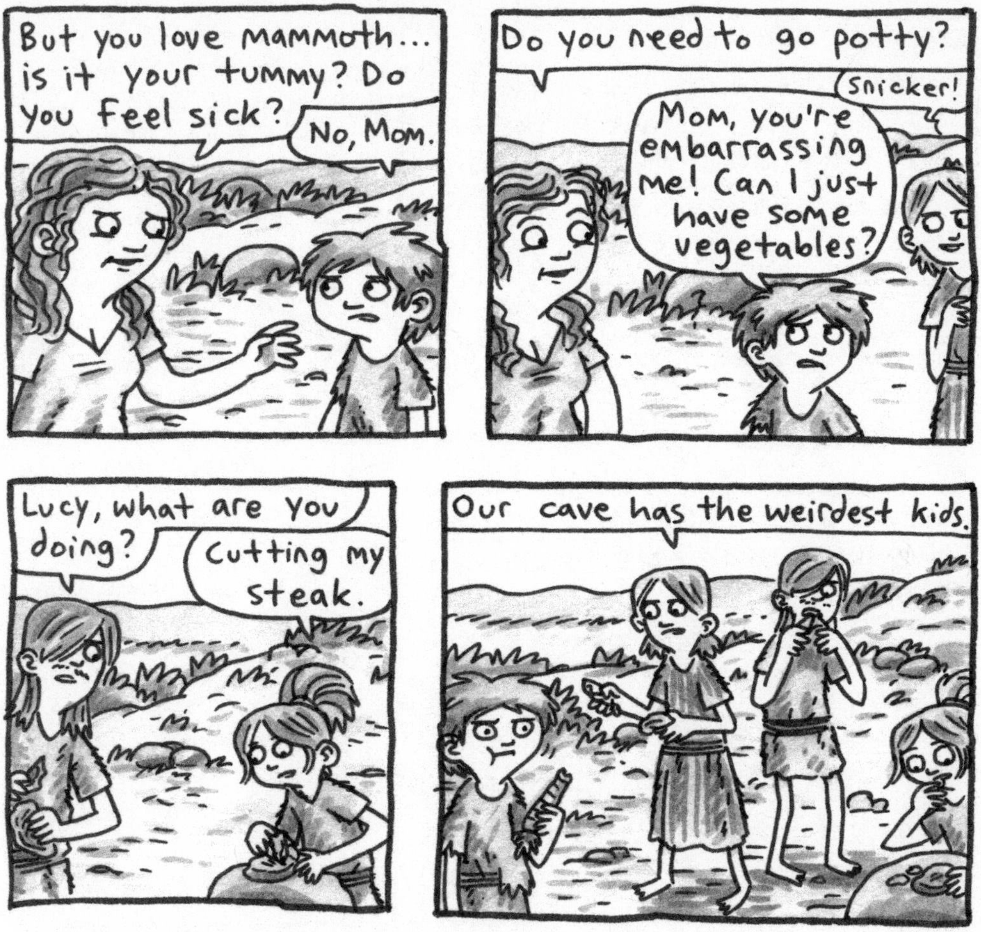
But you love mammoth... is it your tummy? Do you feel sick?
No, Mom.
Do you need to go potty?
Snicker!
Mom, you're embarrassing me! Can I just have some vegetables?
Lucy, what are you doing?
Cutting my steak.
Our cave has the weirdest kids.

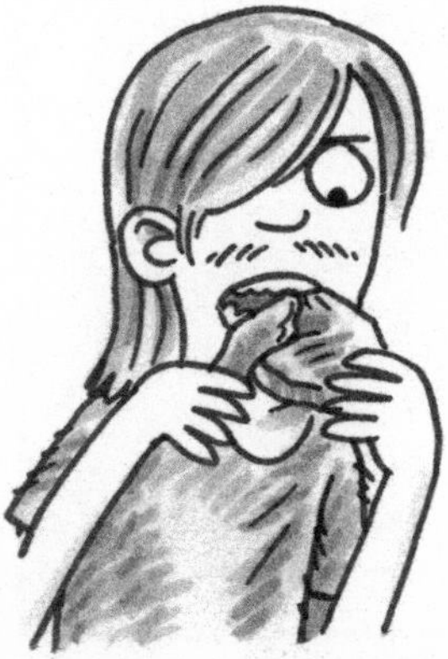

Like some modern-day human hunters, Neanderthals often held food with their teeth while cutting it. Scientists know this from tiny marks on Neanderthal teeth.

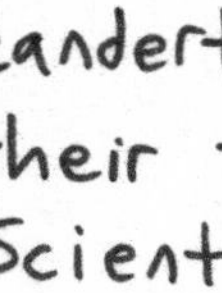

The location and angle of the marks also show that most Neanderthals were right-handed!

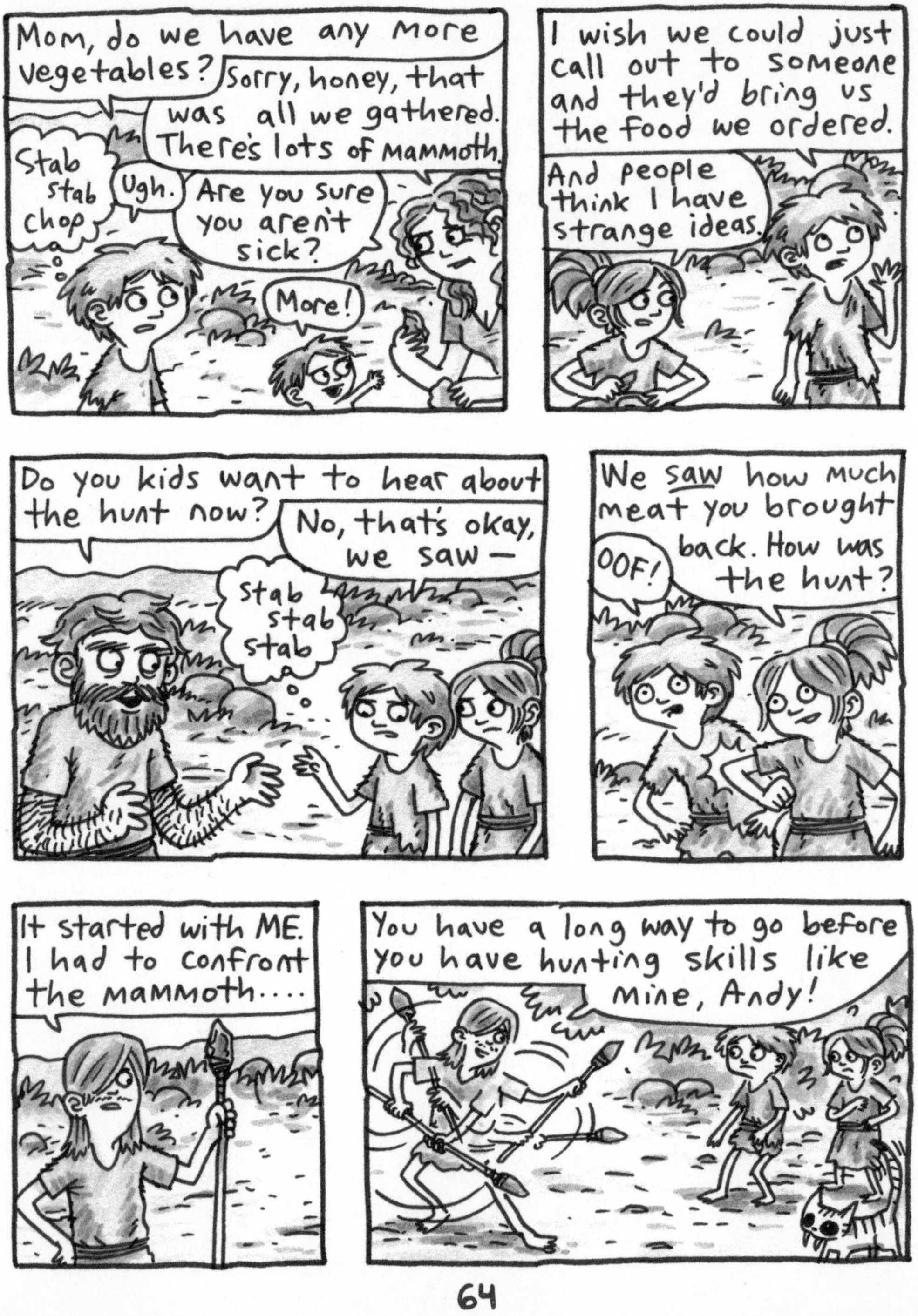
Mom, do we have any more vegetables?
Sorry, honey, that was all we gathered. There's lots of mammoth.
Stab stab chop
Ugh.
Are you sure you aren't sick?
More!
I wish we could just call out to someone and they'd bring us the food we ordered.
And people think I have strange ideas.
Do you kids want to hear about the hunt now?
No, that's okay, we saw—
Stab stab stab
We saw how much meat you brought back. How was the hunt?
OOF!
It started with ME. I had to confront the mammoth....
You have a long way to go before you have hunting skills like mine, Andy!

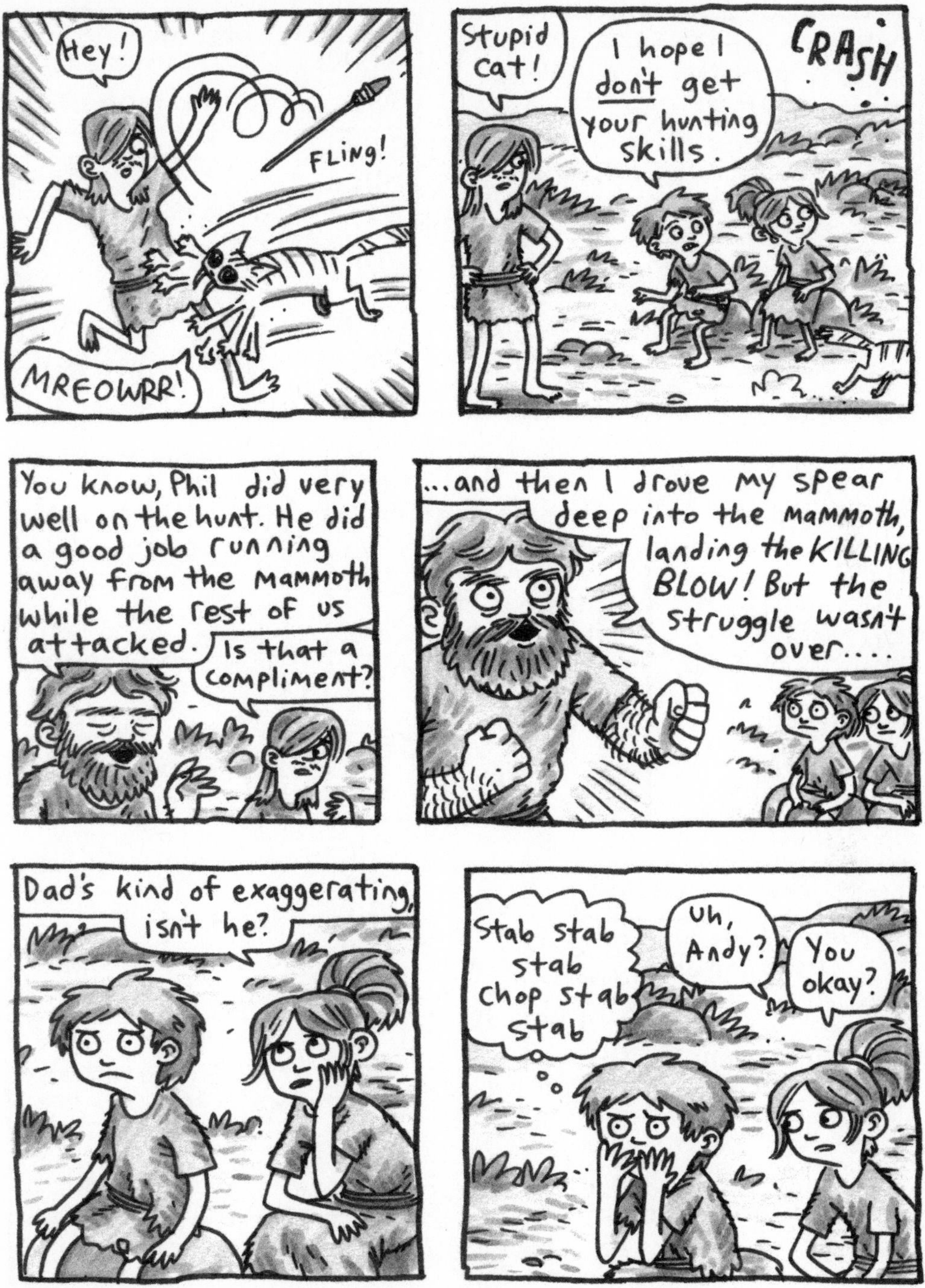
Hey!
FLING!
MREOWRR!
Stupid cat!
I hope I don't get your hunting skills.
CRASH
You know, Phil did very well on the hunt. He did a good job running away from the mammoth while the rest of us attacked.
Is that a compliment?
...and then I drove my spear deep into the mammoth, landing the KILLING BLOW! But the struggle wasn't over....
Dad's kind of exaggerating, isn't he?
Stab stab stab chop stab stab
Uh, Andy?
You okay?

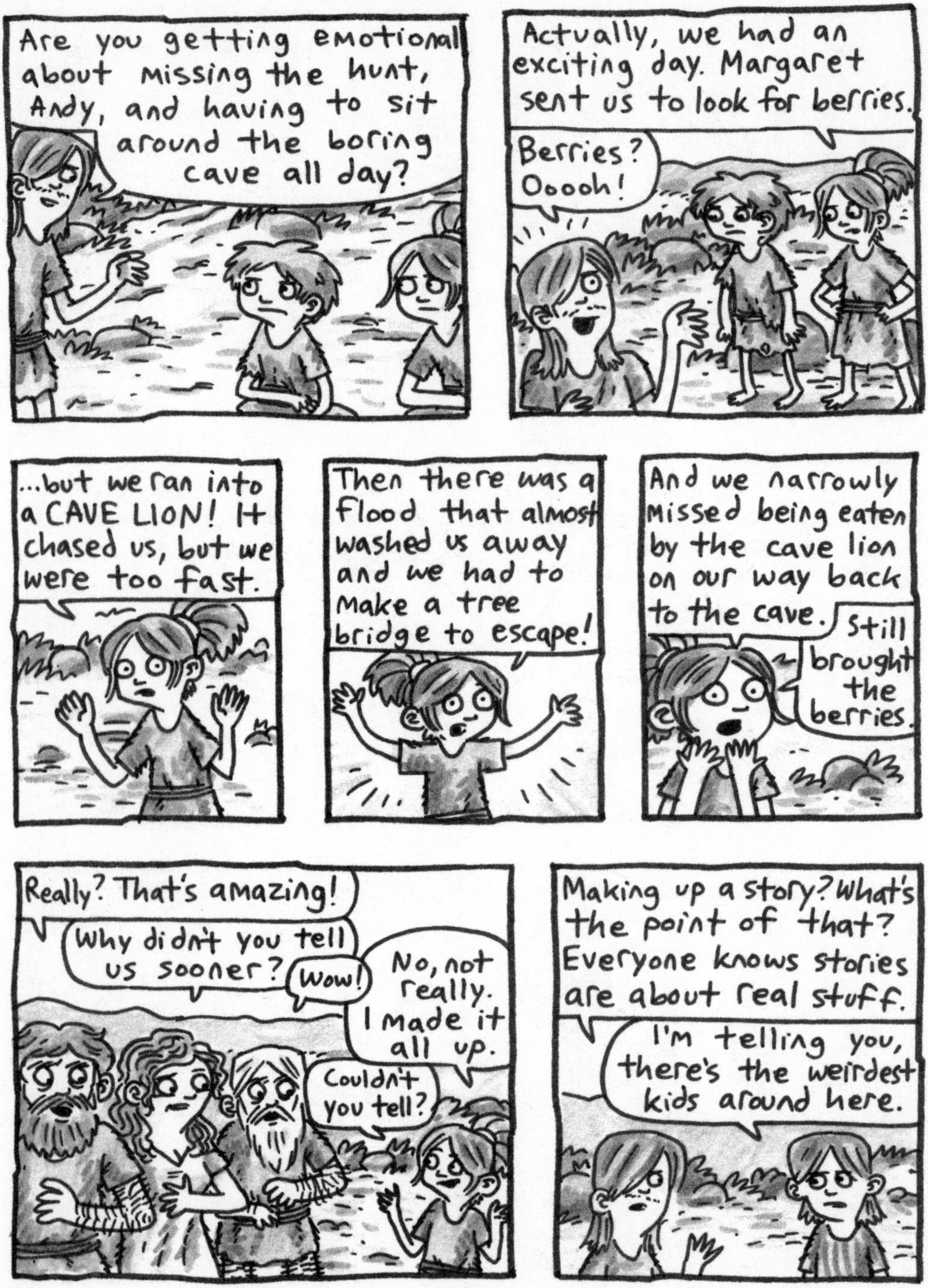

Are you getting emotional about missing the hunt, Andy, and having to sit around the boring cave all day?
Actually, we had an exciting day. Margaret sent us to look for berries.
Berries? Ooooh!
...but we ran into a CAVE LION! It chased us, but we were too fast.
Then there was a flood that almost washed us away and we had to make a tree bridge to escape!
And we narrowly missed being eaten by the cave lion on our way back to the cave.
Still brought the berries.
Really? That's amazing!
Why didn't you tell us sooner?
Wow!
No, not really. I made it all up.
Couldn't you tell?
Making up a story? What's the point of that? Everyone knows stories are about real stuff.
I'm telling you, there's the weirdest kids around here.

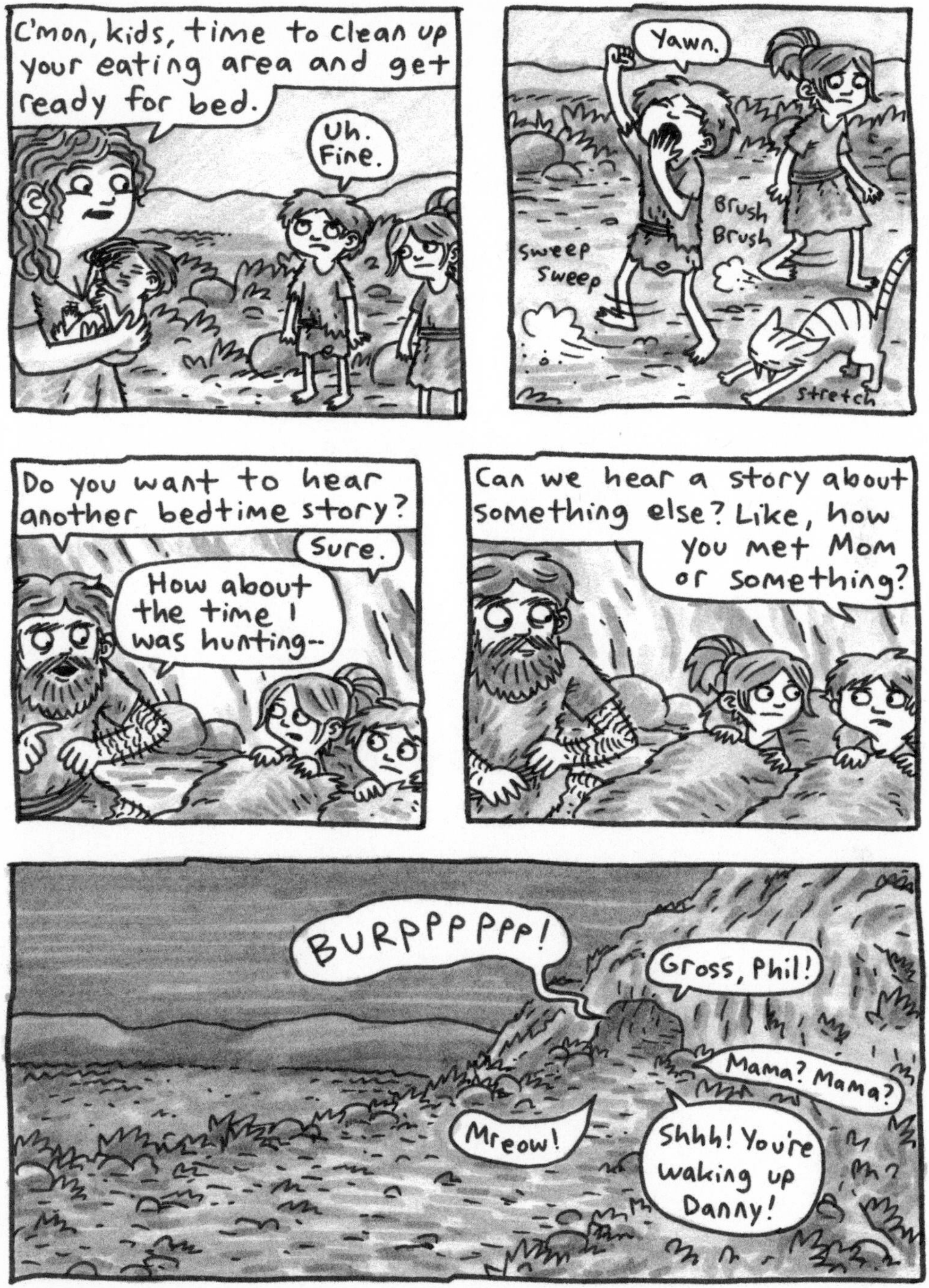
C'mon, kids, time to clean up your eating area and get ready for bed.
Uh. Fine.
Yawn.
Brush Brush
Sweep Sweep
Stretch
Do you want to hear another bedtime story?
Sure.
How about the time I was hunting--
Can we hear a story about something else? Like, how you met Mom or something?
BURPPPPPP!
Gross, Phil!
Mama? Mama?
Mreow!
Shhh! You're waking up Danny!

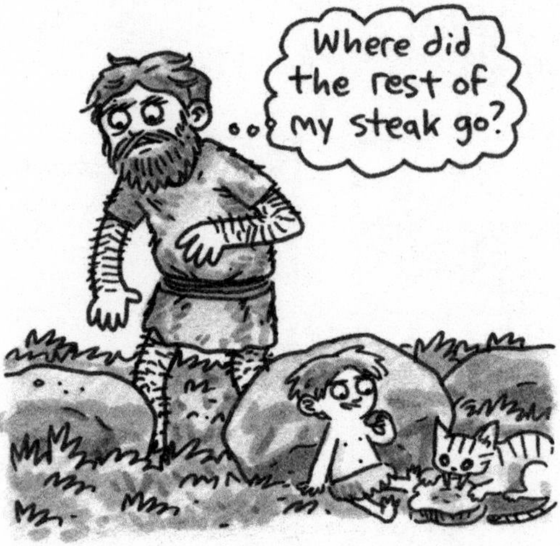
Where did the rest of my steak go?

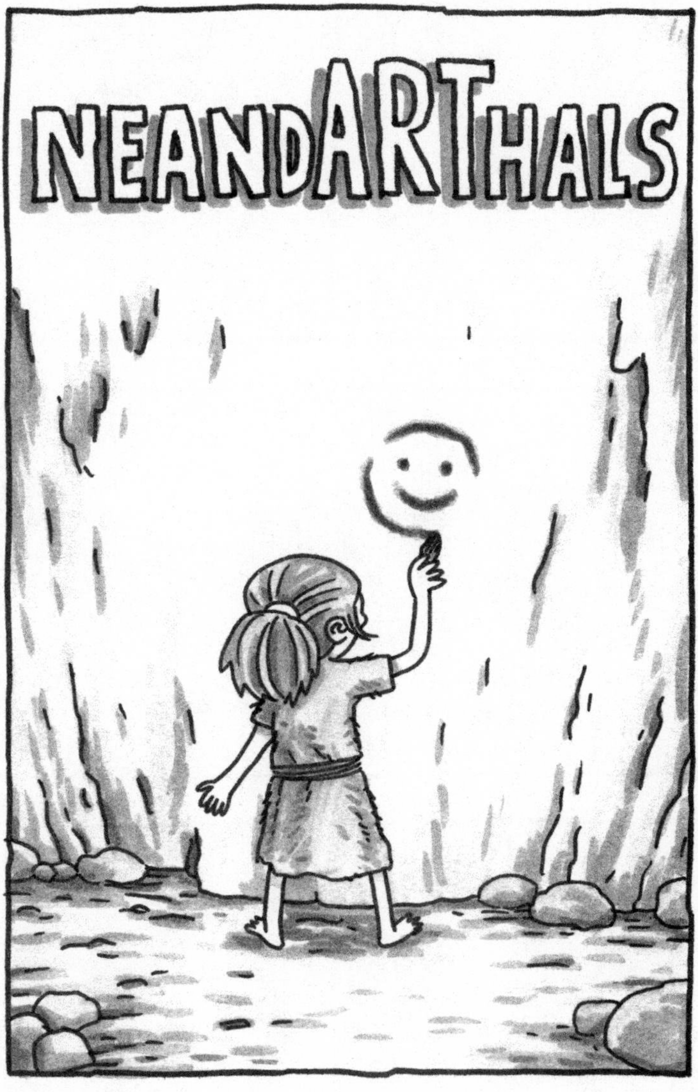
NEANDARTHALS

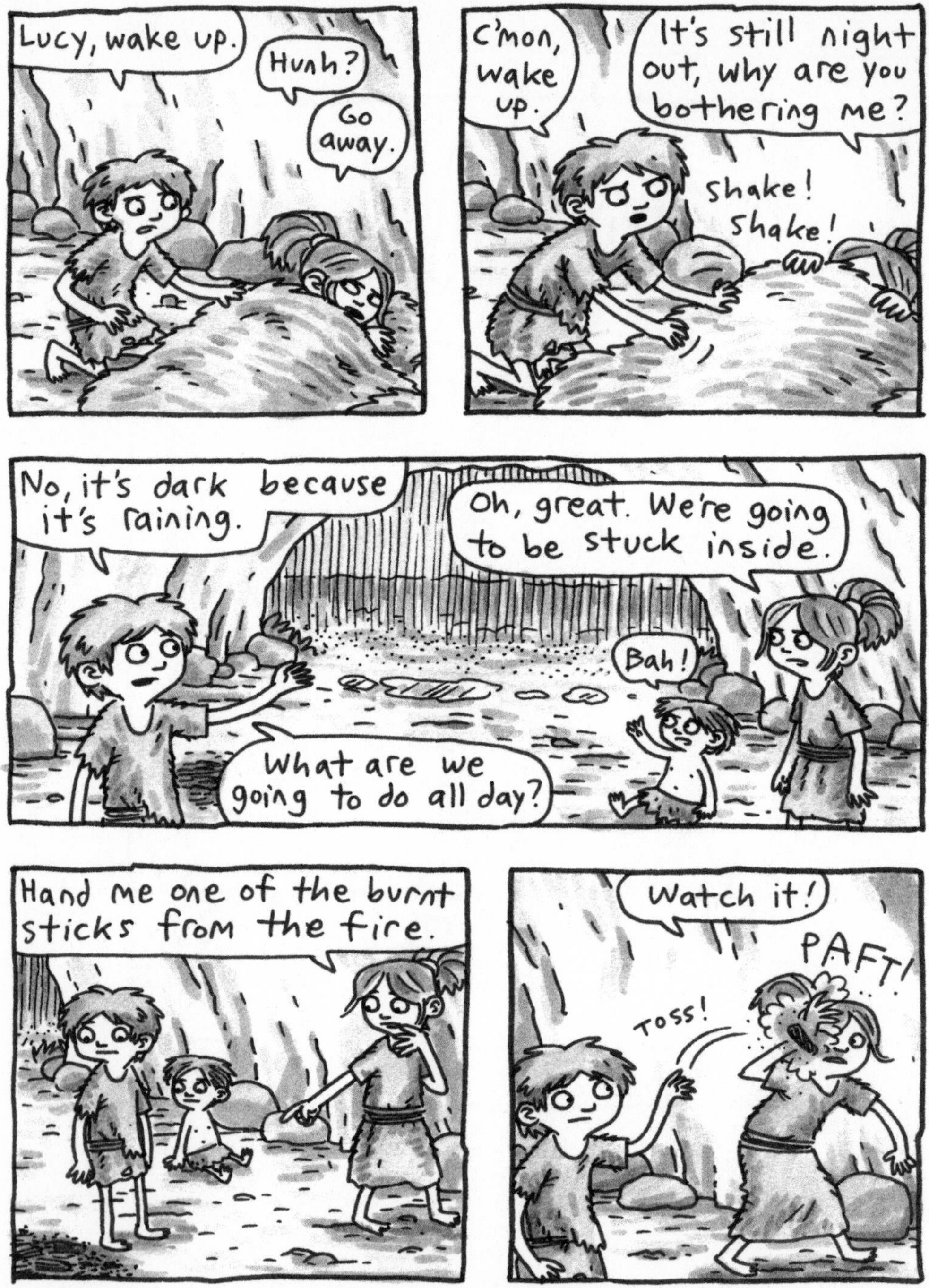
Lucy, wake up.
Hunh?
Go away.
C'mon, wake up.
It's still night out, why are you bothering me?
Shake! Shake!
No, it's dark because it's raining.
Oh, great. We're going to be stuck inside.
Bah!
What are we going to do all day?
Hand me one of the burnt sticks from the fire.
Watch it!
TOSS!
PAFT!

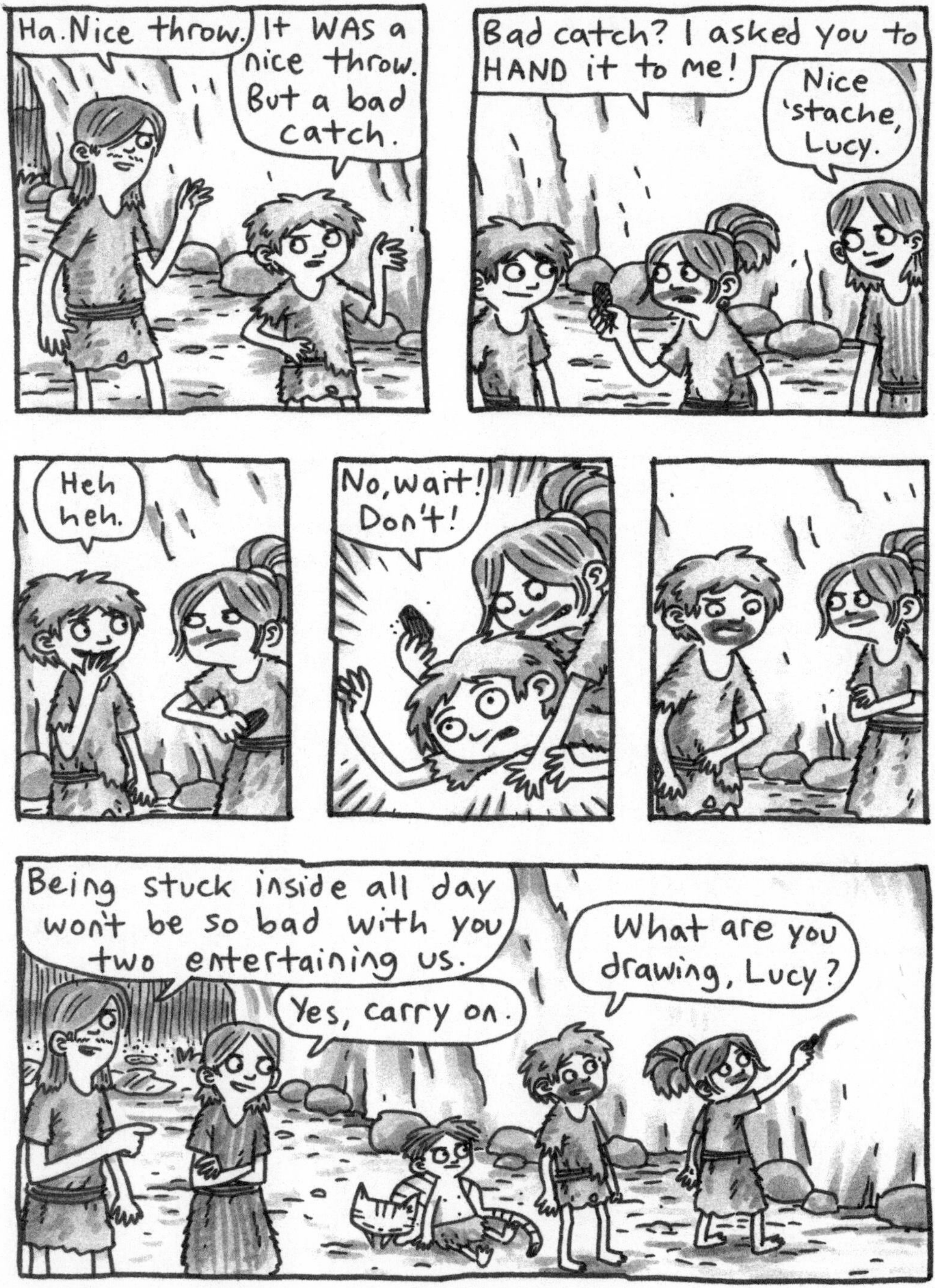
Ha. Nice throw.
It WAS a nice throw. But a bad catch.
Bad catch? I asked you to HAND it to me!
Nice 'stache, Lucy.
Heh heh.
No, wait! Don't!
Being stuck inside all day won't be so bad with you two entertaining us.
Yes, carry on.
What are you drawing, Lucy?

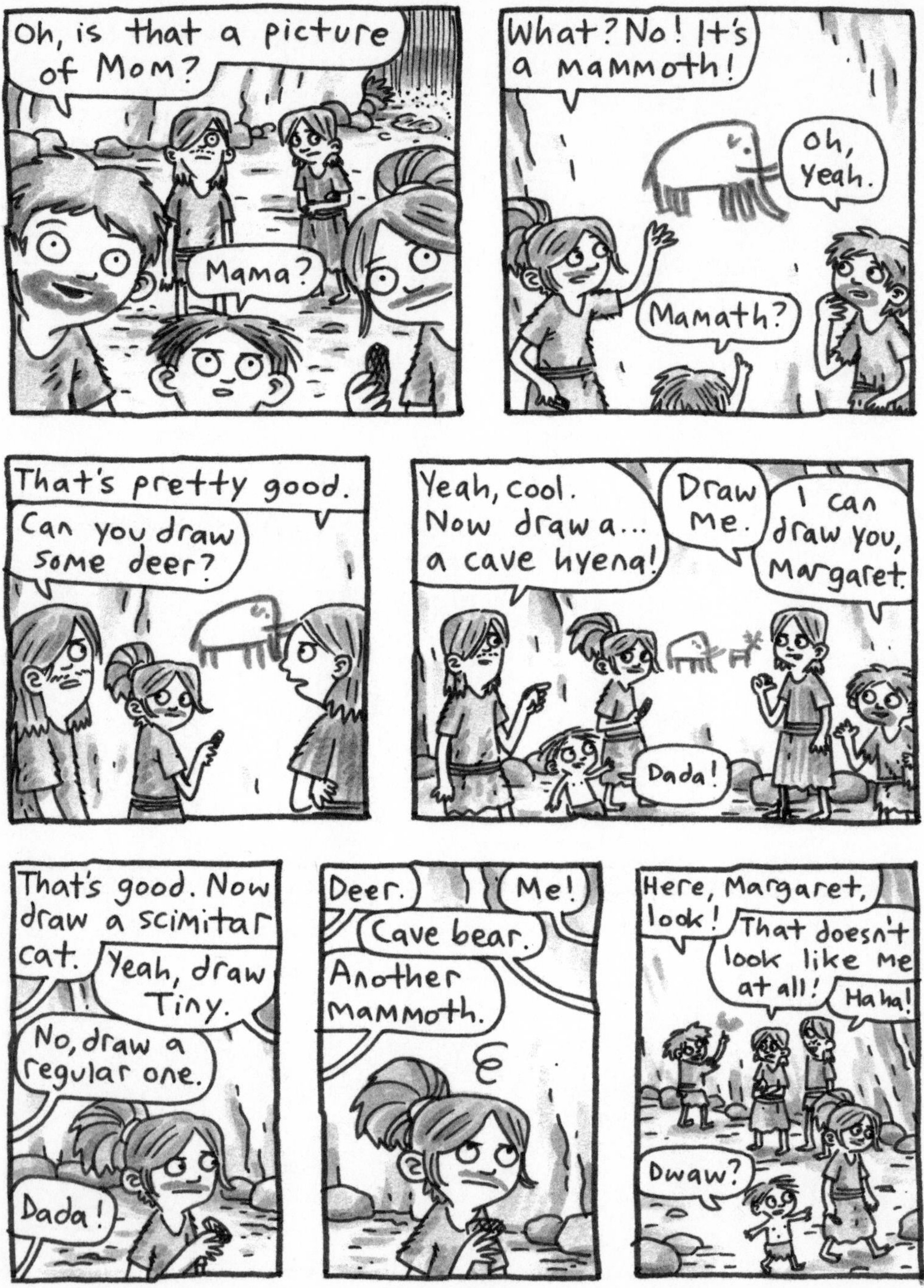
Oh, is that a picture of Mom?
Mama?
What? No! It's a mammoth!
Oh, yeah.
Mamath?
That's pretty good.
Can you draw some deer?
Yeah, cool. Now draw a... a cave hyena!
Draw me.
I can draw you, Margaret.
Dada!
That's good. Now draw a scimitar cat.
Yeah, draw Tiny.
No, draw a regular one.
Dada!
Deer.
Me!
Cave bear.
Another mammoth.
Here, Margaret, look!
That doesn't look like me at all!
Ha ha!
Dwaw?

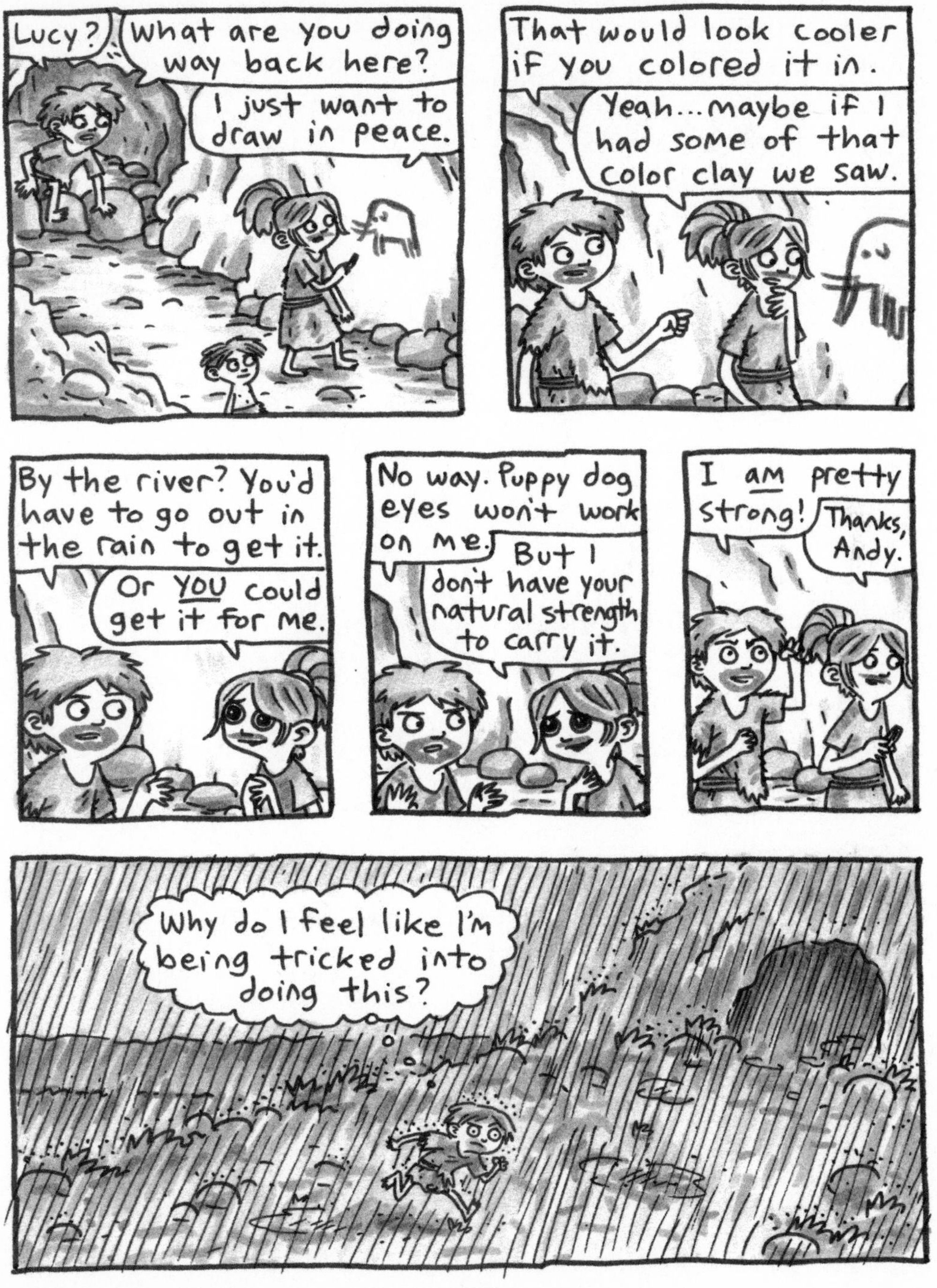
Lucy?
What are you doing way back here?
I just want to draw in peace.
That would look cooler if you colored it in.
Yeah...maybe if I had some of that color clay we saw.
By the river? You'd have to go out in the rain to get it.
Or YOU could get it for me.
No way. Puppy dog eyes won't work on me.
But I don't have your natural strength to carry it.
I AM pretty strong!
Thanks, Andy.
Why do I feel like I'm being tricked into doing this?

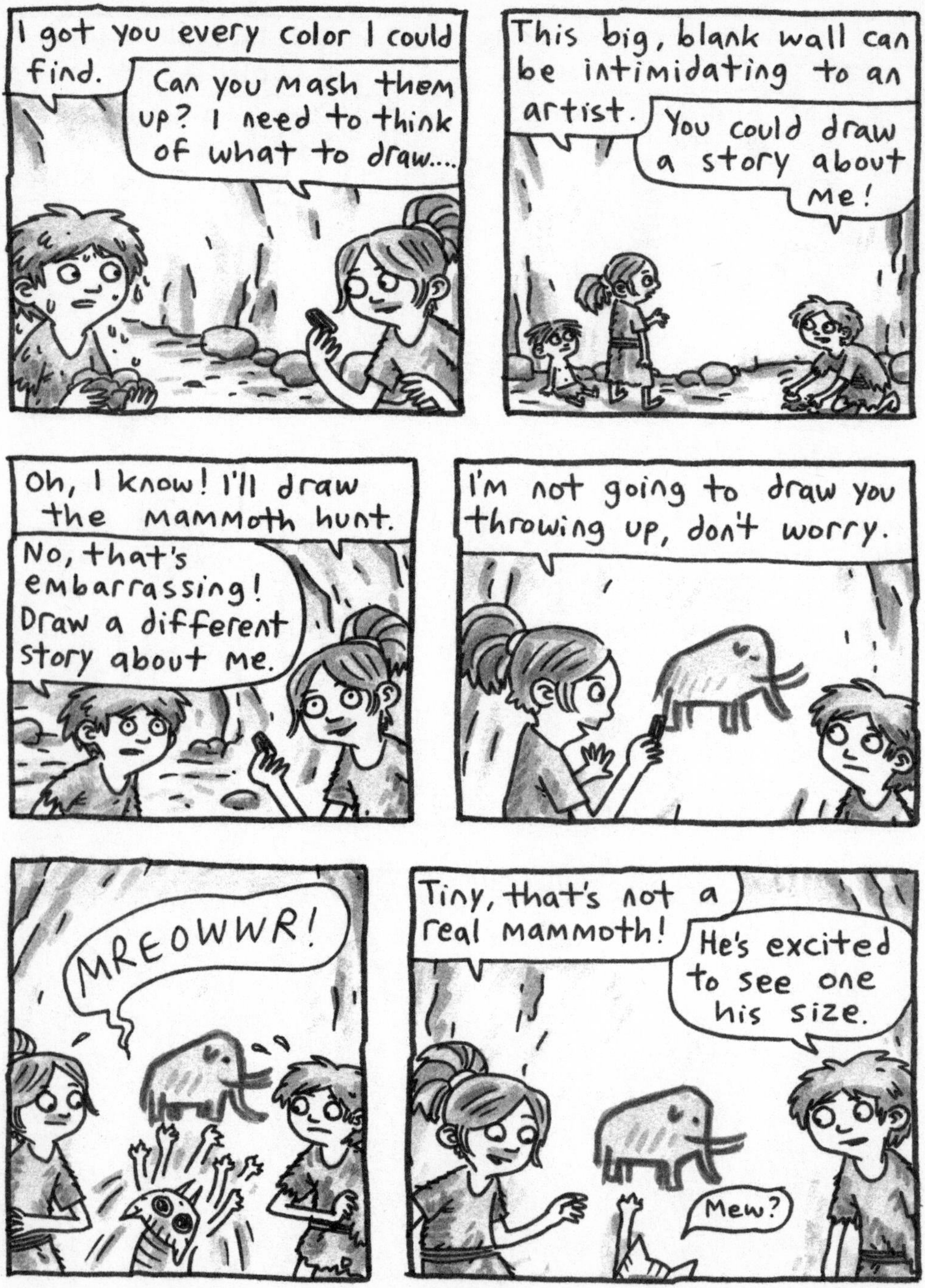
I got you every color I could find.
Can you mash them up? I need to think of what to draw....
This big, blank wall can be intimidating to an artist.
You could draw a story about me!
Oh, I know! I'll draw the mammoth hunt.
No, that's embarrassing! Draw a different story about me.
I'm not going to draw you throwing up, don't worry.
MREOWWR!
Tiny, that's not a real mammoth!
He's excited to see one his size.
Mew?

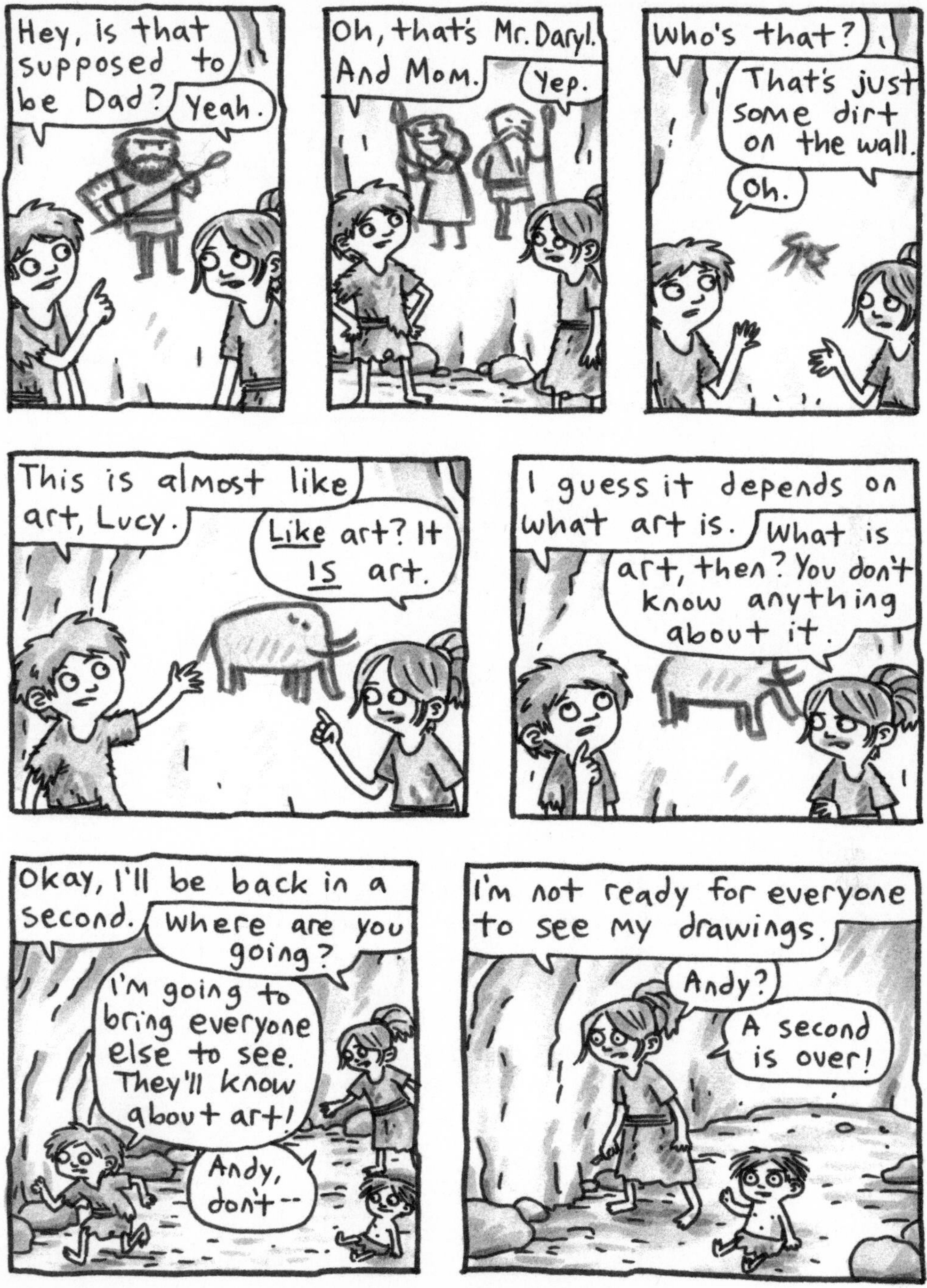

Hey, is that supposed to be Dad?
Yeah.
Oh, that's Mr. Daryl. And Mom.
Yep.
Who's that?
That's just some dirt on the wall.
Oh.
This is almost like art, Lucy.
Like art? It IS art.
I guess it depends on what art is.
What is art, then? You don't know anything about it.
Okay, I'll be back in a second.
Where are you going?
I'm going to bring everyone else to see. They'll know about art!
Andy, don't--
I'm not ready for everyone to see my drawings.
Andy?
A second is over!

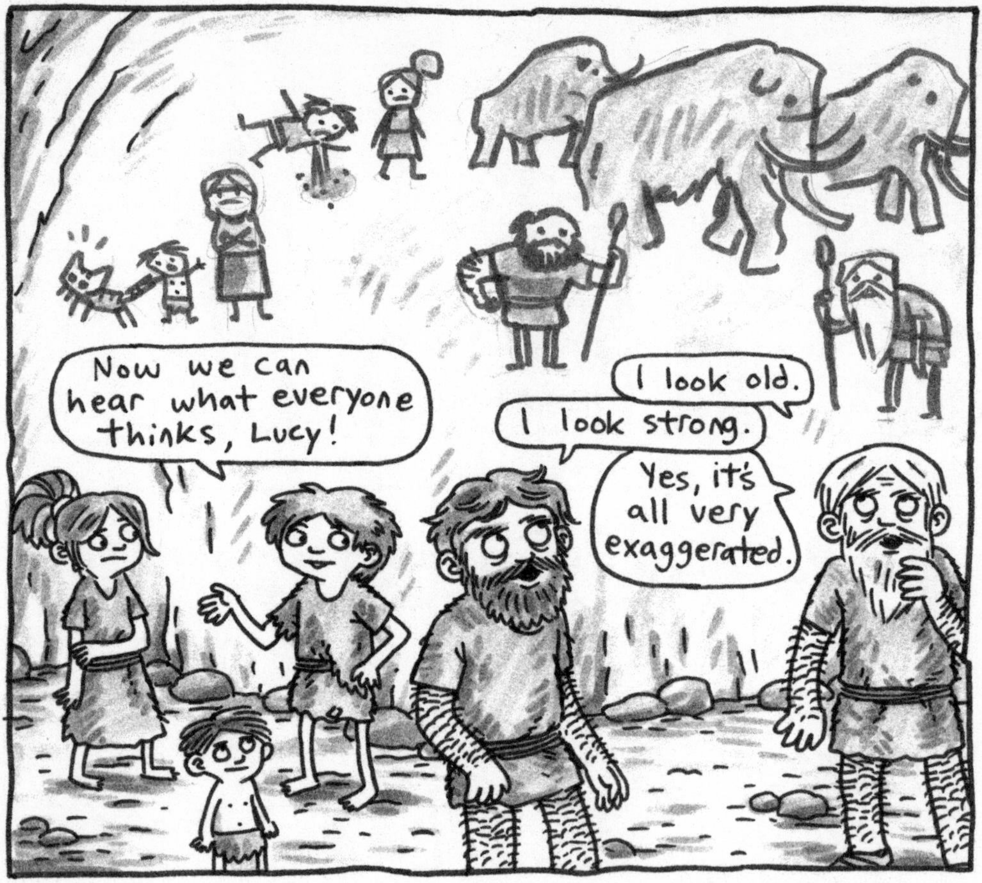
Now we can hear what everyone thinks, Lucy!
I look old.
I look strong.
Yes, it's all very exaggerated.

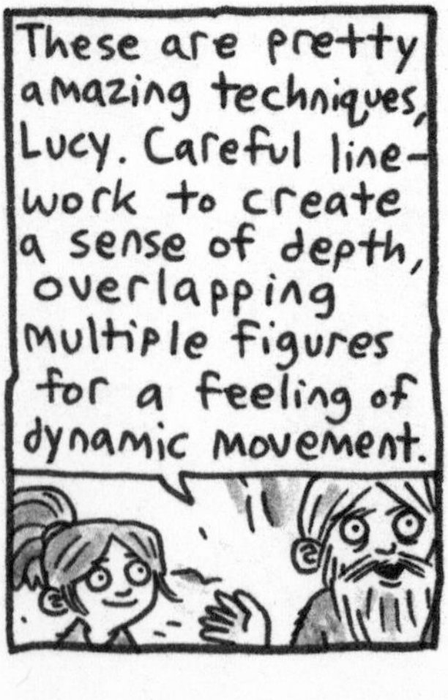
These are pretty amazing techniques, Lucy. Careful line-work to create a sense of depth, overlapping multiple figures for a feeling of dynamic movement.

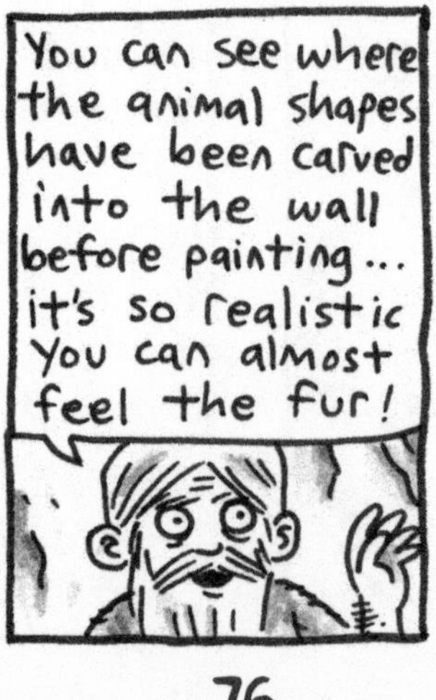
You can see where the animal shapes have been carved into the wall before painting... it's so realistic you can almost feel the fur!

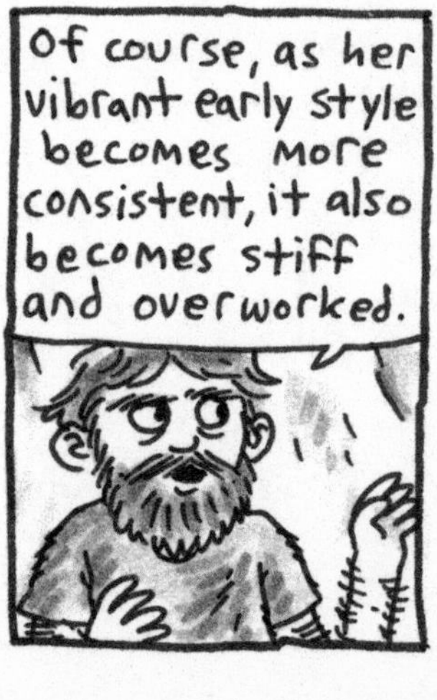
Of course, as her vibrant early style becomes more consistent, it also becomes stiff and overworked.

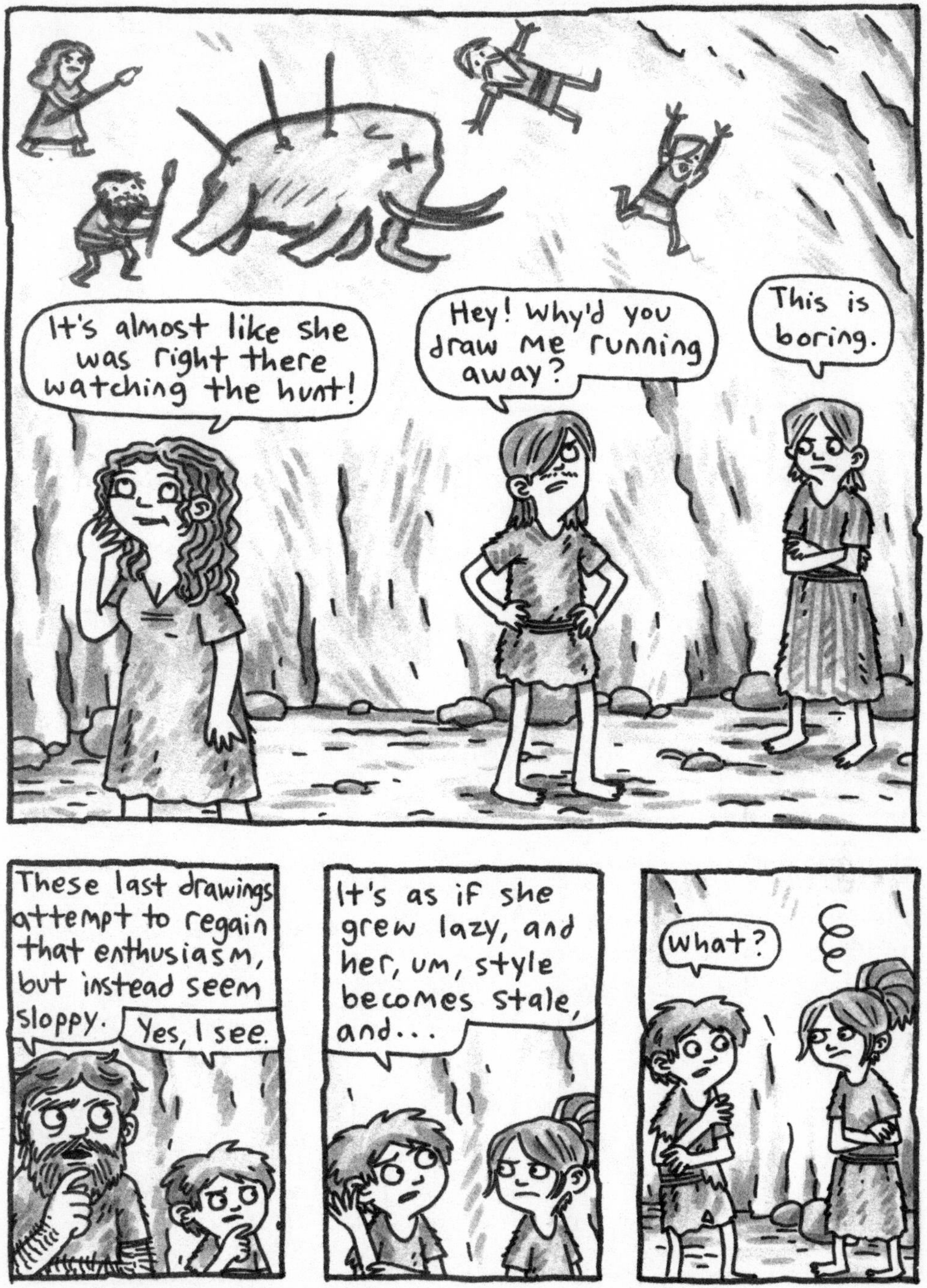

It's almost like she was right there watching the hunt!
Hey! Why'd you draw me running away?
This is boring.
These last drawings attempt to regain that enthusiasm, but instead seem sloppy.
Yes, I see.
It's as if she grew lazy, and her, um, style becomes stale, and...
What?

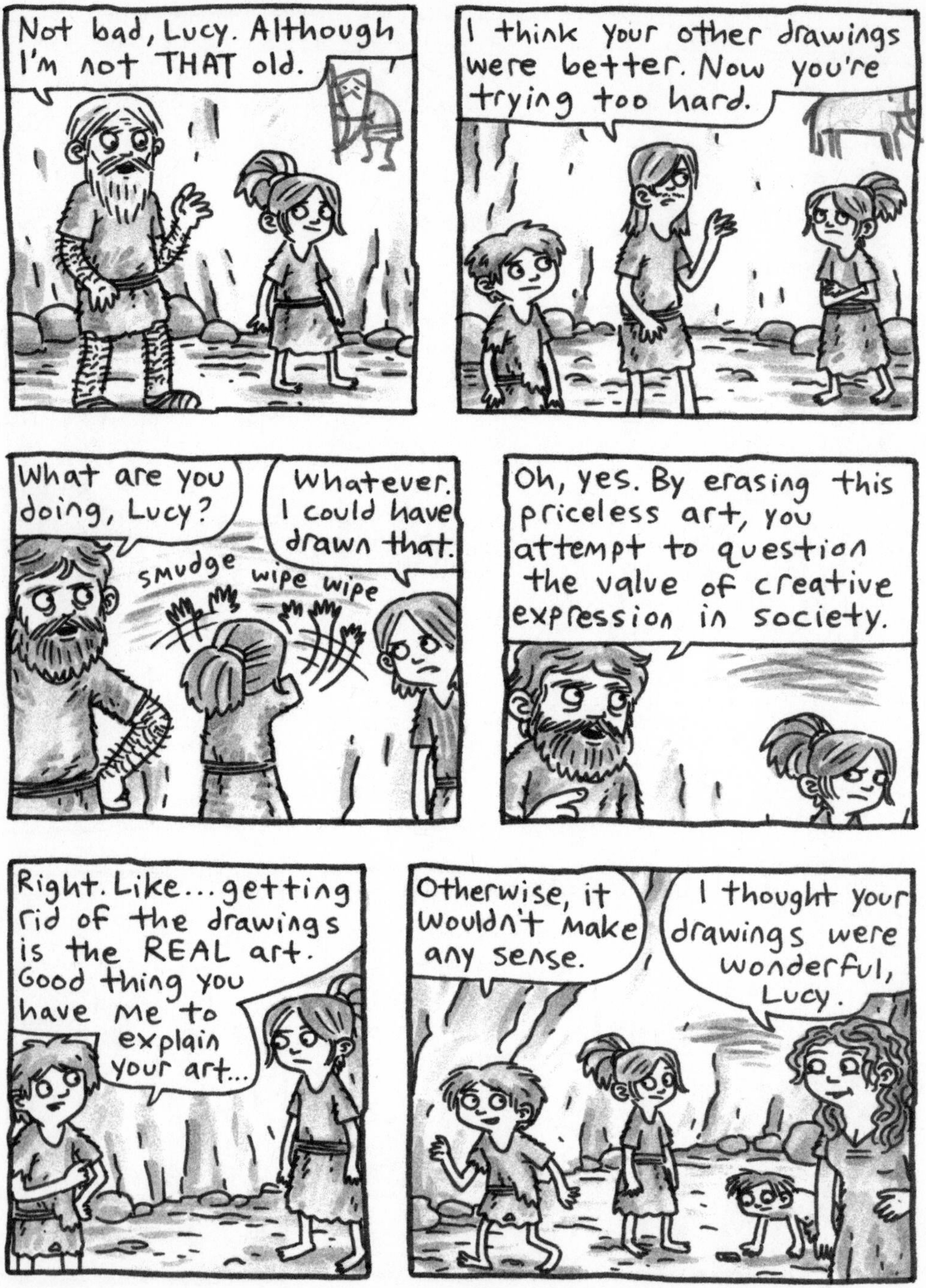

Not bad, Lucy. Although I'm not THAT old.
I think your other drawings were better. Now you're trying too hard.
What are you doing, Lucy?
smudge
wipe wipe
Whatever. I could have drawn that.
Oh, yes. By erasing this priceless art, you attempt to question the value of creative expression in society.
Right. Like... getting rid of the drawings is the REAL art. Good thing you have me to explain your art...
Otherwise, it wouldn't make any sense.
I thought your drawings were wonderful, Lucy.

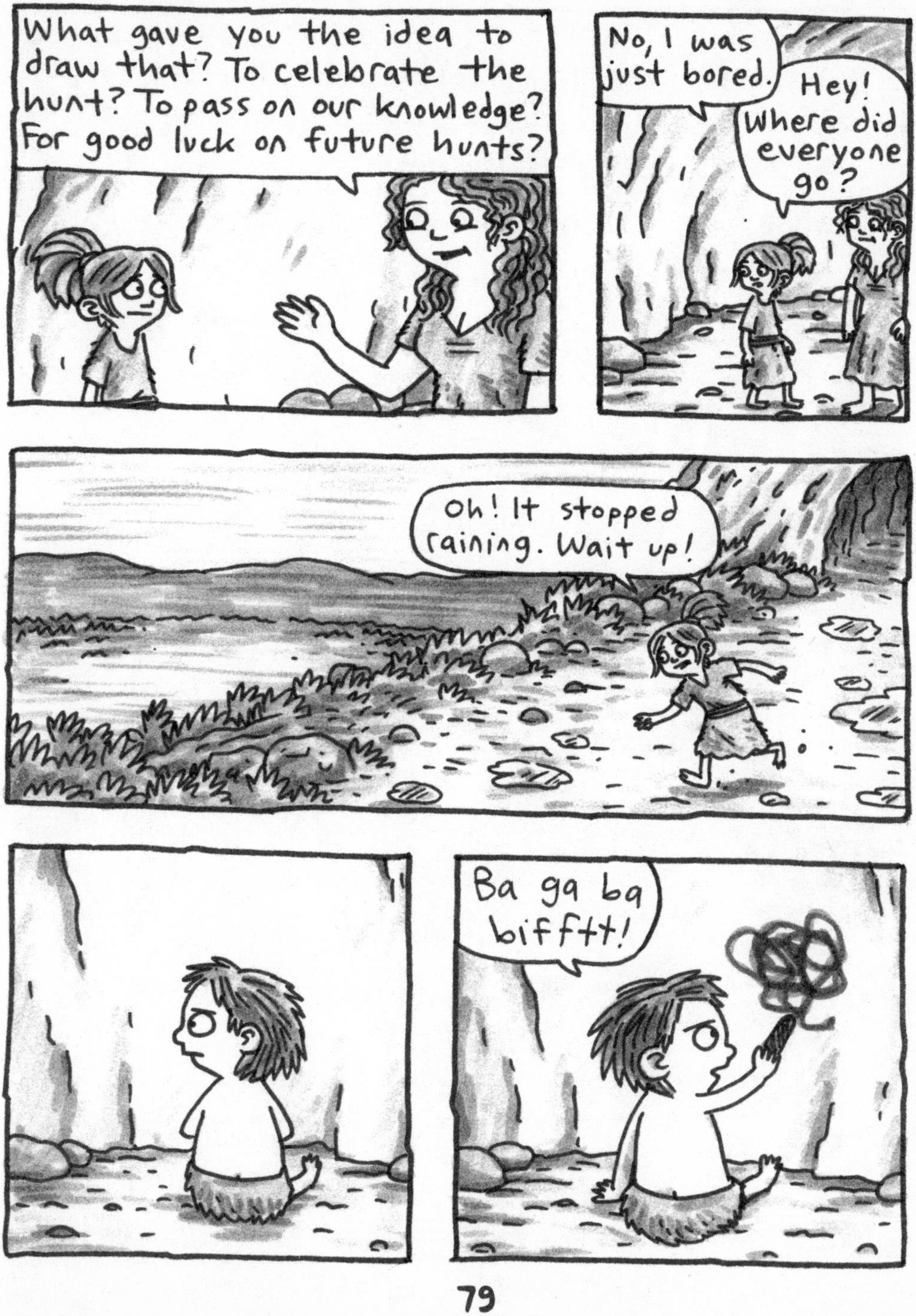
What gave you the idea to draw that? To celebrate the hunt? To pass on our knowledge? For good luck on future hunts?
No, I was just bored.
Hey! Where did everyone go?
Oh! It stopped raining. Wait up!
Ba ga ba bifftt!

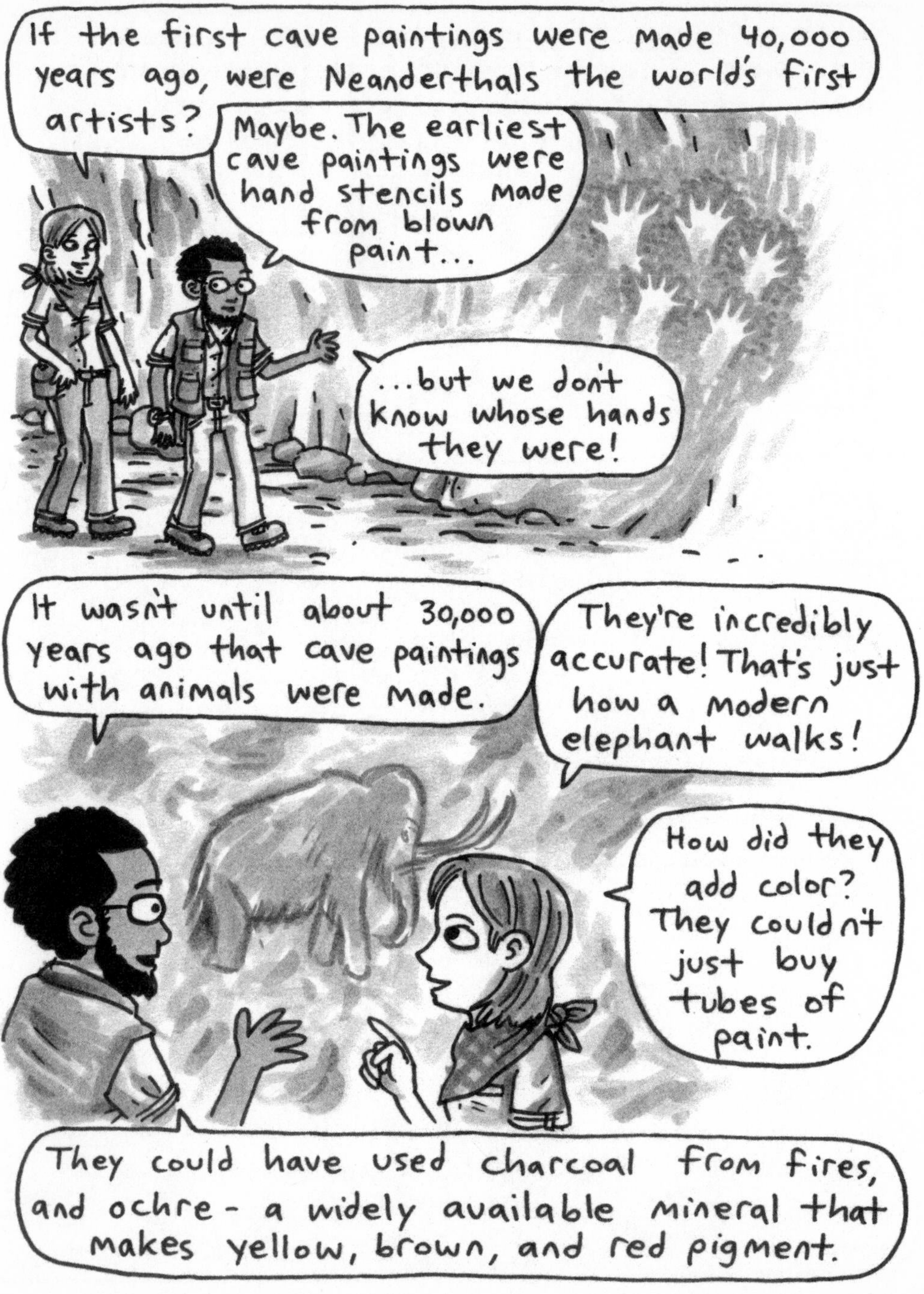
If the first cave paintings were made 40,000 years ago, were Neanderthals the world's first artists?
Maybe. The earliest cave paintings were hand stencils made from blown paint...
...but we don't know whose hands they were!
It wasn't until about 30,000 years ago that cave paintings with animals were made.
They're incredibly accurate! That's just how a modern elephant walks!
How did they add color? They couldn't just buy tubes of paint.
They could have used charcoal from fires, and ochre - a widely available mineral that makes yellow, brown, and red pigment.

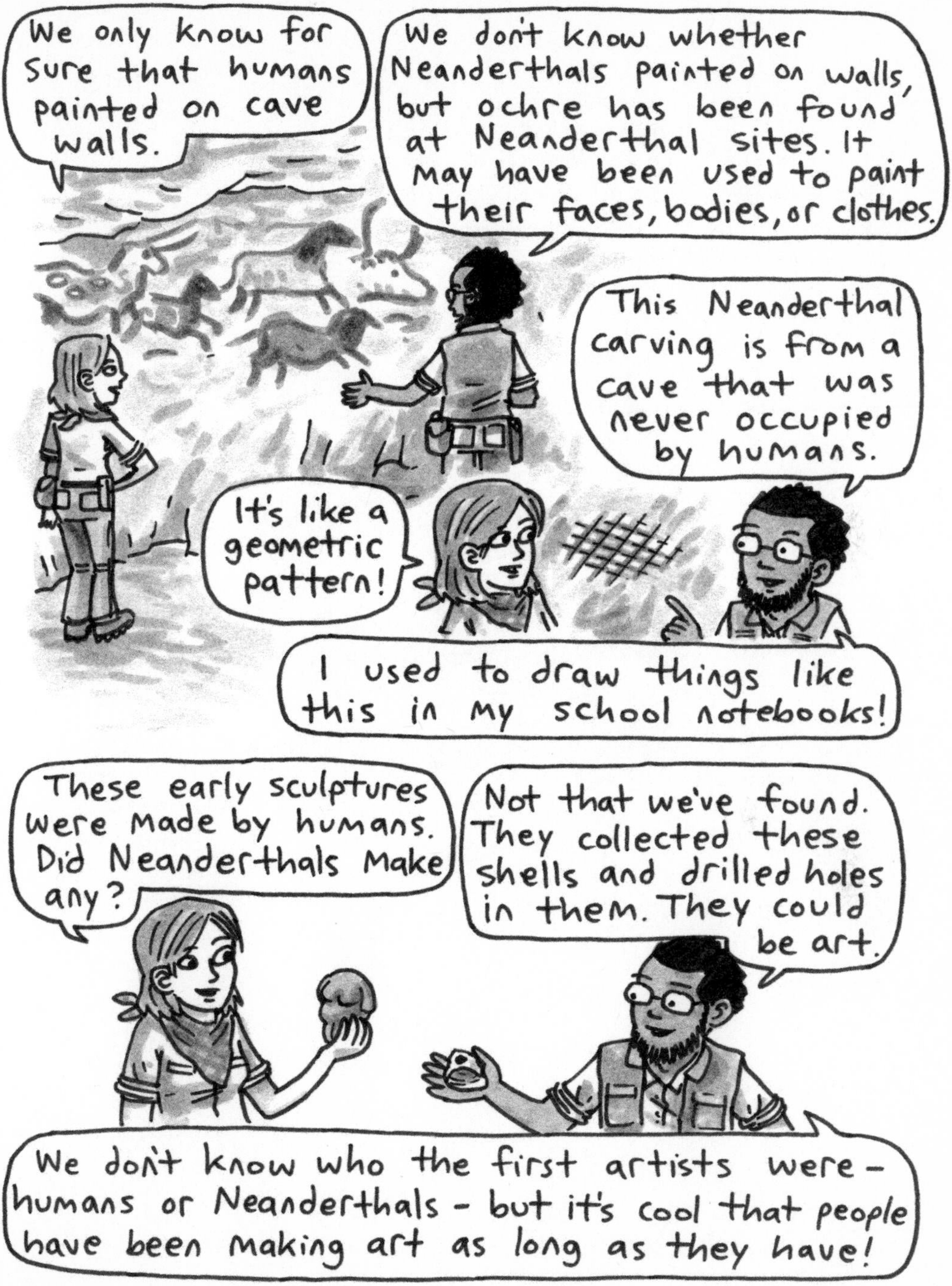
We only know for sure that humans painted on cave walls.
We don't know whether Neanderthals painted on walls, but ochre has been found at Neanderthal sites. It may have been used to paint their faces, bodies, or clothes.
This Neanderthal carving is from a cave that was never occupied by humans.
It's like a geometric pattern!
I used to draw things like this in my school notebooks!
These early sculptures were made by humans. Did Neanderthals make any?
Not that we've found. They collected these shells and drilled holes in them. They could be art.
We don't know who the first artists were - humans or Neanderthals - but it's cool that people have been making art as long as they have!

SUBSTITUTE
BABYSITTERS

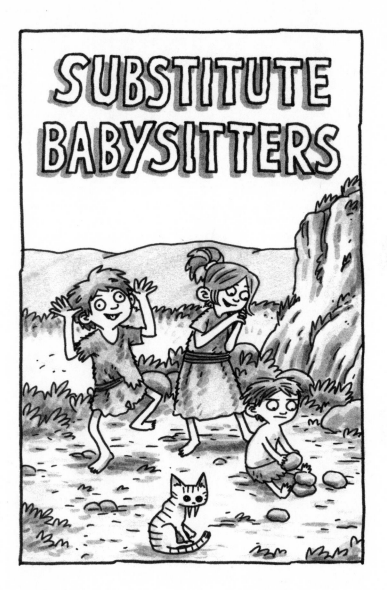

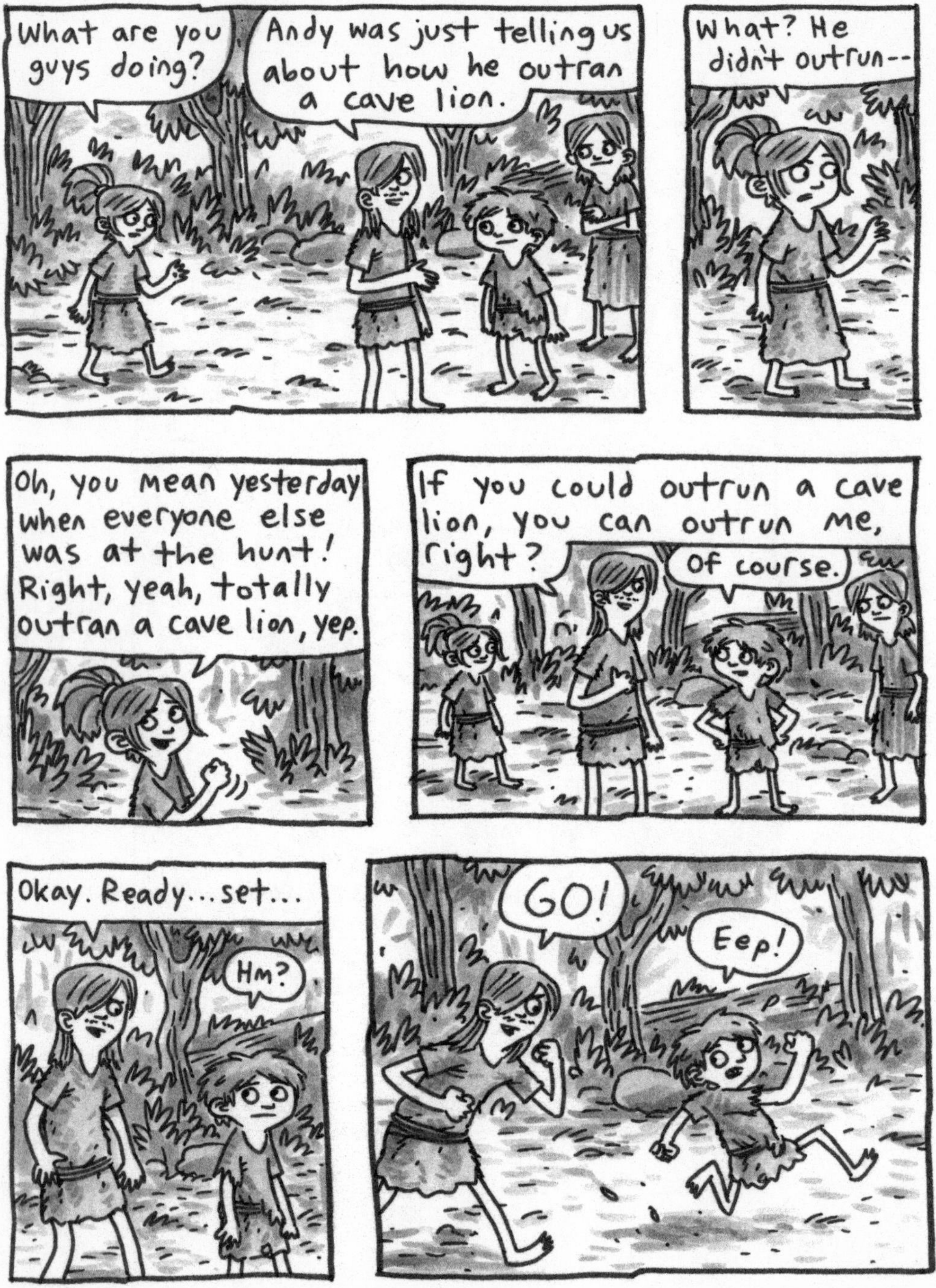
What are you guys doing?
Andy was just telling us about how he outran a cave lion.
What? He didn't outrun--
Oh, you mean yesterday when everyone else was at the hunt! Right, yeah, totally outran a cave lion, yep.
If you could outrun a cave lion, you can outrun me, right?
Of course.
Okay. Ready... set...
Hm?
GO!
Eep!

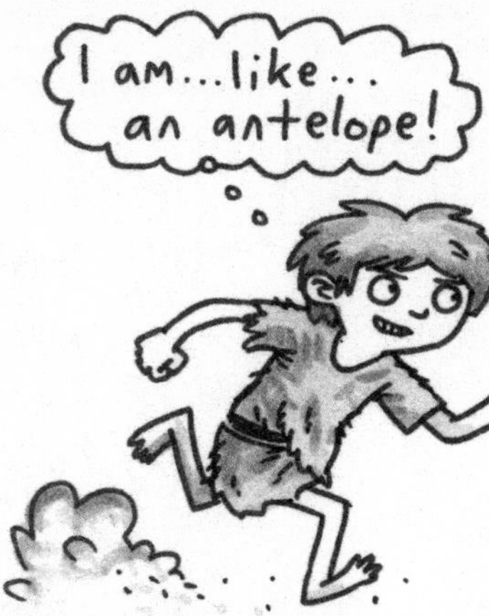
I am...like... an antelope!

Neanderthals may have used more energy for running than humans because they had shorter and thicker limbs.

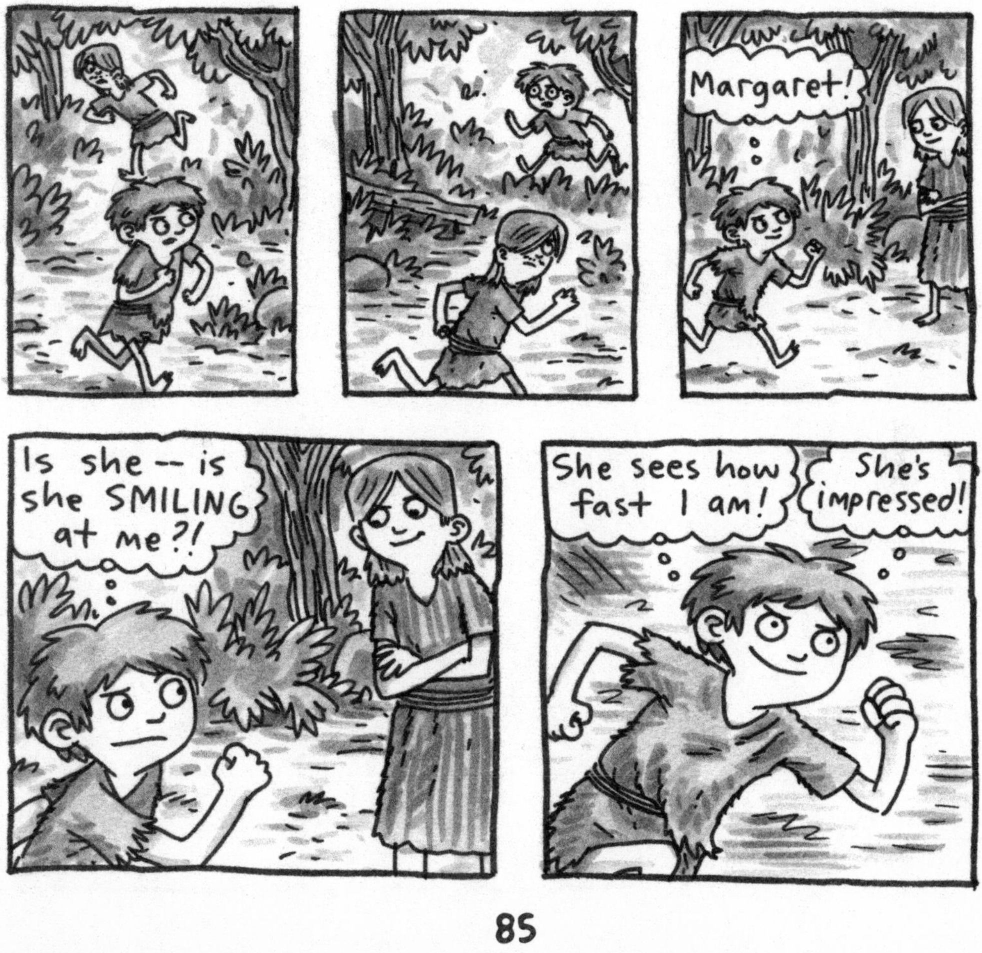
Margaret!
Is she -- is she SMILING at me?!
She sees how fast I am!
She's impressed!

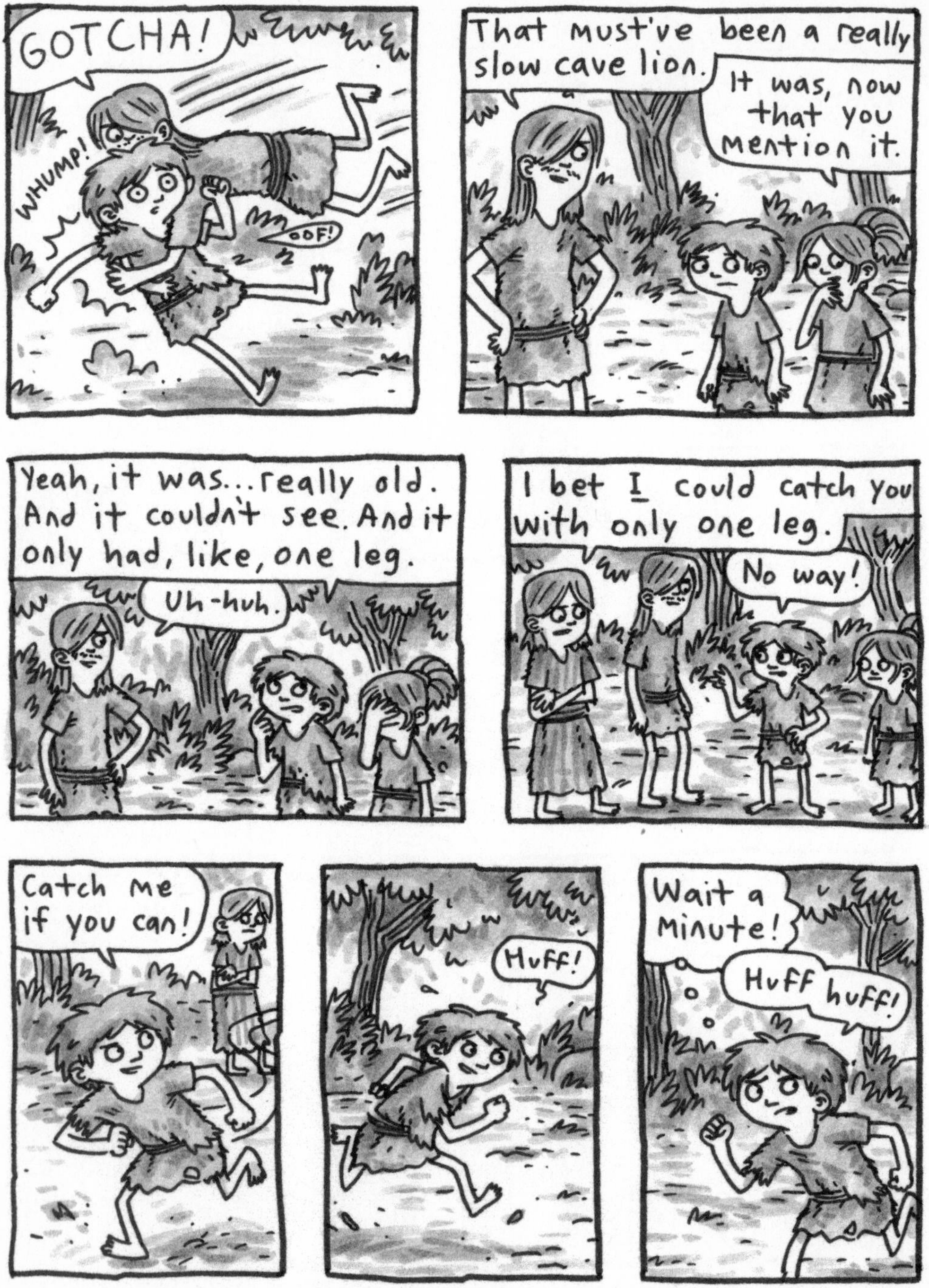
GOTCHA!
WHUMP!
OOF!
That must've been a really slow cave lion.
It was, now that you mention it.
Yeah, it was...really old. And it couldn't see. And it only had, like, one leg.
Uh-huh.
I bet I could catch you with only one leg.
No way!
Catch me if you can!
Huff!
Wait a minute!
Huff huff!

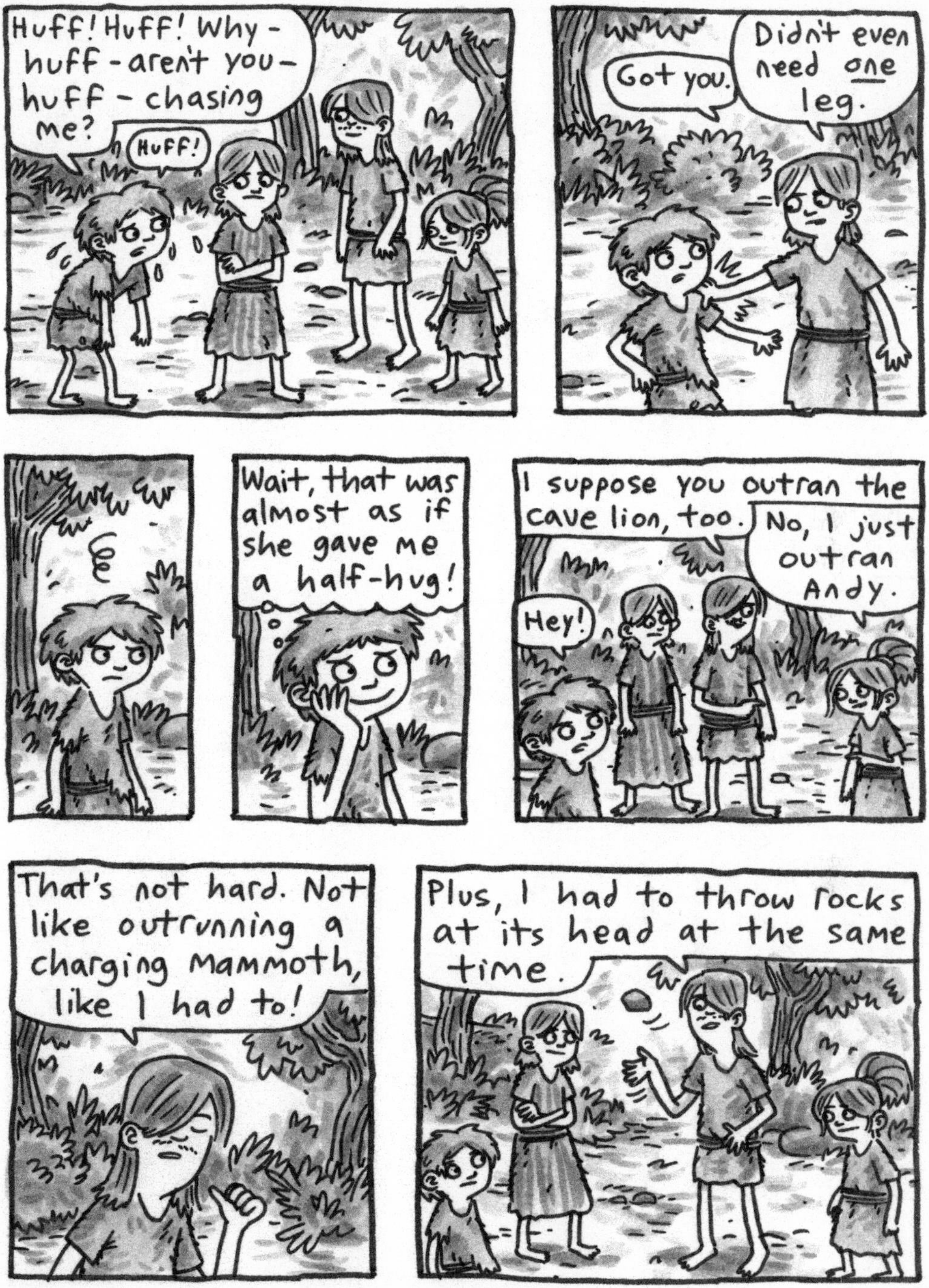
Huff! Huff! Why - huff - aren't you - huff - chasing me?
HUFF!
Got you.
Didn't even need one leg.
Wait, that was almost as if she gave me a half-hug!
I suppose you outran the cave lion, too.
No, I just outran Andy.
Hey!
That's not hard. Not like outrunning a charging mammoth, like I had to!
Plus, I had to throw rocks at its head at the same time.

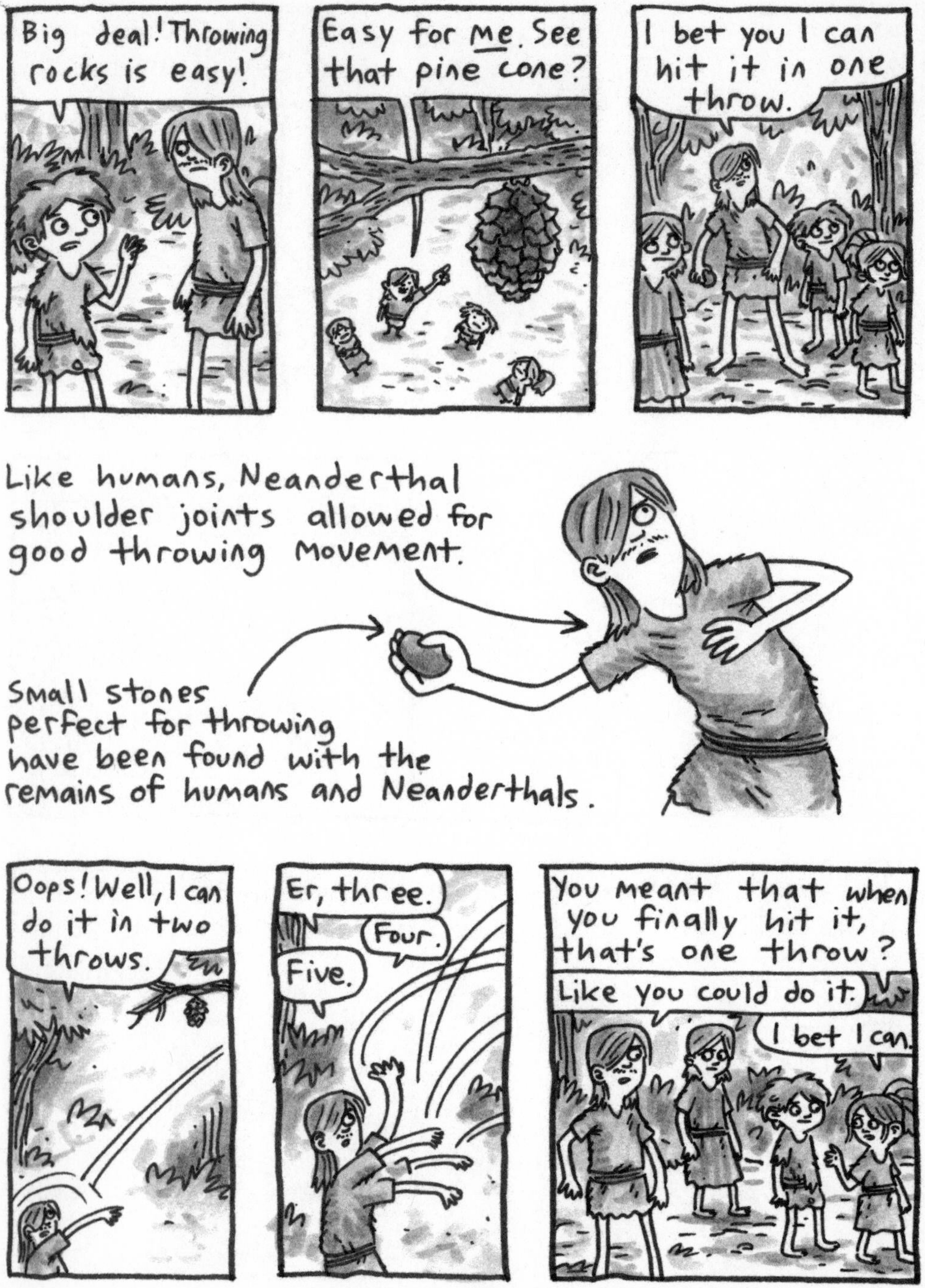
Big deal! Throwing rocks is easy!
Easy for me. See that pine cone?
I bet you I can hit it in one throw.
Like humans, Neanderthal shoulder joints allowed for good throwing movement.
Small stones perfect for throwing have been found with the remains of humans and Neanderthals.
Oops! Well, I can do it in two throws.
Er, three.
Four.
Five.
You meant that when you finally hit it, that's one throw?
Like you could do it.
I bet I can.

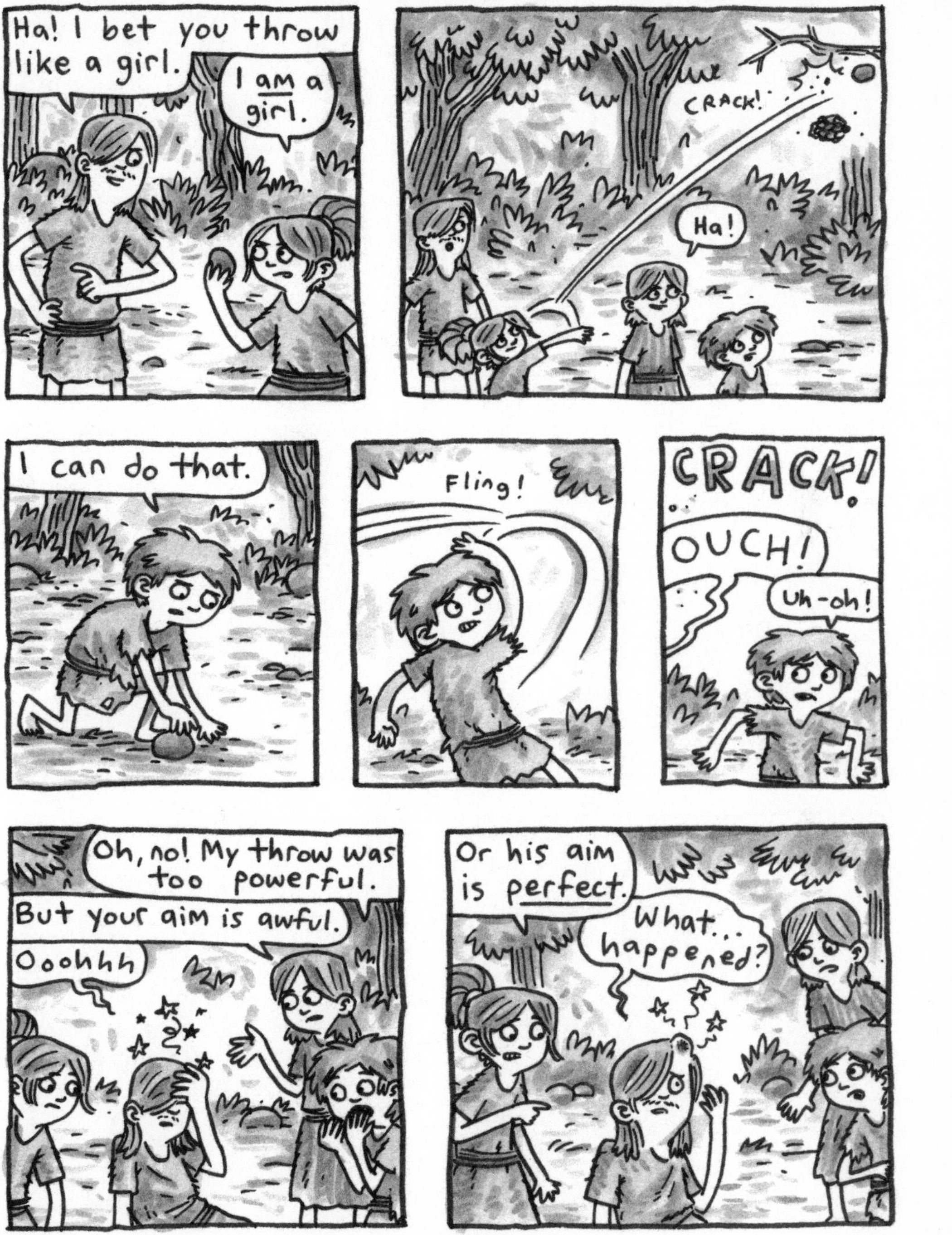
Ha! I bet you throw like a girl.
I am a girl.
CRACK!
Ha!
I can do that.
Fling!
CRACK!
OUCH!
Uh-oh!
Oh, no! My throw was too powerful.
But your aim is awful.
Ooohhh
Or his aim is perfect.
What... happened?

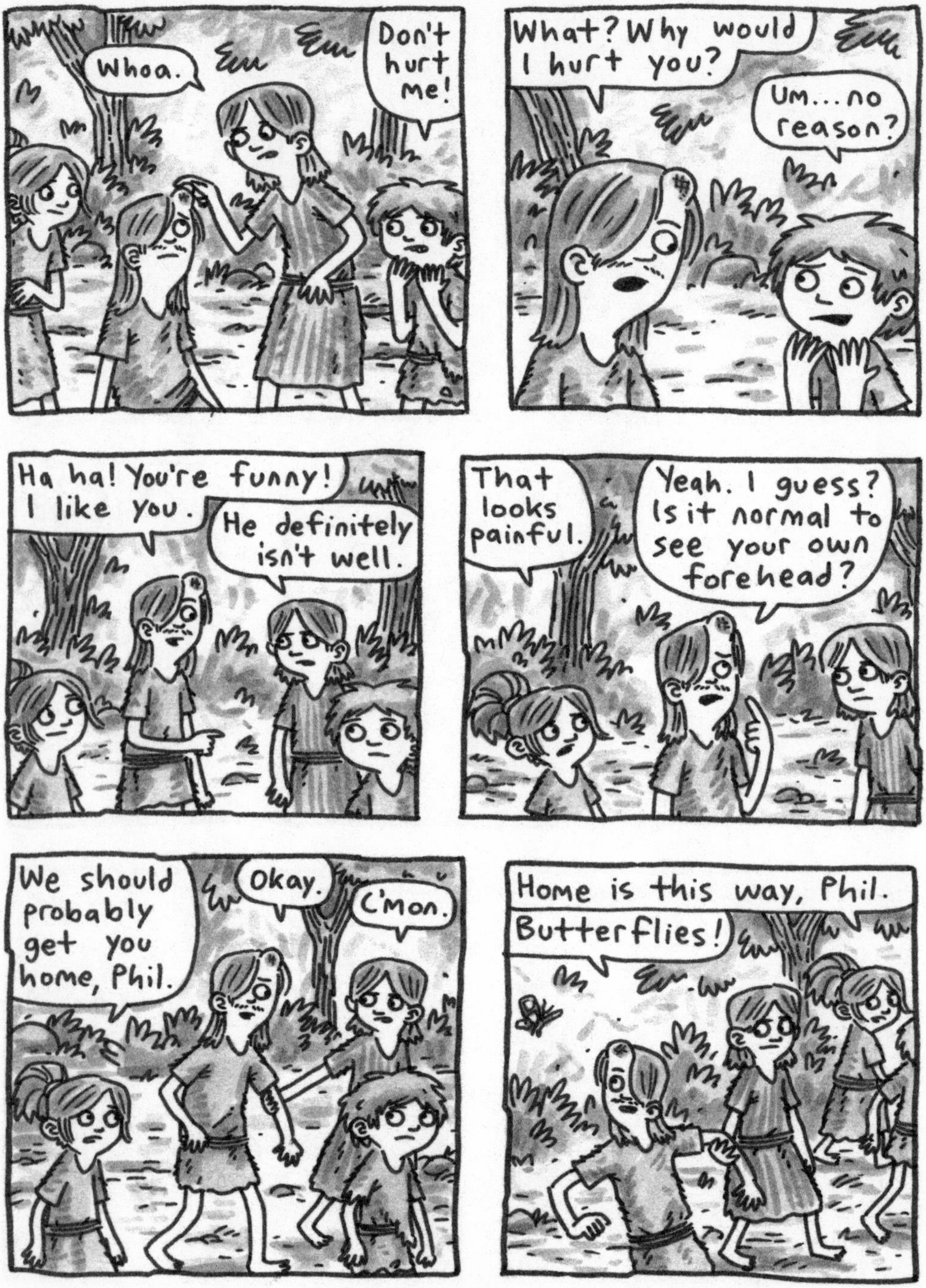
Whoa.
Don't hurt me!
What? Why would I hurt you?
Um... no reason?
Ha ha! You're funny! I like you.
He definitely isn't well.
That looks painful.
Yeah. I guess? Is it normal to see your own forehead?
We should probably get you home, Phil.
Okay.
C'mon.
Home is this way, Phil.
Butterflies!

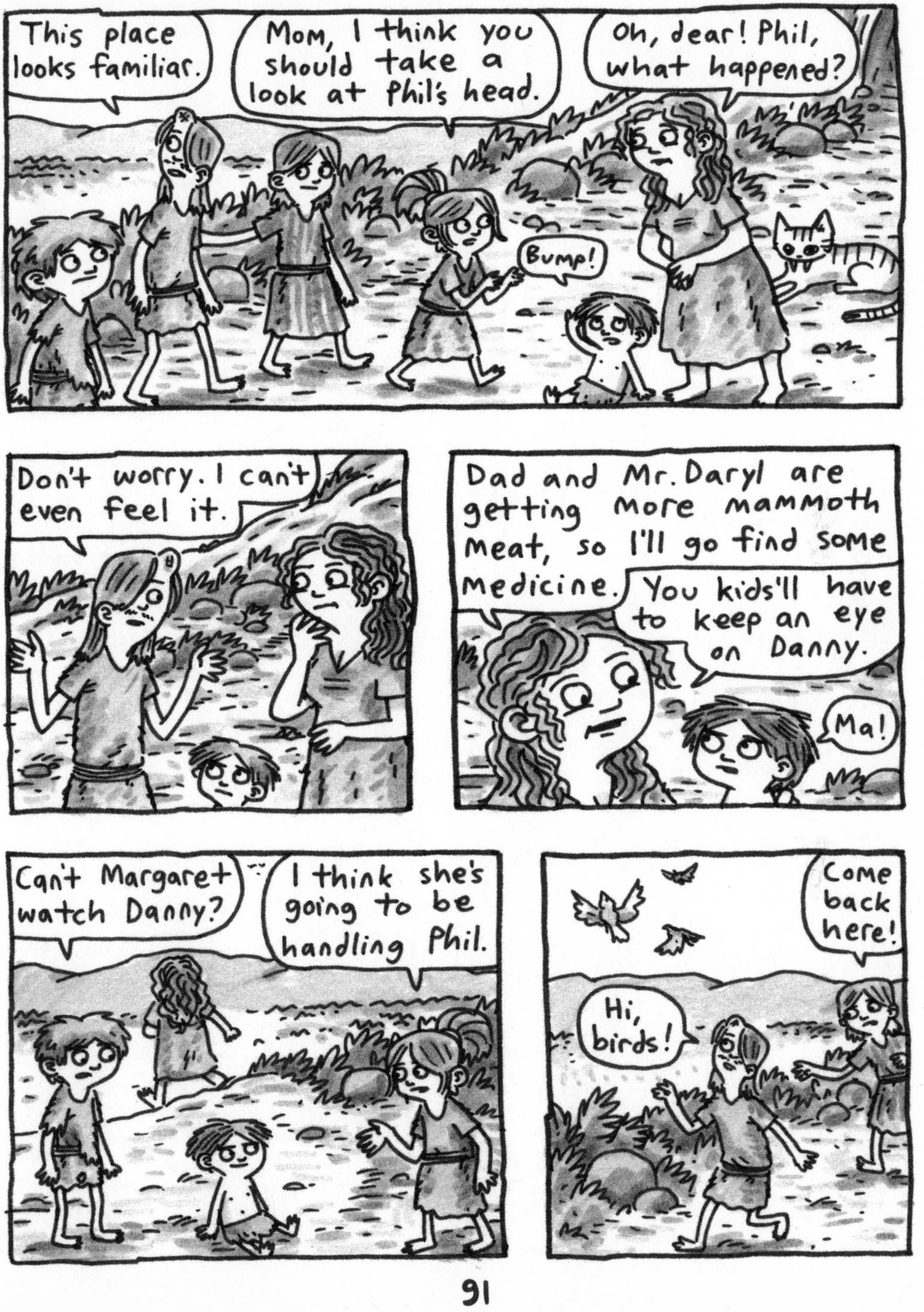
This place looks familiar.
Mom, I think you should take a look at Phil's head.
Oh, dear! Phil, what happened?
Bump!
Don't worry. I can't even feel it.
Dad and Mr. Daryl are getting more mammoth meat, so I'll go find some medicine.
You kids'll have to keep an eye on Danny.
Ma!
Can't Margaret watch Danny?
I think she's going to be handling Phil.
Come back here!
Hi, birds!

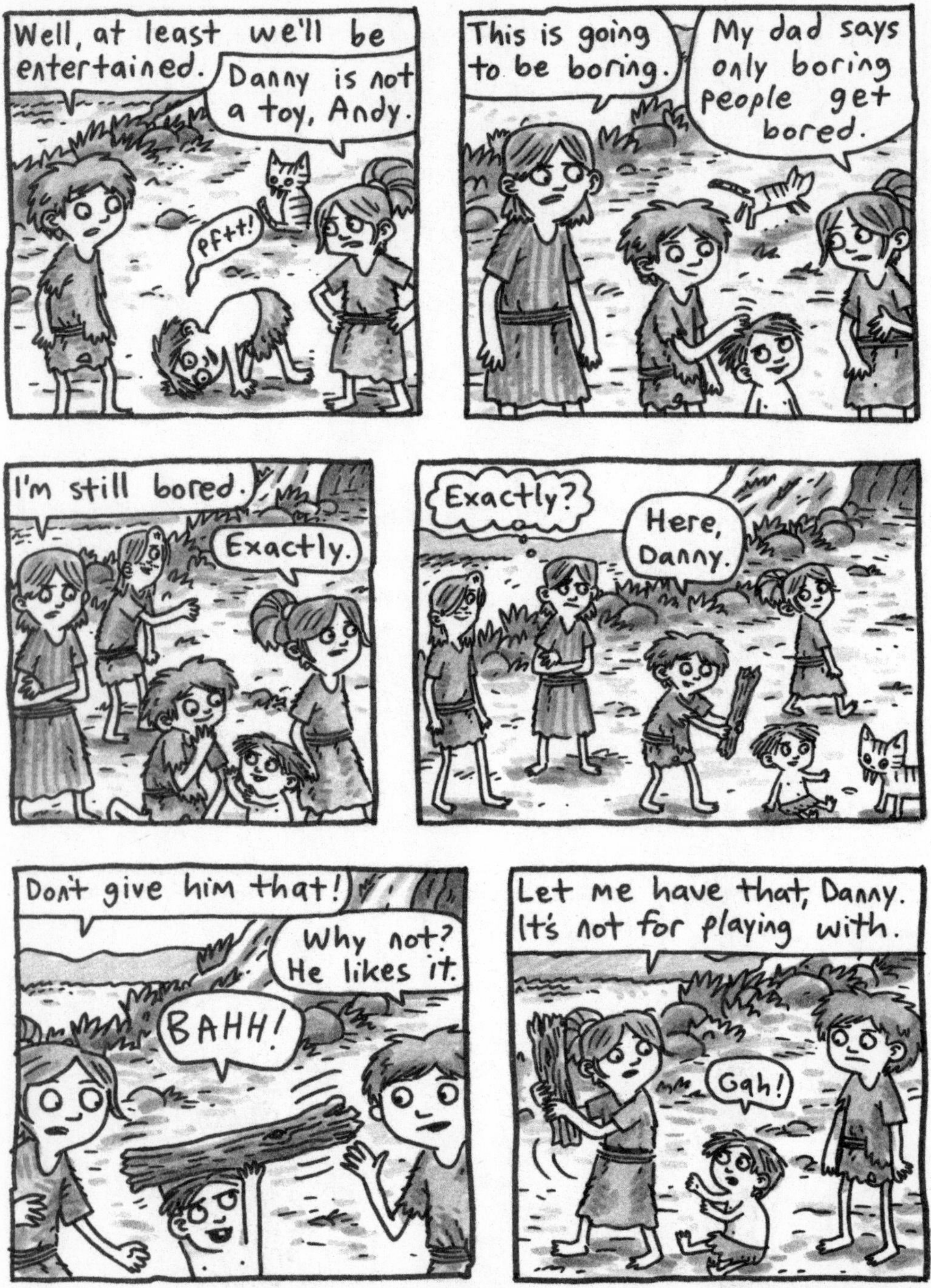
Well, at least we'll be entertained.
Danny is not a toy, Andy.
pftt!
This is going to be boring.
My dad says only boring people get bored.
I'm still bored.
Exactly.
Exactly?
Here, Danny.
Don't give him that!
Why not? He likes it.
BAHH!
Let me have that, Danny. It's not for playing with.
Gah!

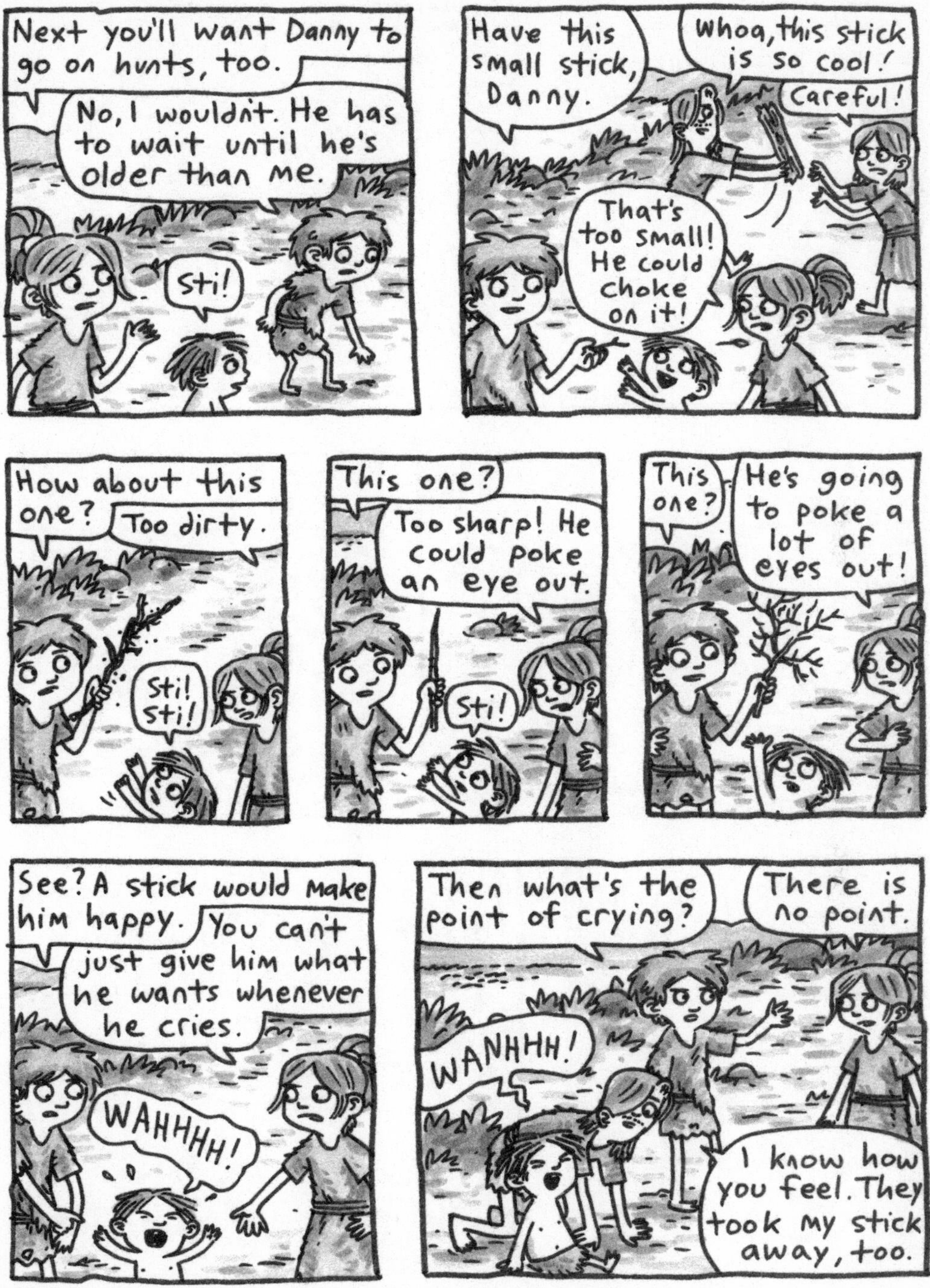
Next you'll want Danny to go on hunts, too.
No, I wouldn't. He has to wait until he's older than me.
Sti!
Have this small stick, Danny.
Whoa, this stick is so cool!
Careful!
That's too small! He could choke on it!
How about this one?
Too dirty.
Sti! Sti!
This one?
Too sharp! He could poke an eye out.
Sti!
This one?
He's going to poke a lot of eyes out!
See? A stick would make him happy.
You can't just give him what he wants whenever he cries.
WAHHHH!
Then what's the point of crying?
There is no point.
WANHHH!
I know how you feel. They took my stick away, too.

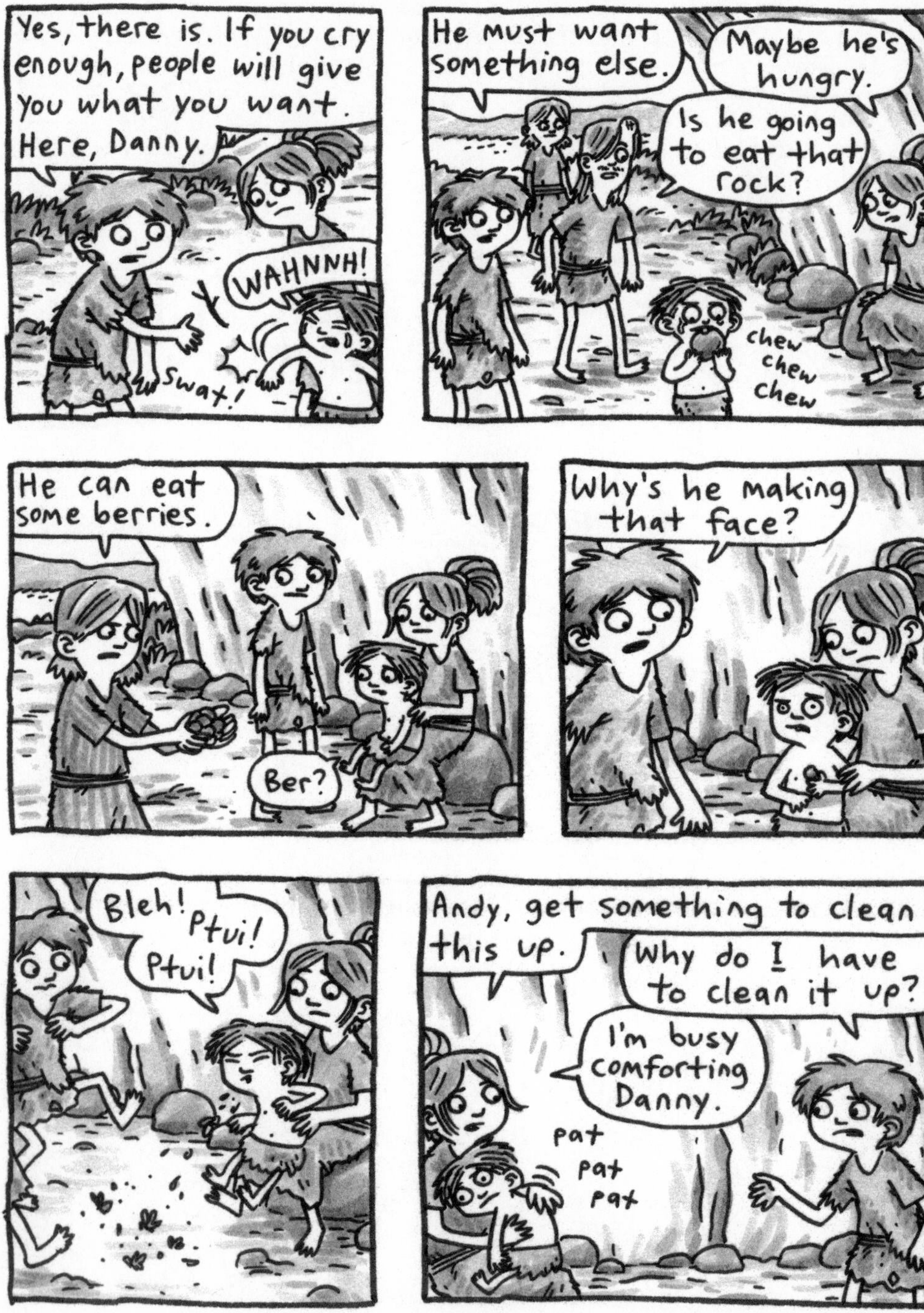
Yes, there is. If you cry enough, people will give you what you want. Here, Danny.
WAHNNH!
Swat!
He must want something else.
Maybe he's hungry.
Is he going to eat that rock?
chew chew chew
He can eat some berries.
Ber?
Why's he making that face?
Bleh!
Ptui!
Ptui!
Andy, get something to clean this up.
Why do I have to clean it up?
I'm busy comforting Danny.
pat
pat
pat

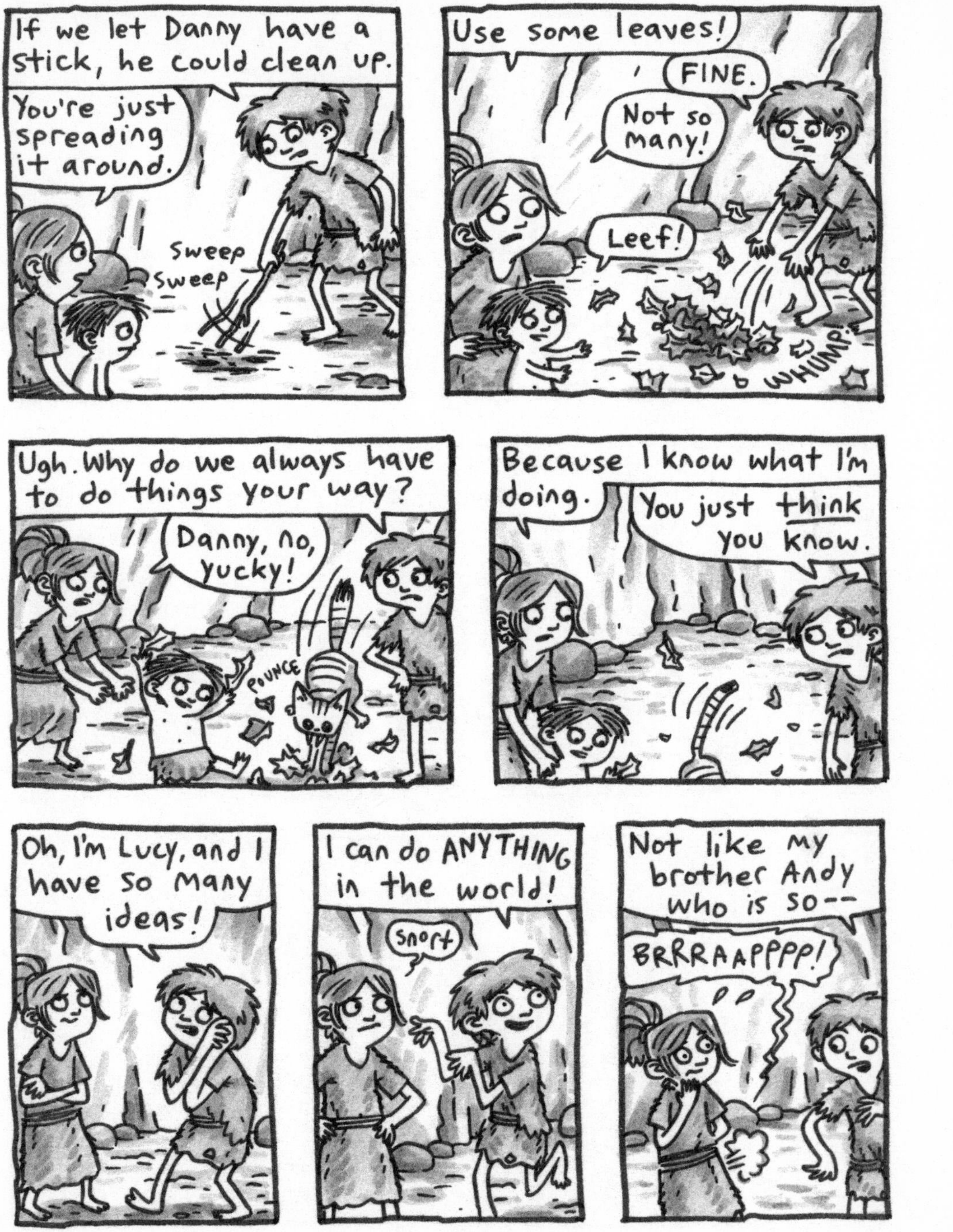

If we let Danny have a stick, he could clean up.
You're just spreading it around.
Sweep
Sweep
Use some leaves!
FINE.
Not so many!
Leef!
WHUMP!
Ugh. Why do we always have to do things your way?
Danny, no, yucky!
POUNCE
Because I know what I'm doing.
You just think you know.
Oh, I'm Lucy, and I have so many ideas!
I can do ANYTHING in the world!
snort
Not like my brother Andy who is so--
BRRRAAPPPP!

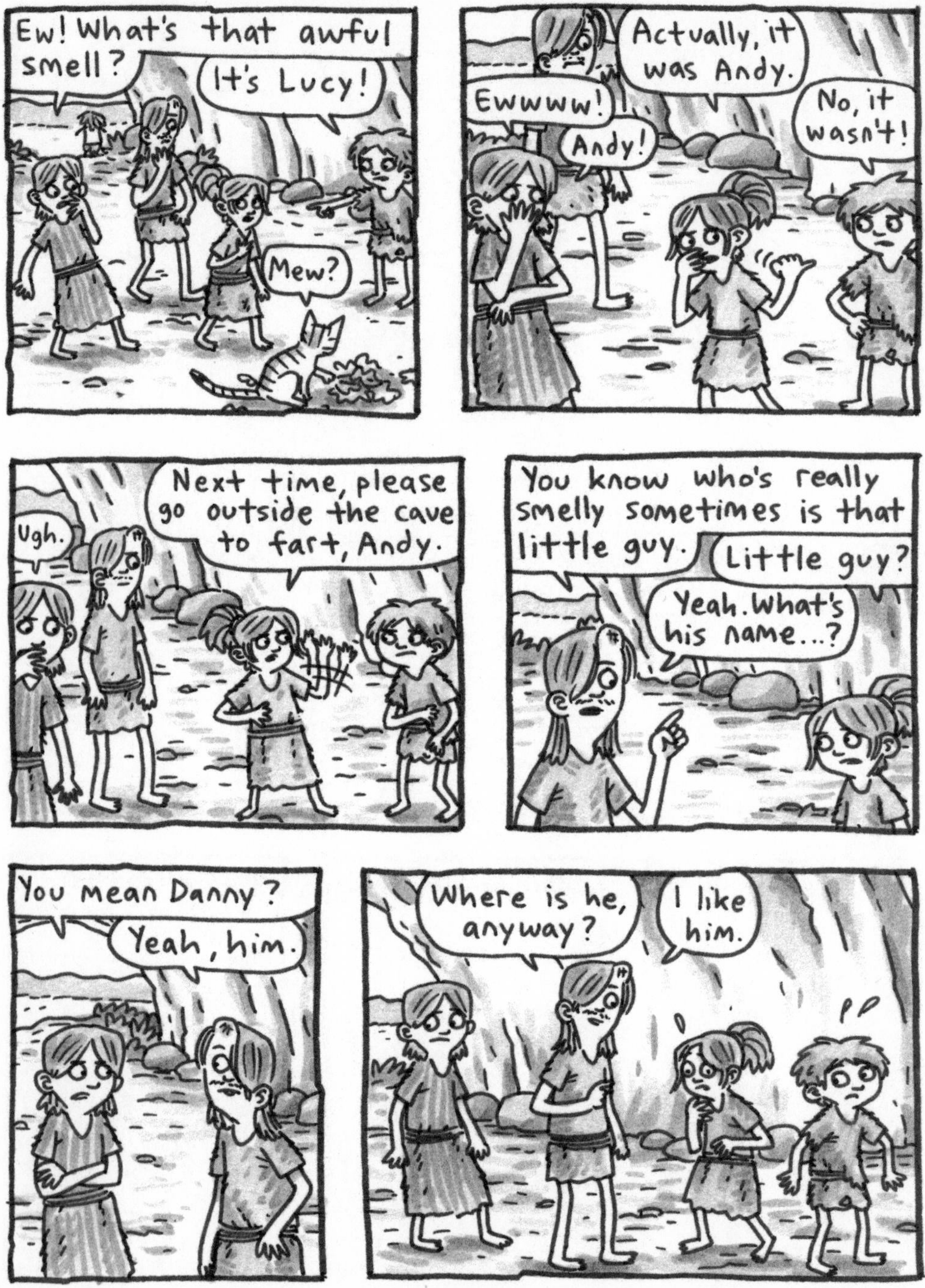
Ew! What's that awful smell?
It's Lucy!
Mew?
Actually, it was Andy.
Ewwww!
Andy!
No, it wasn't!
Ugh.
Next time, please go outside the cave to fart, Andy.
You know who's really smelly sometimes is that little guy.
Little guy?
Yeah. What's his name...?
You mean Danny?
Yeah, him.
Where is he, anyway?
I like him.

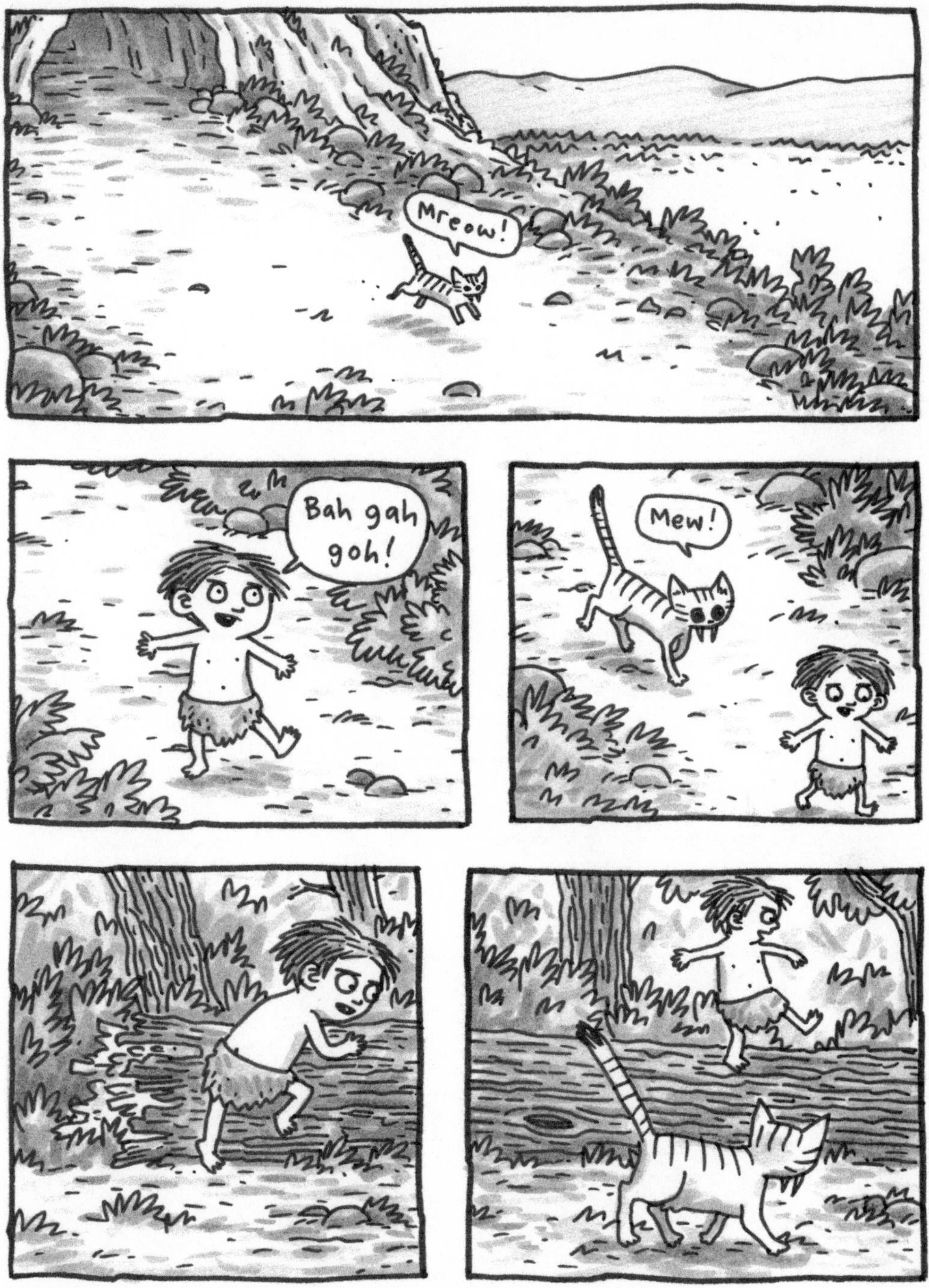
Mreow!
Bah gah goh!
Mew!

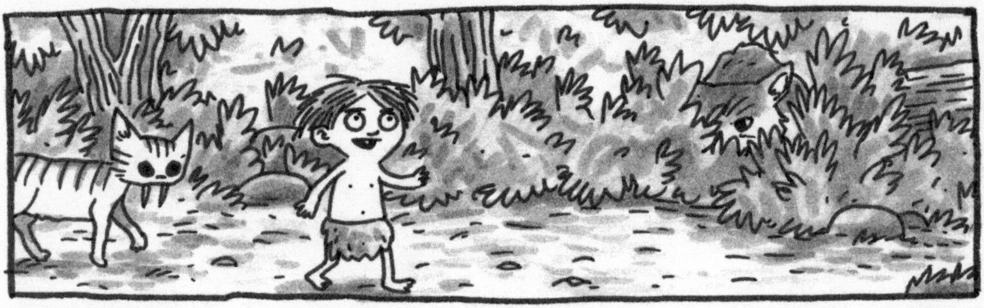

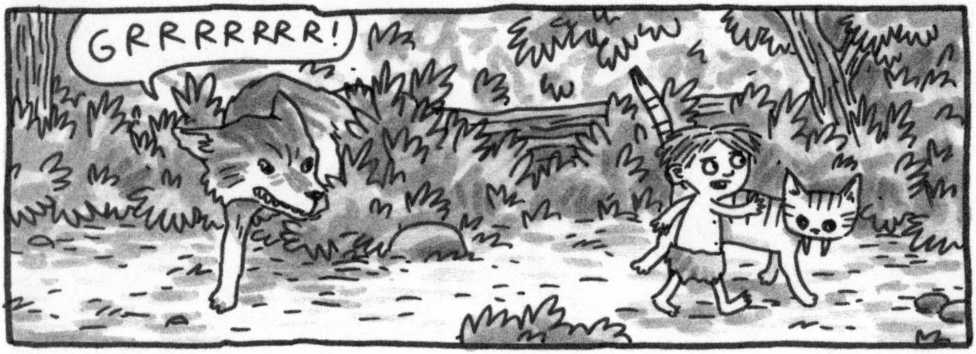
GRRRRRRR!

The largest and deadliest canine to ever live was the dire wolf. Fortunately for Neanderthals, dire wolves lived only in North and South America, while wolves in Europe were more like modern-day wolves.

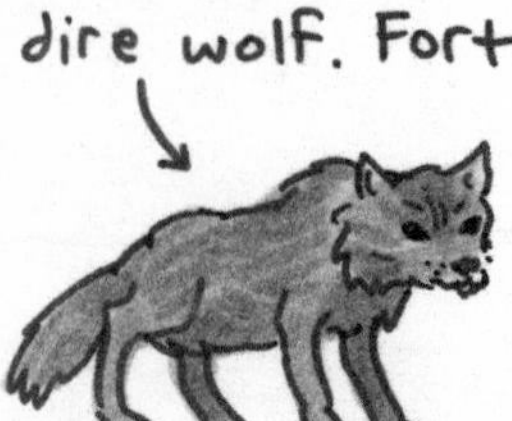

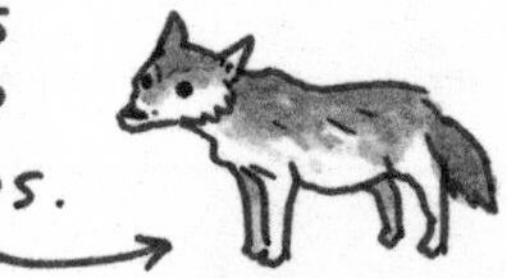

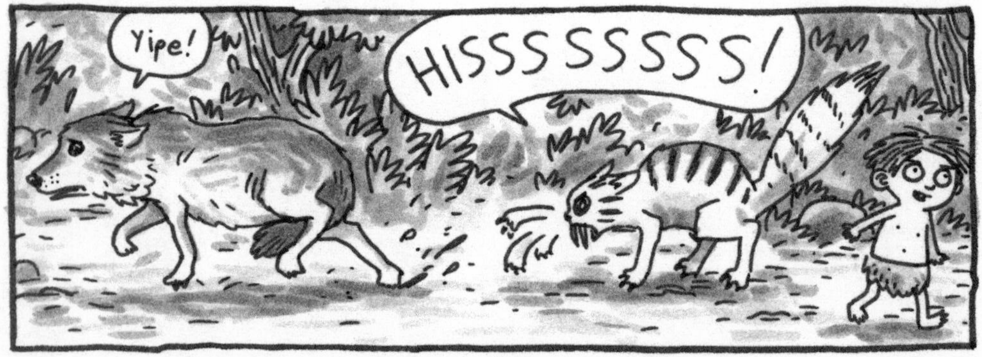
Yipe!
HISSSSSSSSS!

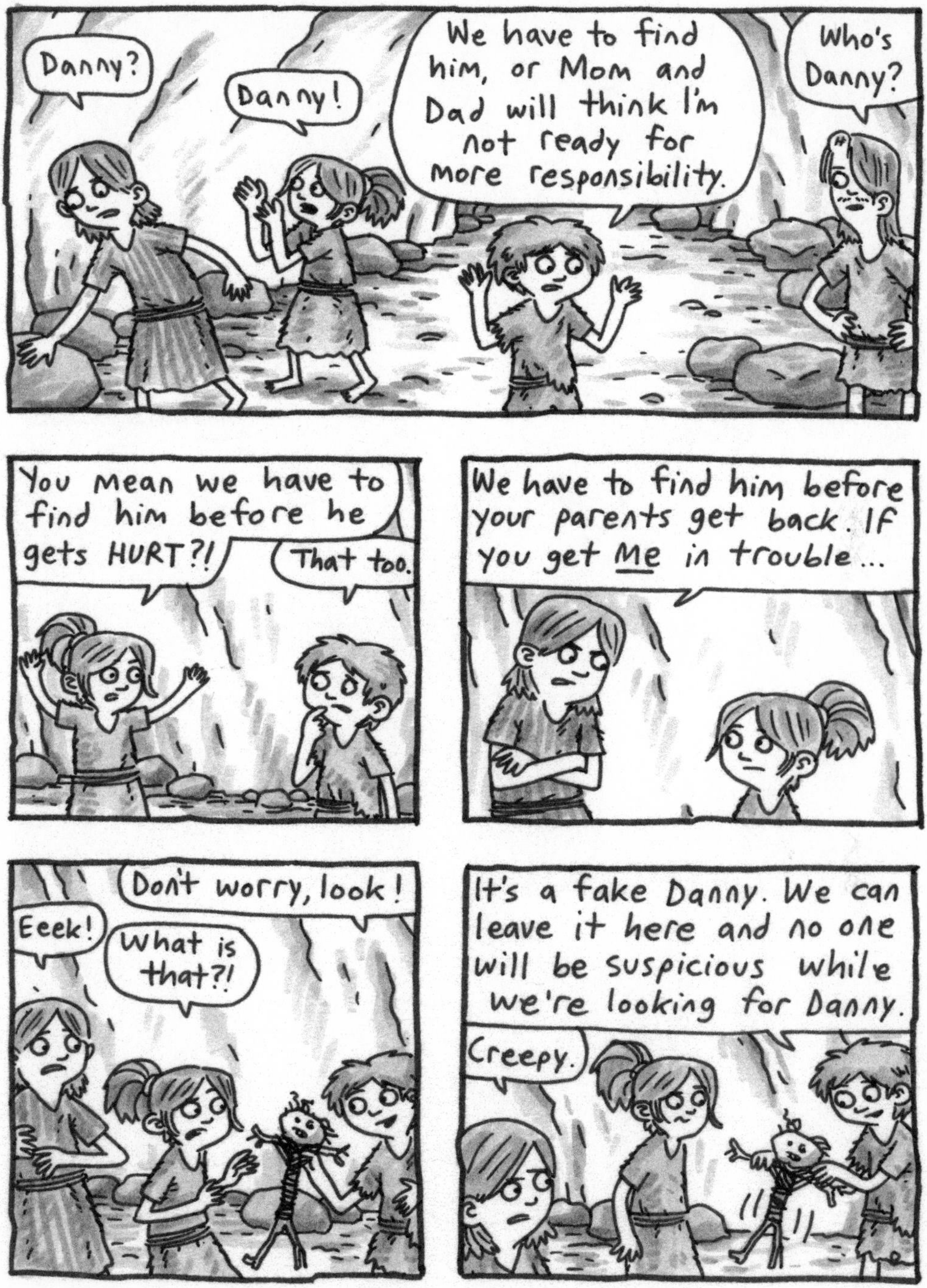
Danny?
Danny!
We have to find him, or Mom and Dad will think I'm not ready for more responsibility.
Who's Danny?
You mean we have to find him before he gets HURT?!
That too.
We have to find him before your parents get back. If you get ME in trouble...
Don't worry, look!
Eeek!
What is that?!
It's a fake Danny. We can leave it here and no one will be suspicious while we're looking for Danny.
Creepy.

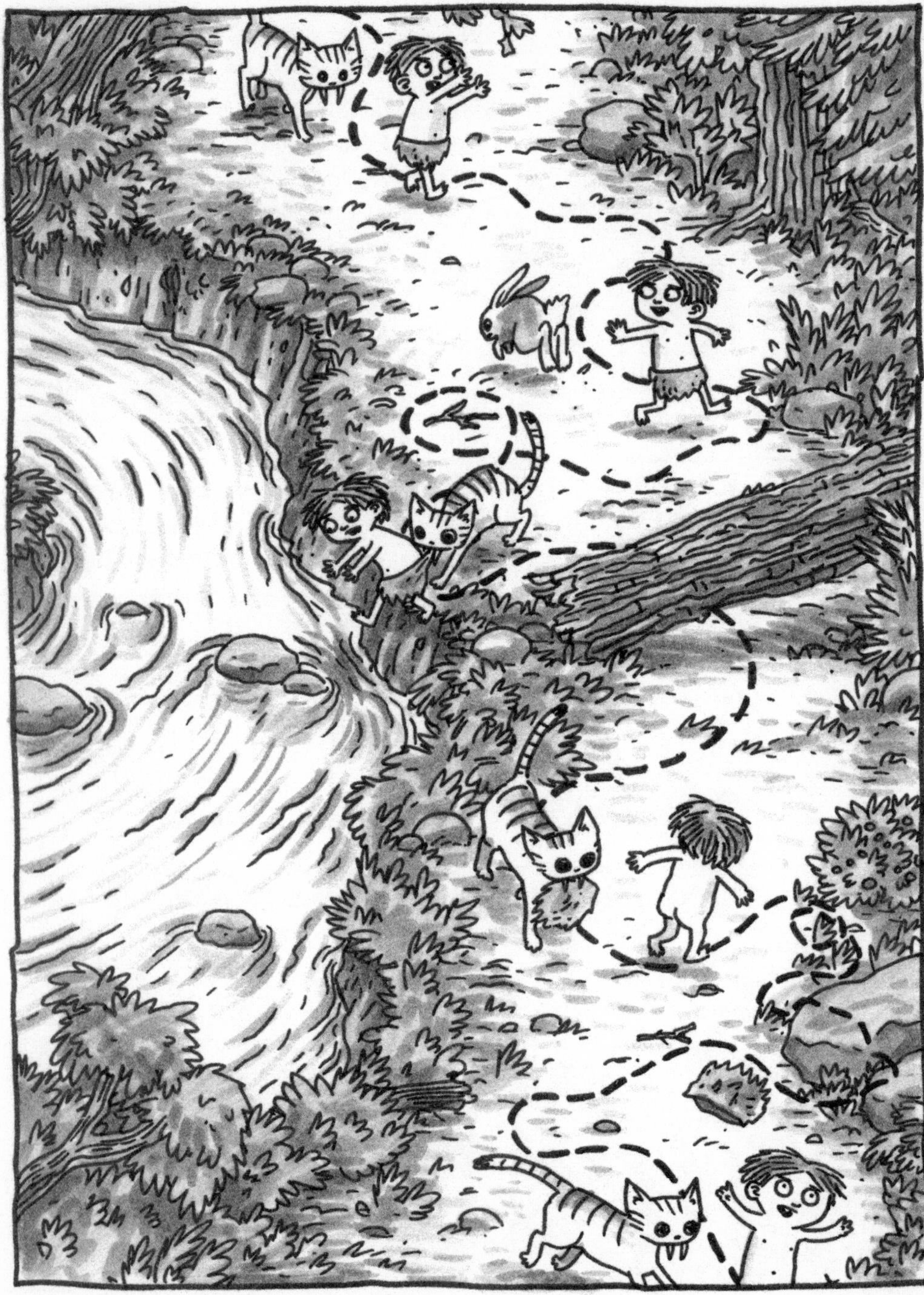

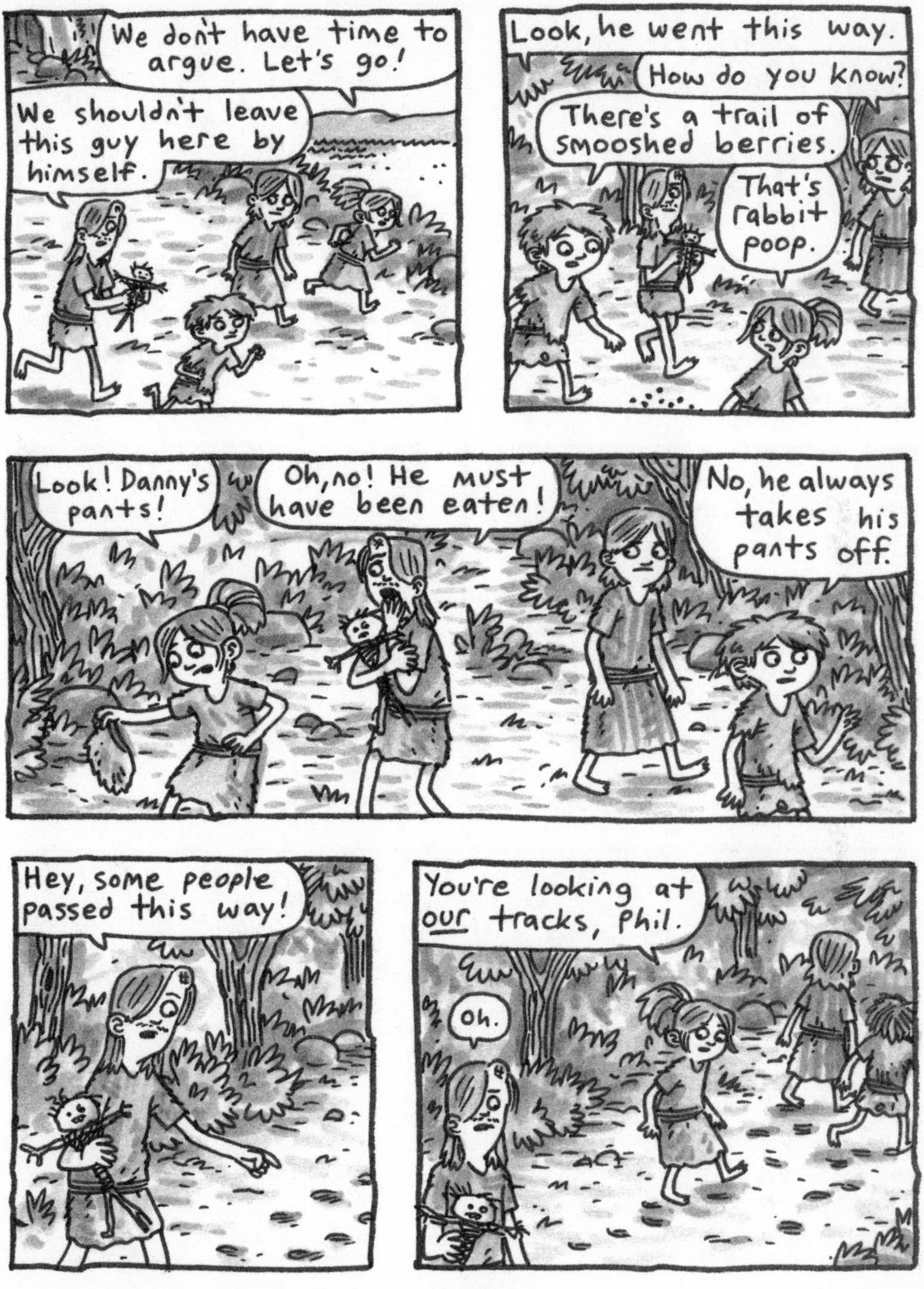

We don't have time to argue. Let's go!
We shouldn't leave this guy here by himself.
Look, he went this way.
How do you know?
There's a trail of smooshed berries.
That's rabbit poop.
Look! Danny's pants!
Oh, no! He must have been eaten!
No, he always takes his pants off.
Hey, some people passed this way!
You're looking at our tracks, Phil.
Oh.

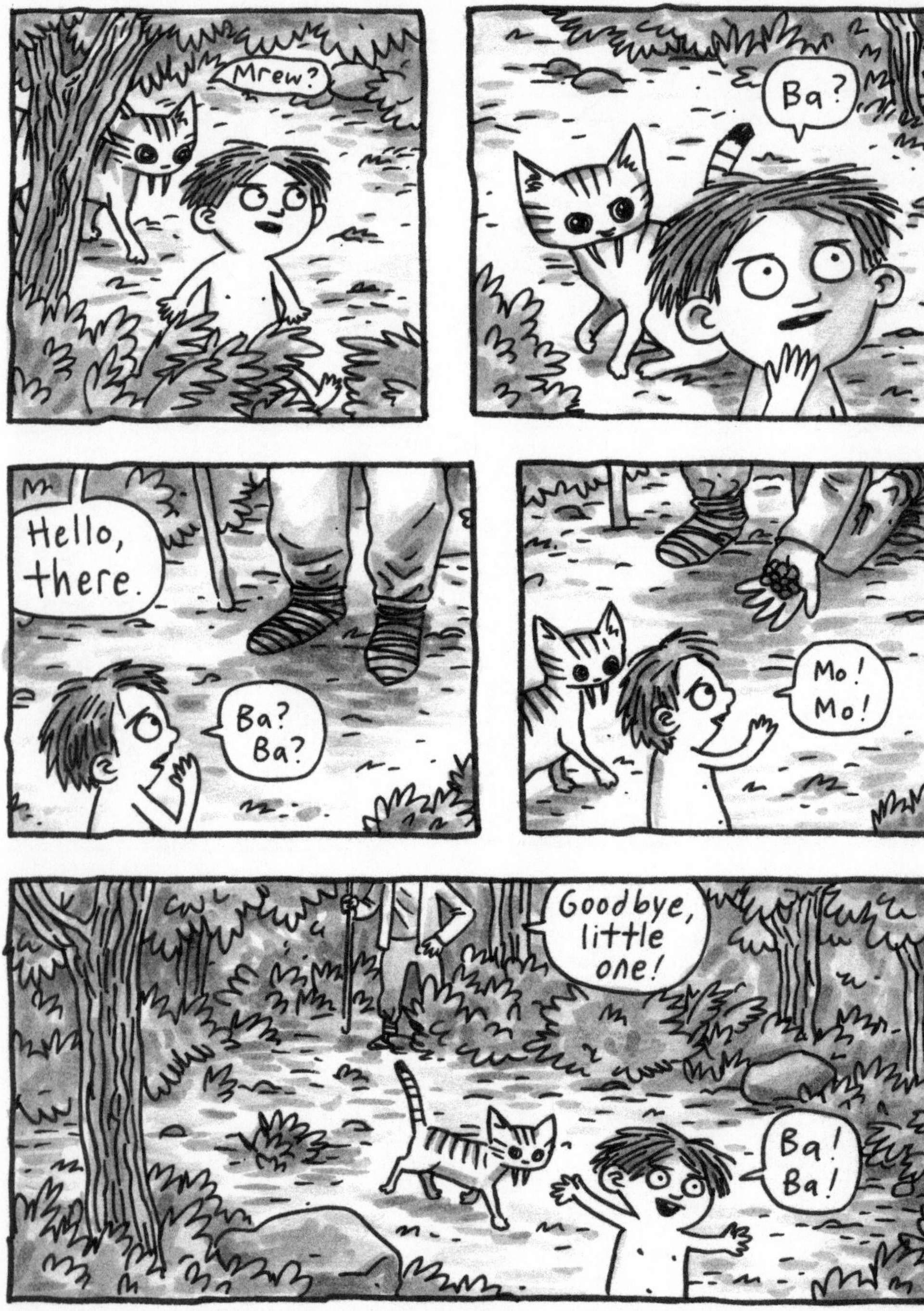
Mrew?
Ba?
Hello, there.
Ba? Ba?
Mo! Mo!
Goodbye, little one!
Ba! Ba!

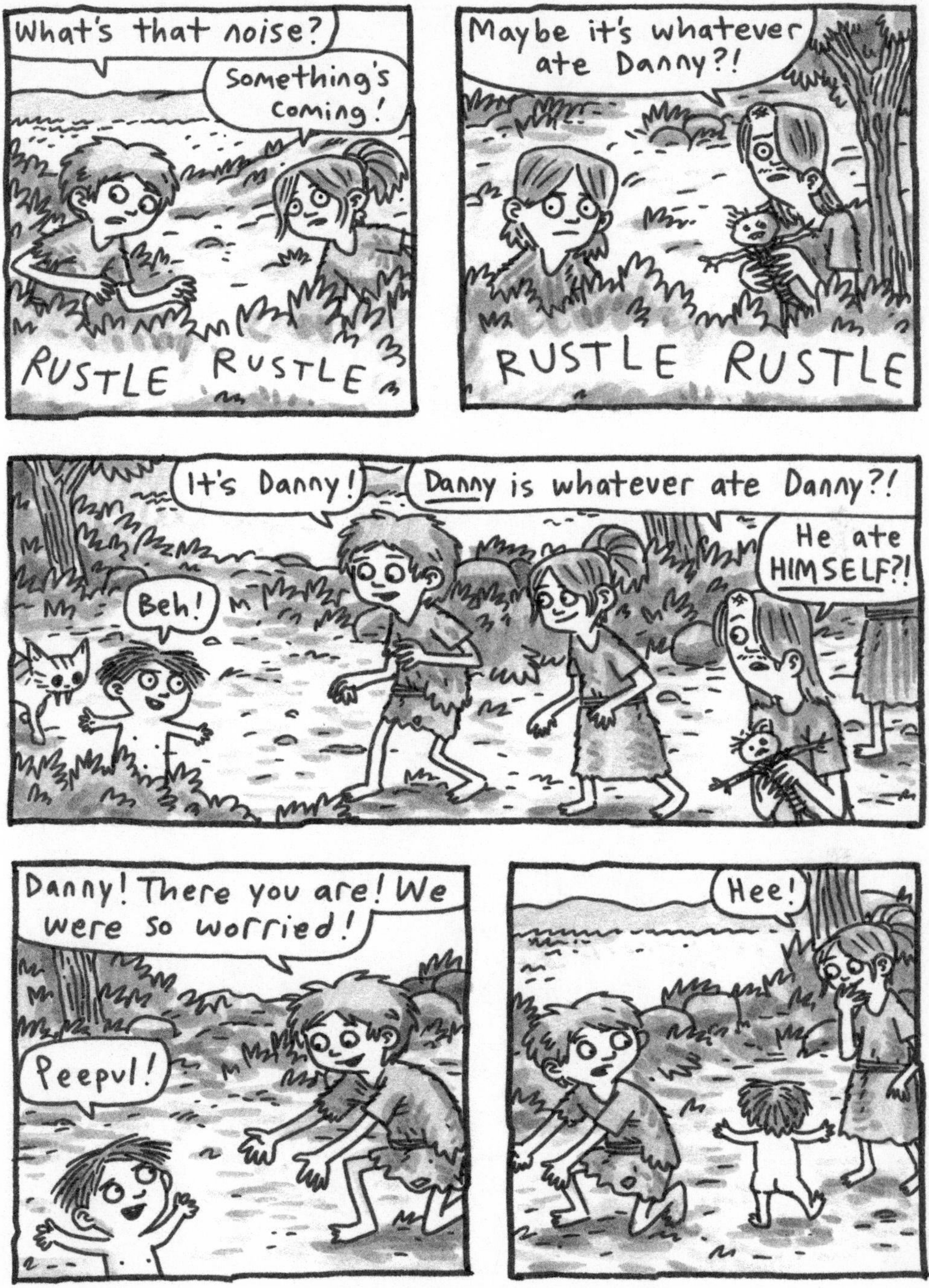
What's that noise?
Something's coming!
RUSTLE RUSTLE
Maybe it's whatever ate Danny?!
RUSTLE RUSTLE
It's Danny!
Danny is whatever ate Danny?!
He ate HIMSELF?!
Beh!
Danny! There you are! We were so worried!
Peepul!
Hee!

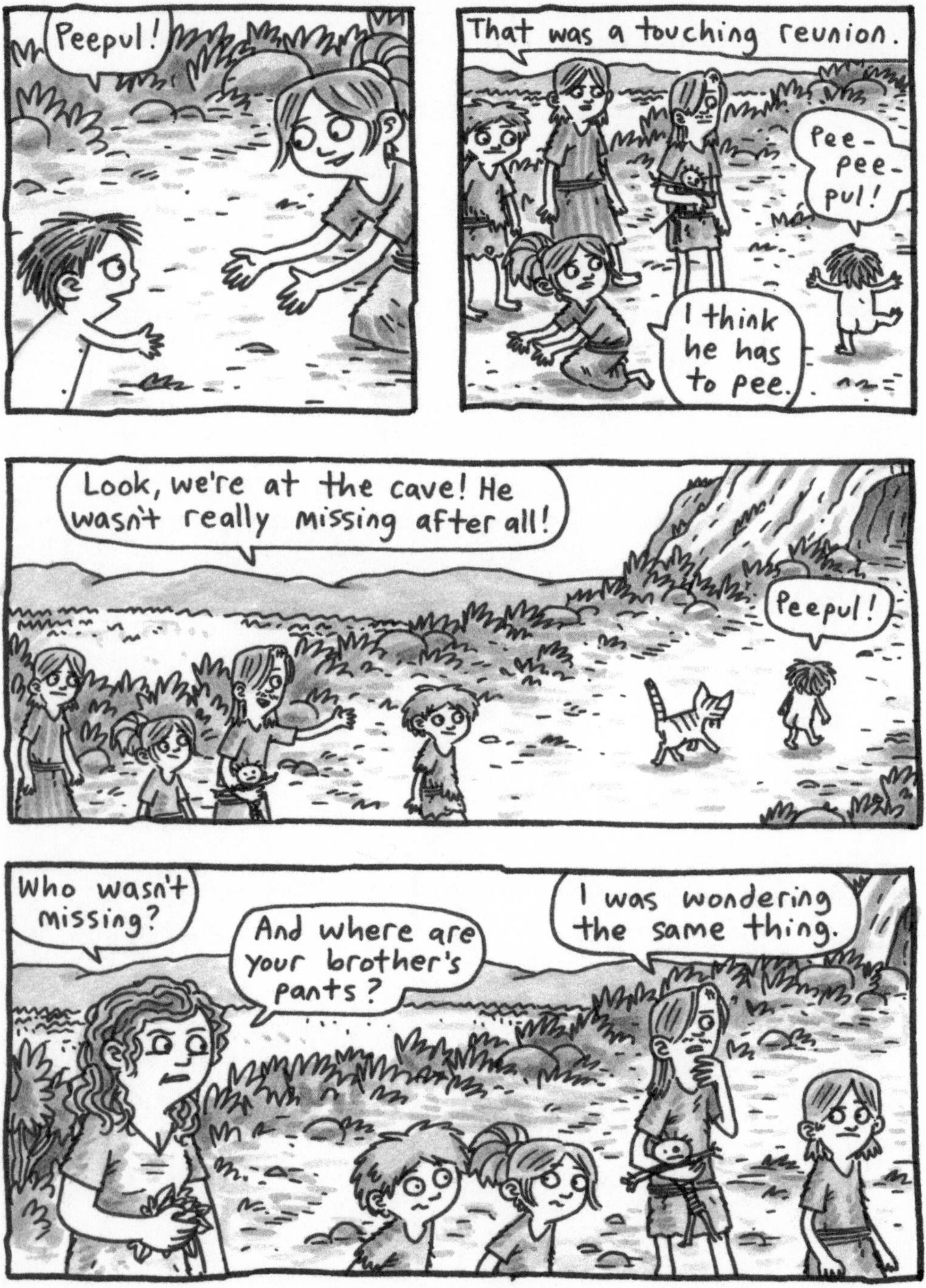
Peepul!
That was a touching reunion.
Pee-pee-pul!
I think he has to pee.
Look, we're at the cave! He wasn't really missing after all!
Peepul!
Who wasn't missing?
And where are your brother's pants?
I was wondering the same thing.

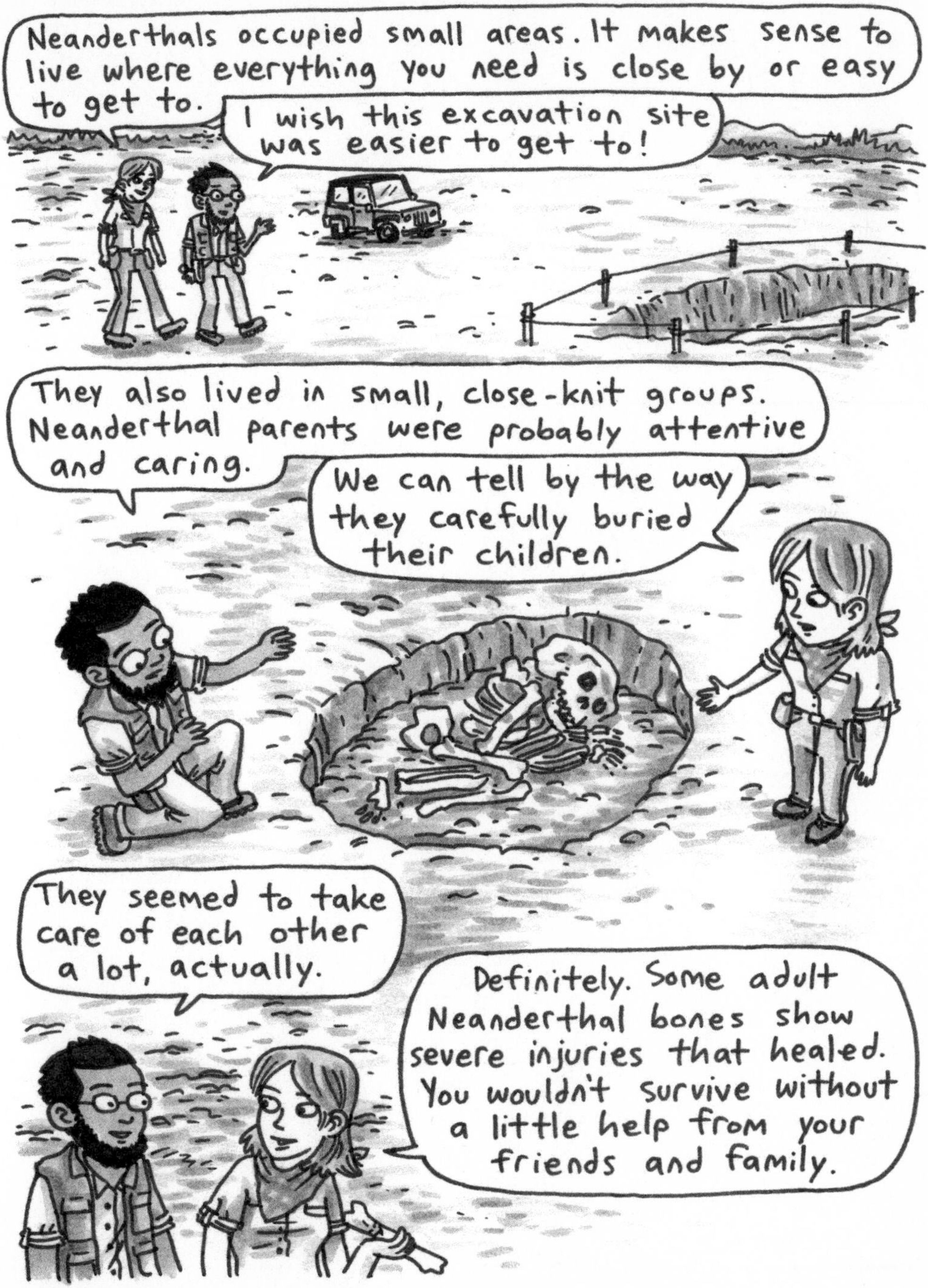
Neanderthals occupied small areas. It makes sense to live where everything you need is close by or easy to get to.
I wish this excavation site was easier to get to!
They also lived in small, close-knit groups. Neanderthal parents were probably attentive and caring.
We can tell by the way they carefully buried their children.
They seemed to take care of each other a lot, actually.
Definitely. Some adult Neanderthal bones show severe injuries that healed. You wouldn't survive without a little help from your friends and family.

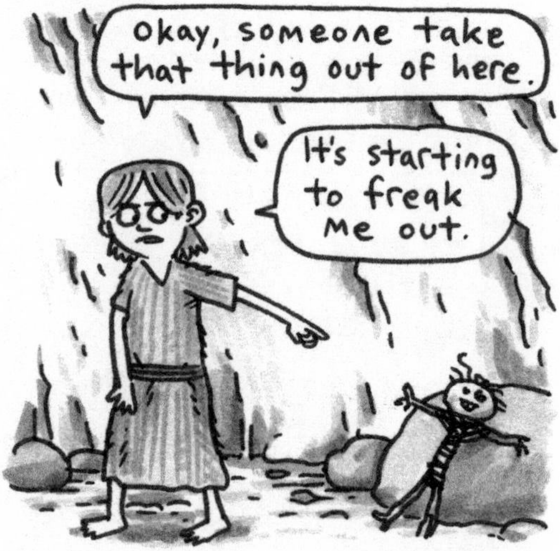
Okay, someone take that thing out of here.
It's starting to freak me out.

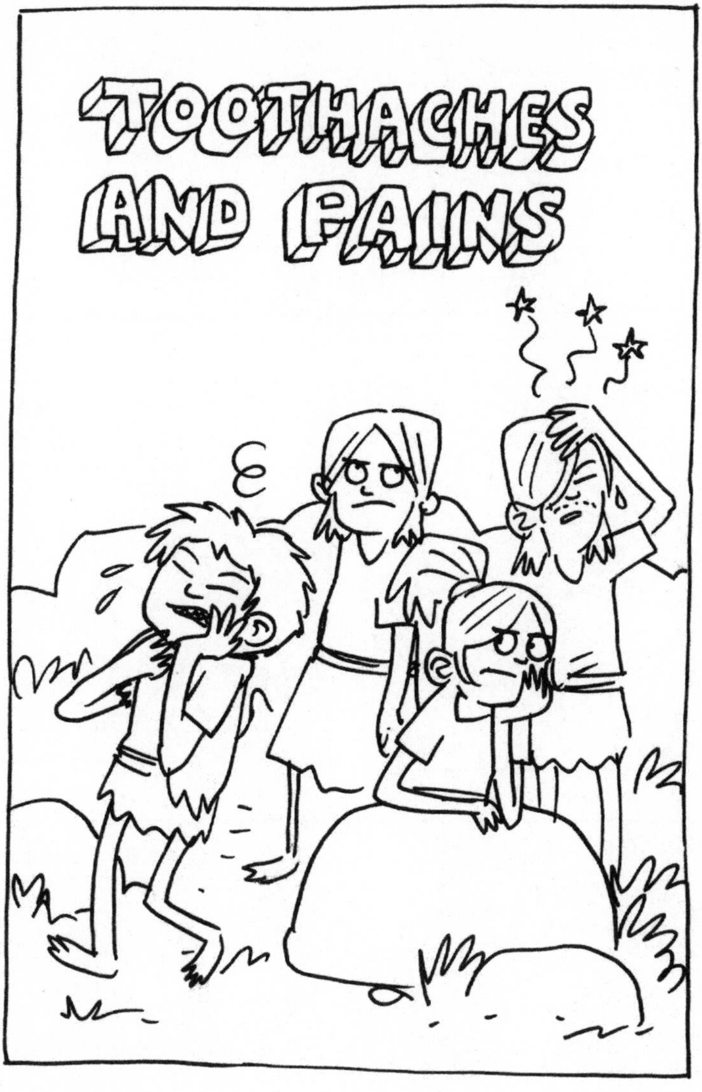
TOOTHACHES AND PAINS

Mom, you're back so soon!
I didn't have to go far to find these plants for Phil's medicine.
Well, everyone is here, see?
But where are Danny's pants?
Mama!
Here they are.
They're all ripped up?
Yeah, something tried to eat him.
What?!
this
Ha ha, Phil's still a little out of it.
Take [redacted] Medicine, Phil.
MMPH!
Keep chewing.
Mmph?
Peepul?

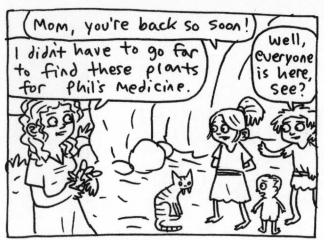

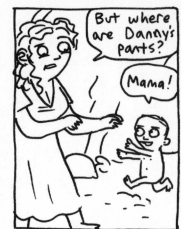

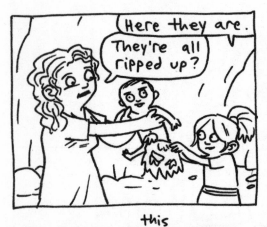

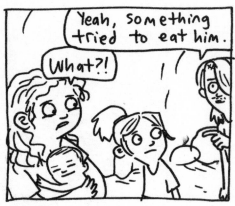

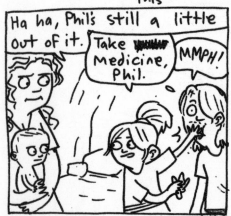

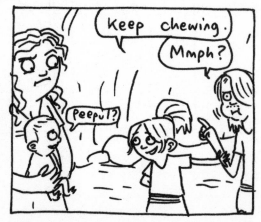

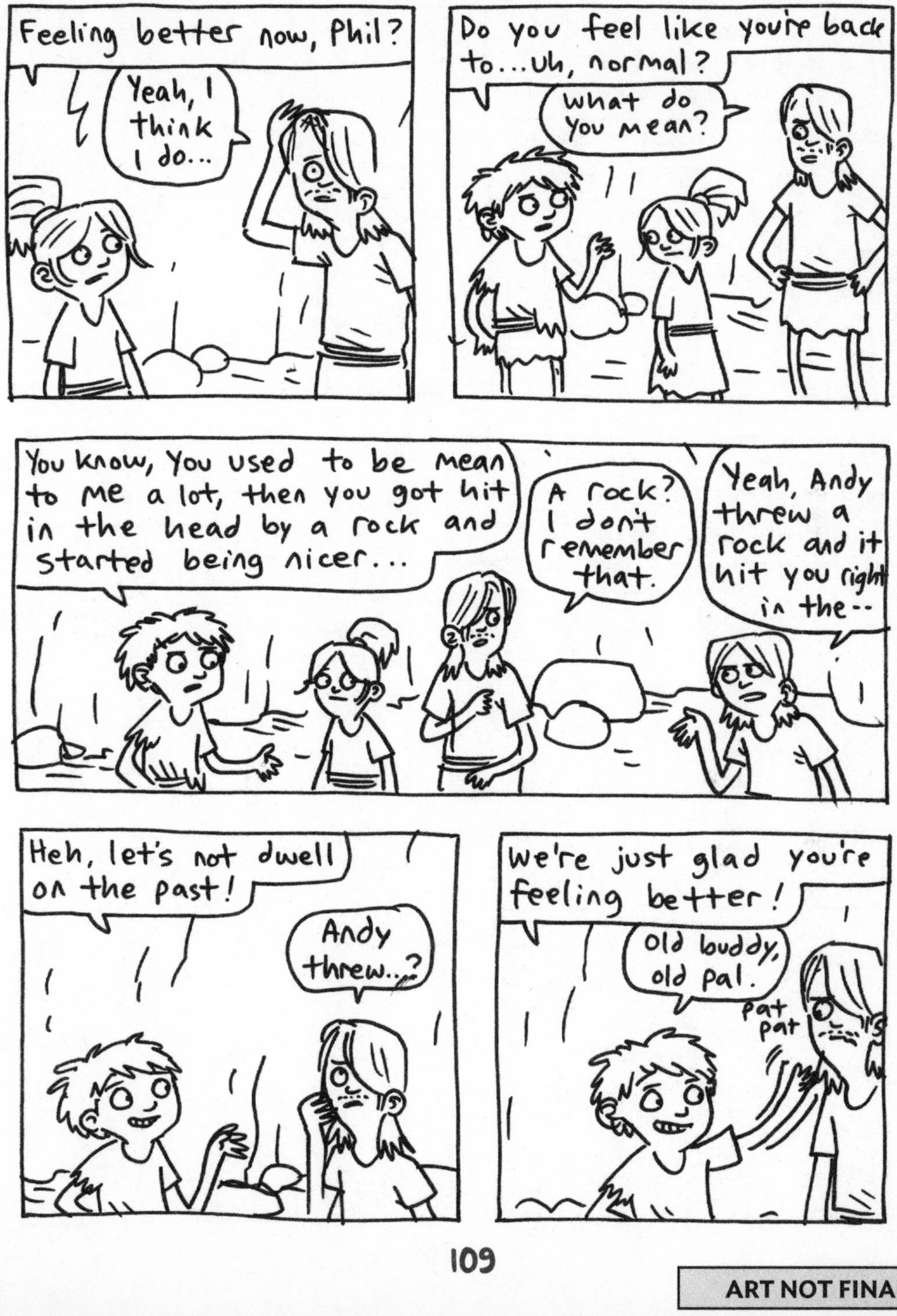
Feeling better now, Phil?
Yeah, I think I do...
Do you feel like you're back to...uh, normal?
What do you mean?
You know, you used to be mean to me a lot, then you got hit in the head by a rock and started being nicer...
A rock? I don't remember that.
Yeah, Andy threw a rock and it hit you right in the--
Heh, let's not dwell on the past!
Andy threw...?
We're just glad you're feeling better!
Old buddy, old pal.
pat pat

ART NOT FINAL

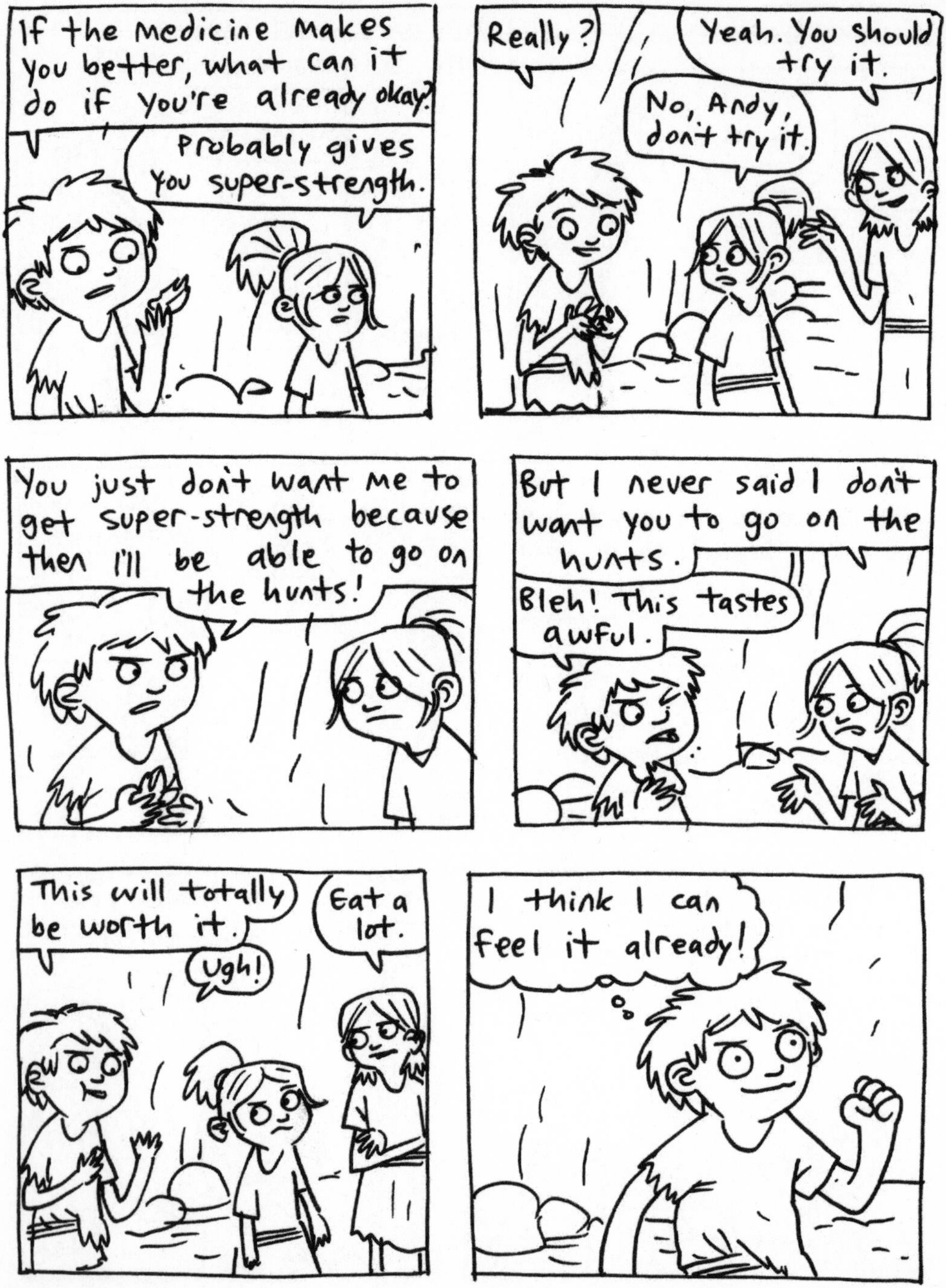
If the medicine makes you better, what can it do if you're already okay?
Probably gives you super-strength.
Really?
Yeah. You should try it.
No, Andy, don't try it.
You just don't want me to get super-strength because then I'll be able to go on the hunts!
But I never said I don't want you to go on the hunts.
Bleh! This tastes awful.
This will totally be worth it.
Eat a lot.
Ugh!
I think I can feel it already!

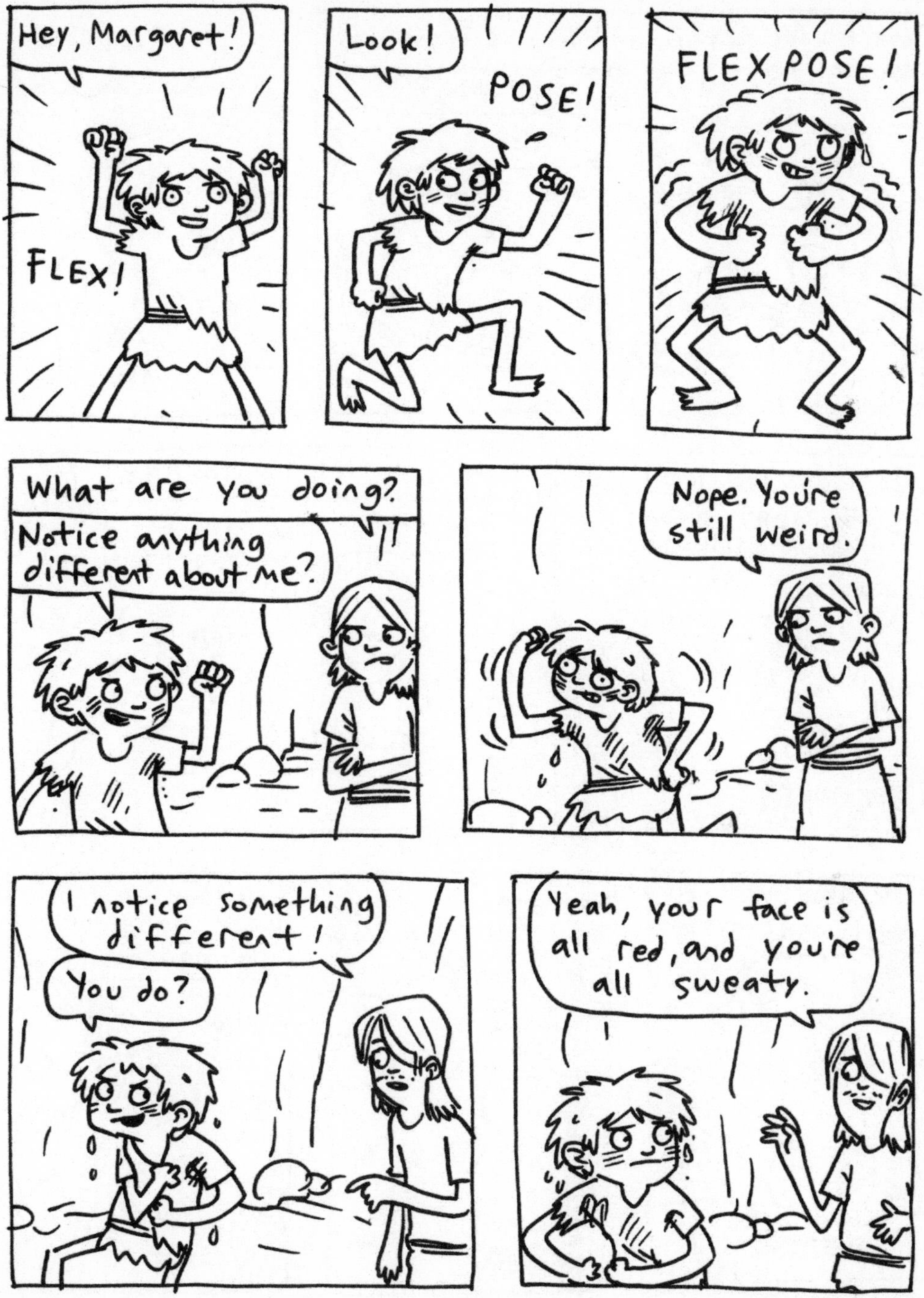
Hey, Margaret!
FLEX!
Look!
POSE!
FLEX POSE!
What are you doing?
Notice anything different about me?
Nope. You're still weird.
I notice something different!
You do?
Yeah, your face is all red, and you're all sweaty.

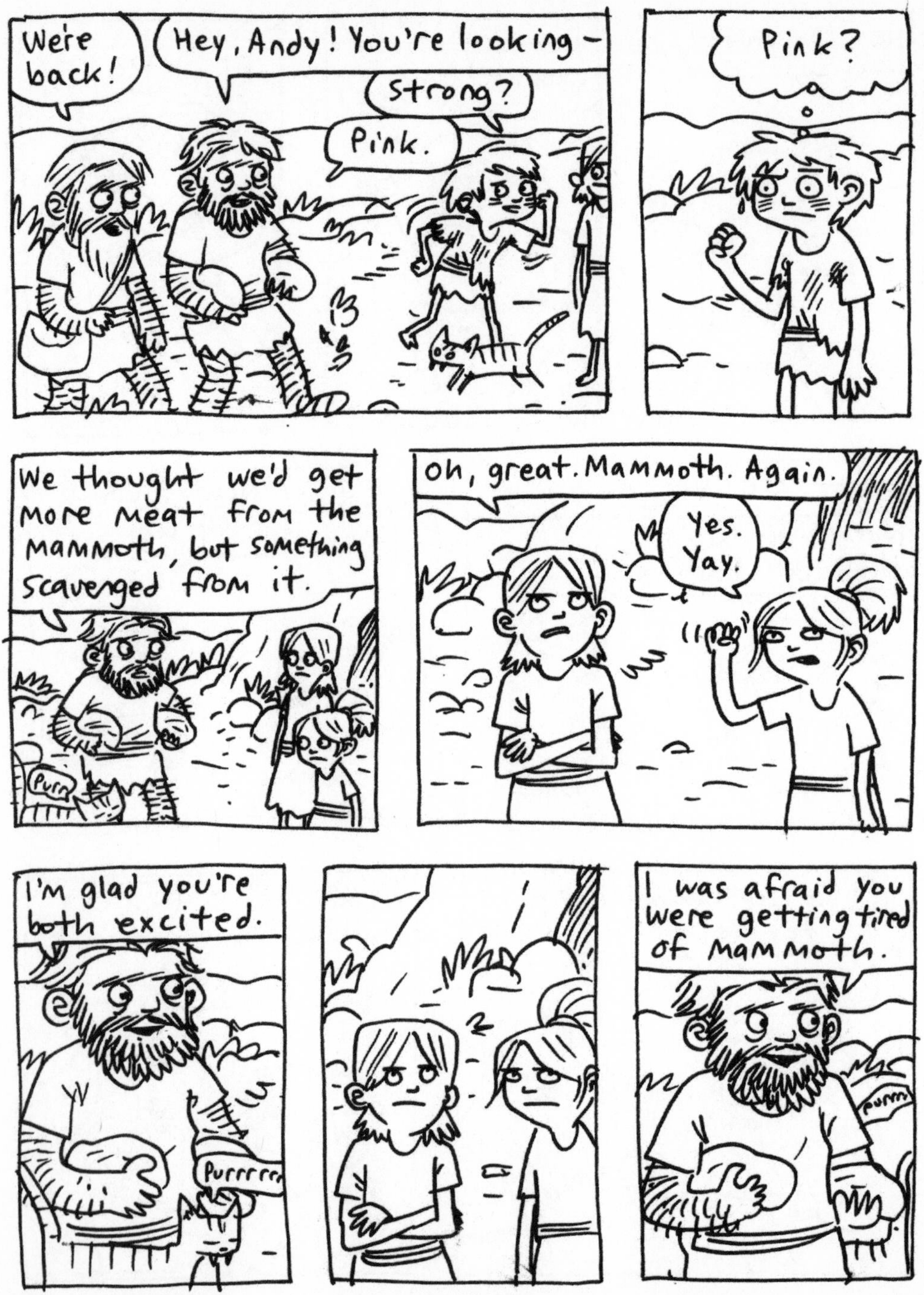
We're back!
Hey, Andy! You're looking—
Strong?
Pink.
Pink?
We thought we'd get more meat from the mammoth, but something scavenged from it.
Purr
Oh, great. Mammoth. Again.
Yes. Yay.
I'm glad you're both excited.
Purrrrrr
I was afraid you were getting tired of mammoth.
Purrrr

ART NOT FINAL

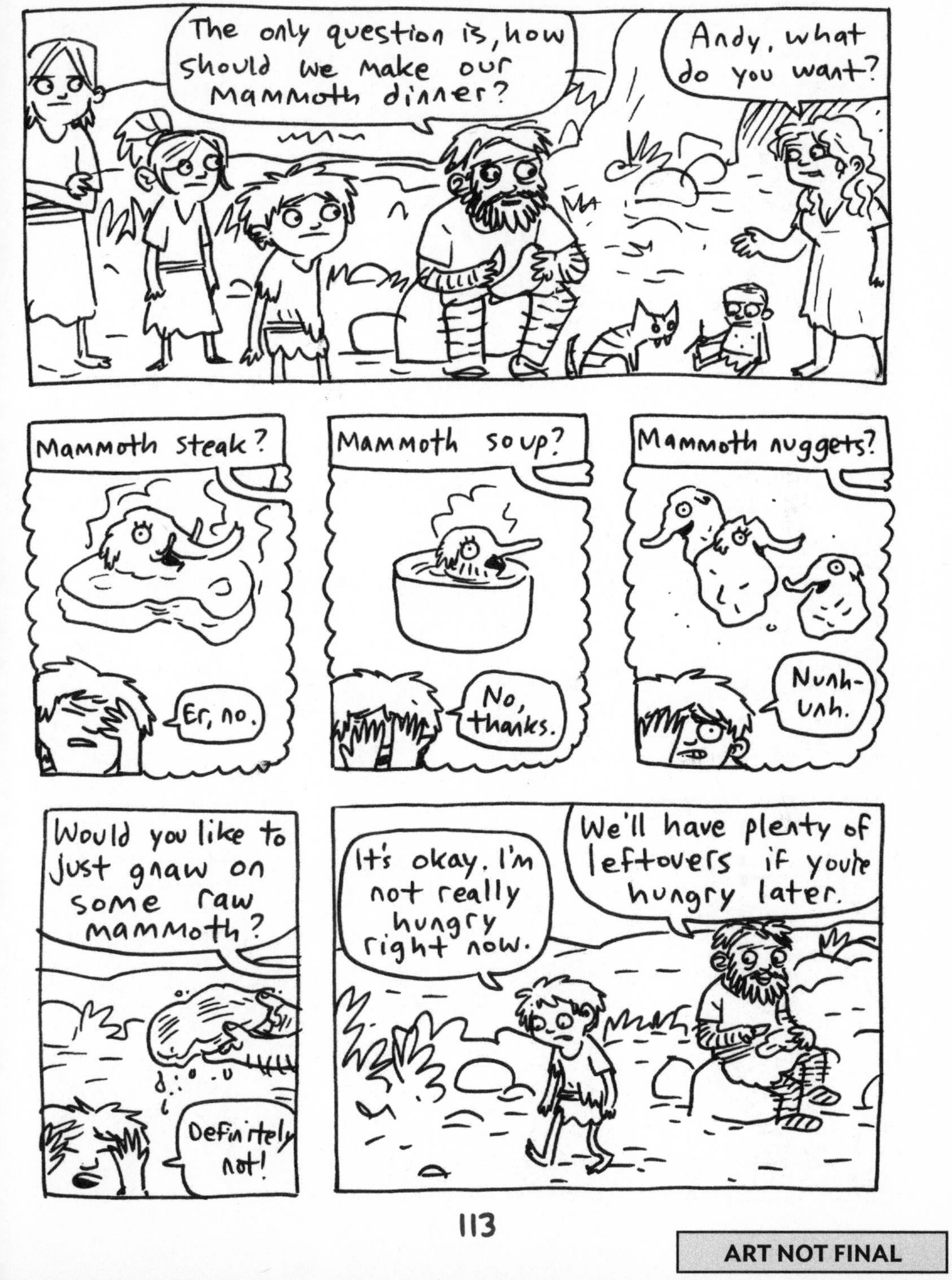
The only question is, how should we make our Mammoth dinner?
Andy, what do you want?
Mammoth steak?
Er, no.
Mammoth soup?
No, thanks.
Mammoth nuggets?
Nunh-Unh.
Would you like to just gnaw on some raw mammoth?
Definitely not!
It's okay. I'm not really hungry right now.
We'll have plenty of leftovers if you're hungry later.

ART NOT FINAL

Sigh.
What's wrong, Andy?
I'm starving, but all there is to eat is mammoth soup, or mammoth steak, or mammoth nuggets..
GRUMBLE
That sounds delicious!
I just wish there was something else to eat.
I have something you might like. Try this.
sniff sniff
Smells okay.
Nibble
chew chew chew
Whoa! This is REALLY good!!
Andy, your face is scaring me.

ART NOT FINAL

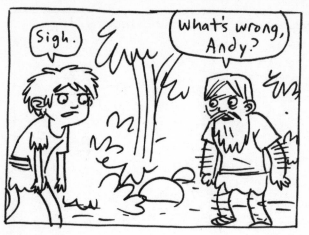

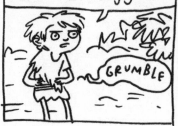

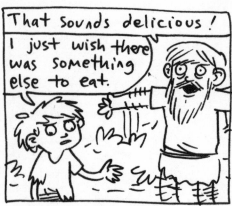

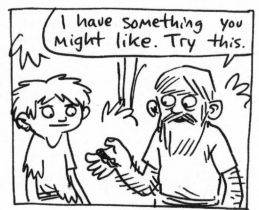

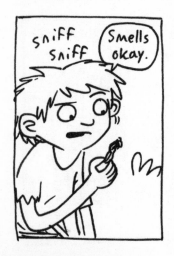

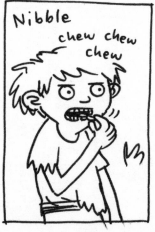

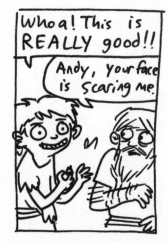

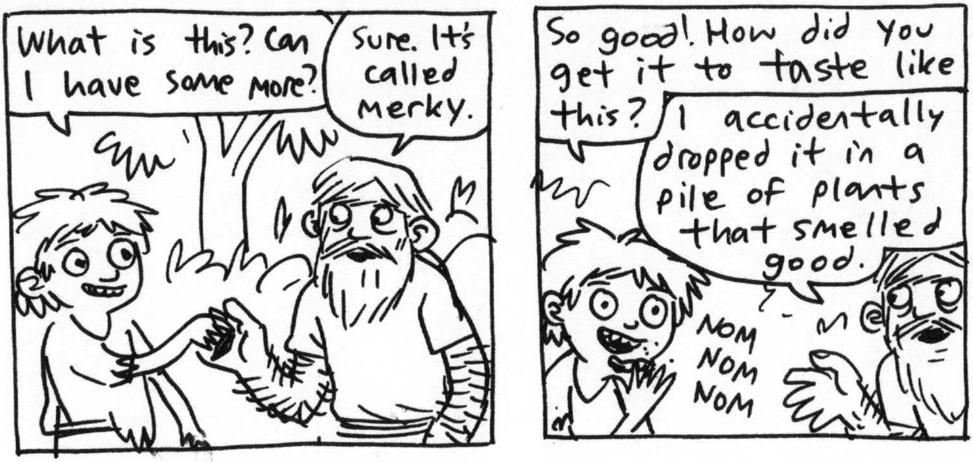
What is this? Can I have some more?
Sure. It's called merky.
So good! How did you get it to taste like this?
I accidentally dropped it in a pile of plants that smelled good.
NOM NOM NOM

Neanderthals didn't seem to use spices. They didn't even have salt or pepper!

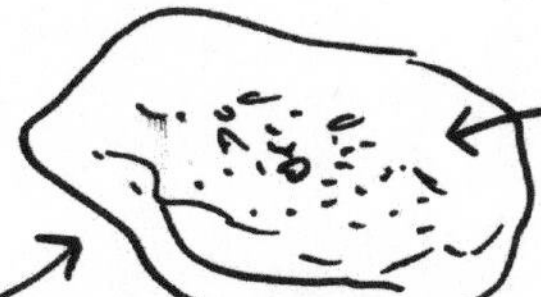
First clear evidence of cooking with spices: 6,000 years ago
Really, really old mustard

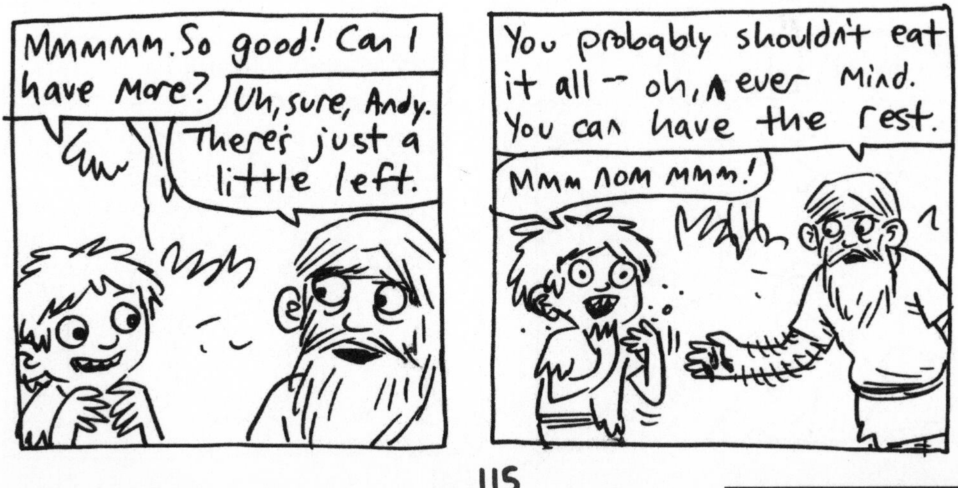
Mmmmm. So good! Can I have more?
Uh, sure, Andy. There's just a little left.
You probably shouldn't eat it all—oh, never mind. You can have the rest.
Mmm nom mmm!

ART NOT FINAL

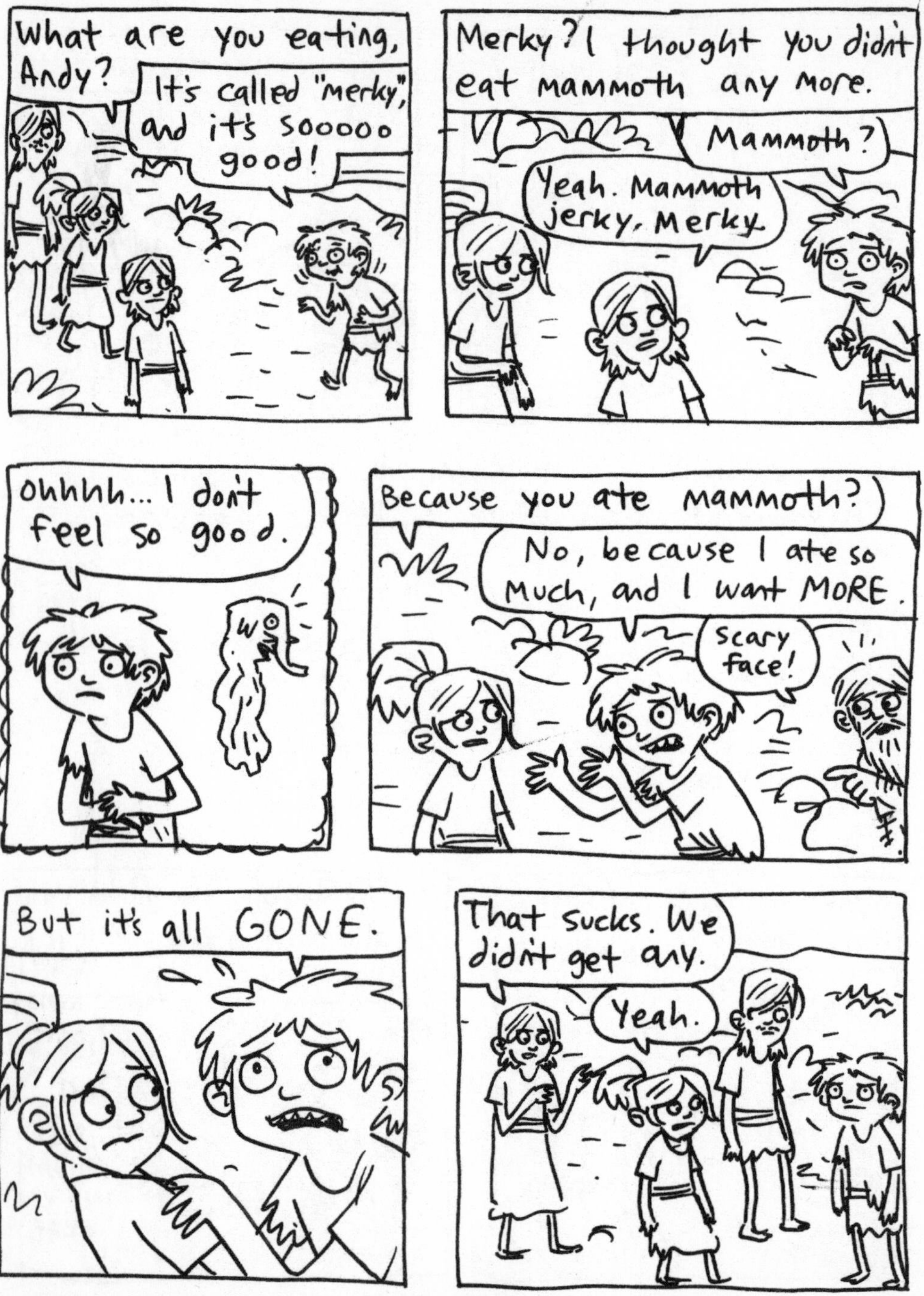
What are you eating, Andy?
It's called "merky," and it's soooooo good!
Merky? I thought you didn't eat mammoth any more.
Mammoth?
Yeah. Mammoth jerky, Merky.
Ohhhh... I don't feel so good.
Because you ate mammoth?
No, because I ate so much, and I want MORE.
Scary face!
But it's all GONE.
That sucks. We didn't get any.
Yeah.

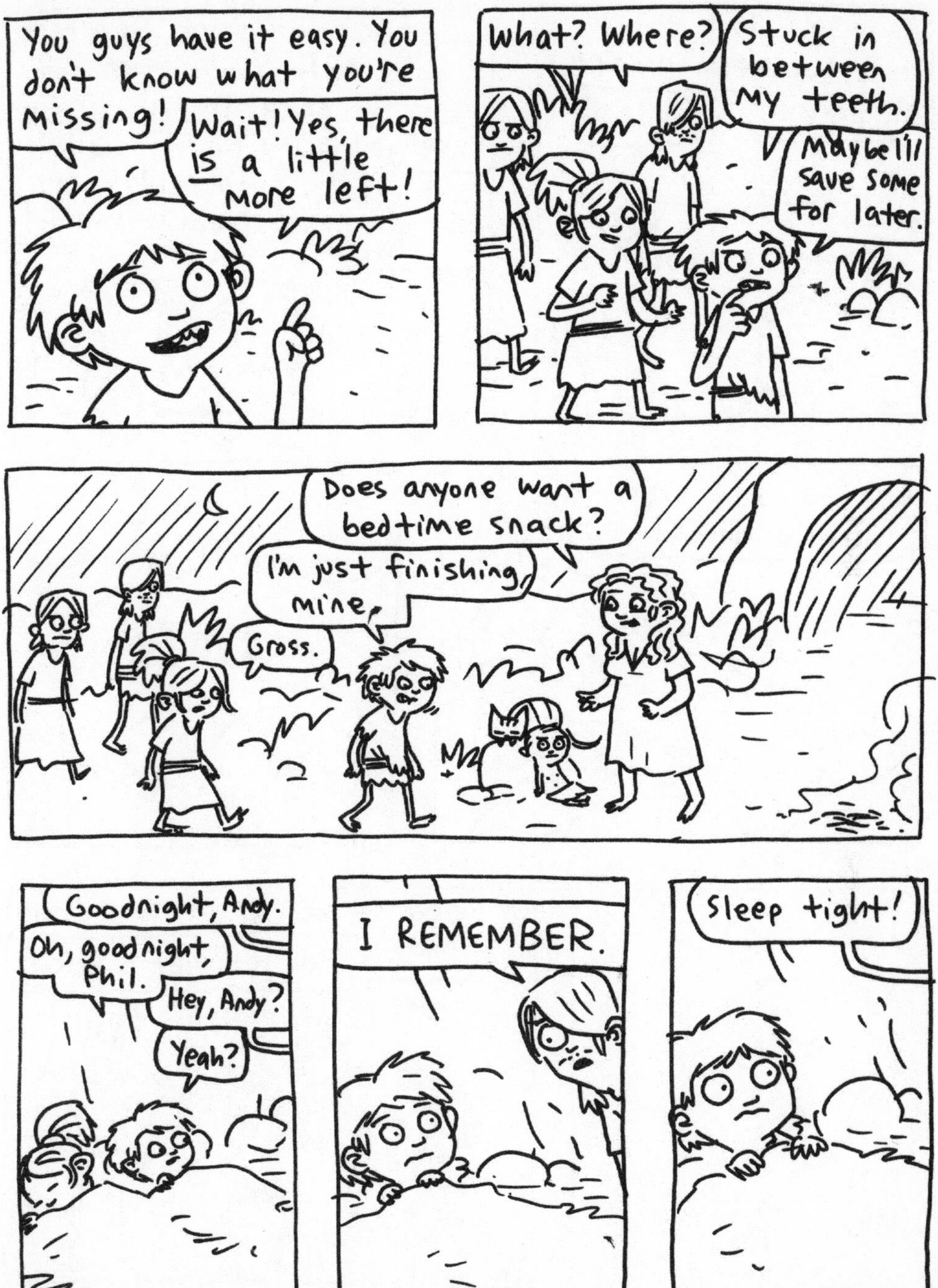
You guys have it easy. You don't know what you're missing!
Wait! Yes, there IS a little more left!
What? Where?
Stuck in between my teeth.
Maybe I'll save some for later.
Does anyone want a bedtime snack?
I'm just finishing mine.
Gross.
Goodnight, Andy.
Oh, goodnight, Phil.
Hey, Andy?
Yeah?
I REMEMBER.
Sleep tight!

ART NOT FINAL

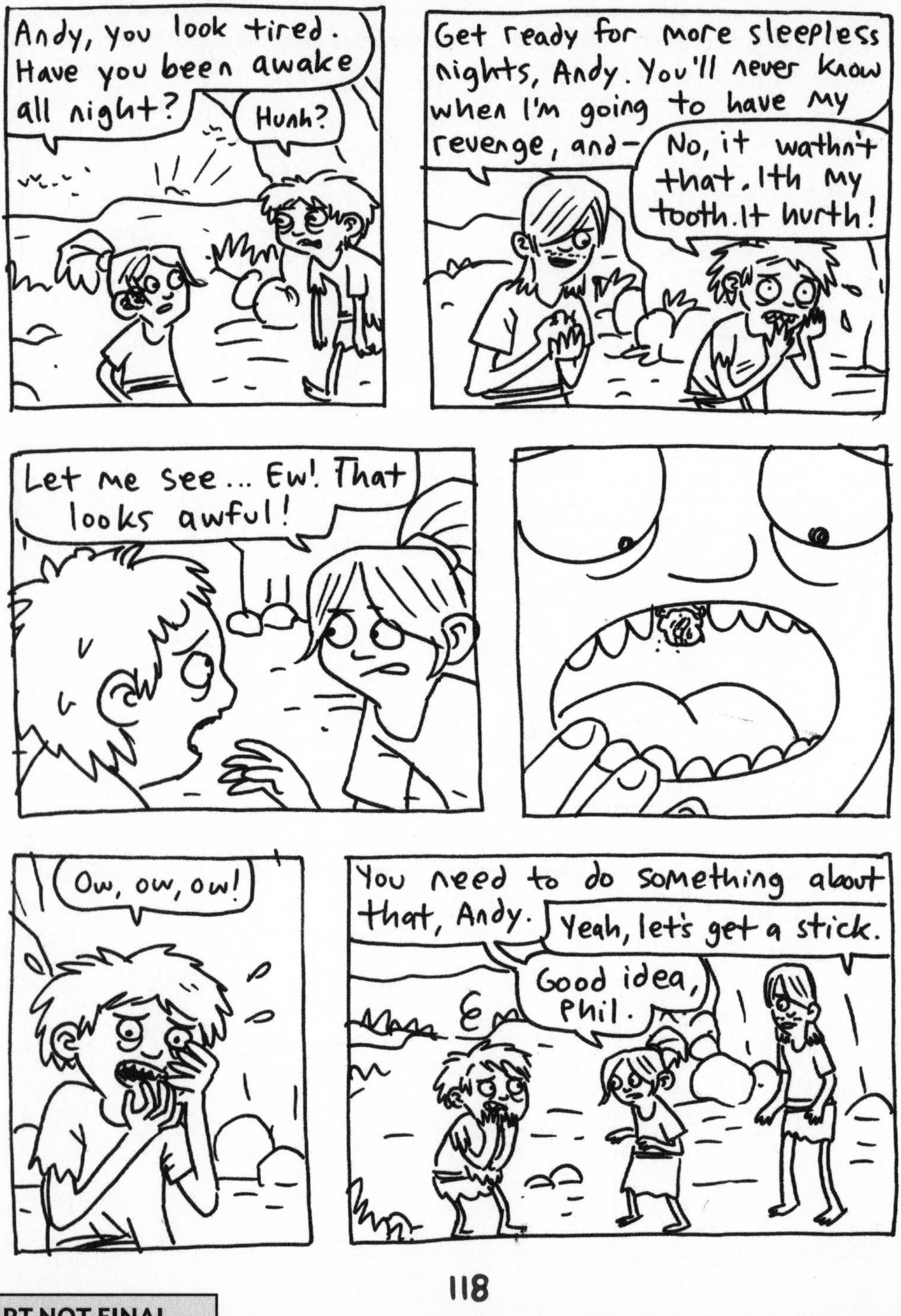
Andy, you look tired. Have you been awake all night?
Hunh?
Get ready for more sleepless nights, Andy. You'll never know when I'm going to have my revenge, and—
No, it wathn't that. Ith my tooth. It hurth!
Let me see... Ew! That looks awful!
Ow, ow, ow!
You need to do something about that, Andy.
Yeah, let's get a stick.
Good idea, Phil.

ART NOT FINAL

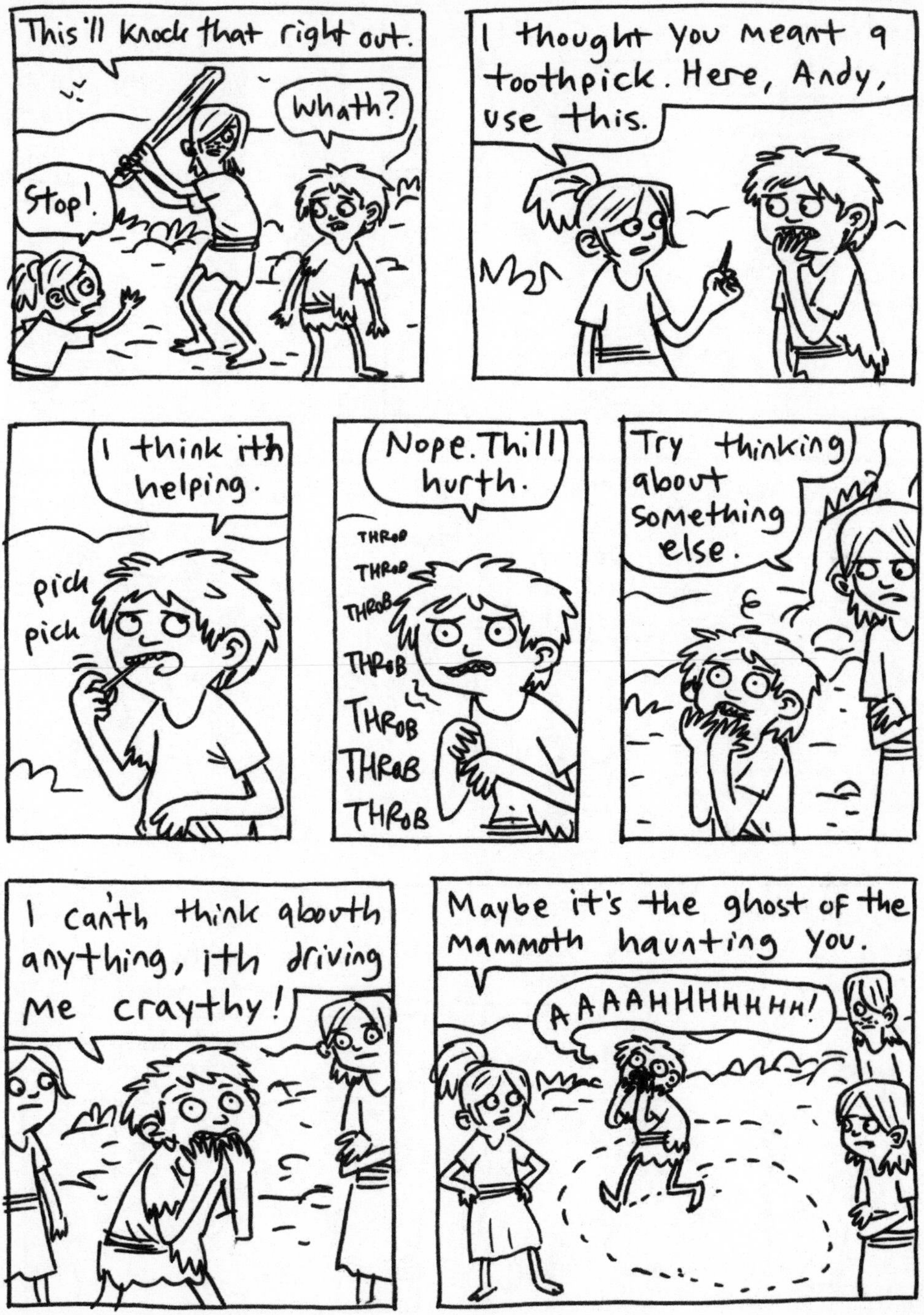
This'll knock that right out.
Whath?
Stop!
I thought you meant a toothpick. Here, Andy, use this.
I think ith helping.
pich pich
Nope. Thill hurth.
THROB
THROB
THROB
THROB
THROB
THROB
THROB
Try thinking about something else.
I canth think abouth anything, ith driving me craythy!
Maybe it's the ghost of the mammoth haunting you.
AAAAHHHHHHH!

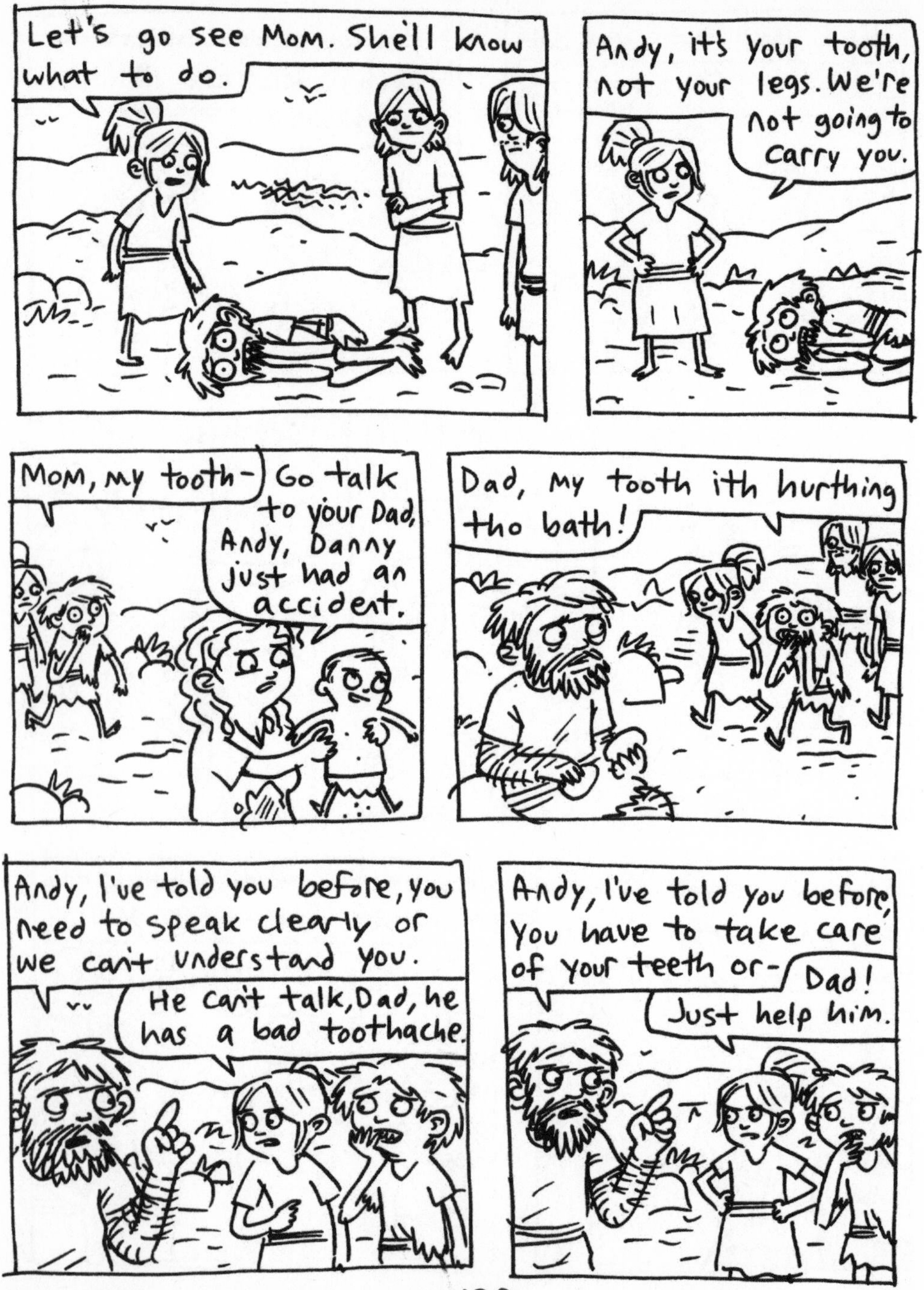
Let's go see Mom. She'll know what to do.
Andy, it's your tooth, not your legs. We're not going to carry you.
Mom, my tooth-
Go talk to your Dad, Andy, Danny just had an accident.
Dad, my tooth ith hurthing tho bath!
Andy, I've told you before, you need to speak clearly or we can't understand you.
He can't talk, Dad, he has a bad toothache.
Andy, I've told you before, you have to take care of your teeth or-
Dad! Just help him.

Okay, okay. Let's take a look.
Thankth.
We just need you to stop Moaning.
YIKES! You're right. We're going to have to pull that out.
I'll just reach in and--
OUCH!!
CHOMP!
Thorry.
Here, Andy, wrap this around your tooth.
I'm almost glad I followed along.
Oth-kay. Nowth what?
Avenge your finger, Dad.

ART NOT FINAL

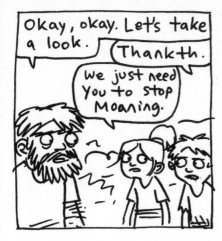

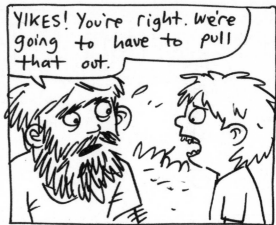

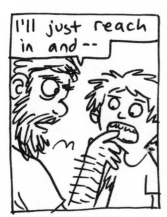

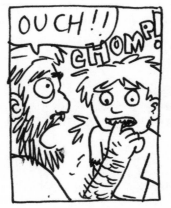

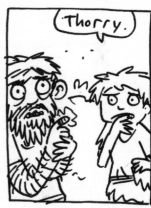

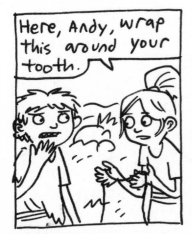

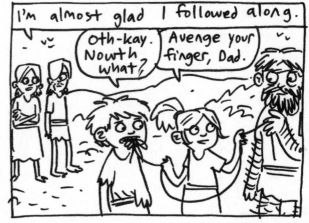

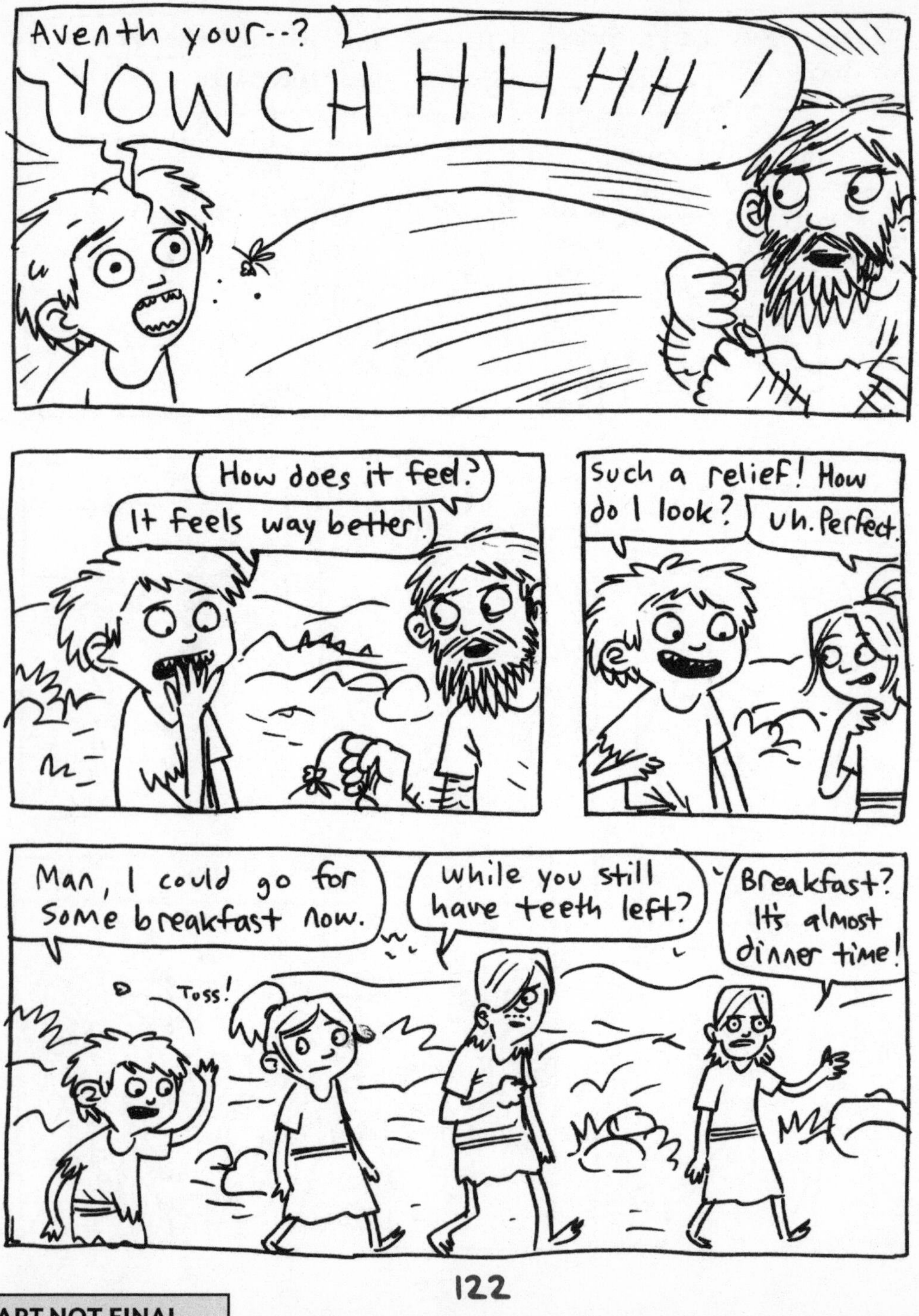

Aventh your--?
YOWCHHHHH!
How does it feel?
It feels way better!
Such a relief! How do I look?
uh. Perfect.
Man, I could go for some breakfast now.
TOSS!
While you still have teeth left?
Breakfast? It's almost dinner time!

ART NOT FINAL

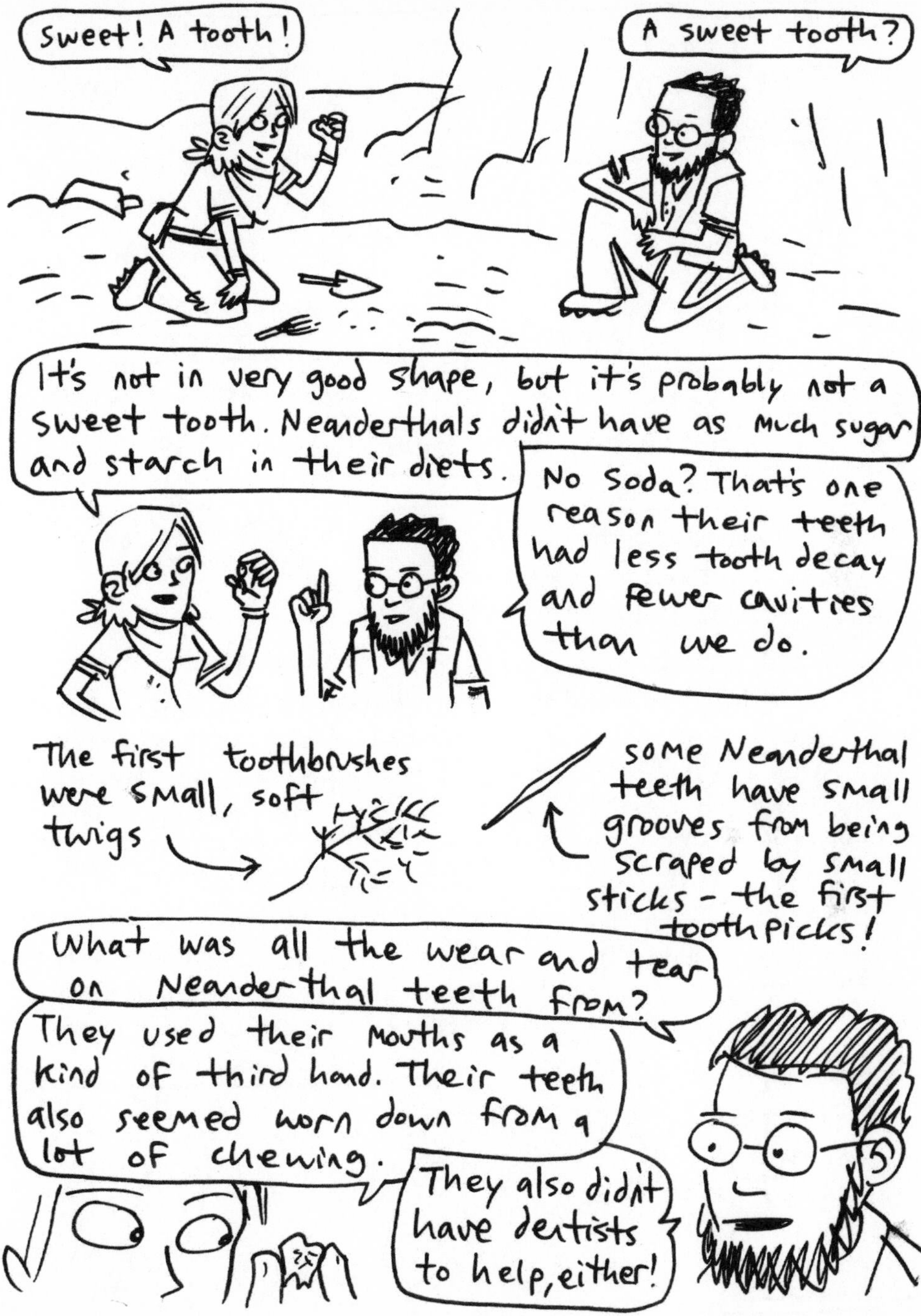
Sweet! A tooth!
A sweet tooth?
It's not in very good shape, but it's probably not a sweet tooth. Neanderthals didn't have as much sugar and starch in their diets.
No soda? That's one reason their teeth had less tooth decay and fewer cavities than we do.
The first toothbrushes were small, soft twigs
Some Neanderthal teeth have small grooves from being scraped by small sticks - the first toothpicks!
What was all the wear and tear on Neanderthal teeth from?
They used their mouths as a kind of third hand. Their teeth also seemed worn down from a lot of chewing.
They also didn't have dentists to help, either!

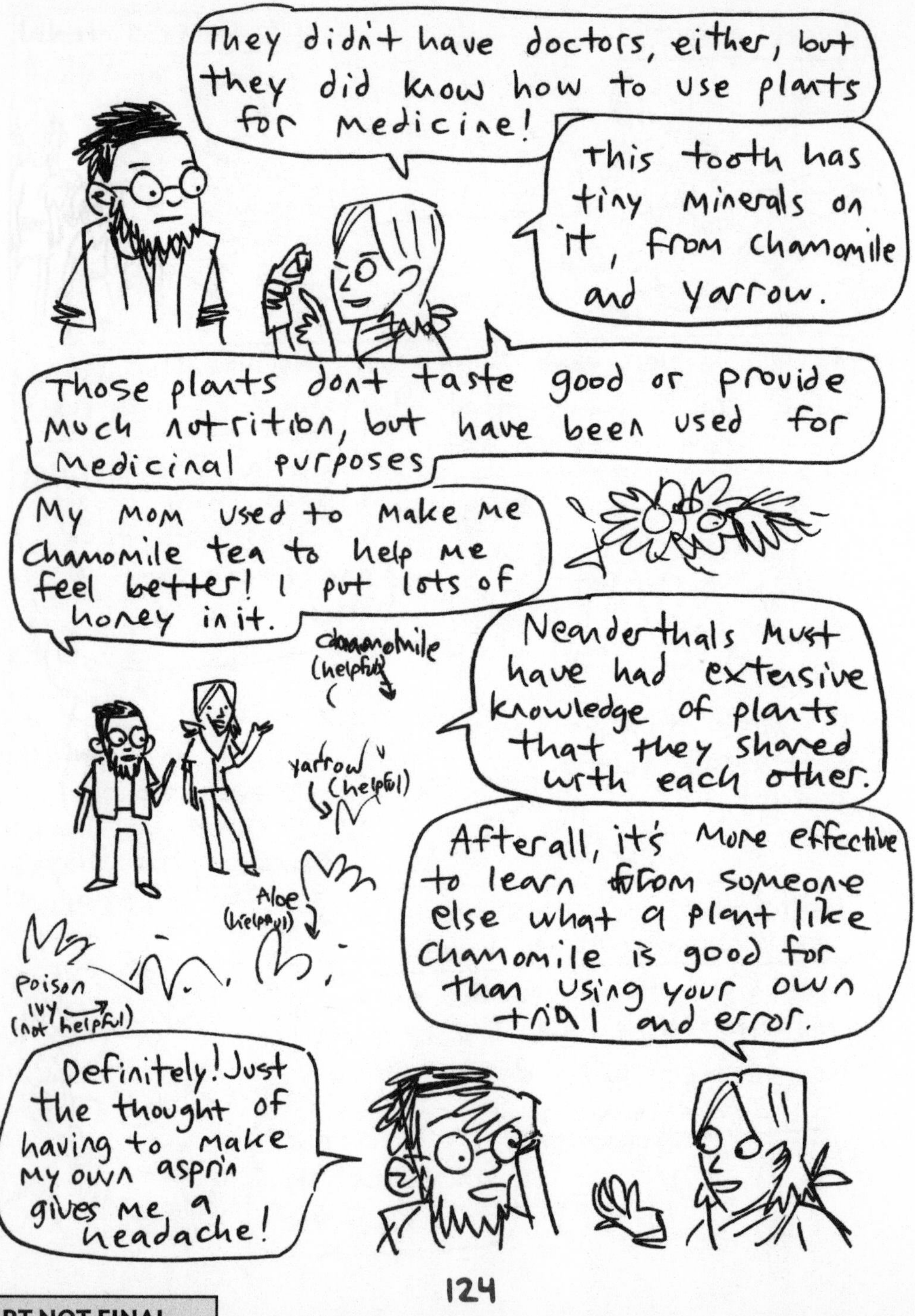
They didn't have doctors, either, but they did know how to use plants for medicine!
this tooth has tiny minerals on it, from chamomile and yarrow.
Those plants dont taste good or provide much nutrition, but have been used for medicinal purposes
My mom used to make me chamomile tea to help me feel better! I put lots of honey in it.
chamomile (helpful)
Neanderthals must have had extensive knowledge of plants that they shared with each other.
yarrow (helpful)
Aloe (helpful)
Poison ivy (not helpful)
Afterall, it's more effective to learn from someone else what a plant like chamomile is good for than using your own trial and error.
Definitely! Just the thought of having to make my own asprin gives me a headache!

ART NOT FINAL

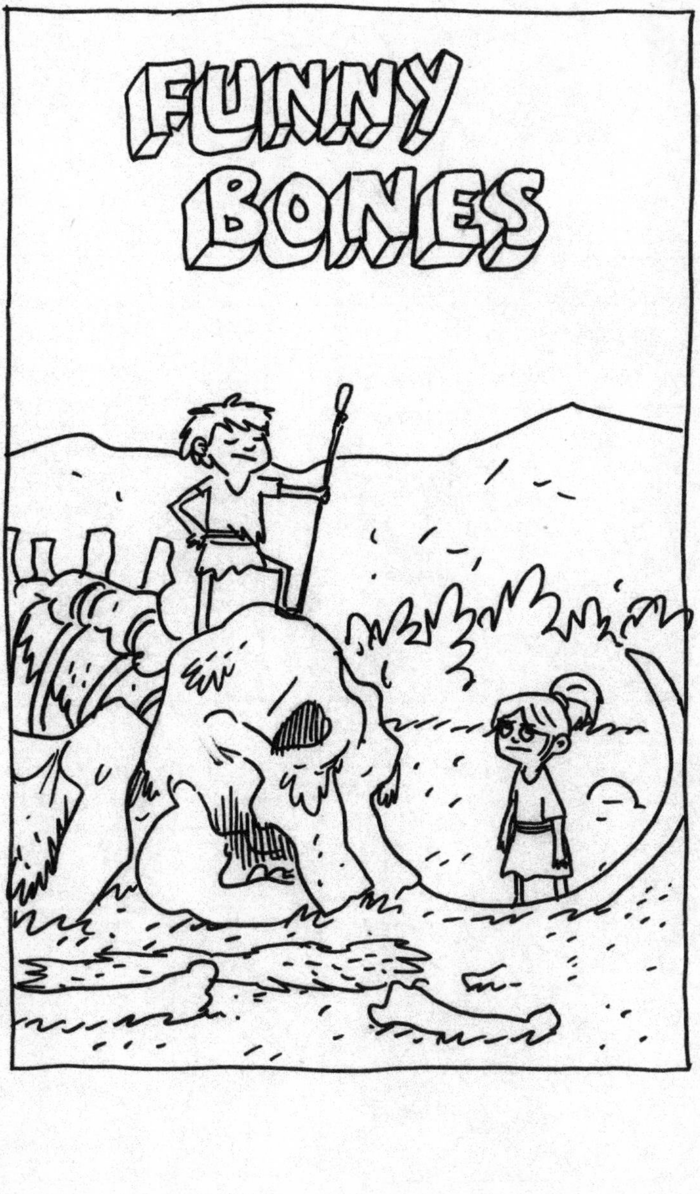
FUNNY
BONES

ART NOT FINAL

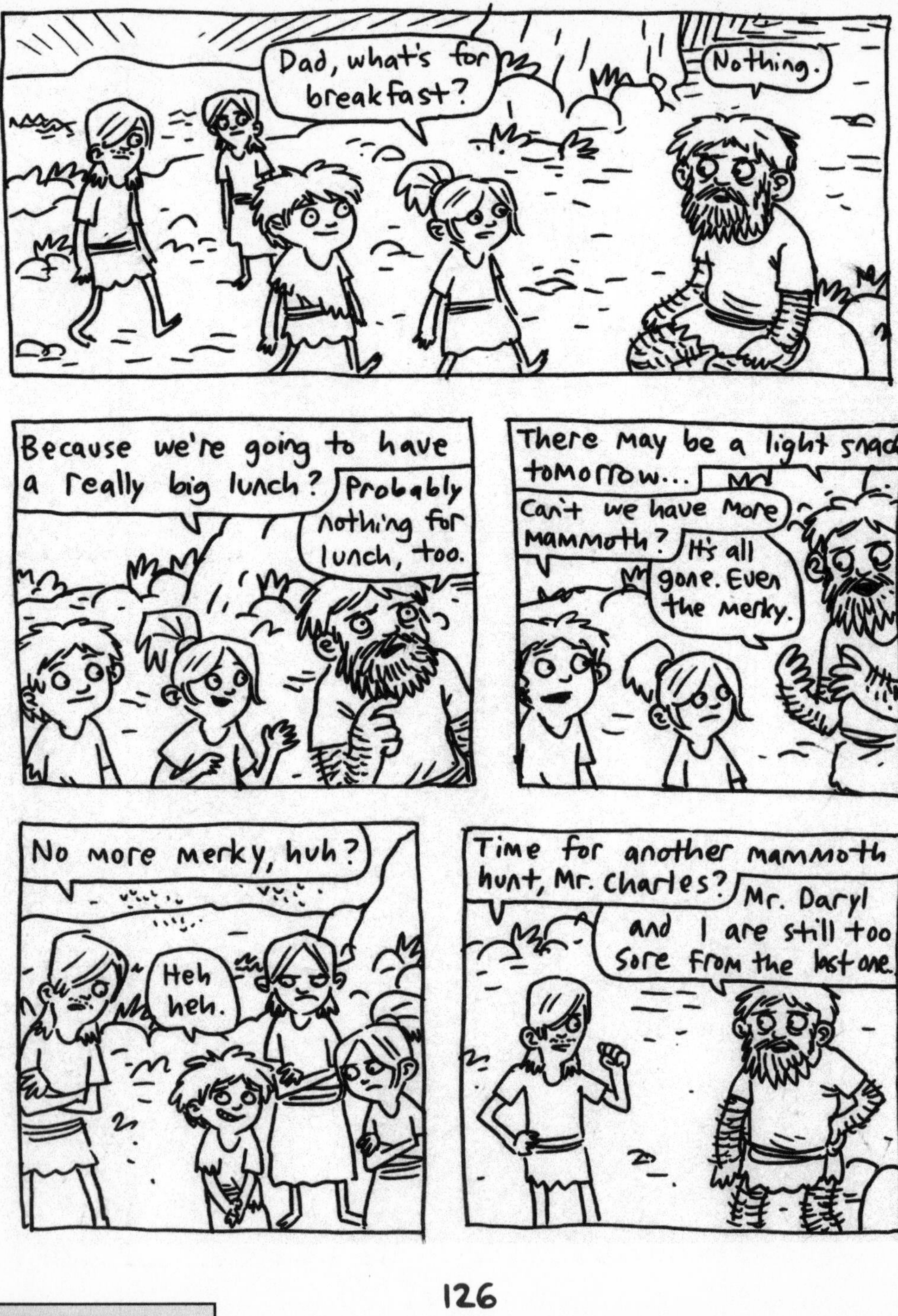
Dad, what's for breakfast?
Nothing.
Because we're going to have a really big lunch?
Probably nothing for lunch, too.
There may be a light snack tomorrow...
Can't we have more mammoth?
It's all gone. Even the merky.
No more merky, huh?
Heh heh.
Time for another mammoth hunt, Mr. Charles?
Mr. Daryl and I are still too sore from the last one.

ART NOT FINAL

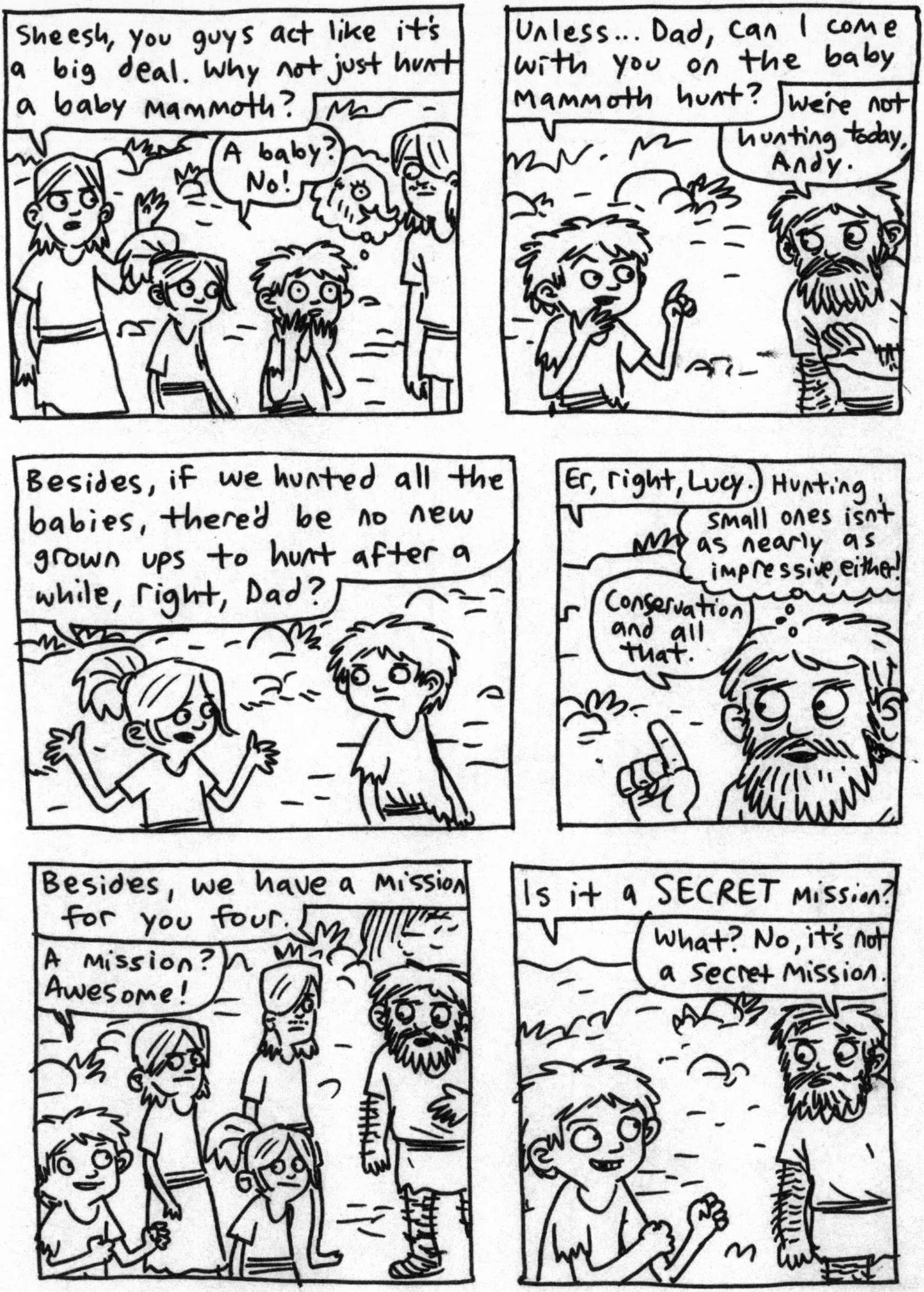
Sheesh, you guys act like it's a big deal. Why not just hunt a baby mammoth?
A baby? No!
Unless... Dad, can I come with you on the baby mammoth hunt?
We're not hunting today, Andy.
Besides, if we hunted all the babies, there'd be no new grown ups to hunt after a while, right, Dad?
Er, right, Lucy.
Hunting small ones isn't as nearly as impressive, either!
Conservation and all that.
Besides, we have a mission for you four.
A mission? Awesome!
Is it a SECRET mission?
What? No, it's not a secret mission.

ART NOT FINAL

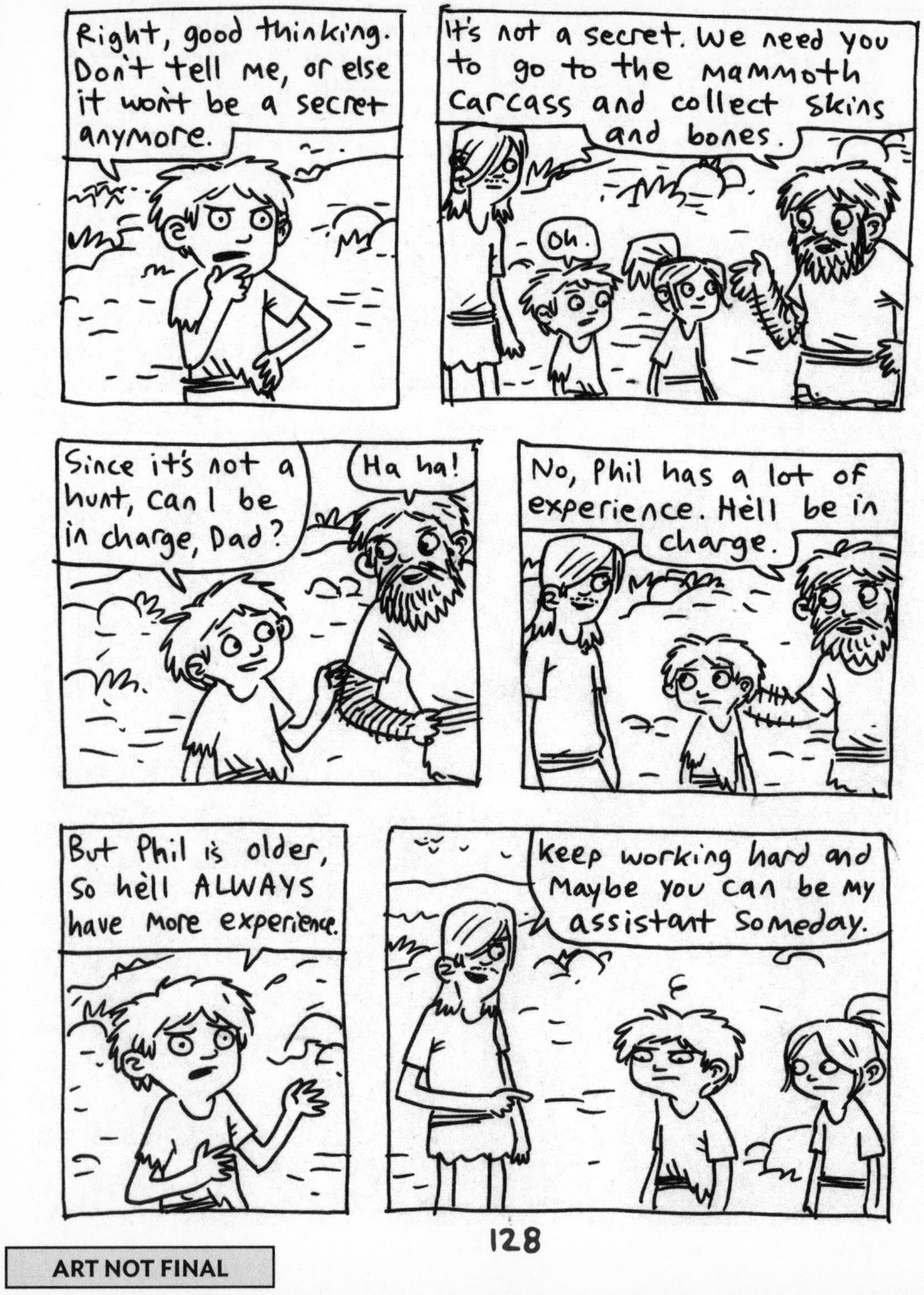
Right, good thinking. Don't tell me, or else it won't be a secret anymore.
It's not a secret. We need you to go to the mammoth carcass and collect skins and bones.
Oh.
Since it's not a hunt, can I be in charge, Dad?
Ha ha!
No, Phil has a lot of experience. He'll be in charge.
But Phil is older, so he'll ALWAYS have more experience.
Keep working hard and maybe you can be my assistant someday.

ART NOT FINAL

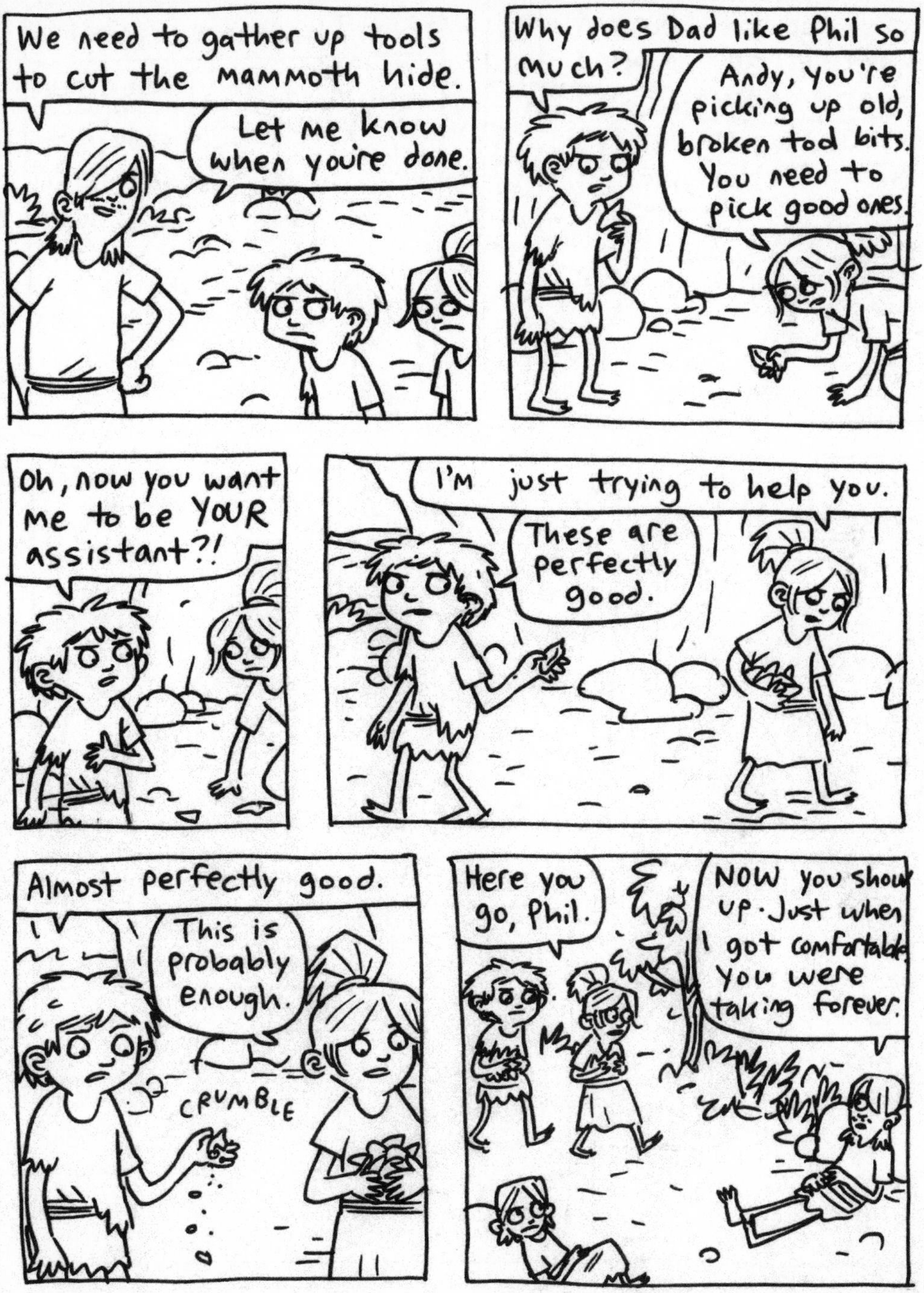
We need to gather up tools to cut the mammoth hide.
Let me know when you're done.
Why does Dad like Phil so much?
Andy, you're picking up old, broken tool bits. You need to pick good ones.
Oh, now you want me to be YOUR assistant?!
I'M just trying to help you.
These are perfectly good.
Almost perfectly good.
This is probably enough.
CRUMBLE
Here you go, Phil.

ART NOT FINAL

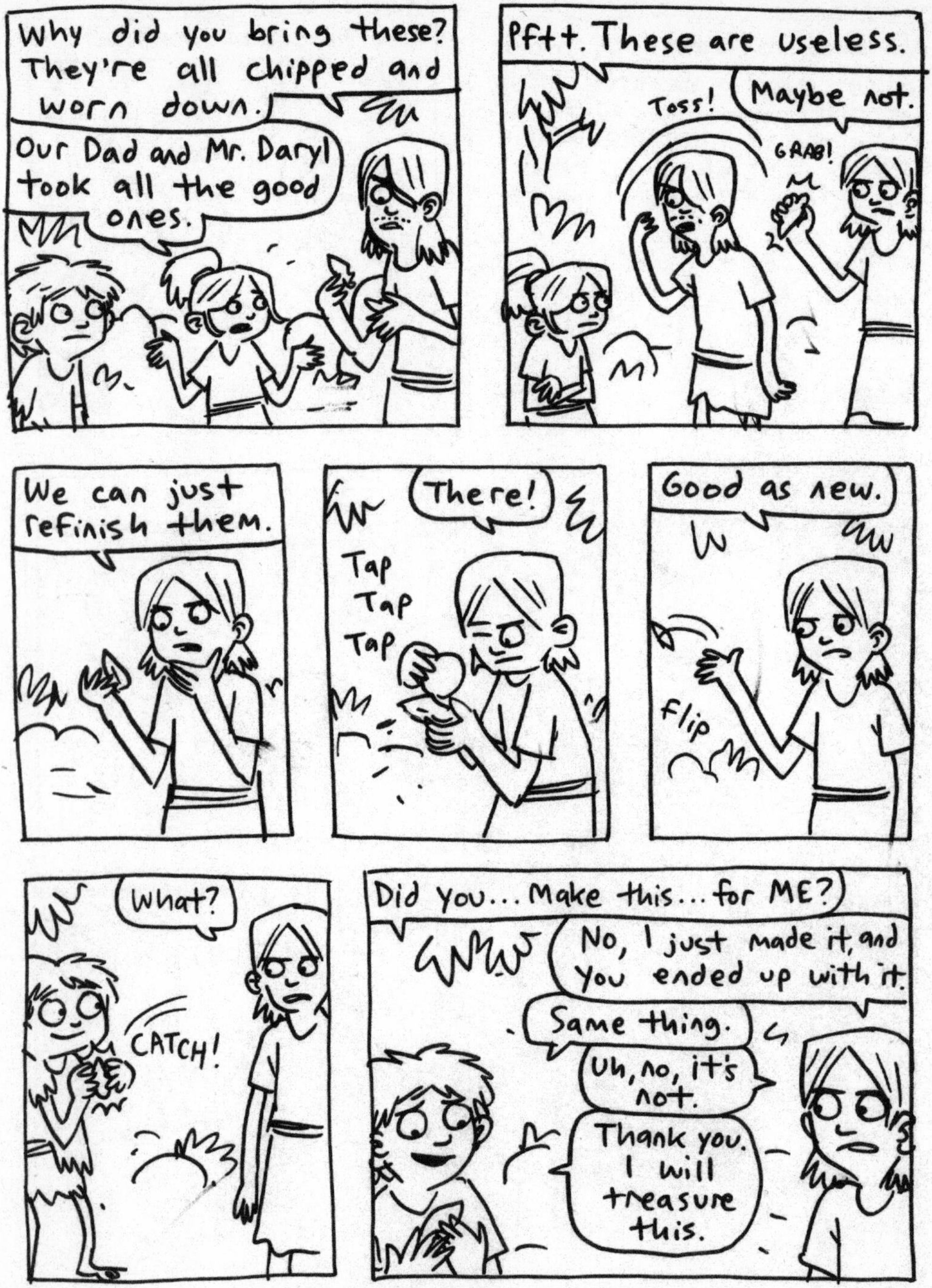

Why did you bring these? They're all chipped and worn down.
Our Dad and Mr. Daryl took all the good ones.
Pftt. These are useless.
Toss!
Maybe not.
GRAB!
We can just refinish them.
There!
Tap
Tap
Tap
Good as new.
Flip
What?
CATCH!
Did you... Make this... for ME?
No, I just made it, and you ended up with it.
Same thing.
Uh, no, it's not.
Thank you. I will treasure this.

Neanderthals were some of the world's first people to recycle!

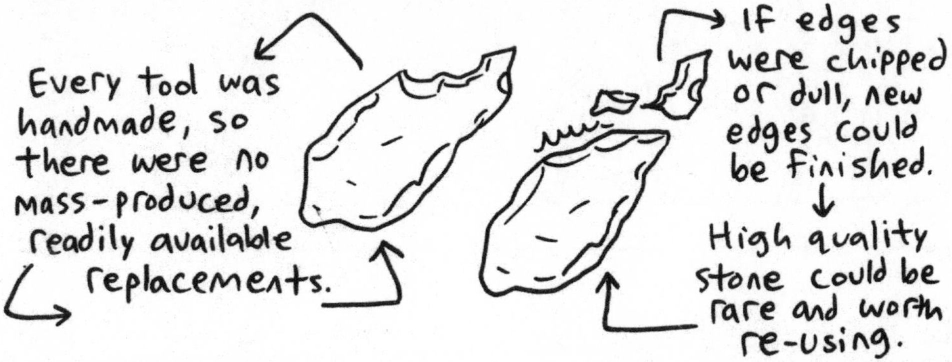
Every tool was handmade, so there were no mass-produced, readily available replacements.
If edges were chipped or dull, new edges could be finished.
High quality stone could be rare and worth re-using.

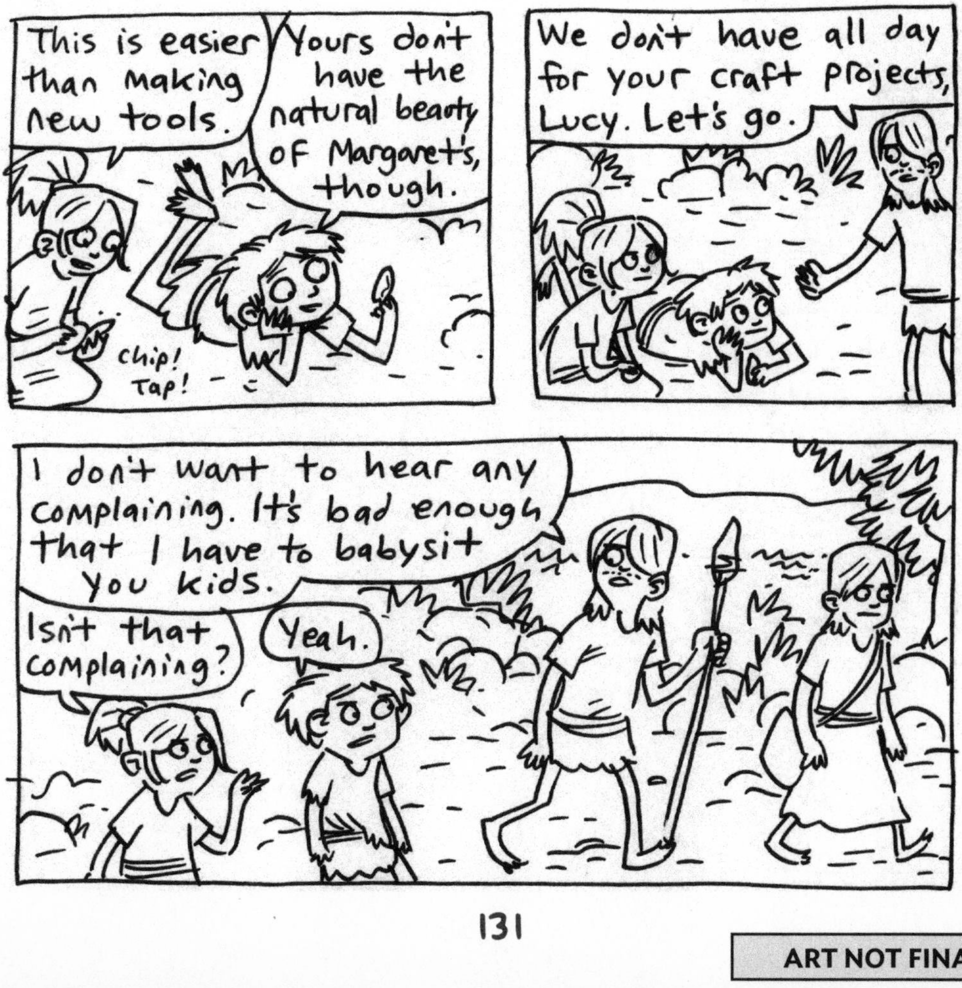
This is easier than making new tools.
Yours don't have the natural beauty of Margaret's, though.
Chip! Tap!
We don't have all day for your craft projects, Lucy. Let's go.
I don't want to hear any complaining. It's bad enough that I have to babysit you kids.
Isn't that complaining?
Yeah.

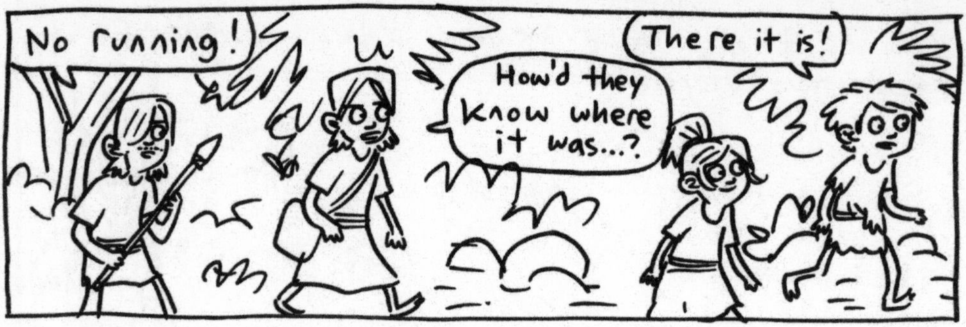
No running!
How'd they know where it was...?
There it is!

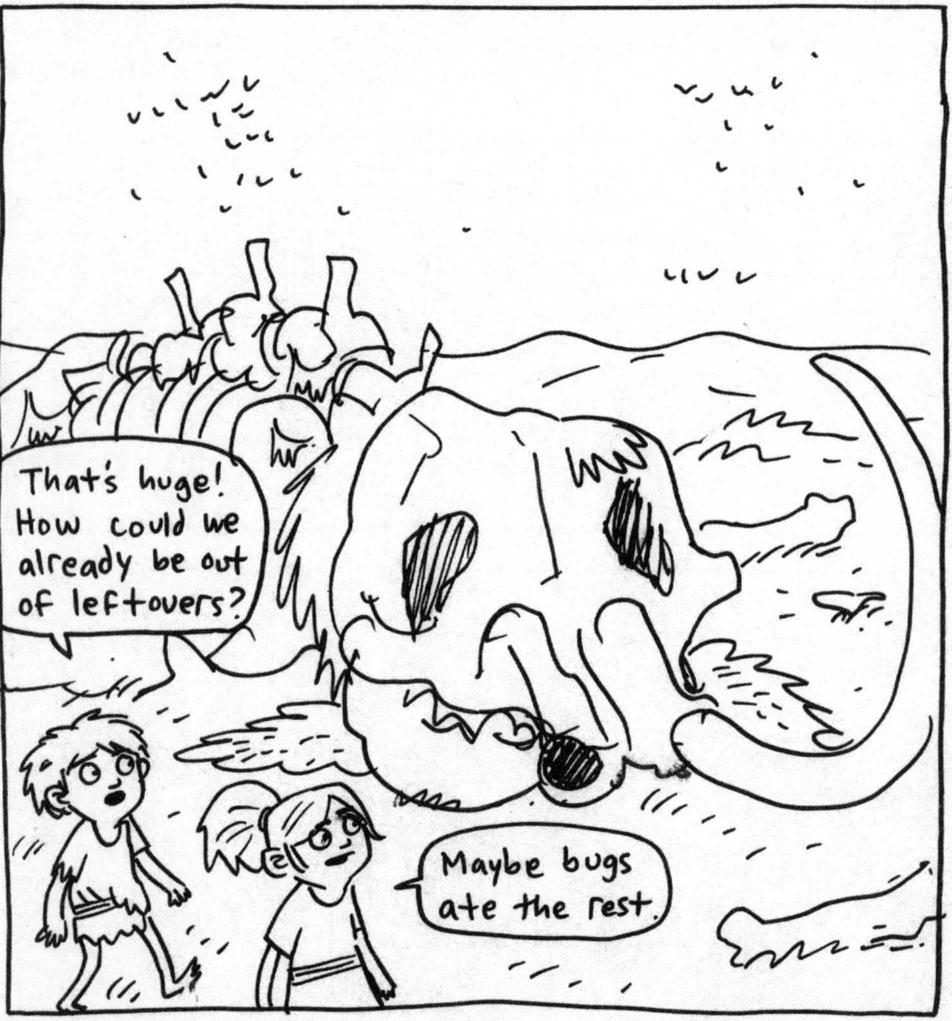
That's huge! How could we already be out of leftovers?
Maybe bugs ate the rest.

ART NOT FINAL

Museums use Dermestid beetles to clean bones of flesh and debris, for easier study!

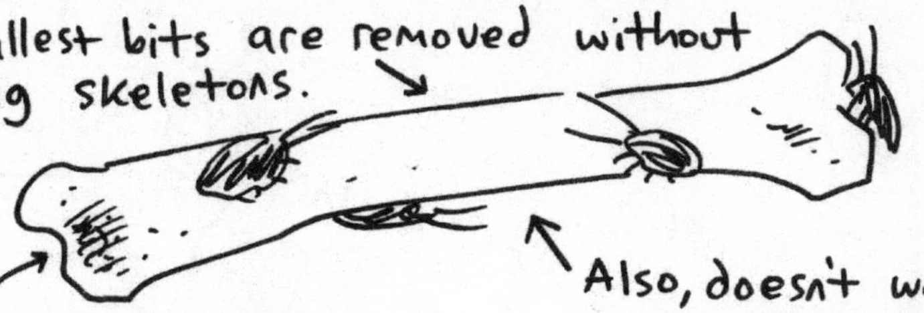
Even smallest bits are removed without damaging skeletons.
Doesn't clean off dirt or rock, though.
Also, doesn't work on large animals like elephants.

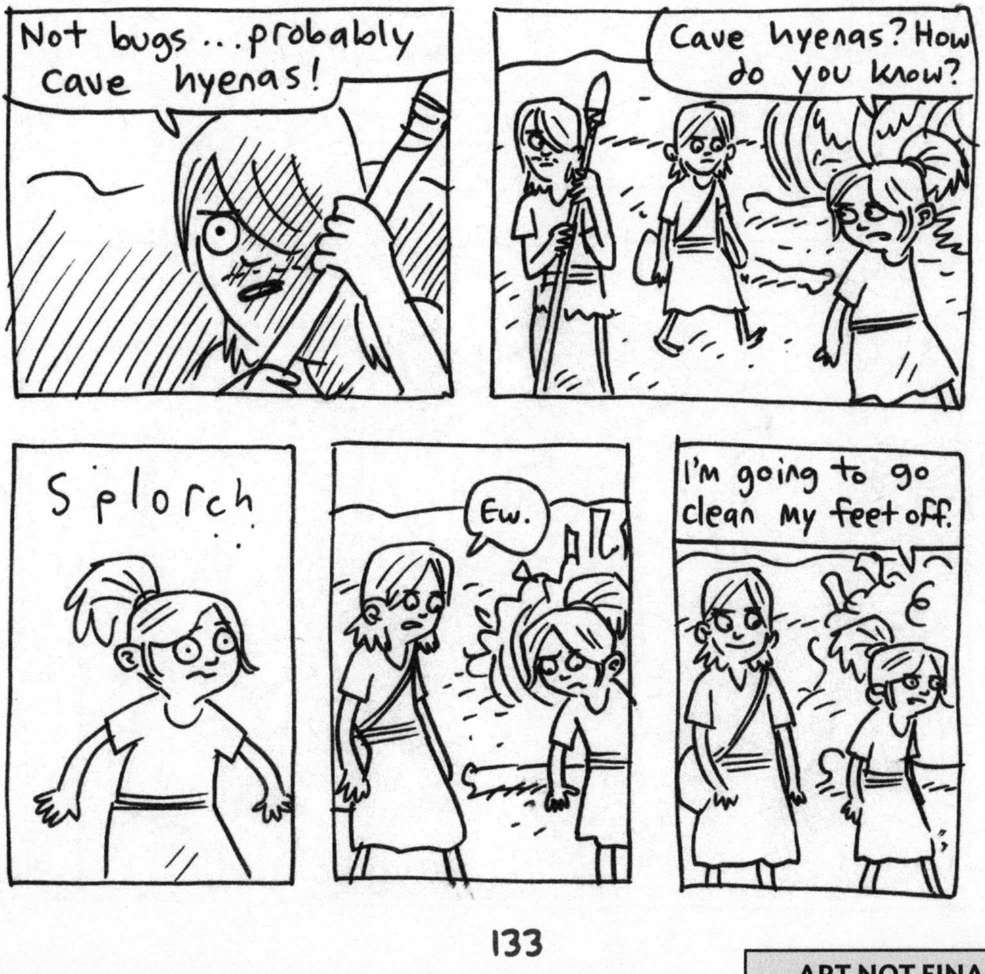
Not bugs...probably cave hyenas!
Cave hyenas? How do you know?
Splorch
Ew.
I'm going to go clean my feet off.

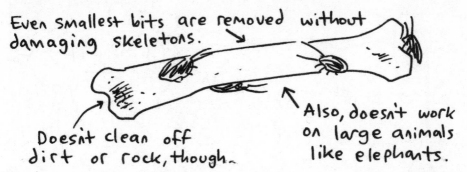

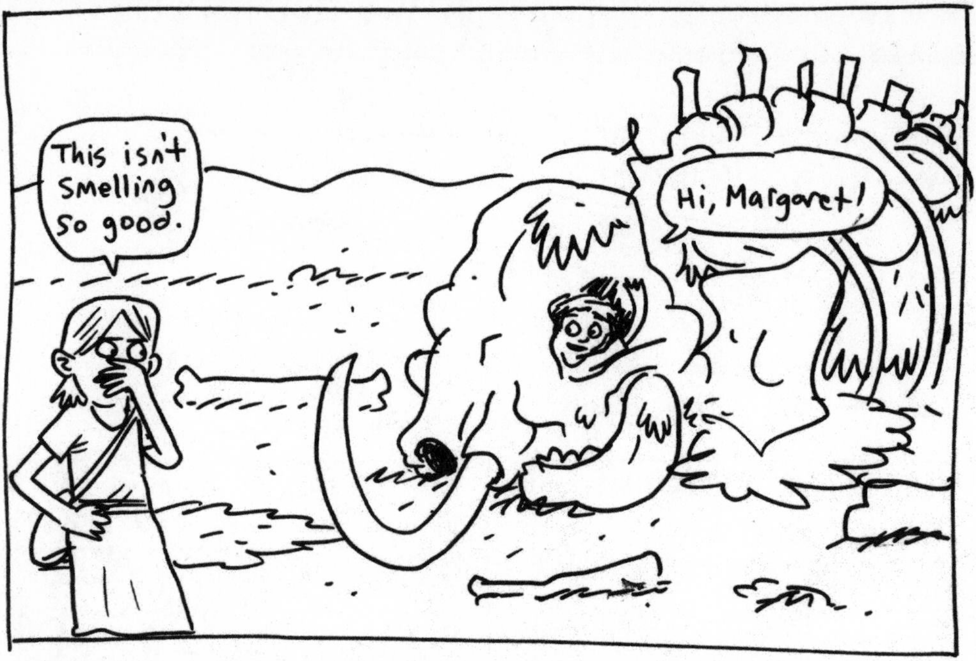
This isn't smelling so good.
Hi, Margaret!

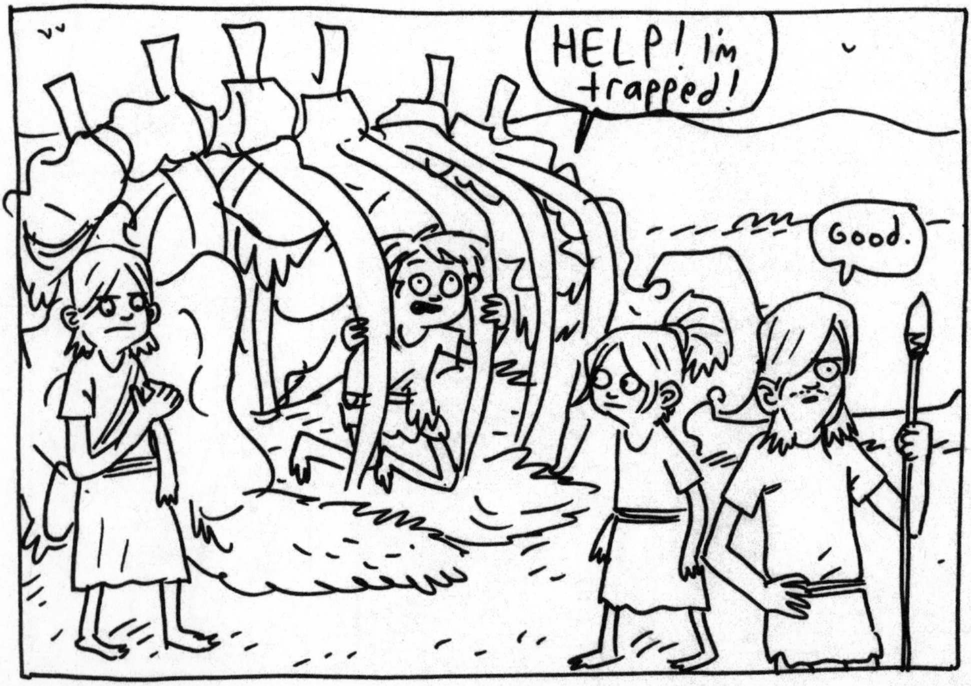
HELP! I'm trapped!
Good.

ART NOT FINAL

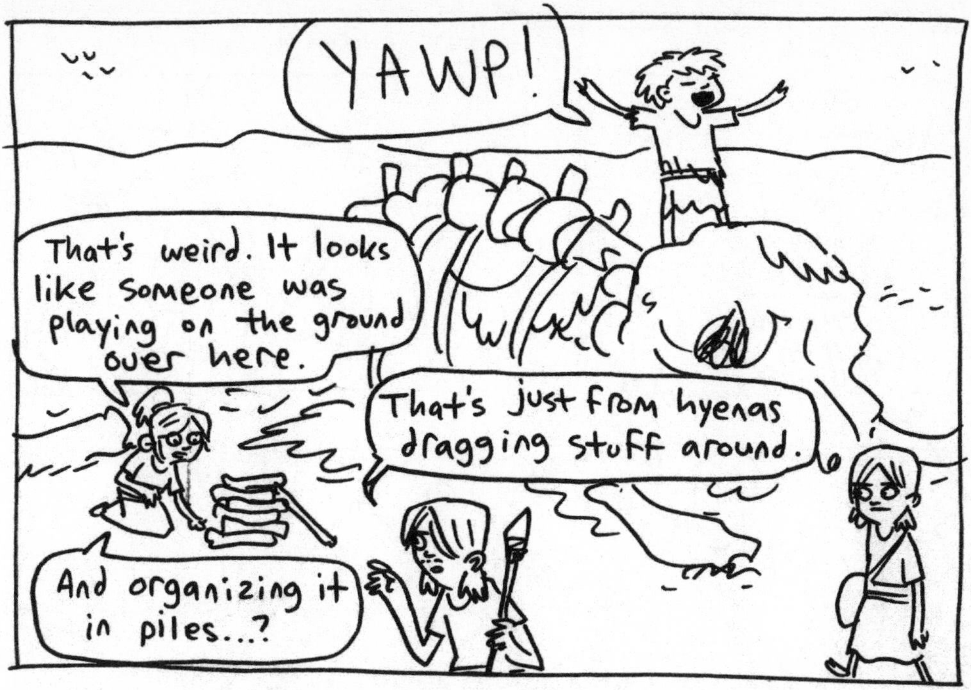
YAWP!
That's weird. It looks like someone was playing on the ground over here.
That's just from hyenas dragging stuff around.
And organizing it in piles...?

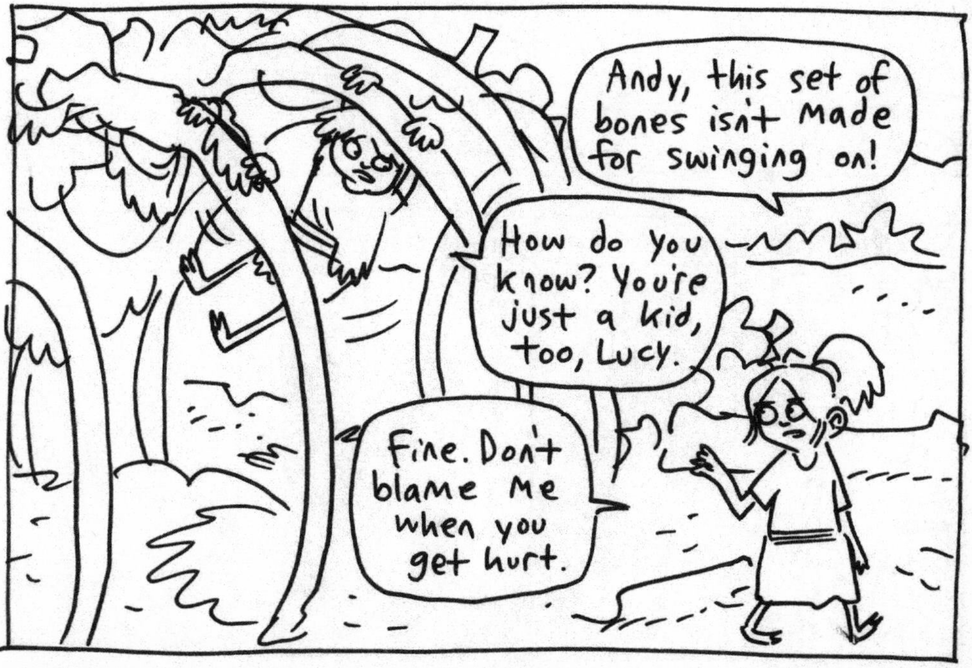
Andy, this set of bones isn't made for swinging on!
How do you know? You're just a kid, too, Lucy.
Fine. Don't blame me when you get hurt.

ART NOT FINAL

What's that noise?
CREEEEEAKKKK
What noise? I don't hear --
CREEEEEE CRACKK!!
--anythinnnnnnggg!
Go ahead. Say it.
Say what?
Rub Rub
You know.
I wasn't going to say anything.
Just say it.
. . .
Oh, okay-
Told you so.

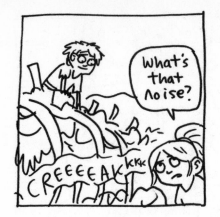

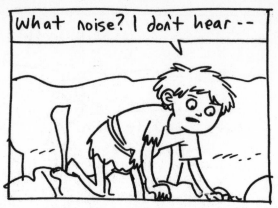

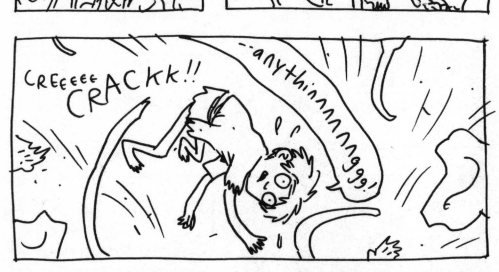

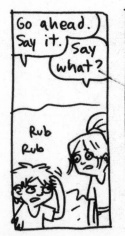

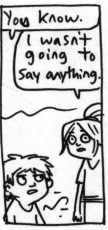

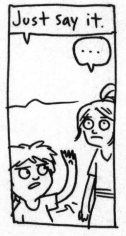

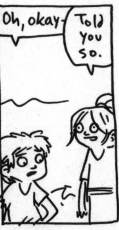

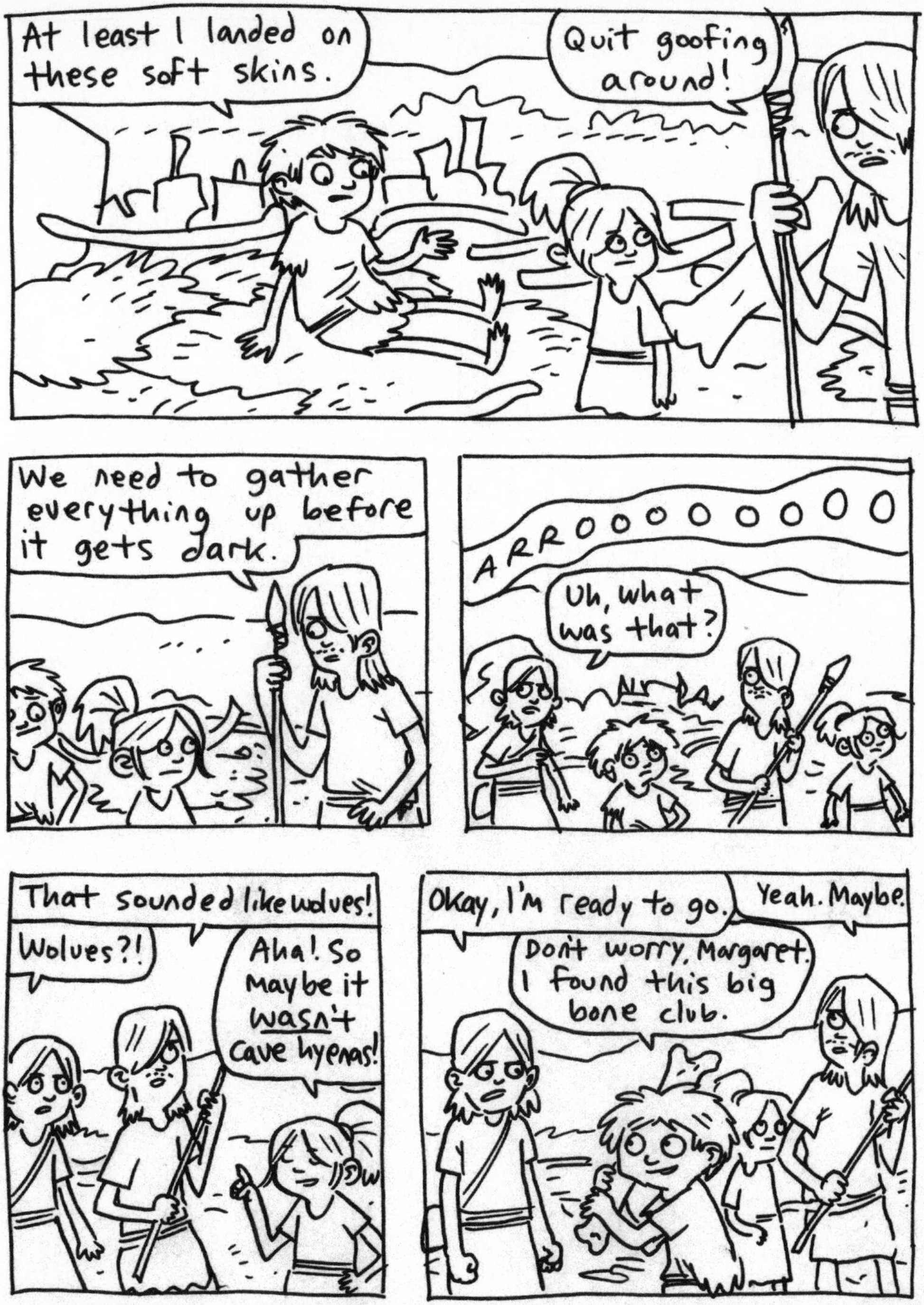

At least I landed on these soft skins.
Quit goofing around!
We need to gather everything up before it gets dark.
ARROOOOOOOOOO
Uh, what was that?
That sounded like wolves!
Wolves?!
Aha! So maybe it WASN'T cave hyenas!
Okay, I'm ready to go.
Don't worry, Margaret. I found this big bone club.
Yeah. Maybe.

ART NOT FINAL

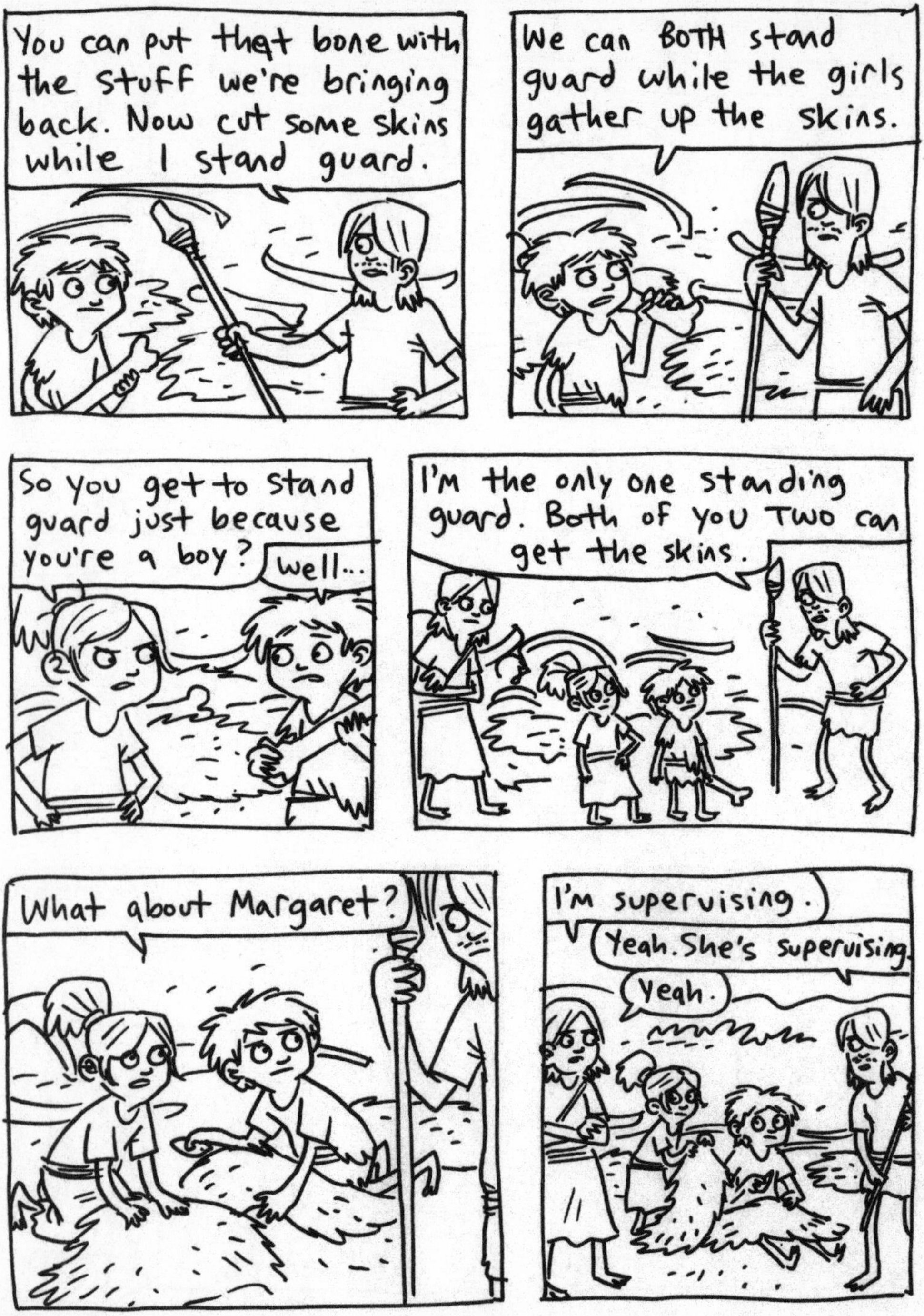
You can put that bone with the stuff we're bringing back. Now cut some skins while I stand guard.
We can BOTH stand guard while the girls gather up the skins.
So you get to stand guard just because you're a boy?
Well...
I'm the only one standing guard. Both of you TWO can get the skins.
What about Margaret?
I'm supervising.
Yeah. She's supervising.
Yeah.

ART NOT FINAL

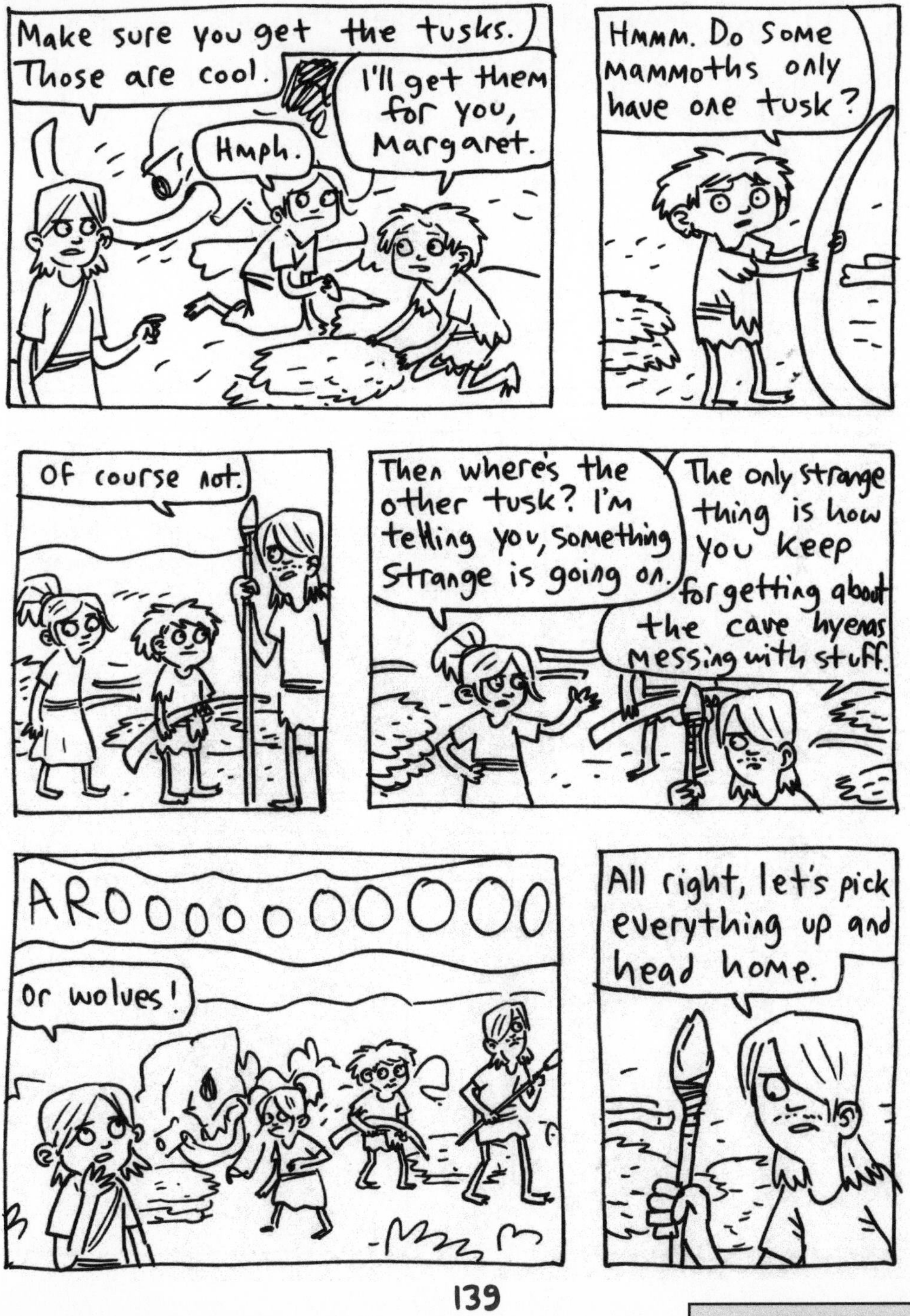
Make sure you get the tusks. Those are cool.
Hmph.
I'll get them for you, Margaret.
Hmmm. Do some mammoths only have one tusk?
Of course not.
Then where's the other tusk? I'm telling you, something strange is going on.
The only strange thing is how you keep forgetting about the cave hyenas messing with stuff.
AROOOOOOOOOOO
Or wolves!
All right, let's pick everything up and head home.

ART NOT FINAL

Okay, let's ALL gather it up.
I'm still standing guard.
I'm still supervising.
Can we take the skull home?
If you carry it.
NGGHHH!
Never Mind.
Let's go. It's almost dark.
Andy, you'll carry my load, right?
Sure!
TOUCH!
Thanks.
Mmphh.

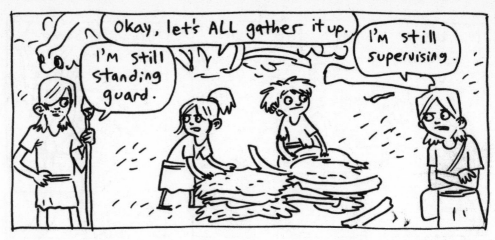

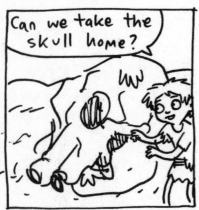

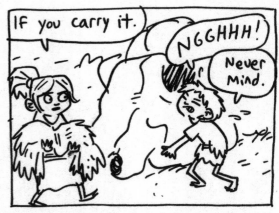

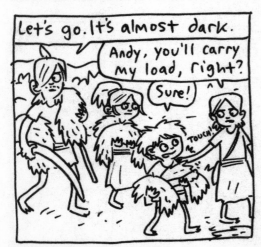

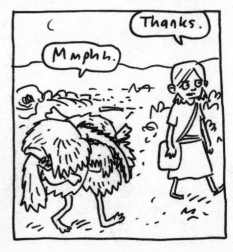

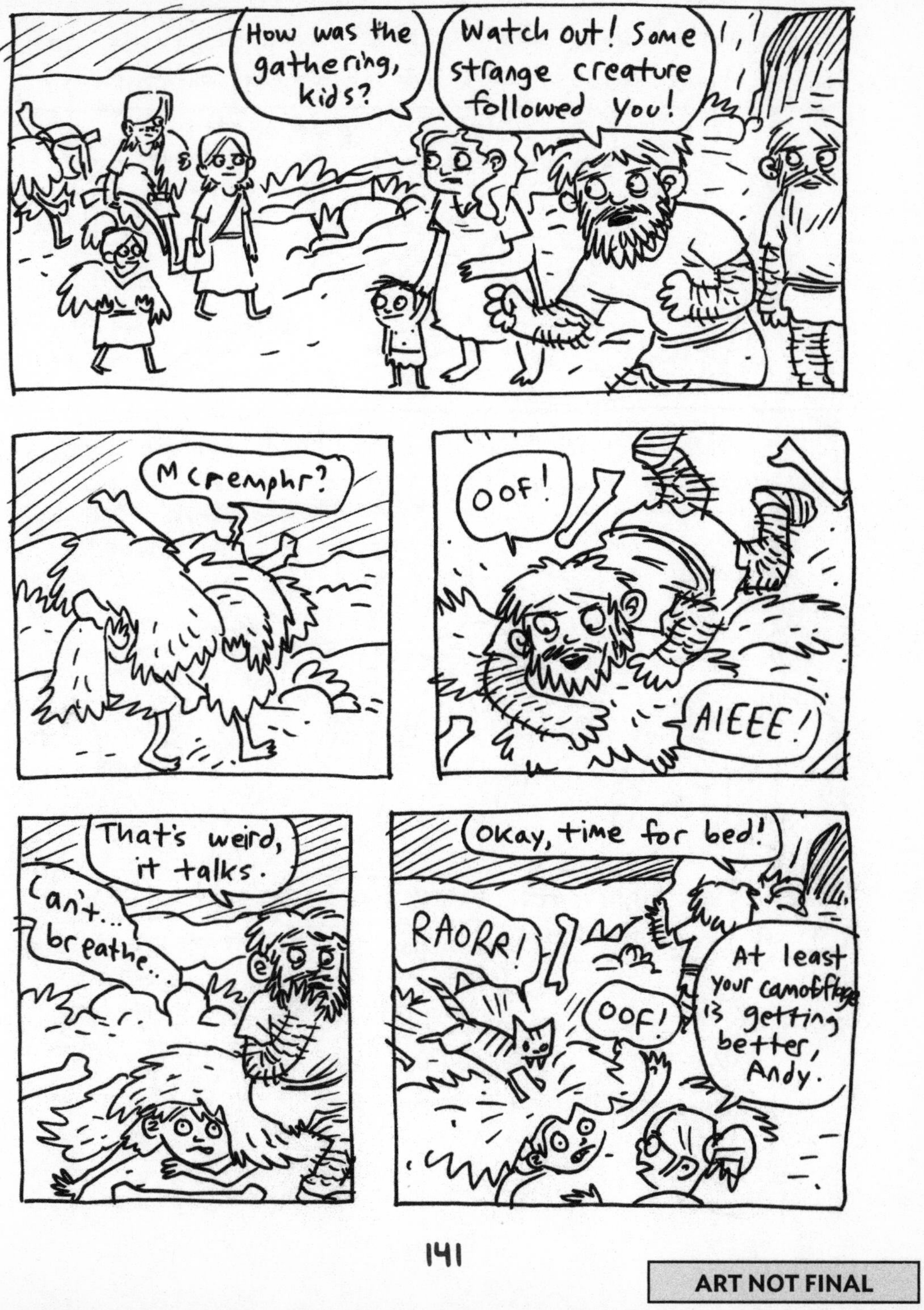
How was the gathering, kids?
Watch out! Some strange creature followed you!
Mcremphr?
OOF!
AIEEE!
That's weird, it talks.
Can't... breathe...
Okay, time for bed!
RAORR!
OOF!
At least your camofflage is getting better, Andy.

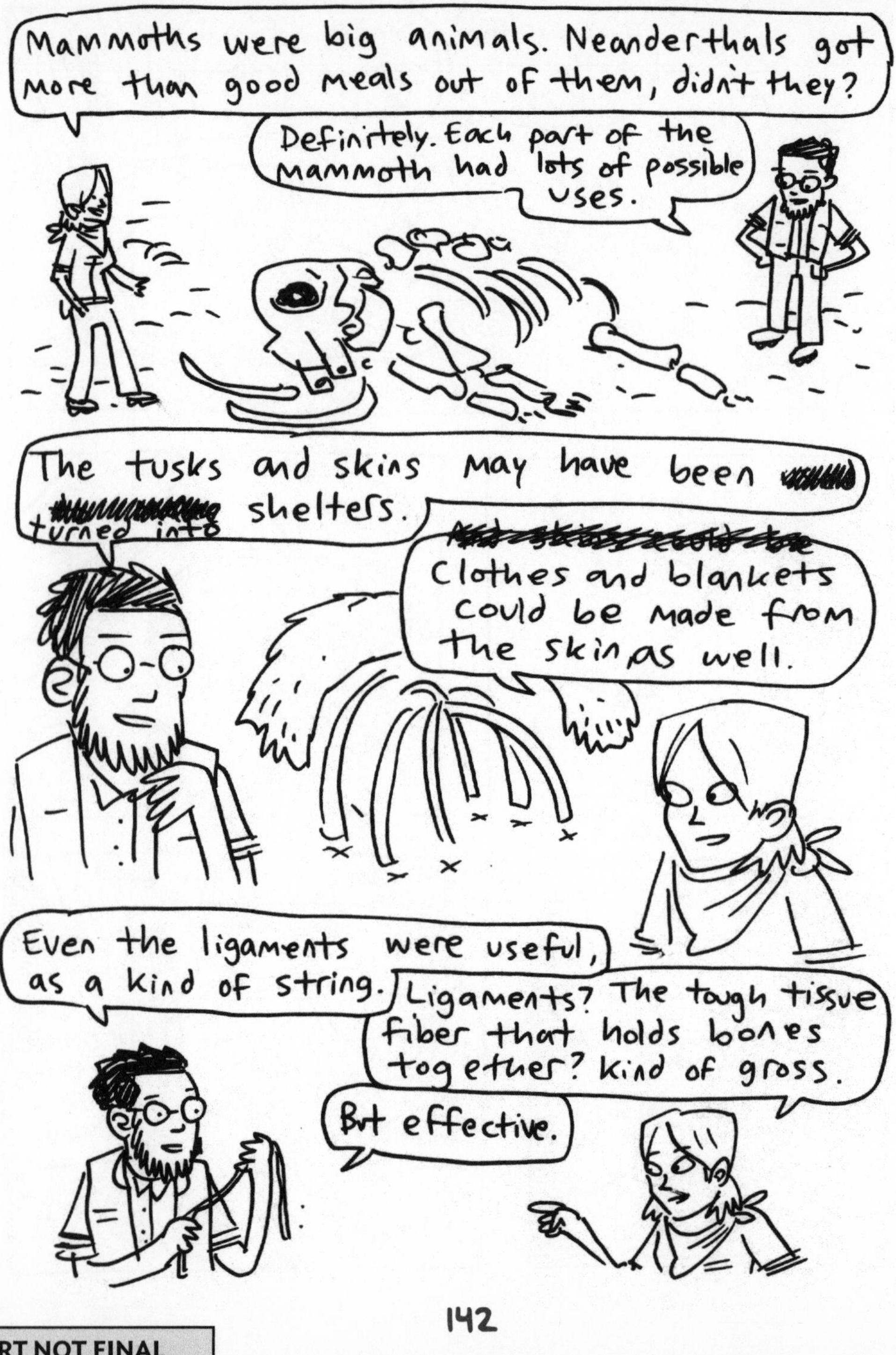
Mammoths were big animals. Neanderthals got more than good meals out of them, didn't they?
Definitely. Each part of the mammoth had lots of possible uses.
The tusks and skins may have been turned into shelters.
Clothes and blankets could be made from the skin as well.
Even the ligaments were useful, as a kind of string.
Ligaments? The tough tissue fiber that holds bones together? Kind of gross.
But effective.

ART NOT FINAL

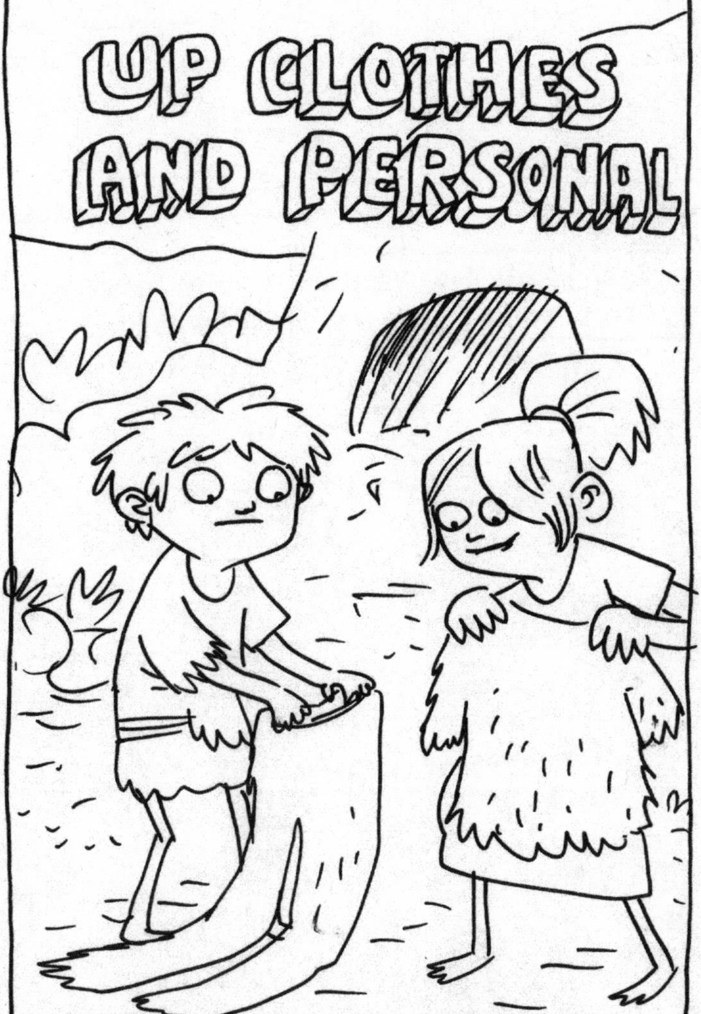
UP CLOTHES
AND PERSONAL

ART NOT FINAL

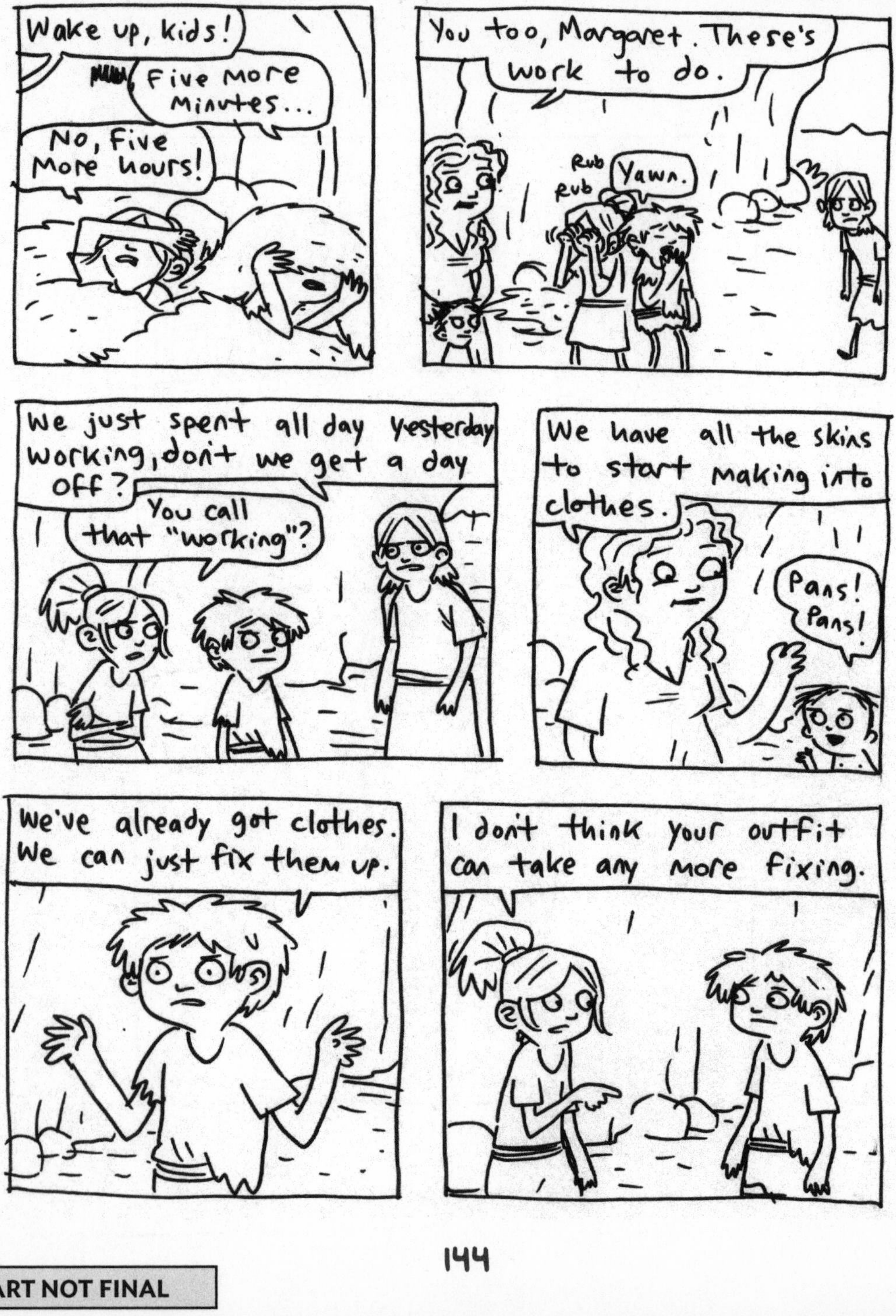

Wake up, kids!
Five more minutes...
No, five more hours!
You too, Margaret. There's work to do.
Rub Rub
Yawn.
We just spent all day yesterday working, don't we get a day off?
You call that "working"?
We have all the skins to start making into clothes.
Pans! Pans!
We've already got clothes. We can just fix them up.
I don't think your outfit can take any more fixing.

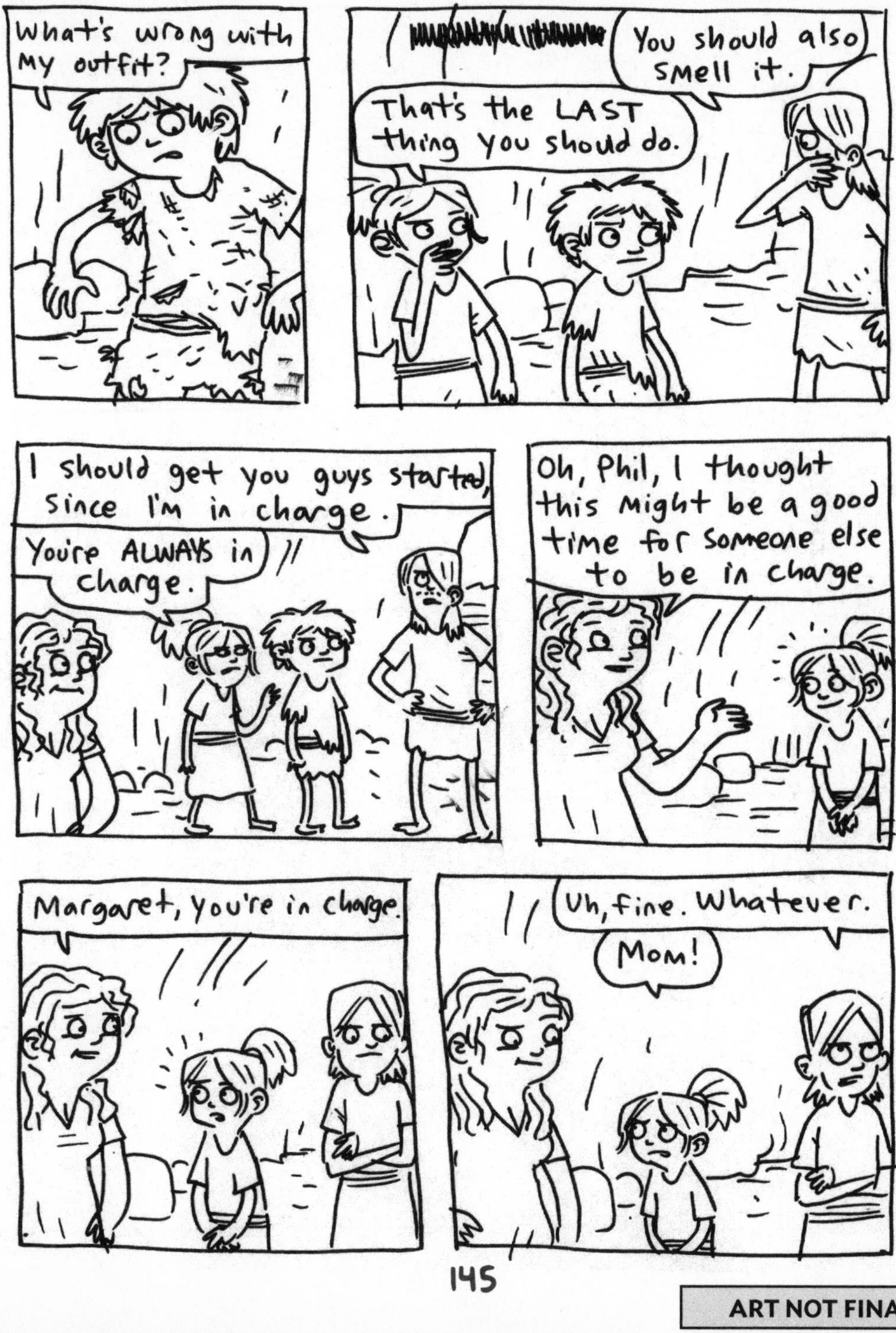
What's wrong with my outfit?
You should also smell it.
That's the LAST thing you should do.
I should get you guys started, since I'm in charge.
You're ALWAYS in charge.
Oh, Phil, I thought this might be a good time for someone else to be in charge.
Margaret, you're in charge.
Uh, fine. Whatever.
Mom!

ART NOT FINAL

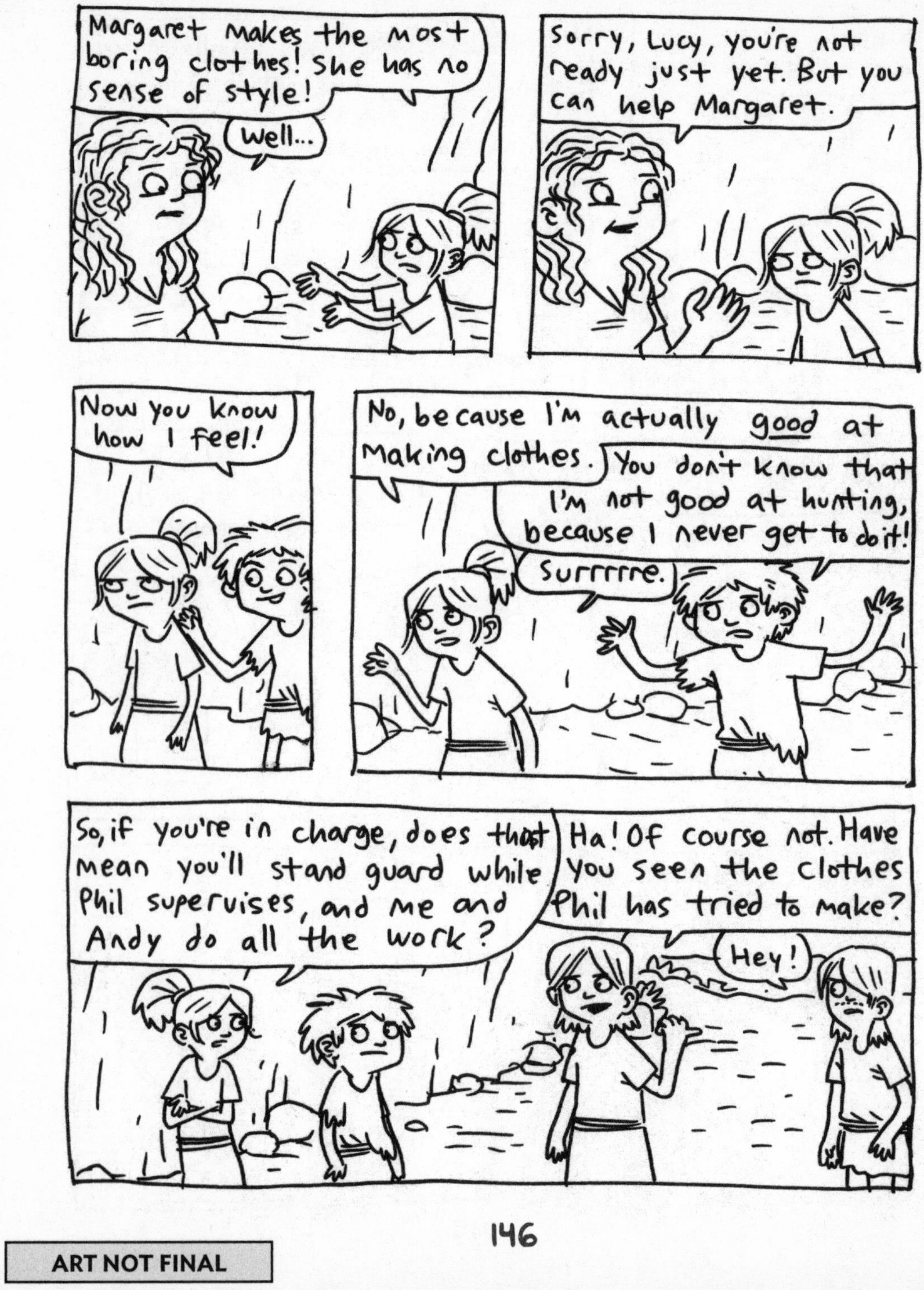
Margaret makes the most boring clothes! She has no sense of style!
Well...
Sorry, Lucy, you're not ready just yet. But you can help Margaret.
Now you know how I feel!
No, because I'm actually good at making clothes.
You don't know that I'm not good at hunting, because I never get to do it!
Surrrrre.
So, if you're in charge, does that mean you'll stand guard while Phil supervises, and me and Andy do all the work?
Ha! Of course not. Have you seen the clothes Phil has tried to make?
Hey!

ART NOT FINAL

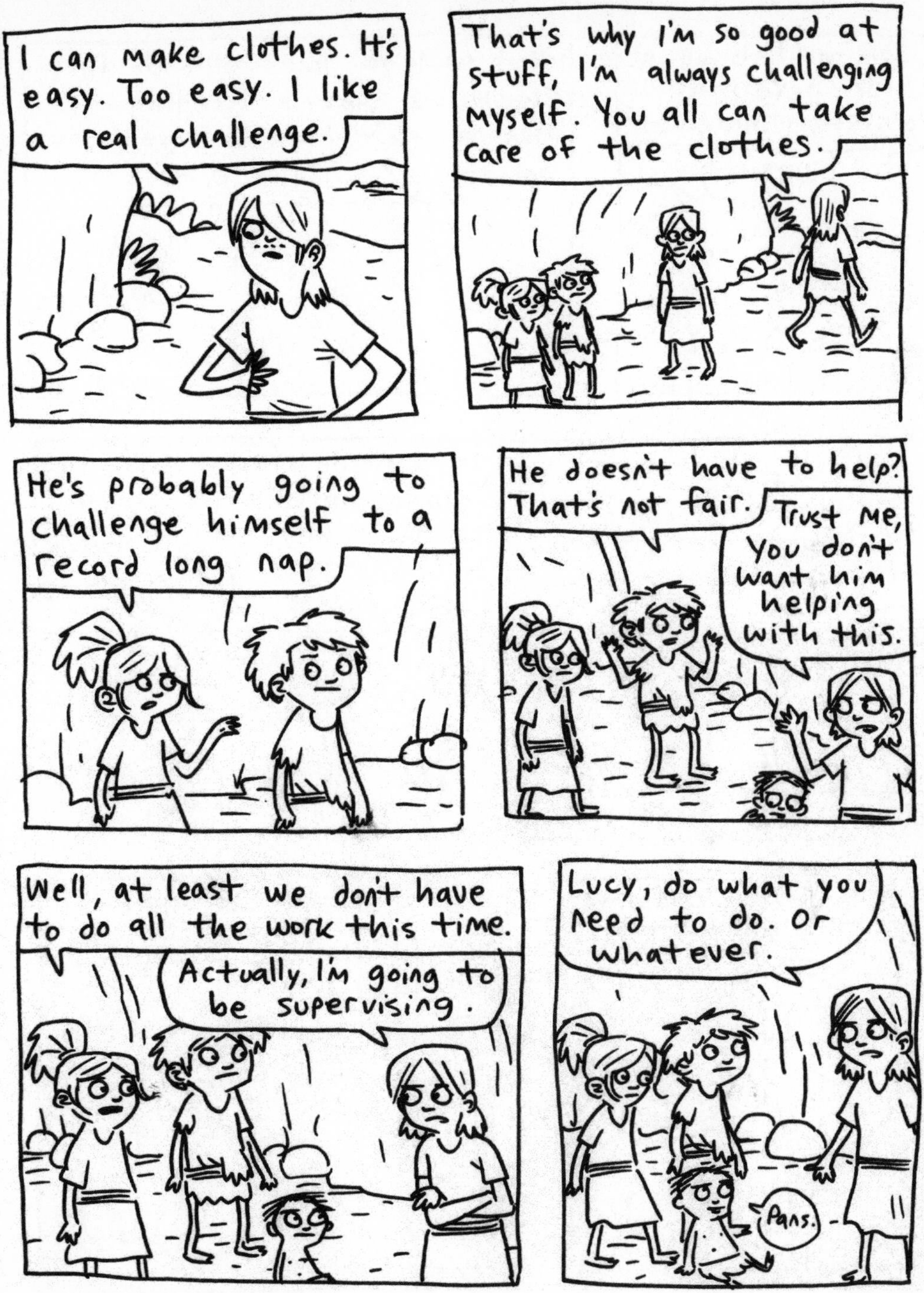
I can make clothes. It's easy. Too easy. I like a real challenge.
That's why I'm so good at stuff, I'm always challenging myself. You all can take care of the clothes.
He's probably going to challenge himself to a record long nap.
He doesn't have to help? That's not fair.
Trust me, you don't want him helping with this.
Well, at least we don't have to do all the work this time.
Actually, I'm going to be supervising.
Lucy, do what you need to do. Or whatever.
Pans.

ART NOT FINAL

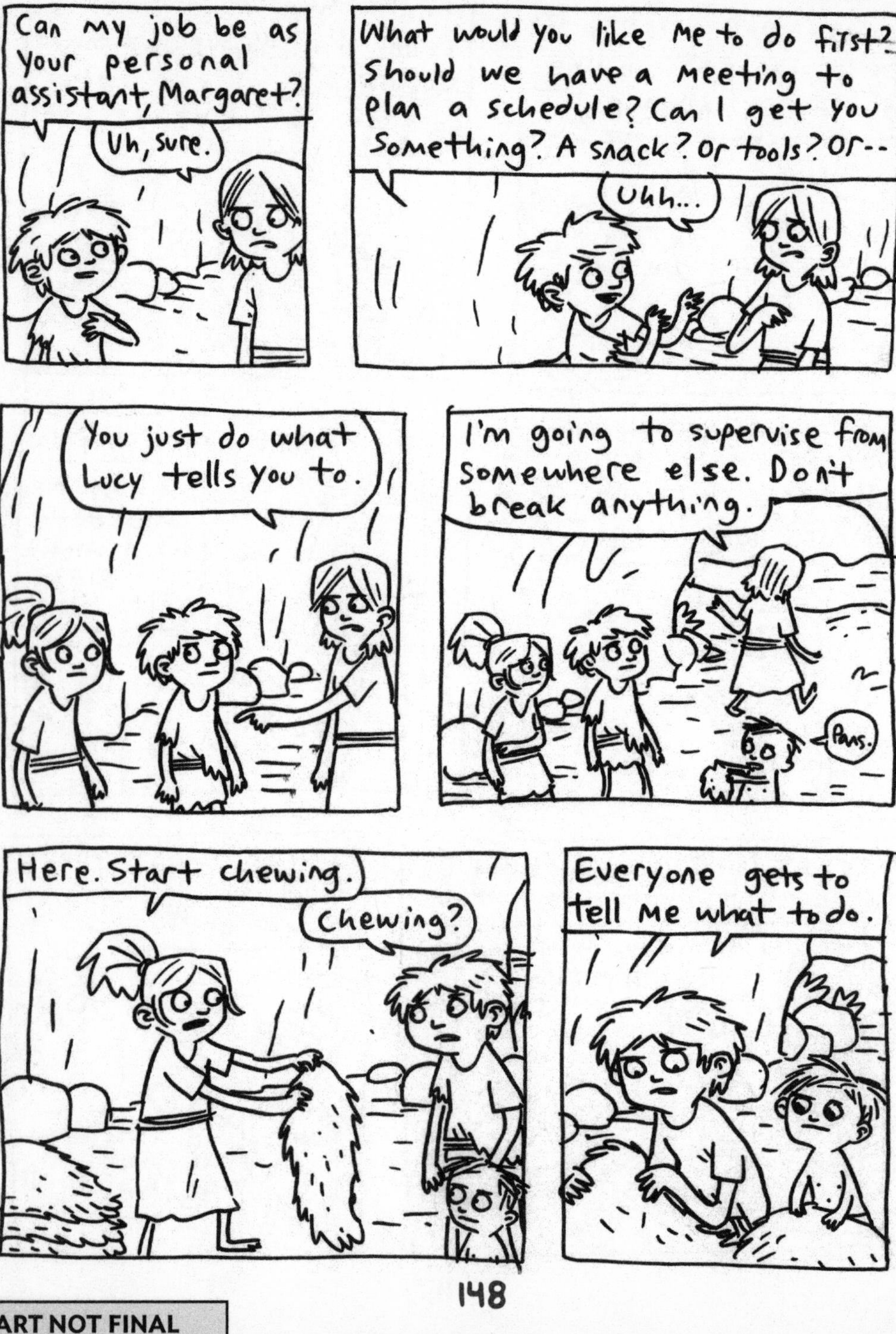
Can my job be as your personal assistant, Margaret?
Uh, sure.
What would you like me to do first? Should we have a meeting to plan a schedule? Can I get you something? A snack? Or tools? Or--
Uhh...
You just do what Lucy tells you to.
I'm going to supervise from somewhere else. Don't break anything.
Here. Start chewing.
Chewing?
Everyone gets to tell me what to do.

Start chewing, Danny.

Ickth, chewy.

chew chew

chew chew chew

Chew

chew Chew chew chew

Chewing on animal skins softened them, making them easier to work on.

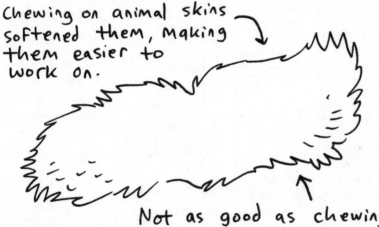

Neanderthal teeth have marks showing they chewed on skins.

Not as good as chewing gum!

What are you guys doing?

Chewing the hides, of course.

But you don't have to slobber so much. Gross! And you didn't finish cleaning the skins off.

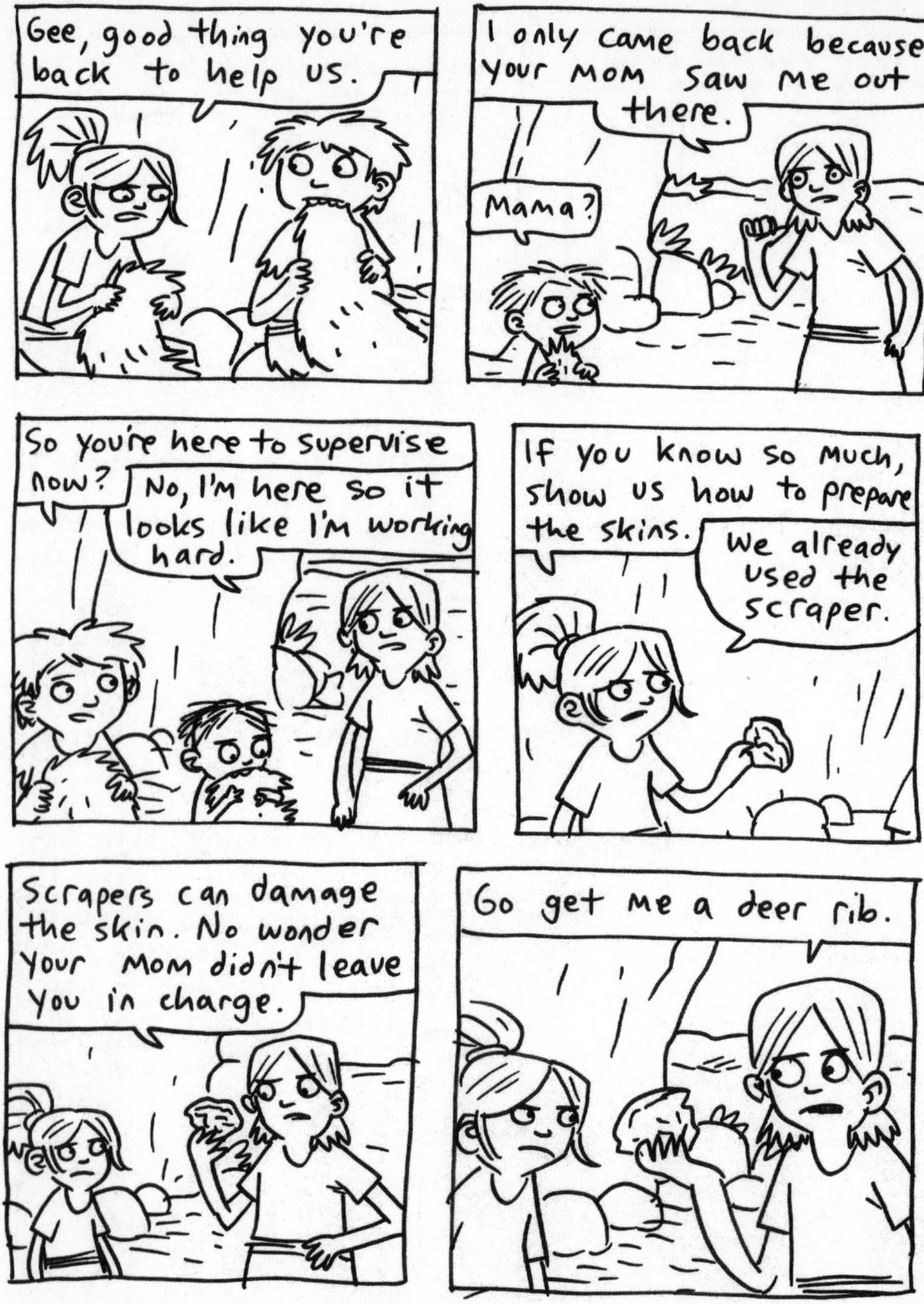
Gee, good thing you're back to help us.
I only came back because your MOM saw me out there.
Mama?
So you're here to supervise now?
No, I'm here so it looks like I'm working hard.
If you know so much, show us how to prepare the skins.
We already used the scraper.
Scrapers can damage the skin. No wonder your MOM didn't leave you in charge.
Go get me a deer rib.

ART NOT FINAL

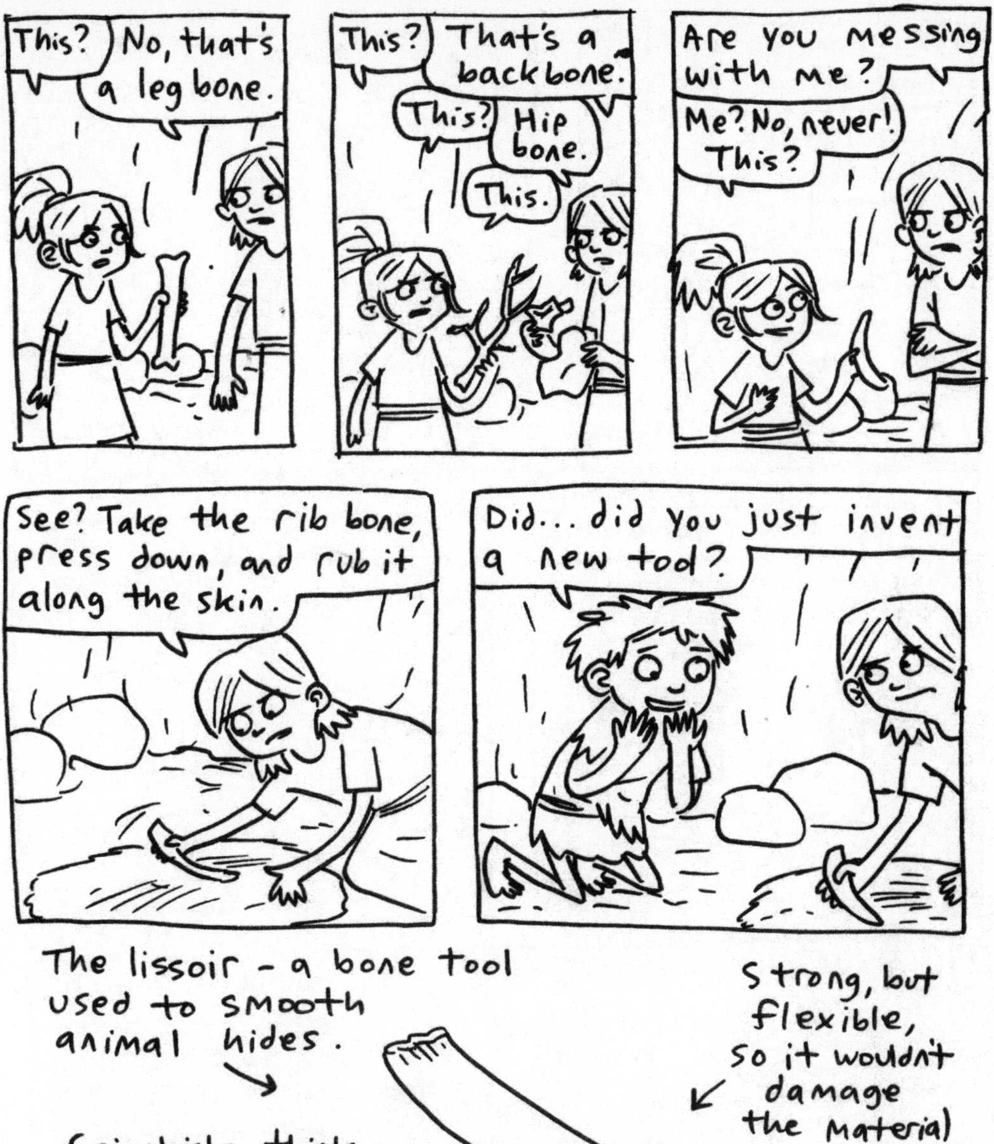
This?
No, that's a leg bone.
This?
That's a backbone.
This?
Hip bone.
This.
Are you messing with me?
Me? No, never! This?
See? Take the rib bone, press down, and rub it along the skin.
Did... did you just invent a new tool?

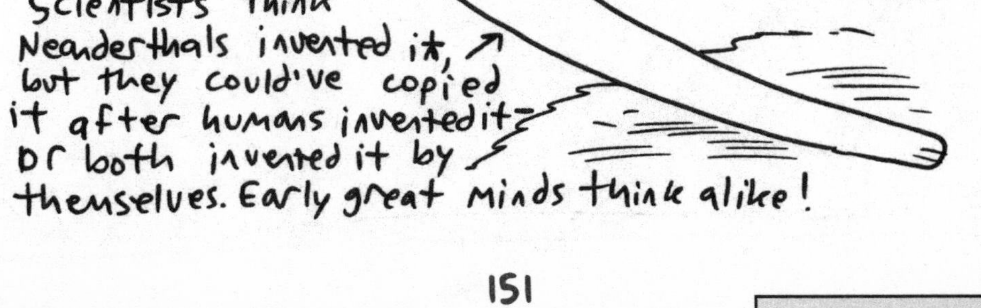
The lissoir - a bone tool used to smooth animal hides.
Strong, but flexible, so it wouldn't damage the material
Scientists think Neanderthals invented it, but they could've copied it after humans invented it or both invented it by themselves. Early great minds think alike!

ART NOT FINAL

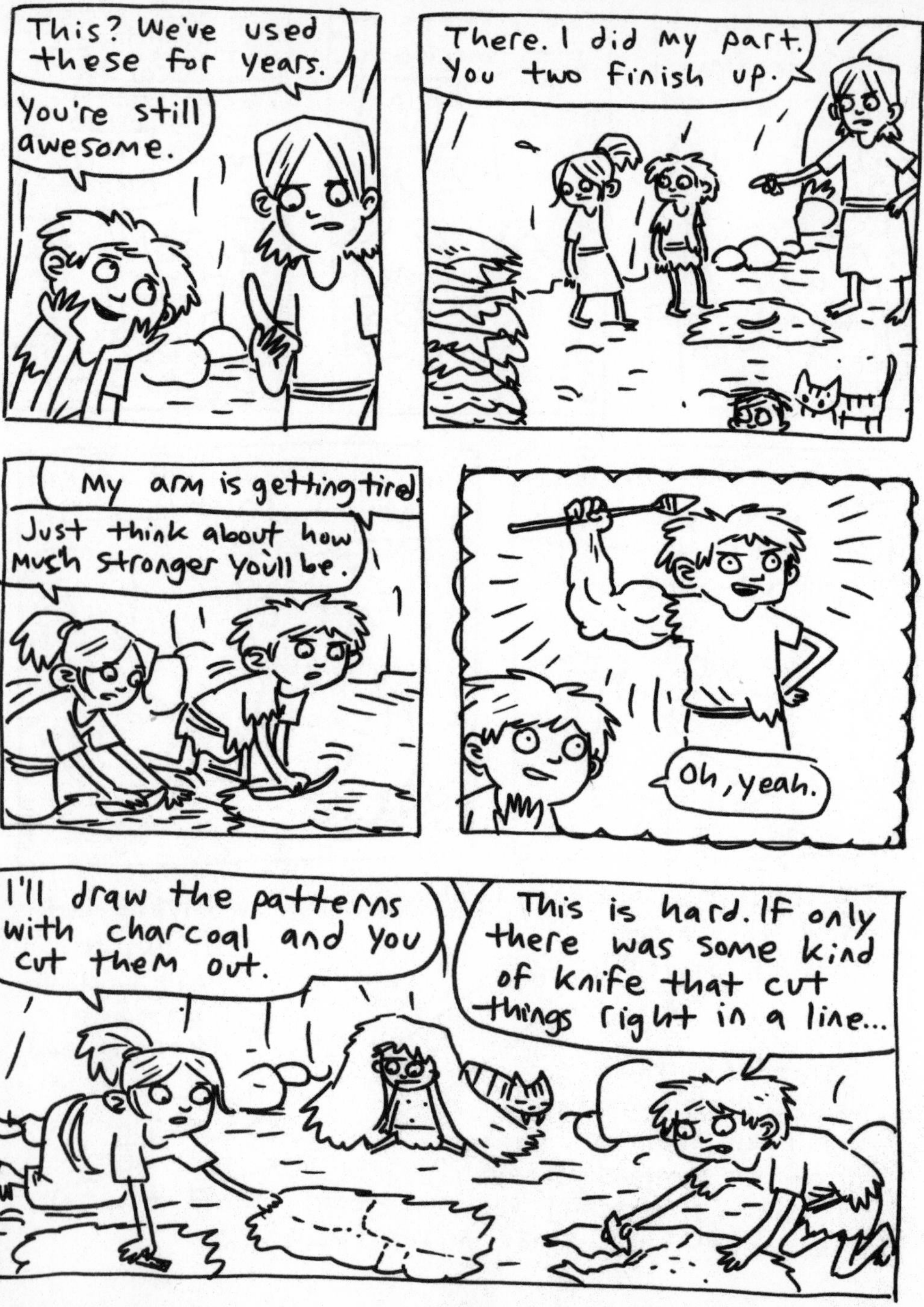
This? We've used these for years.
You're still awesome.
There. I did my part. You two finish up.
My arm is getting tired.
Just think about how mush stronger you'll be.
Oh, yeah.
I'll draw the patterns with charcoal and you cut them out.
This is hard. If only there was some kind of knife that cut things right in a line...

ART NOT FINAL

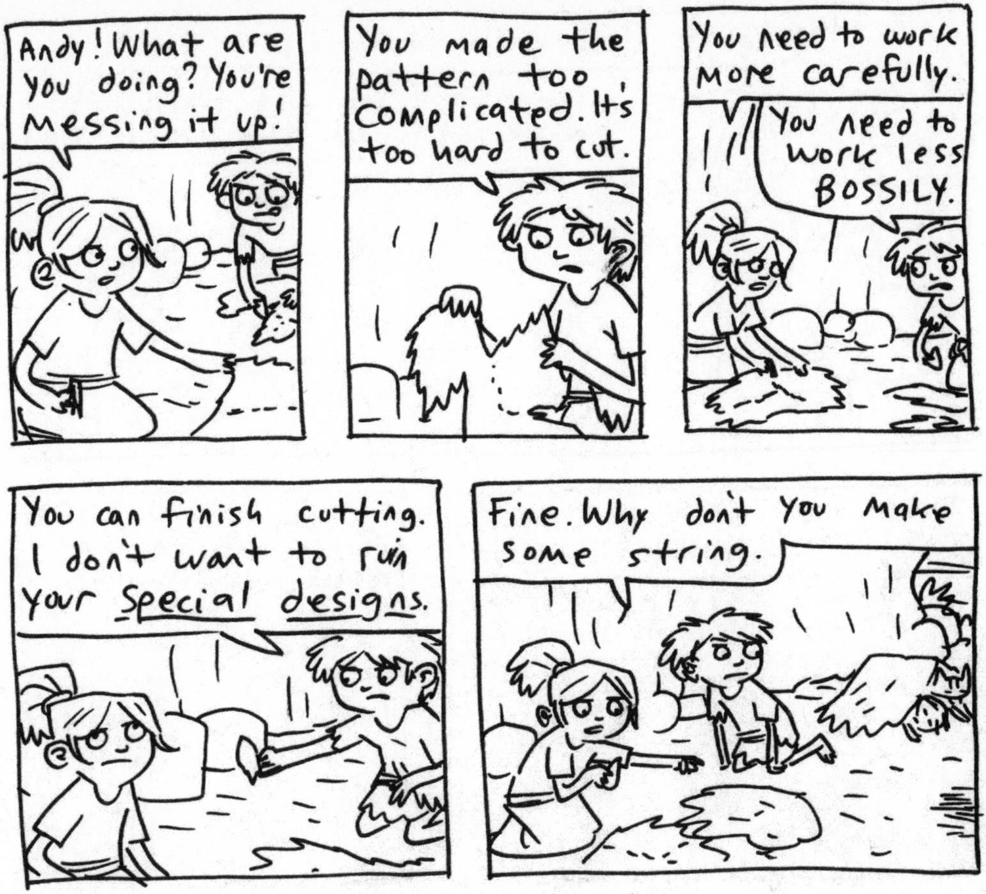
Andy! What are you doing? You're messing it up!
You made the pattern too complicated. It's too hard to cut.
You need to work more carefully.
You need to work less BOSSILY.
You can finish cutting. I don't want to ruin your special designs.
Fine. Why don't you make some string.

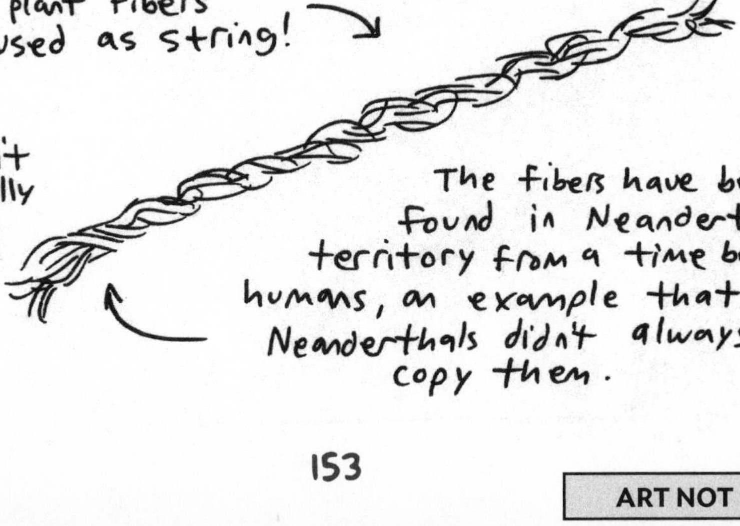
Twisted plant fibers were used as string!
Doesn't naturally grow that way.
The fibers have been found in Neanderthal territory from a time before humans, an example that Neanderthals didn't always copy them.

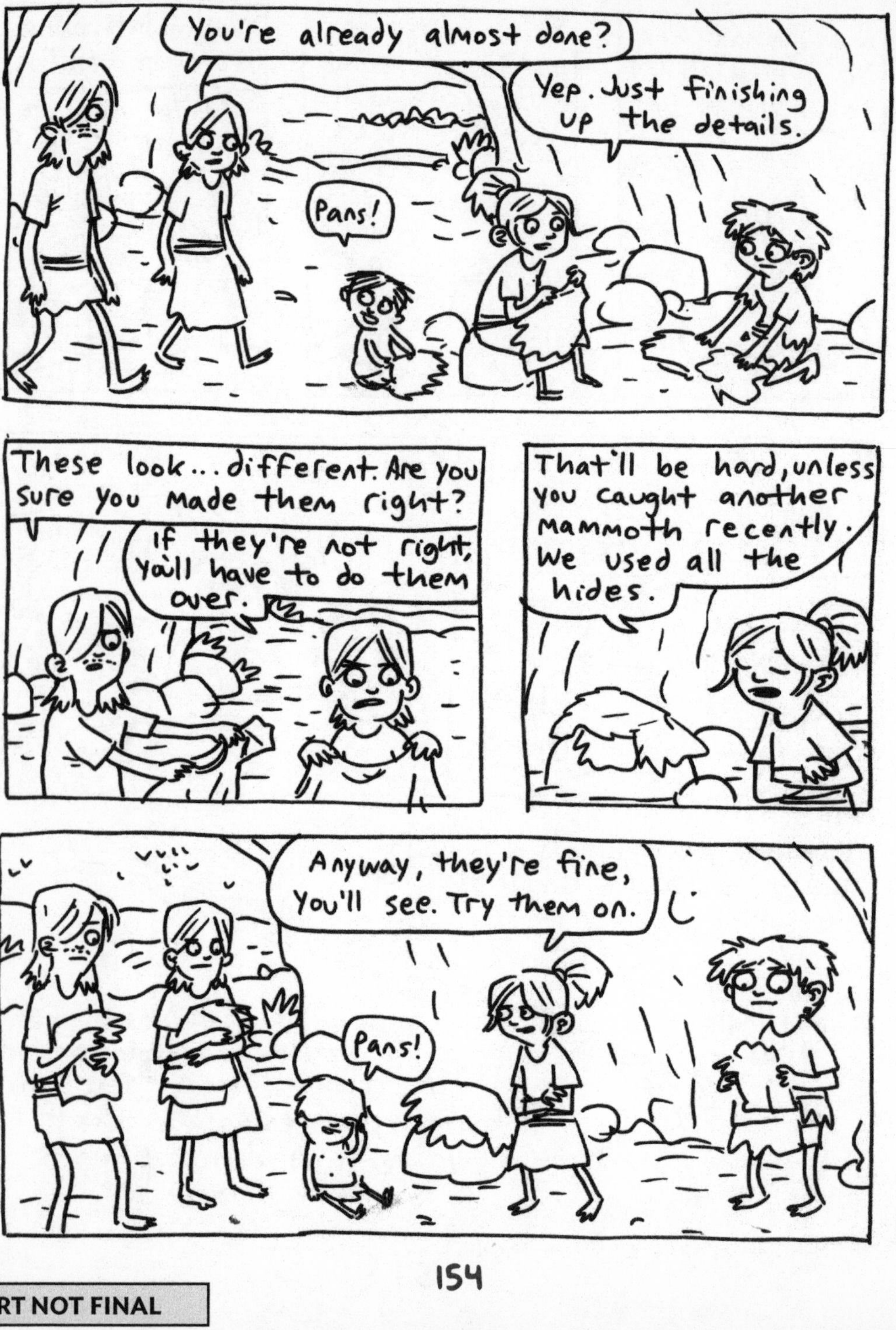
You're already almost done?
Yep. Just finishing up the details.
Pans!
These look... different. Are you sure you made them right?
If they're not right, you'll have to do them over.
That'll be hard, unless you caught another mammoth recently. We used all the hides.
Anyway, they're fine, You'll see. Try them on.
Pans!

ART NOT FINAL

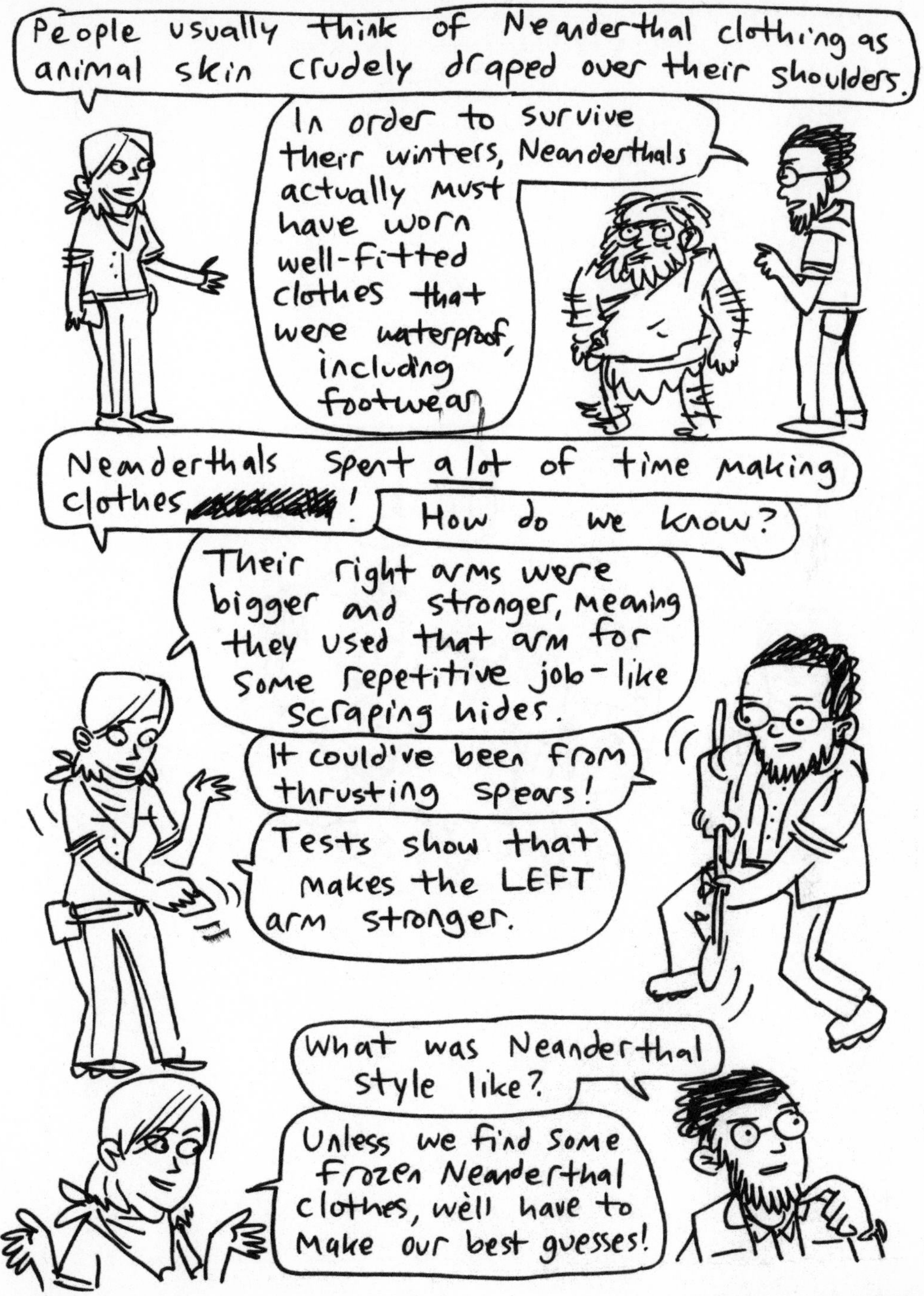
People usually think of Neanderthal clothing as animal skin crudely draped over their shoulders.
In order to survive their winters, Neanderthals actually must have worn well-fitted clothes that were waterproof, including footwear.
Neanderthals spent a lot of time making clothes !
How do we know?
Their right arms were bigger and stronger, meaning they used that arm for some repetitive job-like scraping hides.
It could've been from thrusting spears!
Tests show that makes the LEFT arm stronger.
What was Neanderthal style like?
Unless we find some frozen Neanderthal clothes, we'll have to make our best guesses!

ART NOT FINAL

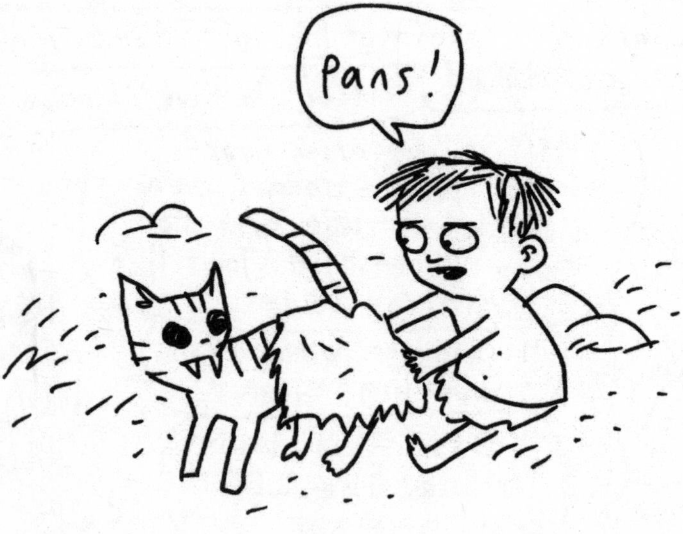
Pans!

ART NOT FINAL

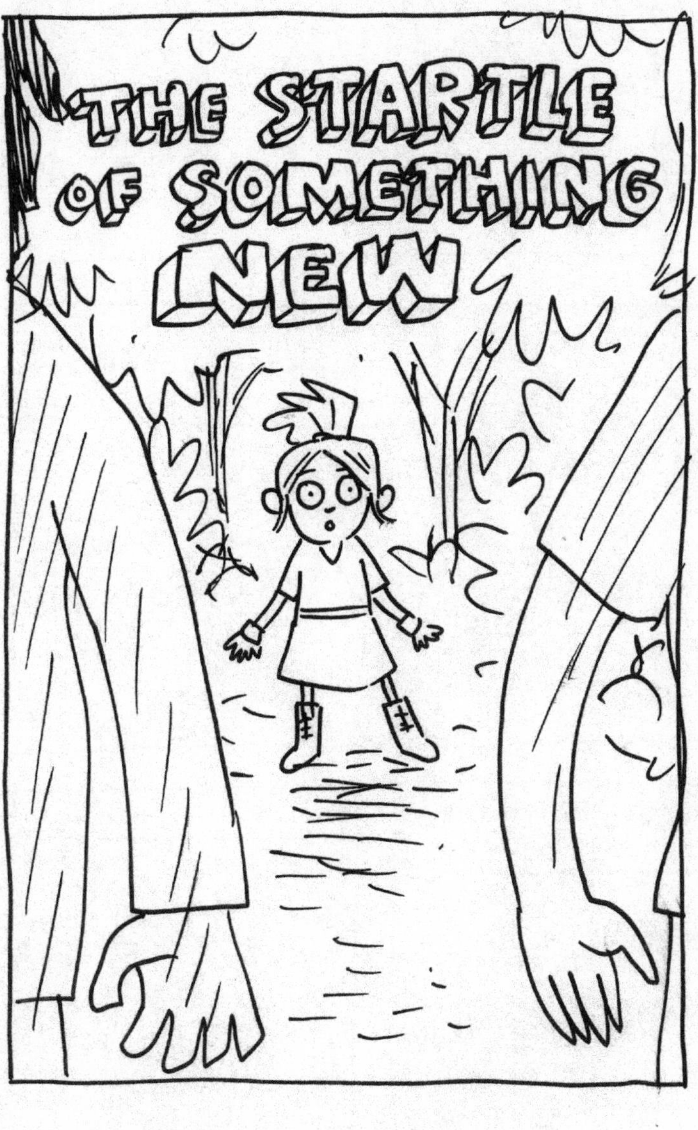
THE STARTLE OF SOMETHING NEW

ART NOT FINAL

Ready?
Okay.
Well, what do you think?
This is, like, the most comfortable outfit I've ever worn.
Uh, good job.
Pans!
You must feel comfortable looking weird.
I feel ridiculous.
But comfy!

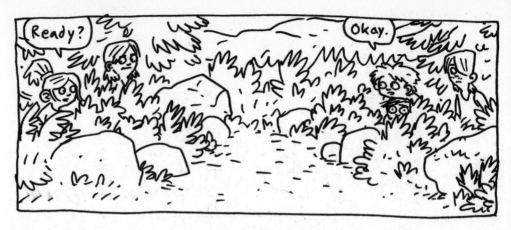

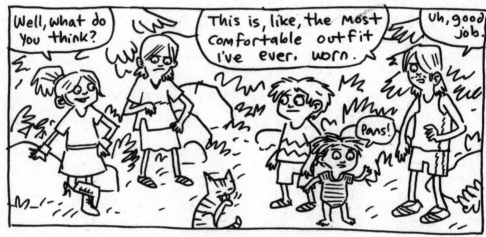

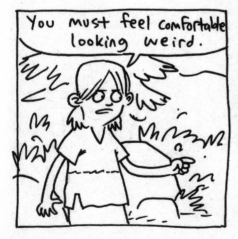

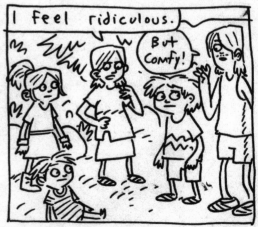

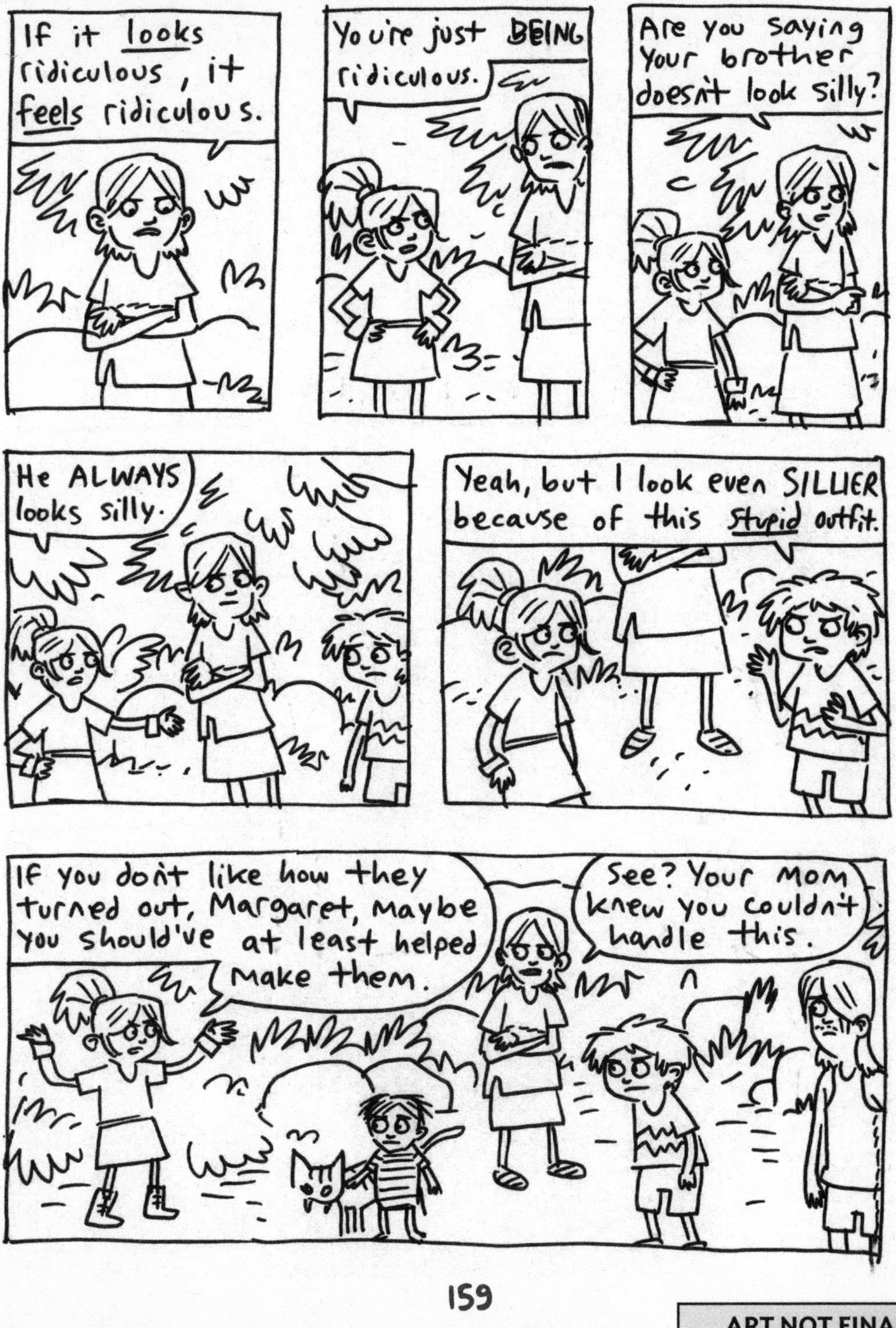
If it looks ridiculous, it feels ridiculous.
You're just BEING ridiculous.
Are you saying your brother doesn't look silly?
He ALWAYS looks silly.
Yeah, but I look even SILLIER because of this stupid outfit.
If you don't like how they turned out, Margaret, maybe you should've at least helped make them.
See? Your MOM knew you couldn't handle this.

ART NOT FINAL

What are you upset about, Lucy?
Mom put Margaret in charge of making clothes instead of me.
Lucy didn't listen to Margaret.
That's because she didn't take charge. She didn't even help!
I tried to, Mr. Charles, but Lucy didn't want my help unless SHE could be the boss.
That's not true! I did all of the work.
YOU did all of it?
Lucy just bossed me around. Right, Margaret?
Uh!
Yep.
Lucy?

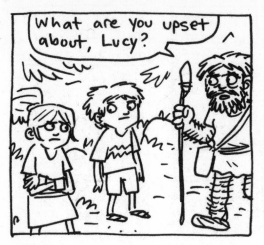

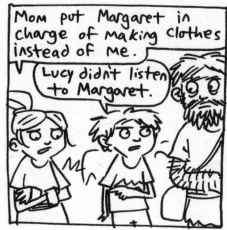

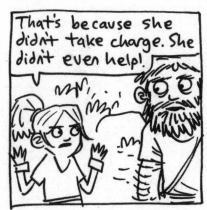

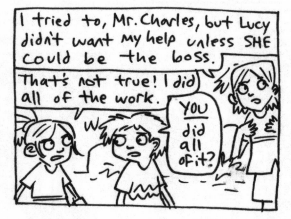

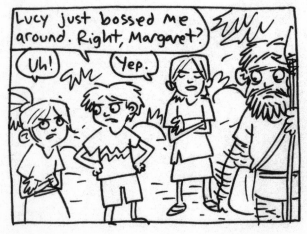

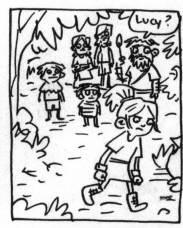

ART NOT FINAL

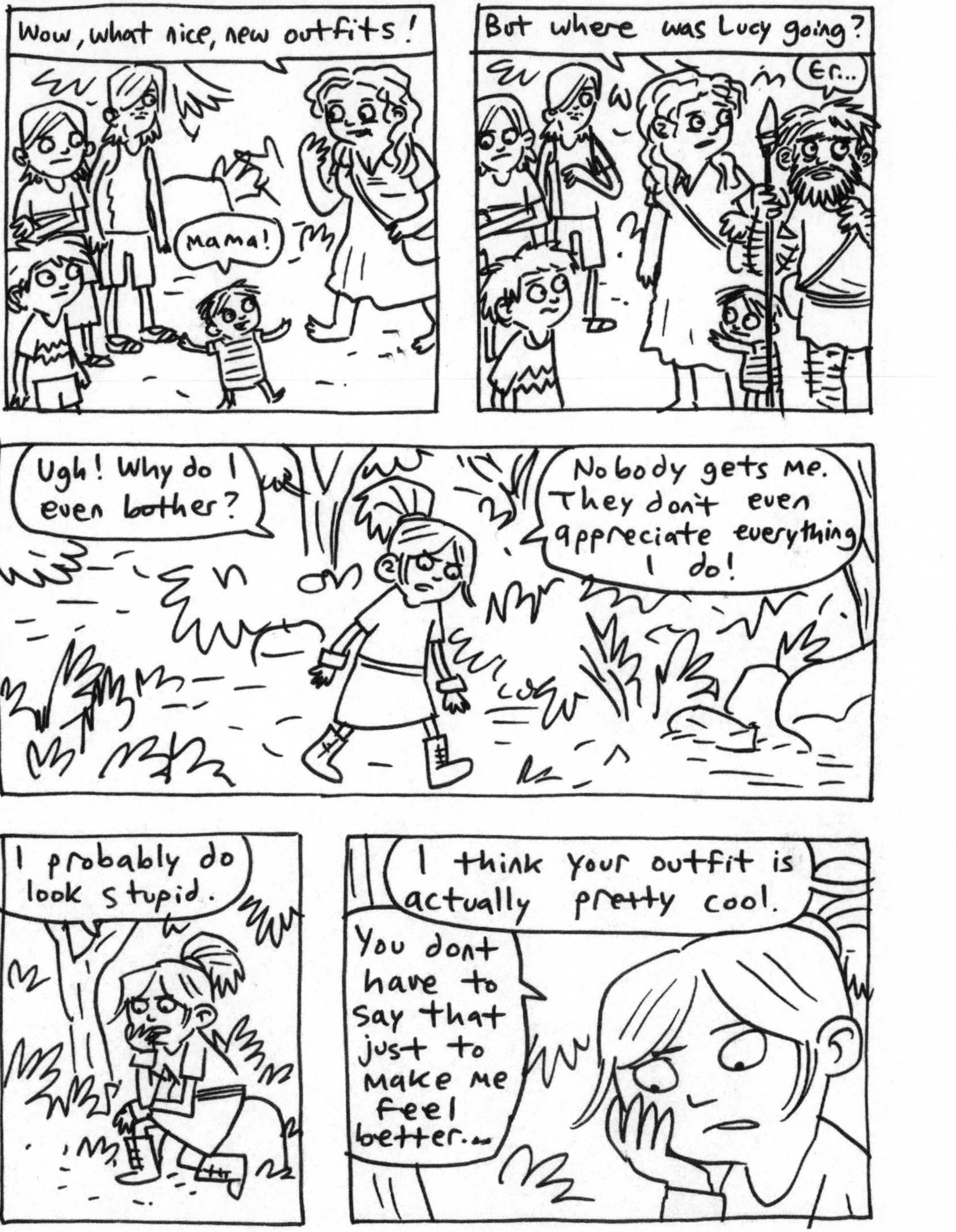

Wow, what nice, new outfits!
Mama!
But where was Lucy going?
Er...
Ugh! Why do I even bother?
Nobody gets me. They don't even appreciate everything I do!
I probably do look stupid.
I think your outfit is actually pretty cool.
You dont have to say that just to make me feel better...

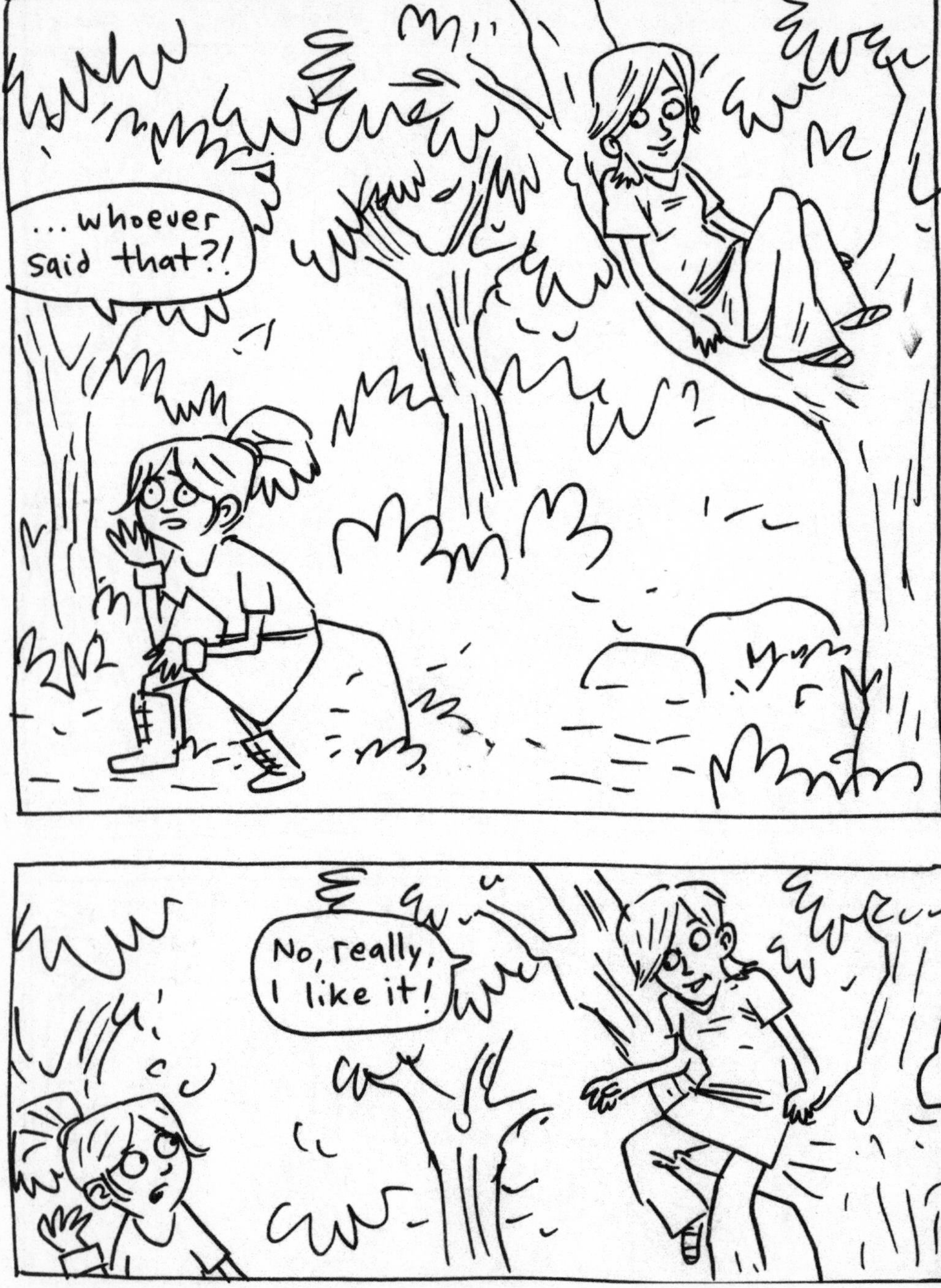
...whoever said that?!
No, really, I like it!

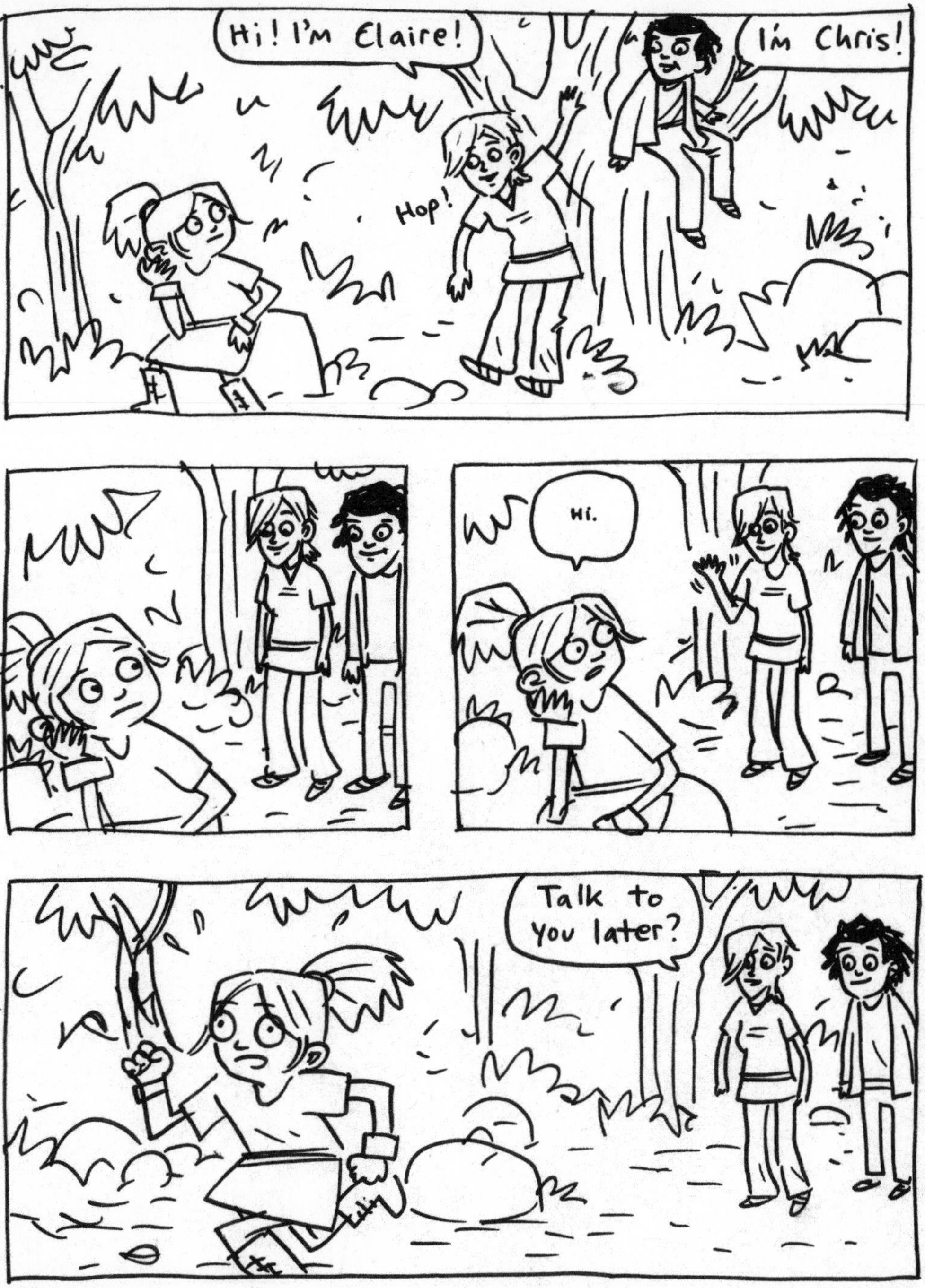
Hi! I'm Elaire!
I'm Chris!
Hop!
Hi.
Talk to you later?

ART NOT FINAL

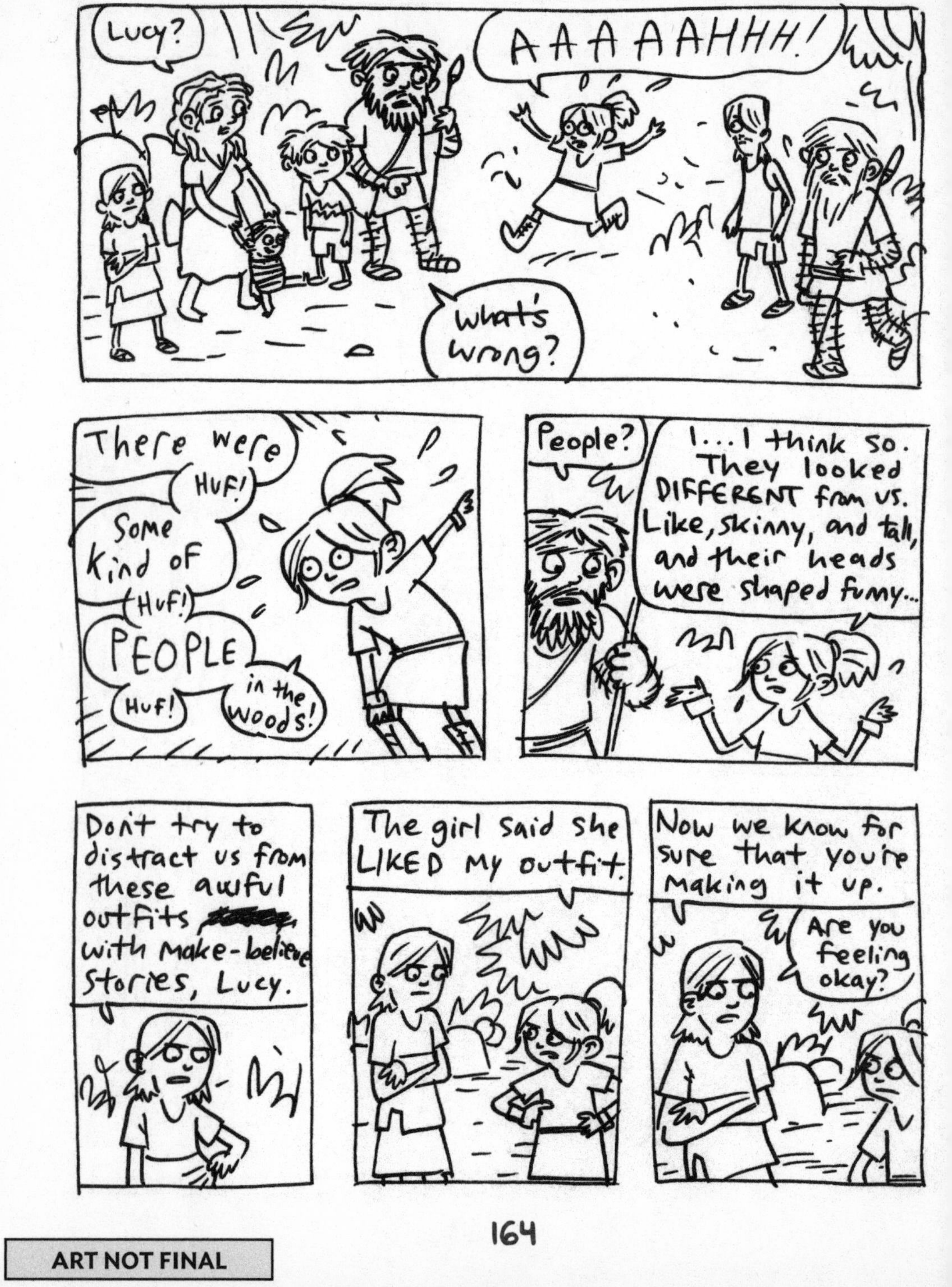
Lucy?
AAAAAHHH!
What's wrong?
There were
HUF!
Some kind of
HUF!
PEOPLE
HUF!
in the woods!
People?
I...I think so. They looked DIFFERENT from us. Like, skinny, and tall, and their heads were shaped funny...
Don't try to distract us from these awful outfits [redacted] with make-believe stories, Lucy.
The girl said she LIKED my outfit.
Now we know for sure that you're making it up.
Are you feeling okay?

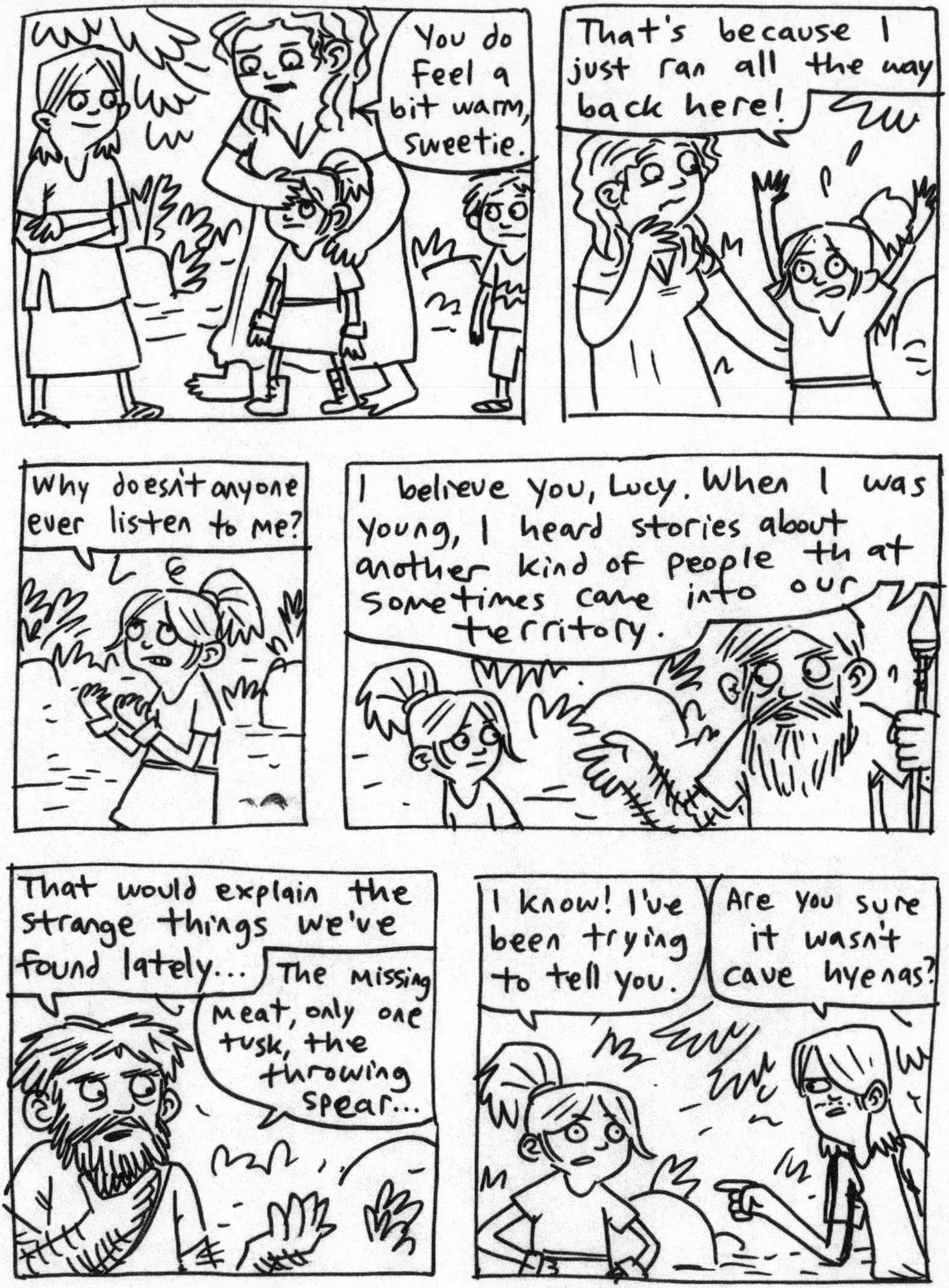
You do feel a bit warm, sweetie.
That's because I just ran all the way back here!
Why doesn't anyone ever listen to me?
I believe you, Lucy. When I was young, I heard stories about another kind of people that sometimes came into our territory.
That would explain the strange things we've found lately...
The missing meat, only one tusk, the throwing spear...
I know! I've been trying to tell you.
Are you sure it wasn't cave hyenas?

ART NOT FINAL

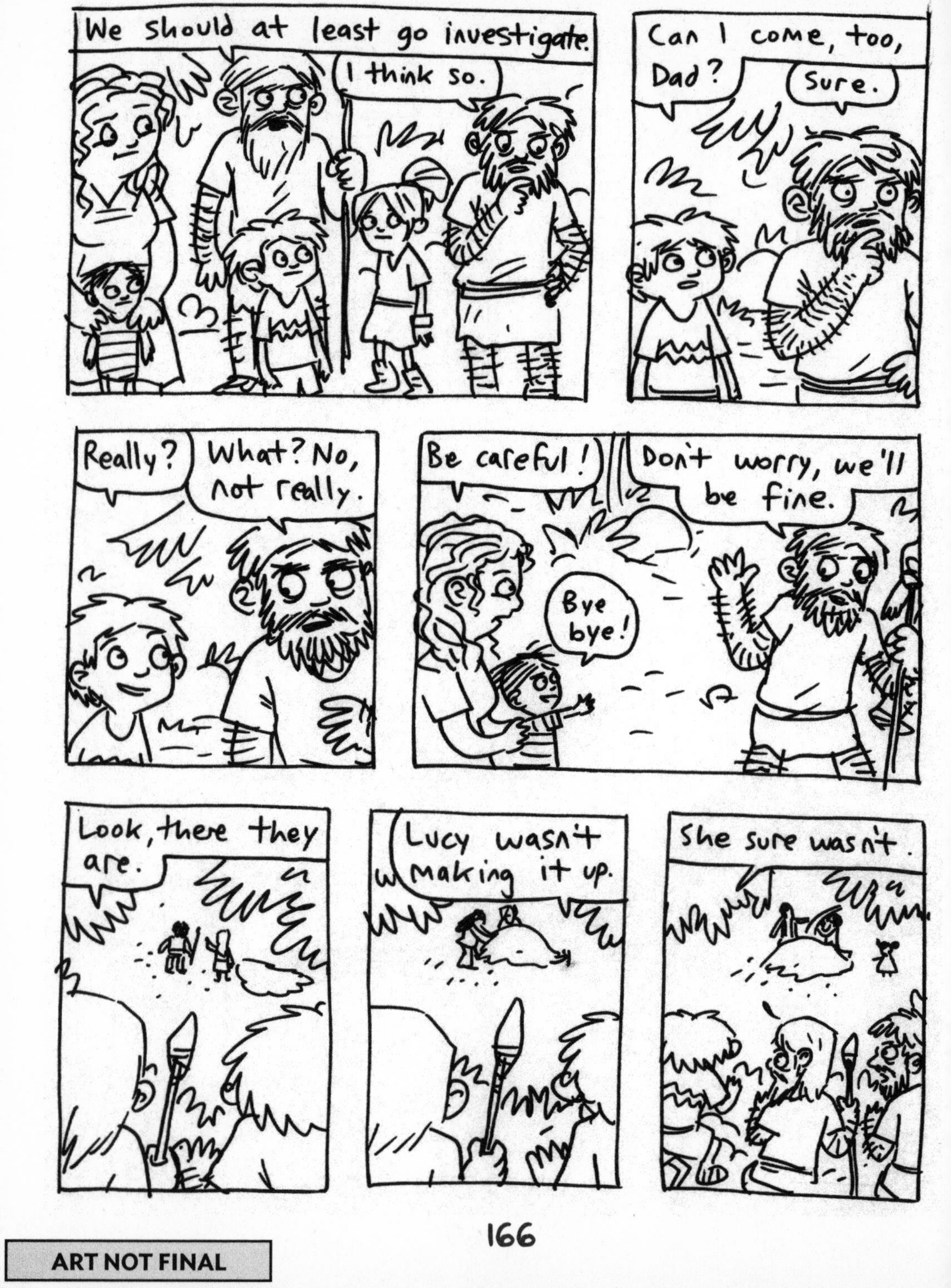
We should at least go investigate.
I think so.
Can I come, too, Dad?
Sure.
Really?
What? No, not really.
Be careful!
Don't worry, we'll be fine.
Bye bye!
Look, there they are.
Lucy wasn't making it up.
She sure wasn't.

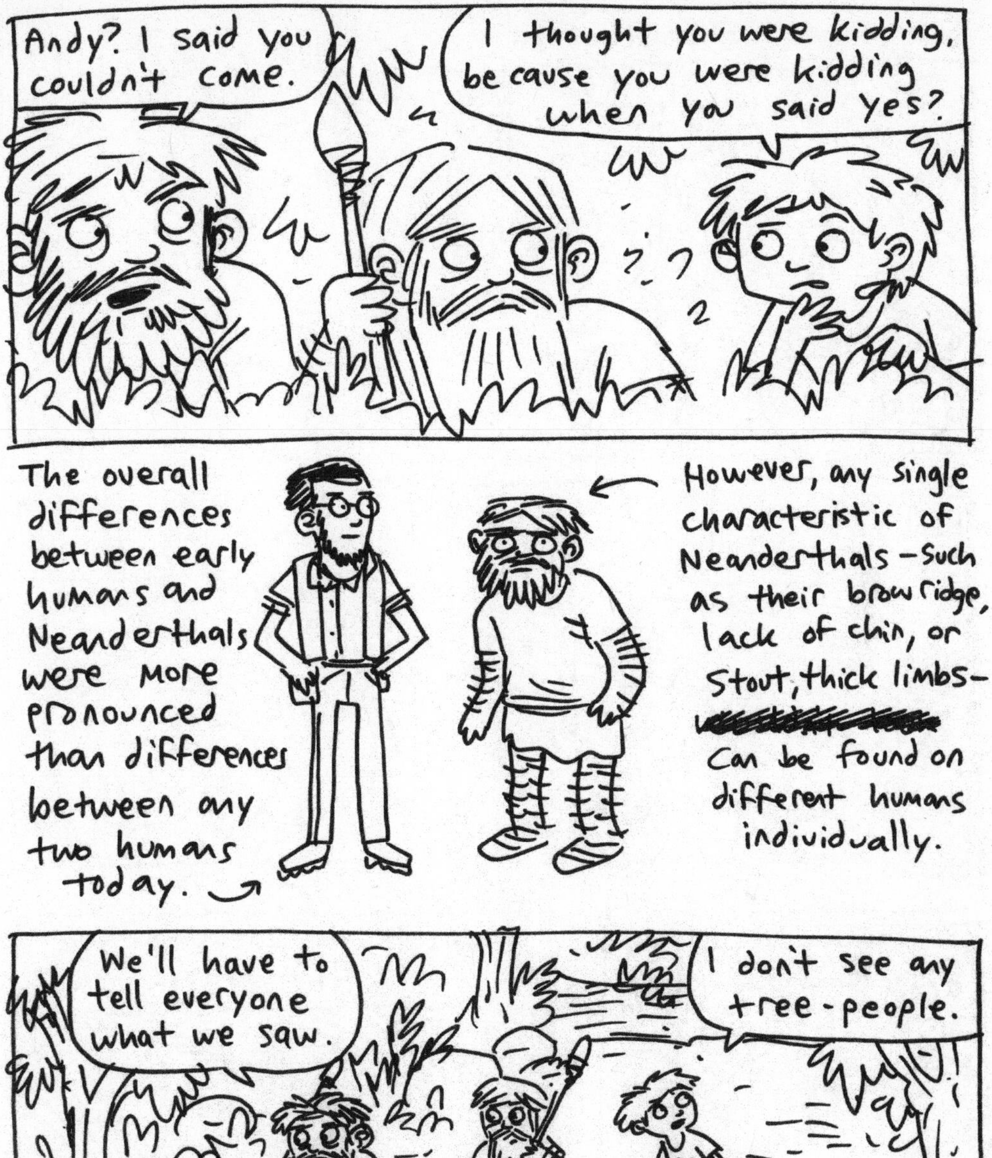
Andy? I said you couldn't come.
I thought you were kidding, because you were kidding when you said yes?
The overall differences between early humans and Neanderthals were more pronounced than differences between any two humans today.
However, any single characteristic of Neanderthals—such as their brow ridge, lack of chin, or stout, thick limbs—
[redacted]
can be found on different humans individually.
We'll have to tell everyone what we saw.
I don't see any tree-people.

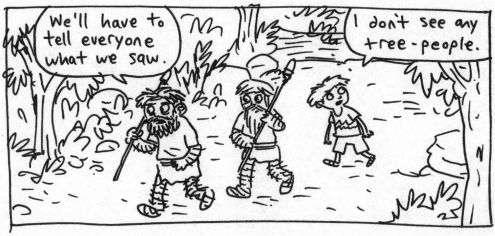

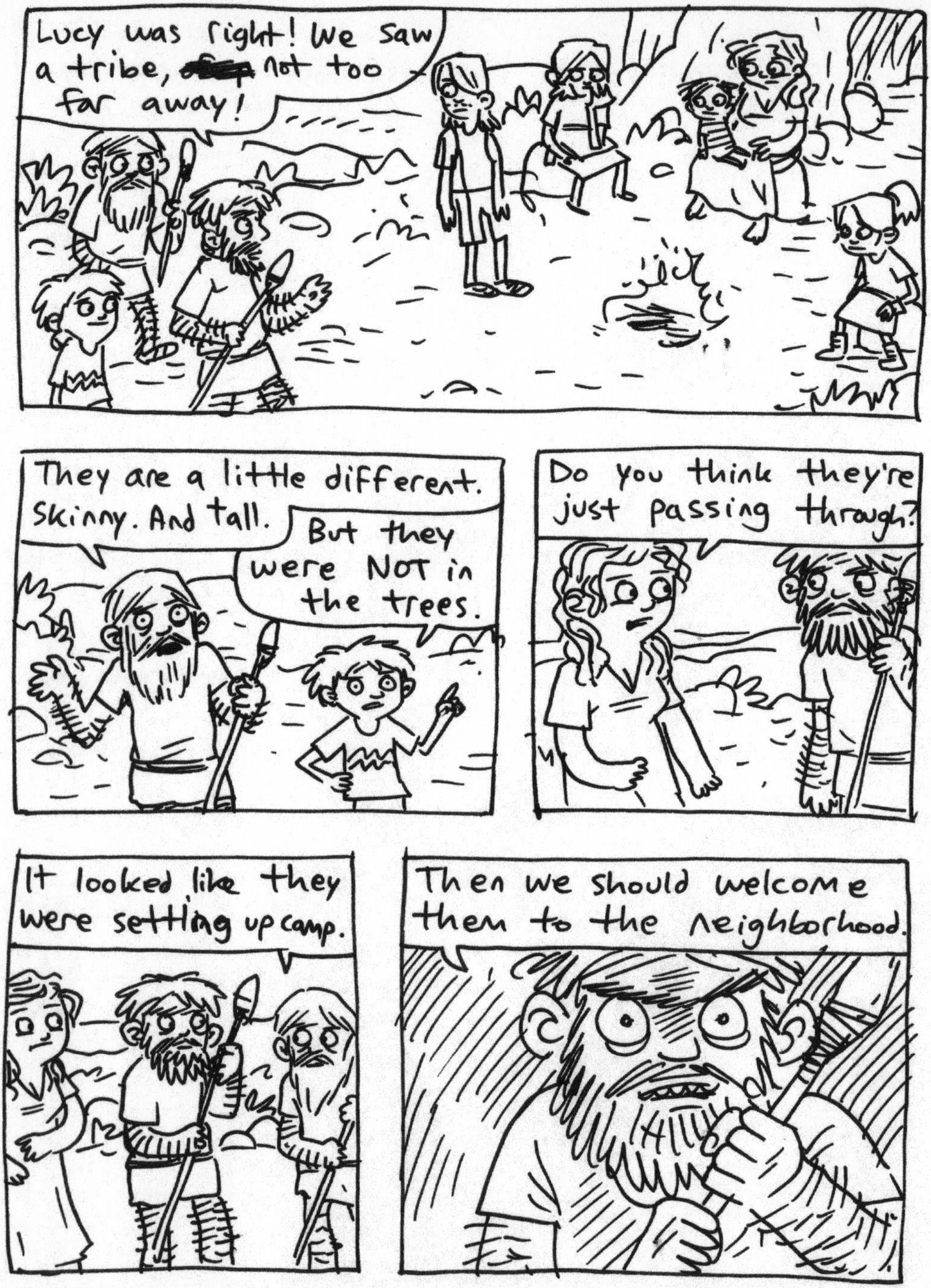
Lucy was right! We saw a tribe, [redacted] not too far away!
They are a little different. Skinny. And tall.
But they were NOT in the trees.
Do you think they're just passing through?
It looked like they were setting up camp.
Then we should welcome them to the neighborhood.

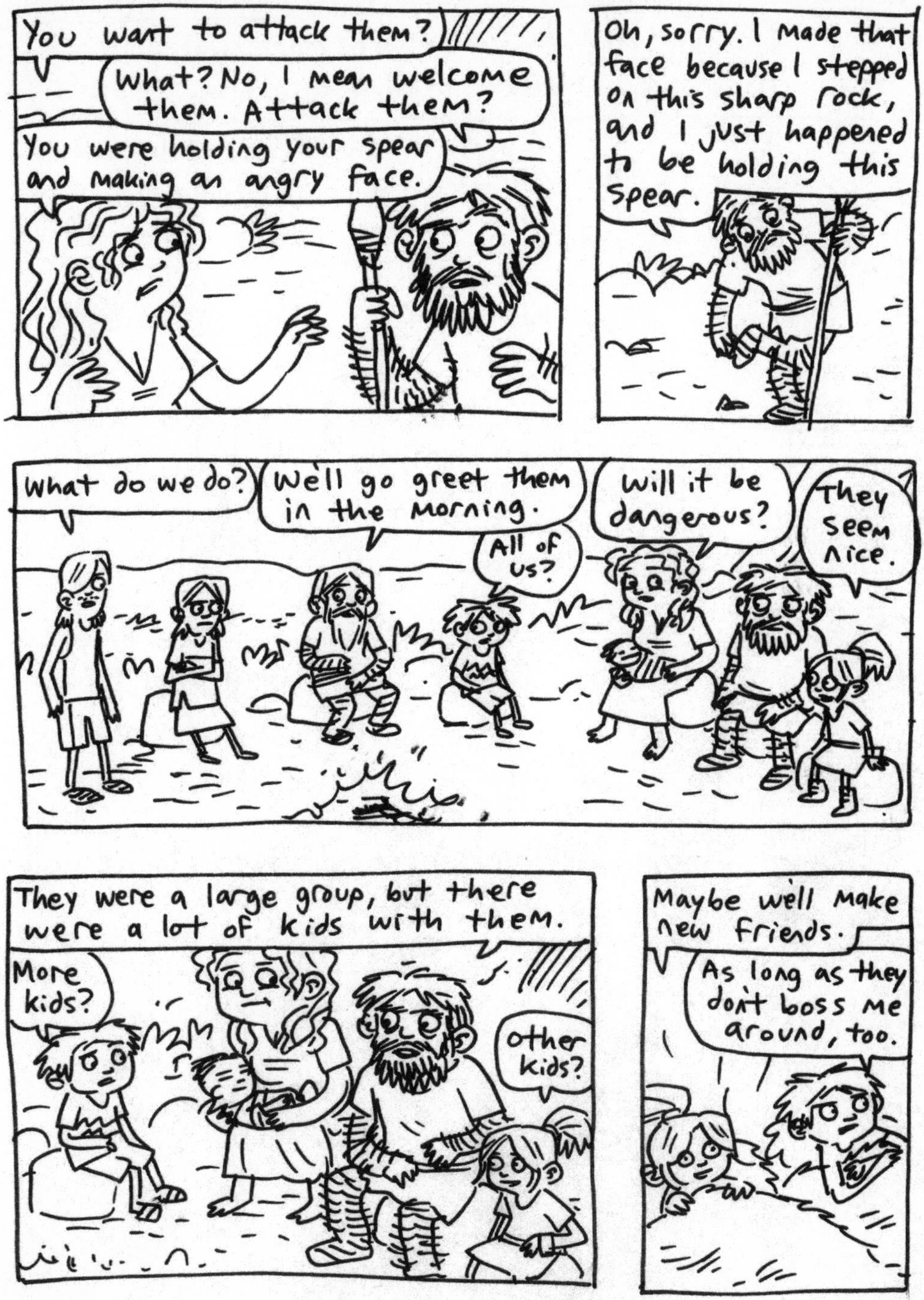
You want to attack them?
What? No, I mean welcome them. Attack them?
You were holding your spear and making an angry face.
Oh, sorry. I made that face because I stepped on this sharp rock, and I just happened to be holding this spear.
What do we do?
We'll go greet them in the morning.
All of us?
Will it be dangerous?
They seem nice.
They were a large group, but there were a lot of kids with them.
More kids?
Other kids?
Maybe we'll make new friends.
As long as they don't boss me around, too.

ART NOT FINAL

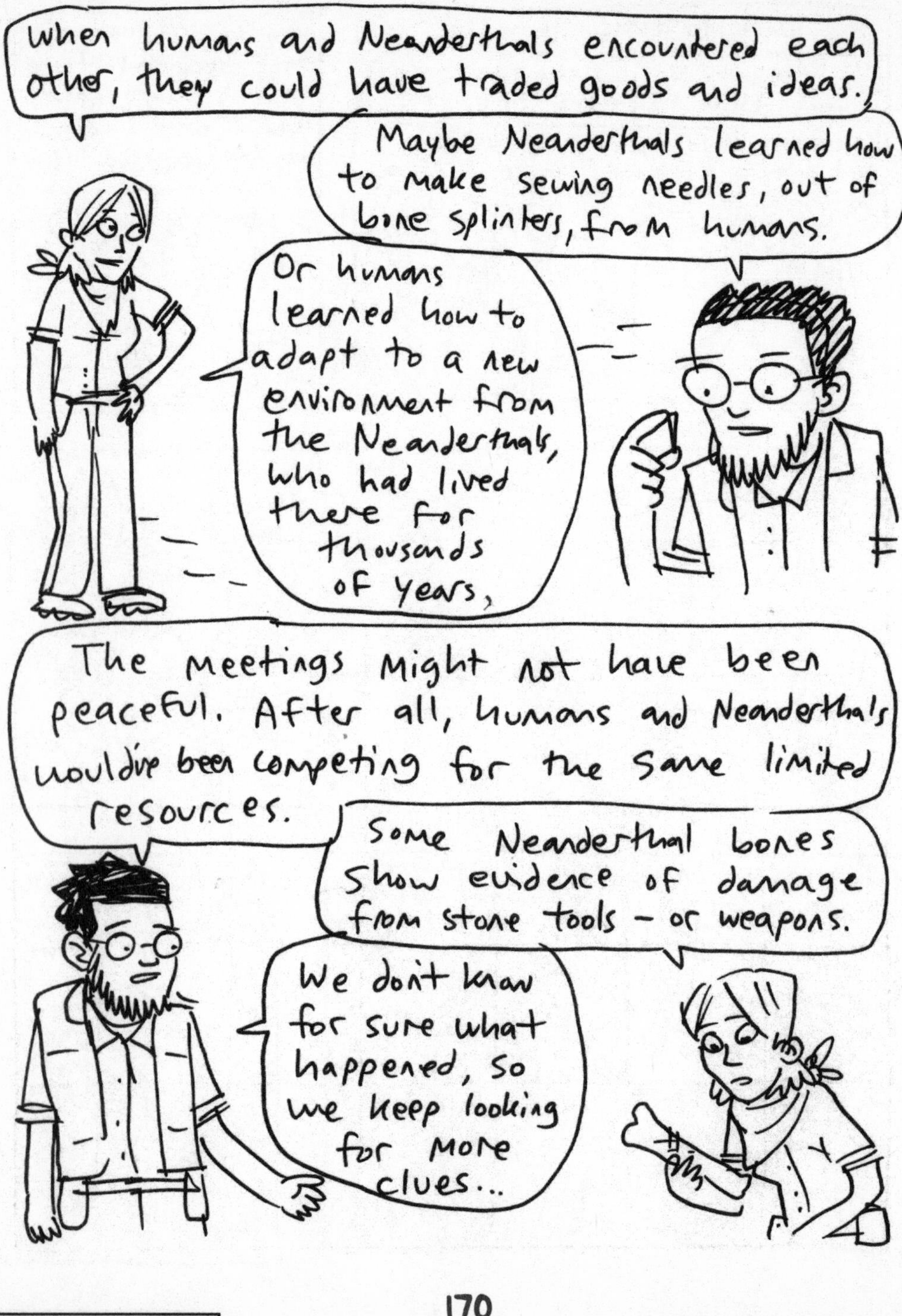
When humans and Neanderthals encountered each other, they could have traded goods and ideas.
Maybe Neanderthals learned how to make sewing needles, out of bone splinters, from humans.
Or humans learned how to adapt to a new environment from the Neanderthals, who had lived there for thousands of years,
The meetings might not have been peaceful. After all, humans and Neanderthals would've been competing for the same limited resources.
Some Neanderthal bones show evidence of damage from stone tools – or weapons.
We don't know for sure what happened, so we keep looking for more clues...

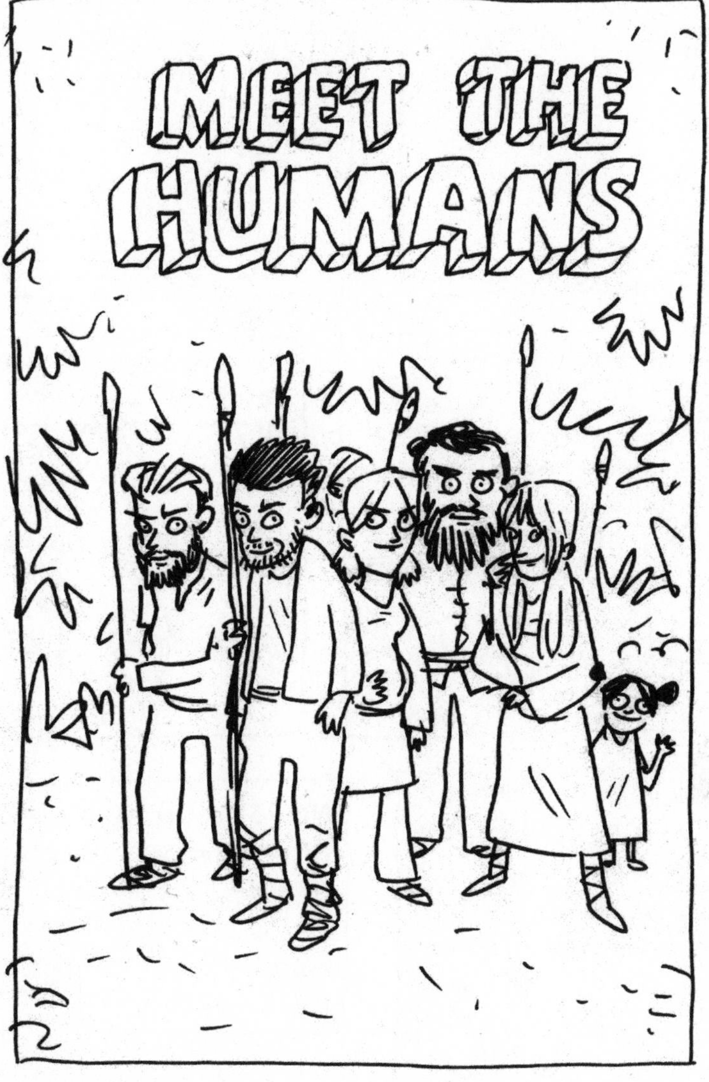
MEET THE HUMANS

ART NOT FINAL

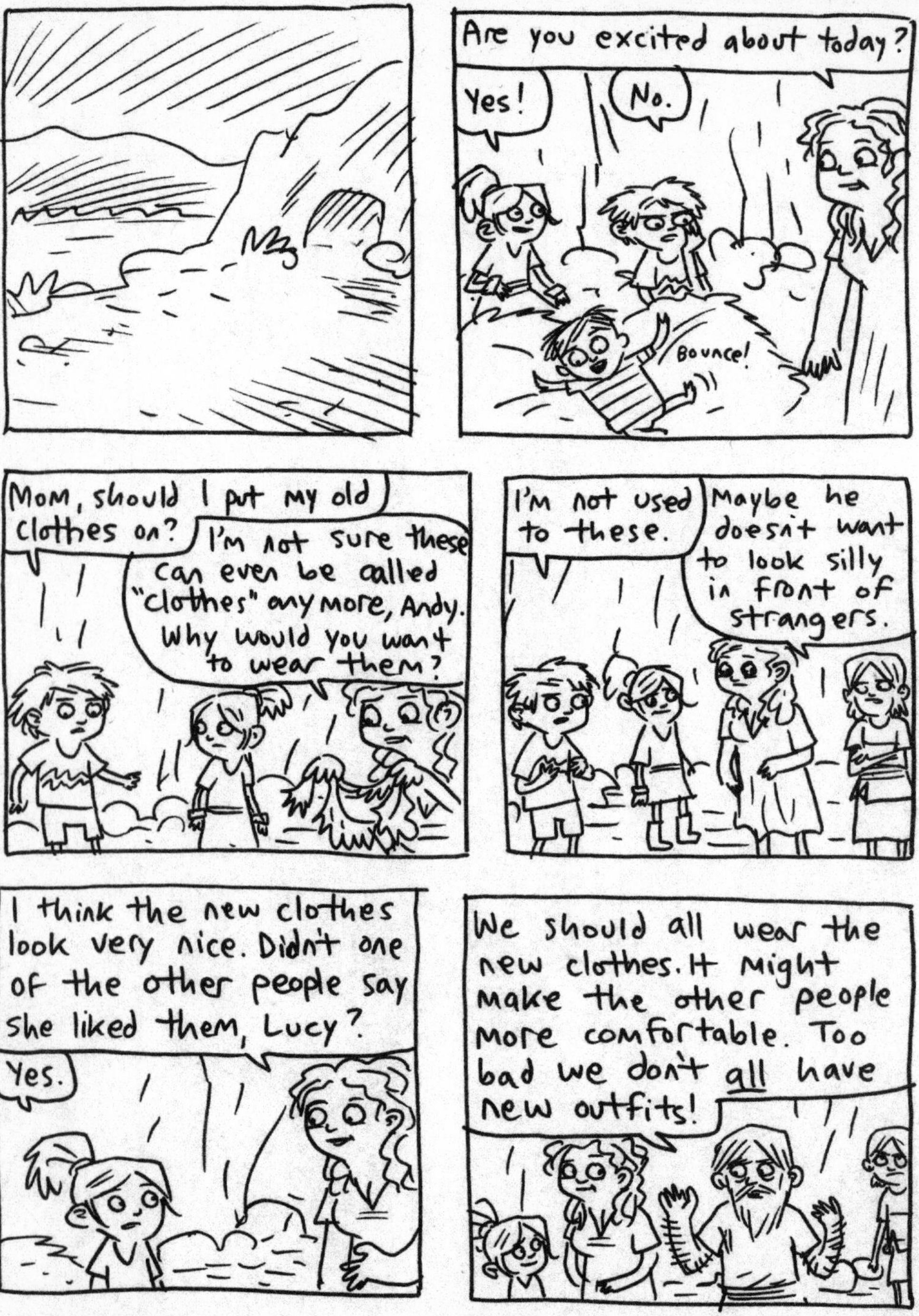
Are you excited about today?
Yes!
No.
Bounce!
Mom, should I put my old clothes on?
I'm not sure these can even be called "clothes" anymore, Andy. Why would you want to wear them?
I'm not used to these.
Maybe he doesn't want to look silly in front of strangers.
I think the new clothes look very nice. Didn't one of the other people say she liked them, Lucy?
Yes.
We should all wear the new clothes. It might make the other people more comfortable. Too bad we don't all have new outfits!

ART NOT FINAL

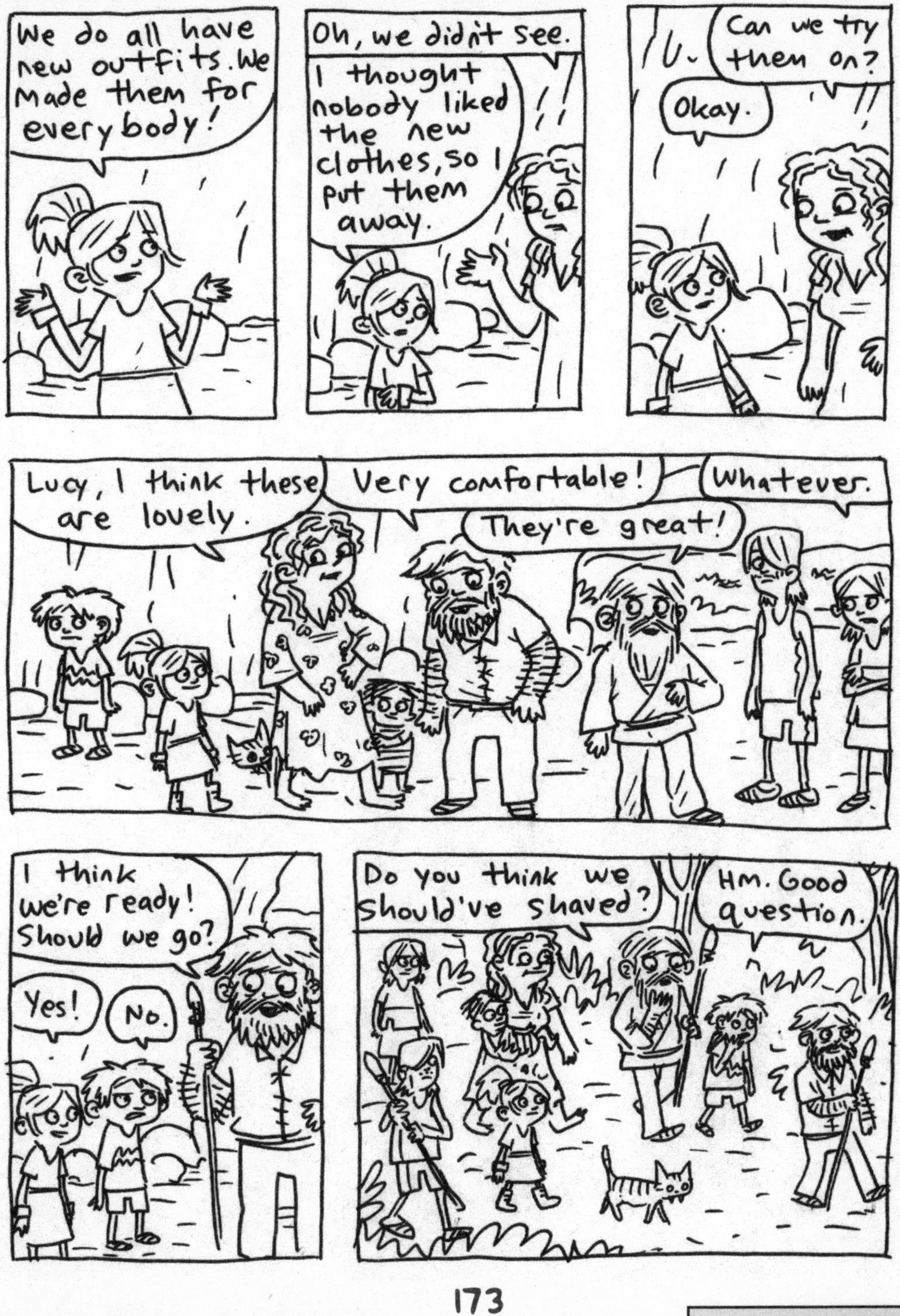

We do all have new outfits. We made them for everybody!
Oh, we didn't see.
I thought nobody liked the new clothes, so I put them away.
Can we try them on?
Okay.
Lucy, I think these are lovely.
Very comfortable!
Whatever.
They're great!
I think we're ready! Should we go?
Yes!
No.
Do you think we should've shaved?
Hm. Good question.

ART NOT FINAL

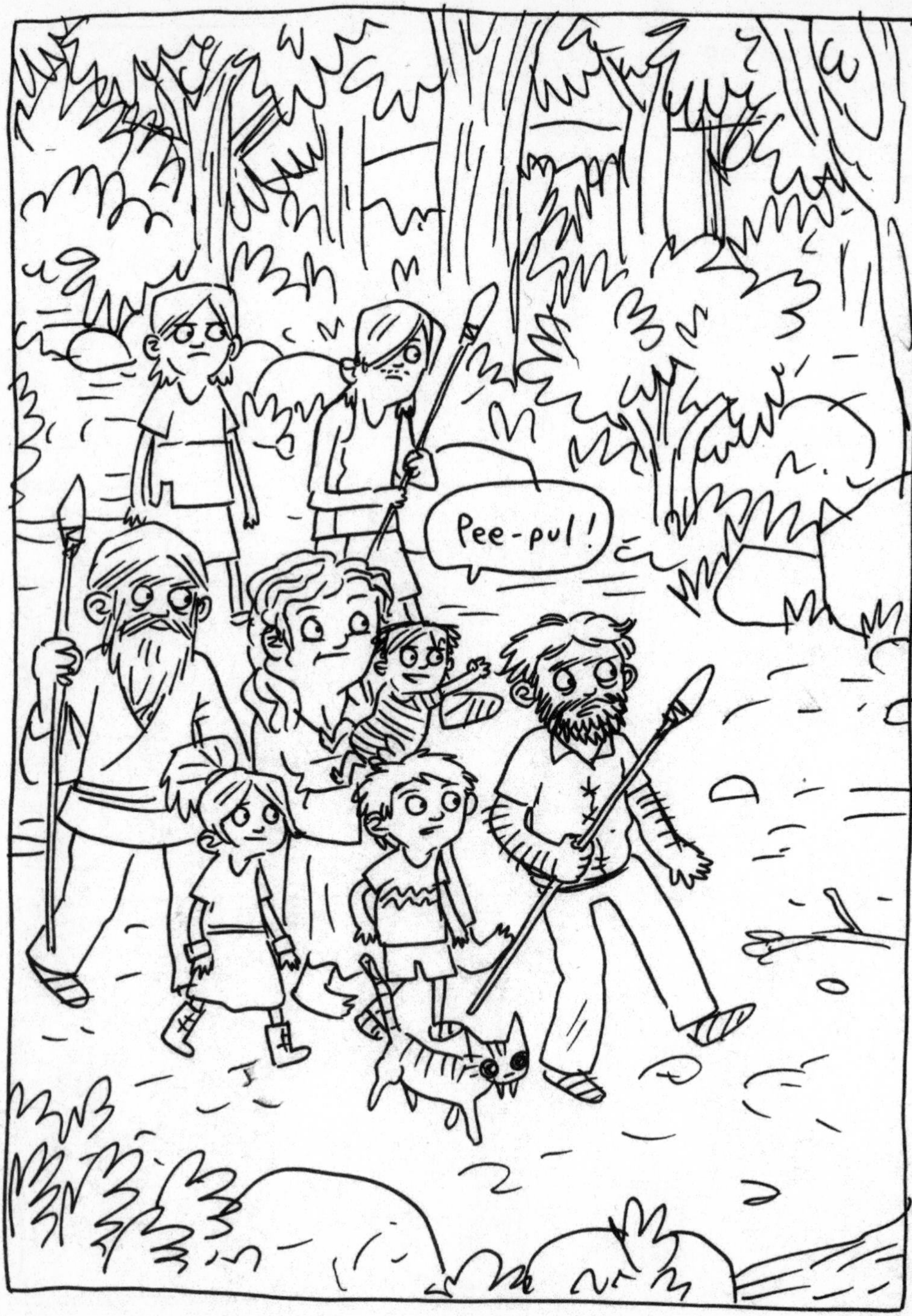
Pee-pul!

ART NOT FINAL

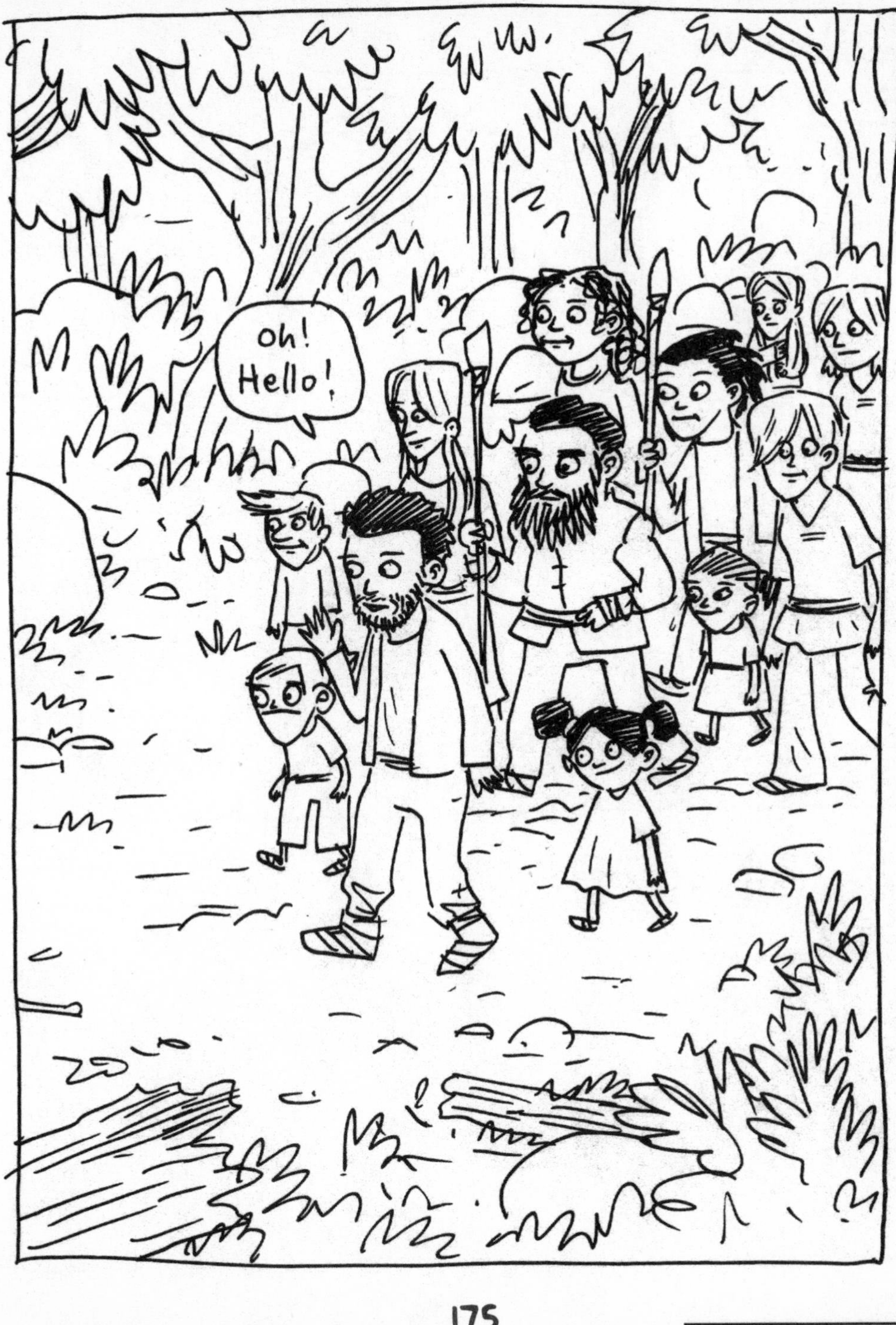
Oh! Hello!

ART NOT FINAL

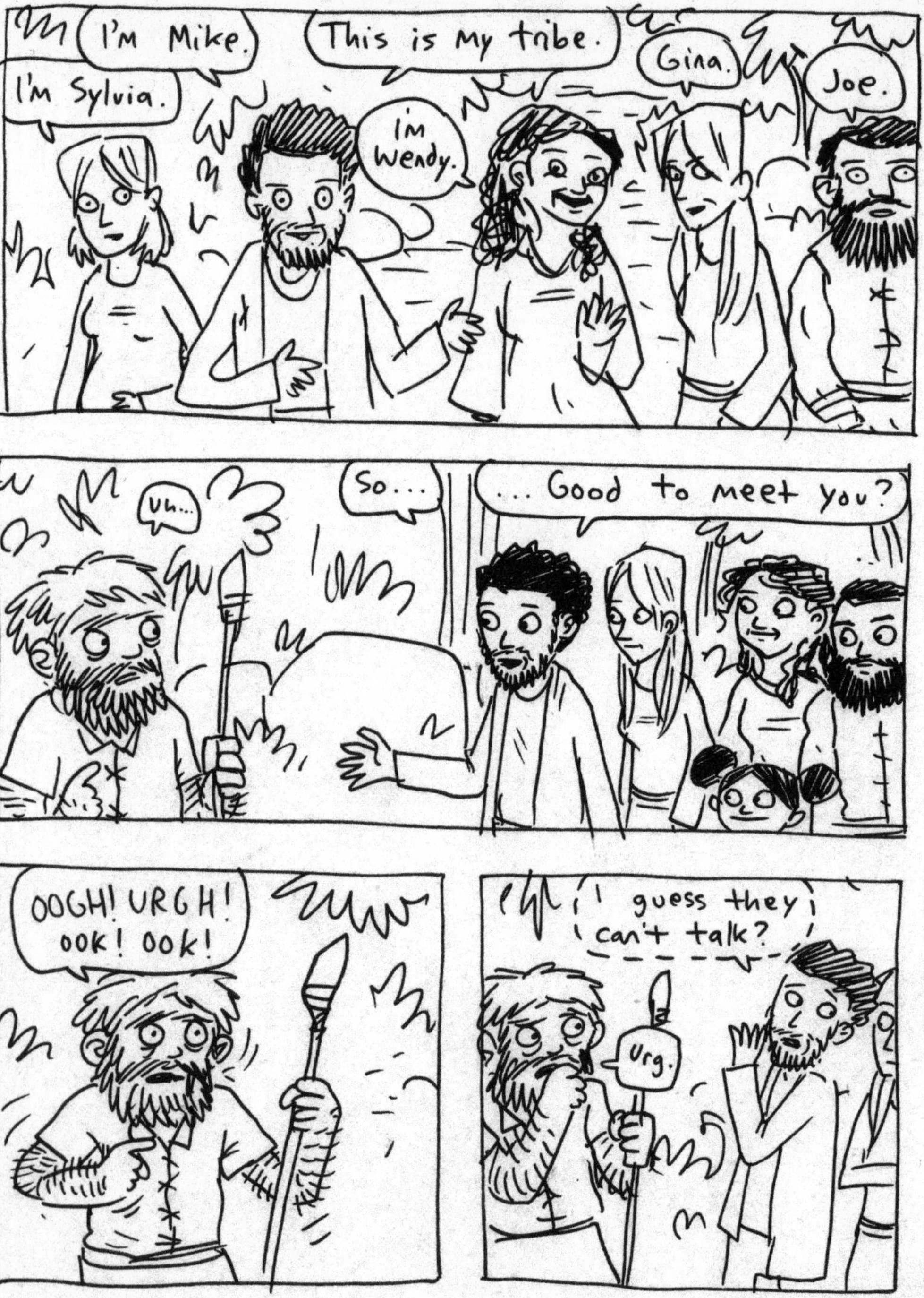
I'm Mike.
I'm Sylvia.
This is my tribe.
I'm Wendy.
Gina.
Joe.
Uh...
So...
... Good to meet you?
OOGH! URGH! OOK! OOK!
guess they can't talk?
Urg.

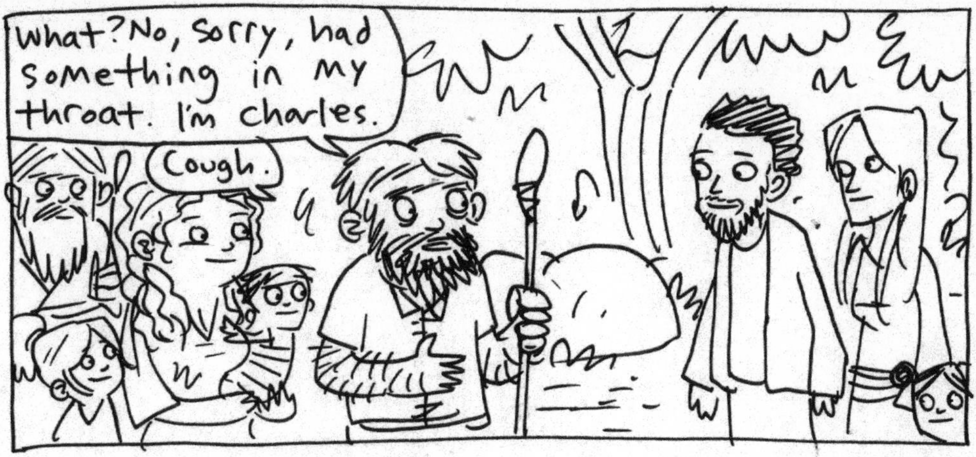
What? No, sorry, had something in my throat. I'm Charles.
Cough.

Human have a hyoid bone - a small bone allowing the mouth and tongue to create complex sounds.

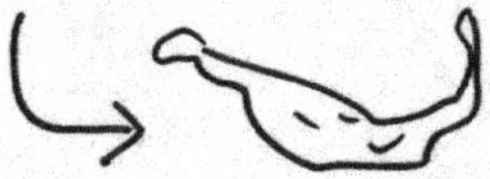

Scientists have discovered Neanderthals had a similar hyoid bone.

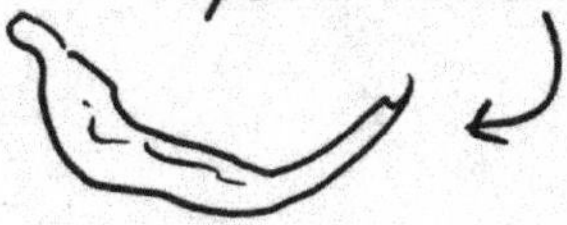

Neanderthals may not have been able to make the same range of sounds as humans, but they communicated in more than simple grunts and pointing!

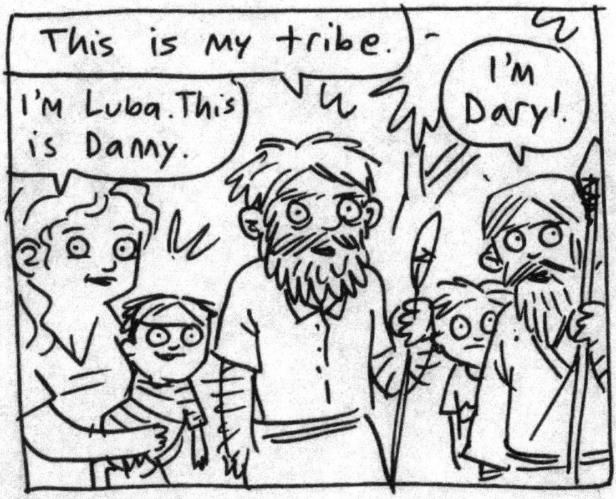
This is my tribe.
I'm Luba. This is Danny.
I'm Dary!.

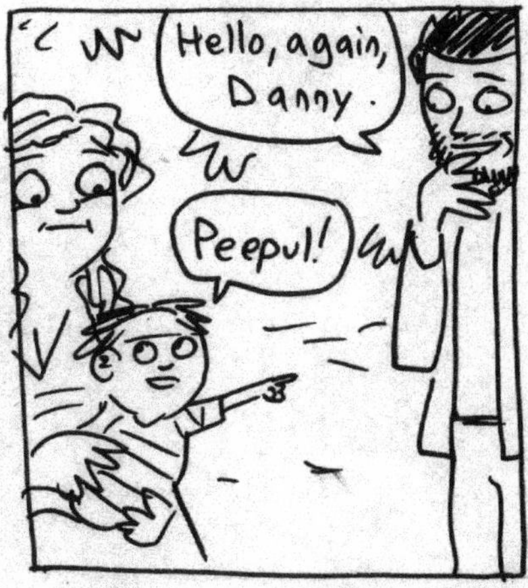
Hello, again, Danny.
Peepul!

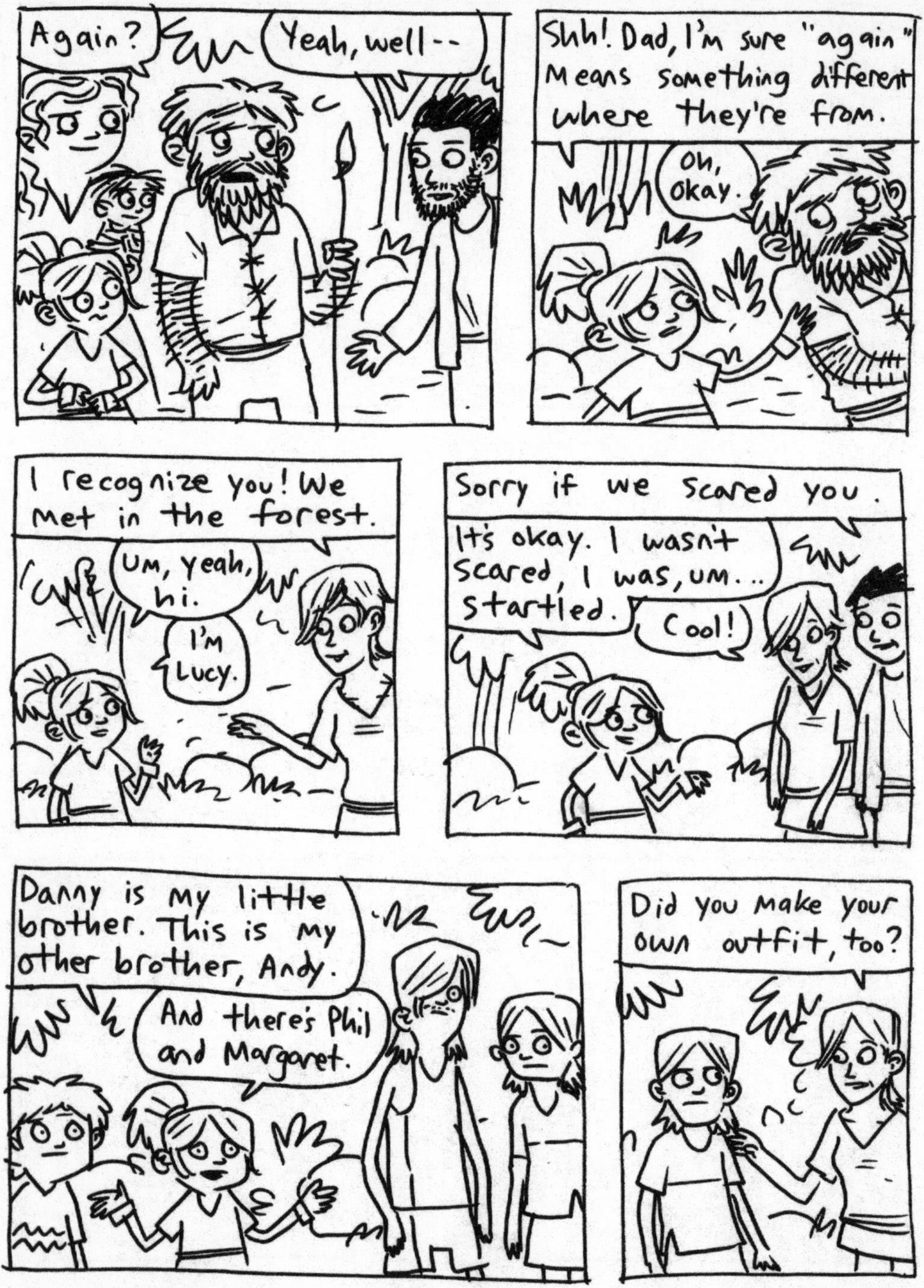
Again?
Yeah, well--
Shh! Dad, I'm sure "again" Means something different where they're from.
Oh, okay.
I recognize you! We met in the forest.
Um, yeah, hi.
I'm Lucy.
Sorry if we scared you.
It's okay. I wasn't scared, I was, um... startled.
Cool!
Danny is my little brother. This is my other brother, Andy.
And there's Phil and Margaret.
Did you make your own outfit, too?

ART NOT FINAL

No way. Lucy did all — It looks great on you.

—but I helped. Nice.

You guys should meet the other kids. I'm Sasha. Chuck. Richard. Tommy. Kathy. Jamie.

That's a lots of kids. Where'd they all come from?

Our parents, duh. Be nice, Richard. I'm just kidding.

ART NOT FINAL

Where did you come from, Mike?

Let's see. We used to live by this big river, but followed that, went by the shore of the sea, came over mountains.

Wow, that's—

And then...

After going through some valleys, we travelled across the plains...

Into a large forest...

Another mountain pass...

Zzzzzzz

Uh, so, really far away.

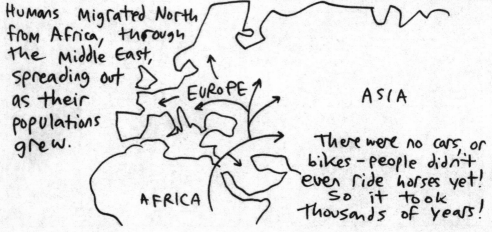

Humans migrated north from Africa, through the Middle East, spreading out as their populations grew.

EUROPE

ASIA

AFRICA

There were no cars, or bikes — people didn't even ride horses yet! So it took thousands of years!

180

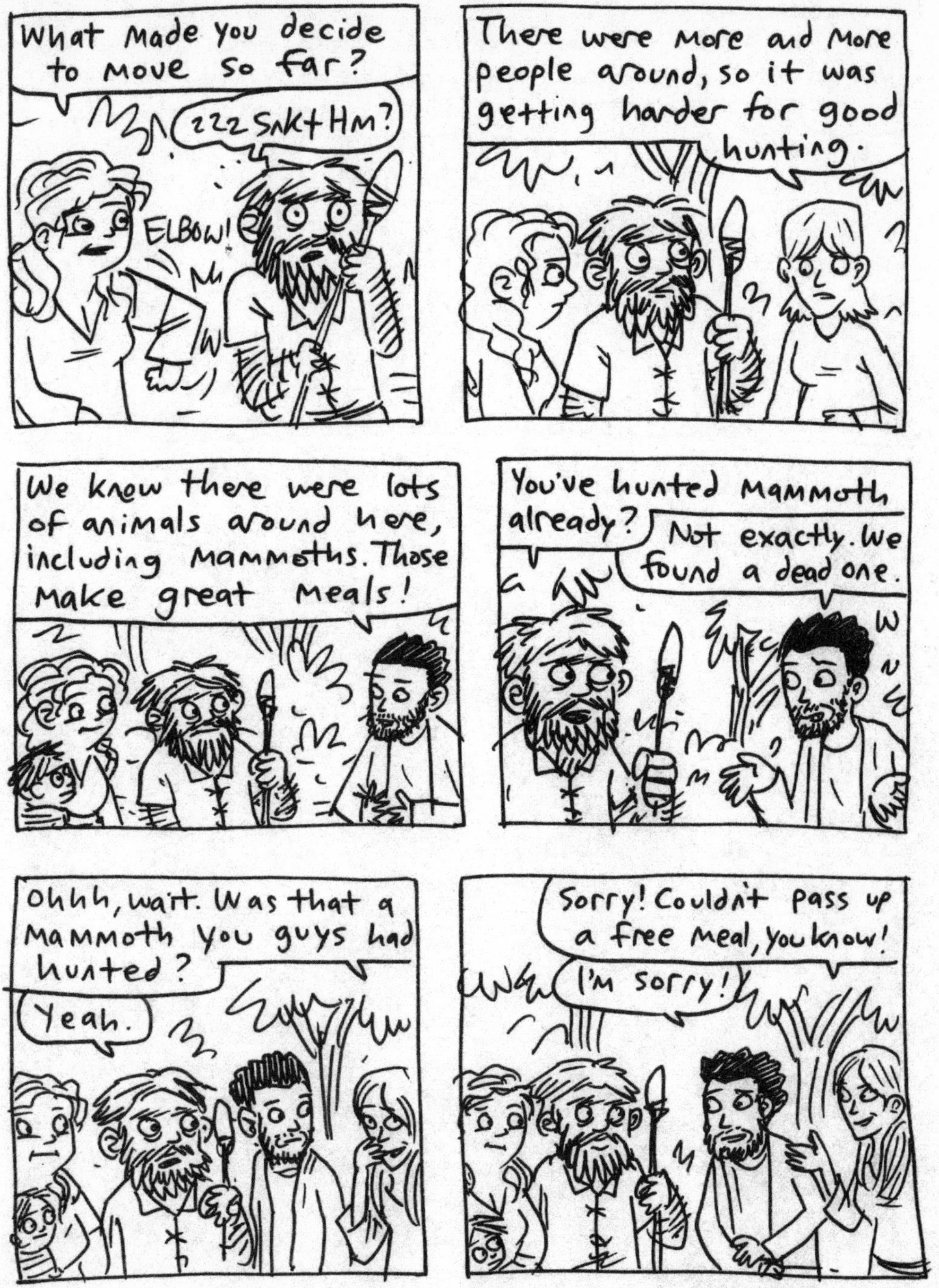
What made you decide to move so far?
zzzSnkt Hm?
ELBOW!
There were more and more people around, so it was getting harder for good hunting.
We know there were lots of animals around here, including mammoths. Those make great meals!
You've hunted mammoth already?
Not exactly. We found a dead one.
Ohhh, wait. Was that a mammoth you guys had hunted?
Yeah.
Sorry! Couldn't pass up a free meal, you know!
I'm sorry!

ART NOT FINAL

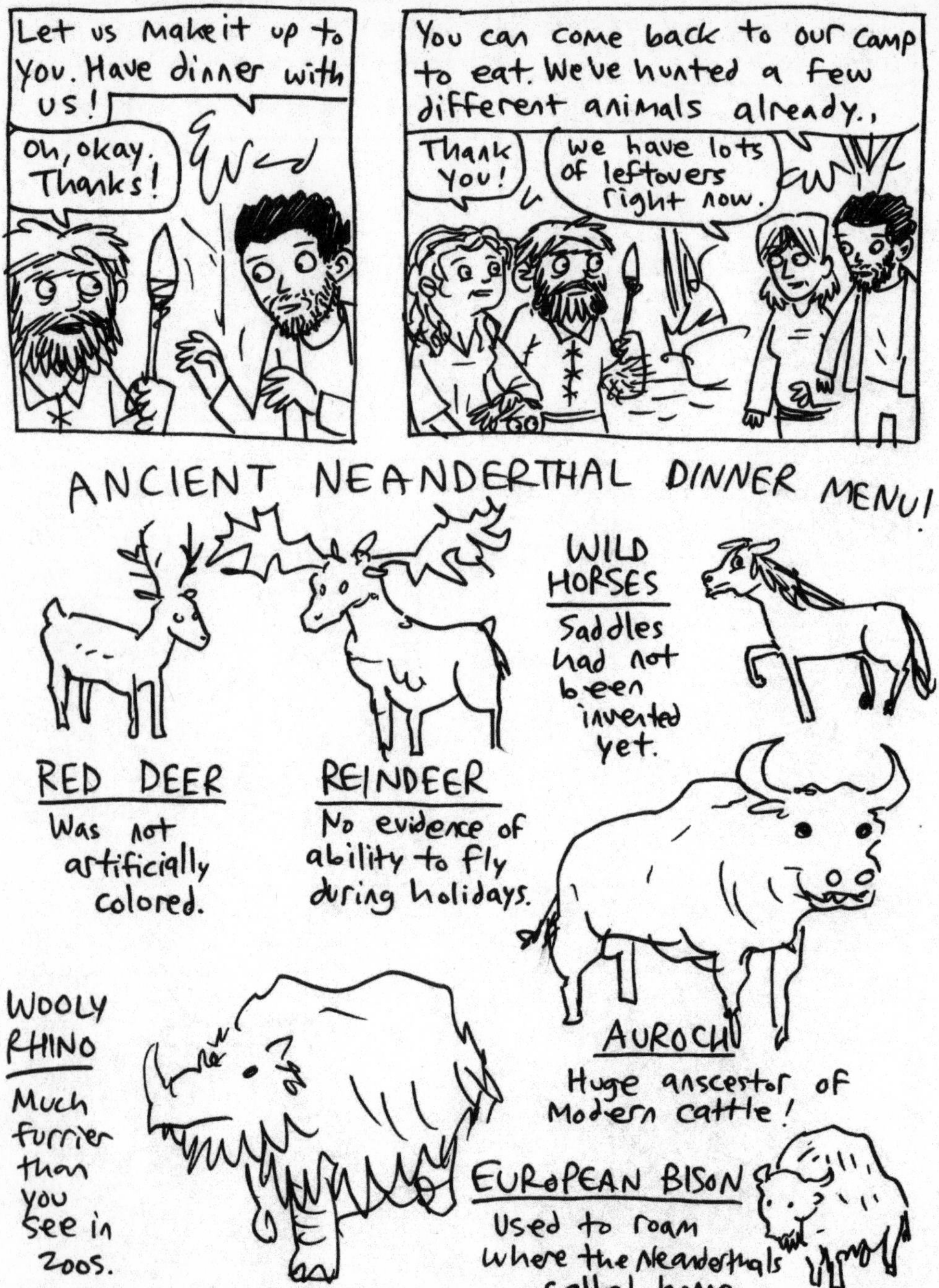
Let us make it up to you. Have dinner with us!
Oh, okay. Thanks!
You can come back to our camp to eat. We've hunted a few different animals already.,
Thank you!
We have lots of leftovers right now.
ANCIENT NEANDERTHAL DINNER MENU!
WILD HORSES
Saddles had not been invented yet.
RED DEER
Was not artificially colored.
REINDEER
No evidence of ability to fly during holidays.
WOOLY RHINO
Much furrier than you see in zoos.
AUROCH
Huge anscestor of modern cattle!
EUROPEAN BISON
Used to roam where the Neanderthals called home.

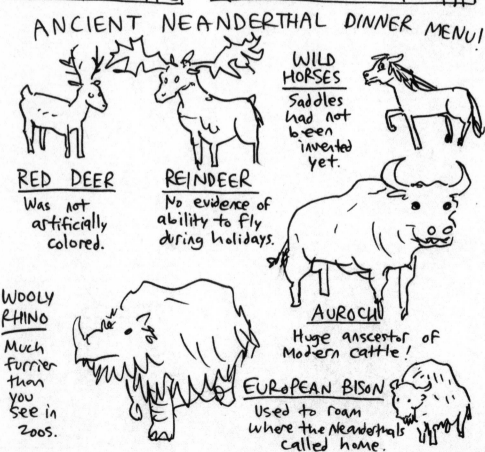

ART NOT FINAL

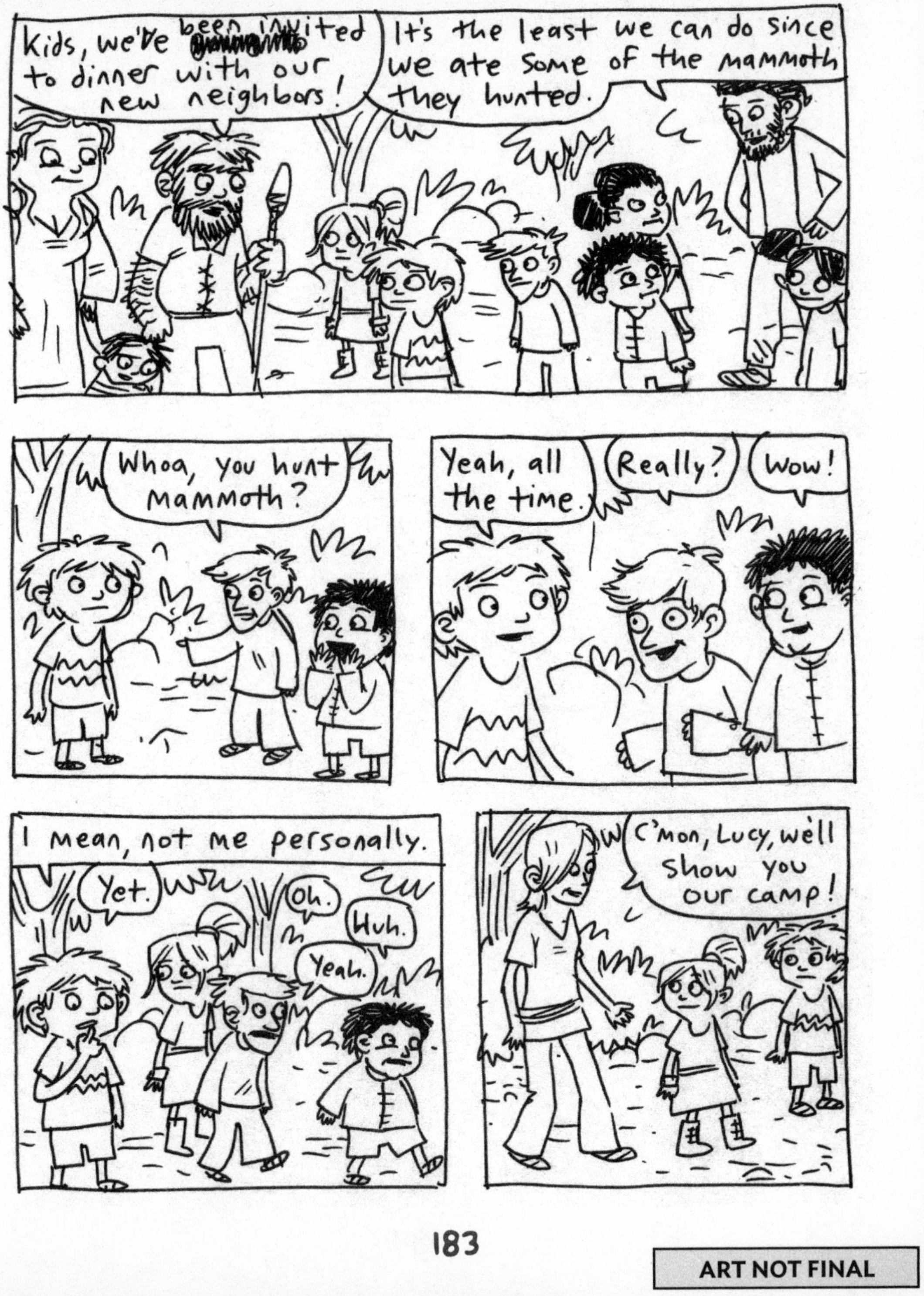
Kids, we've been invited to dinner with our new neighbors!
It's the least we can do since we ate some of the mammoth they hunted.
Whoa, you hunt mammoth?
Yeah, all the time.
Really?
Wow!
I mean, not me personally.
Yet.
Oh.
Huh.
Yeah.
C'mon, Lucy, we'll show you our camp!

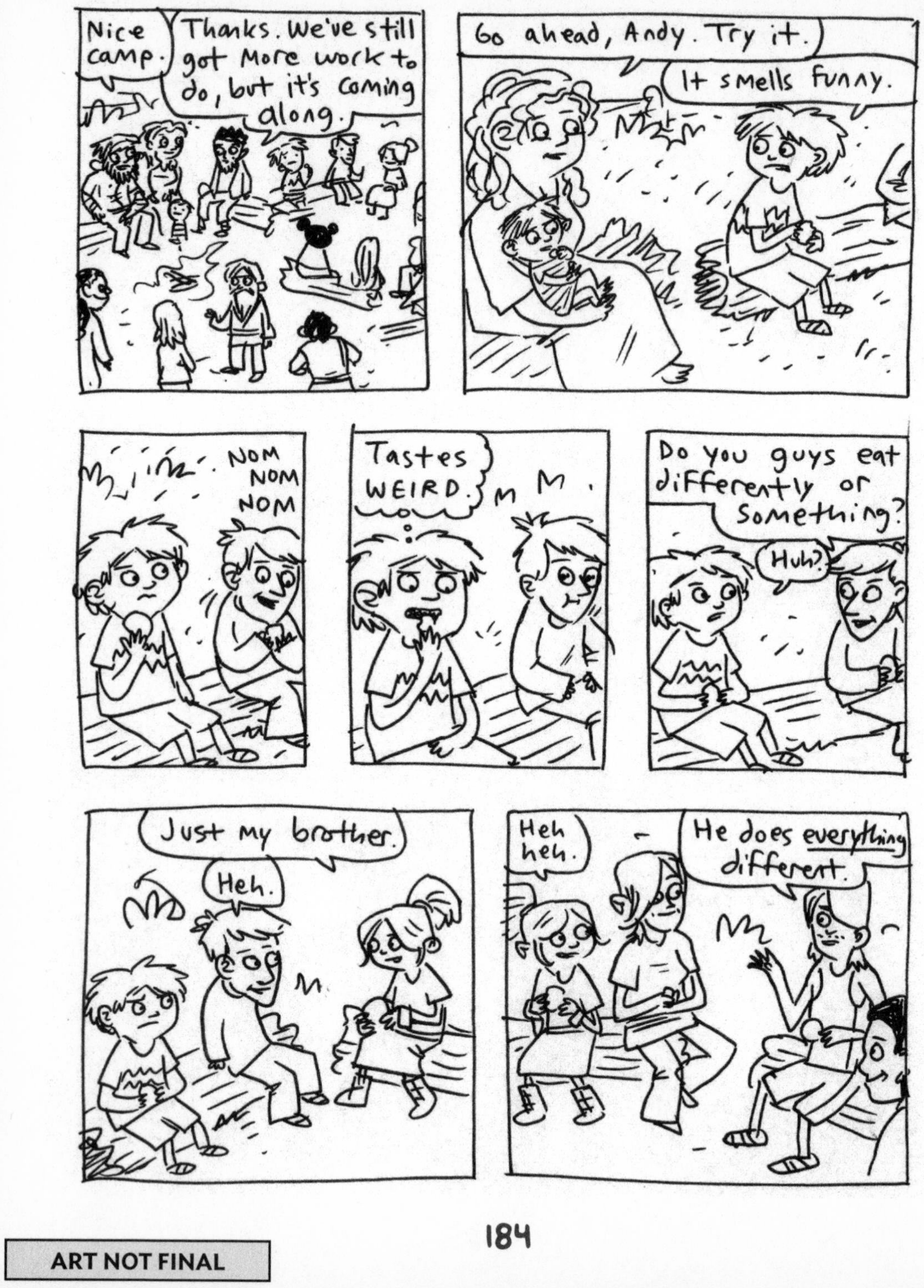
Nice camp.
Thanks. We've still got more work to do, but it's coming along.
Go ahead, Andy. Try it.
It smells funny.
NOM NOM NOM
Tastes WEIRD.
Do you guys eat differently or something?
Huh?
Just my brother.
Heh.
Heh heh.
He does everything different.

Don't listen to them, Andy. Different is good!
sigh.
MMM, this food is really different!
Groan.
AROOOOOOOO
Wolves?
I'll show them!
GRAB!
Andy?
What's he doing?!
The hero prepares to nobly sacrifice himself...
Come back!

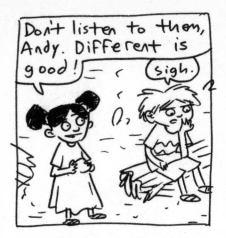

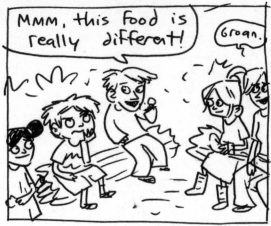

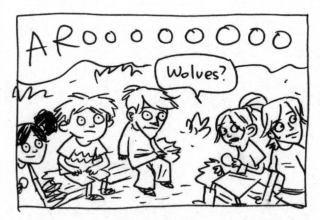

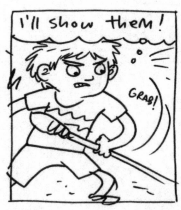

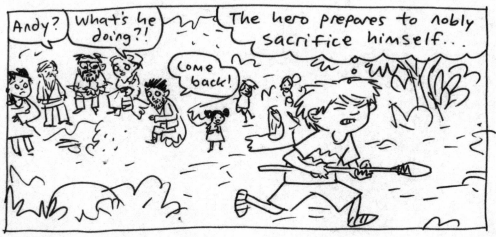

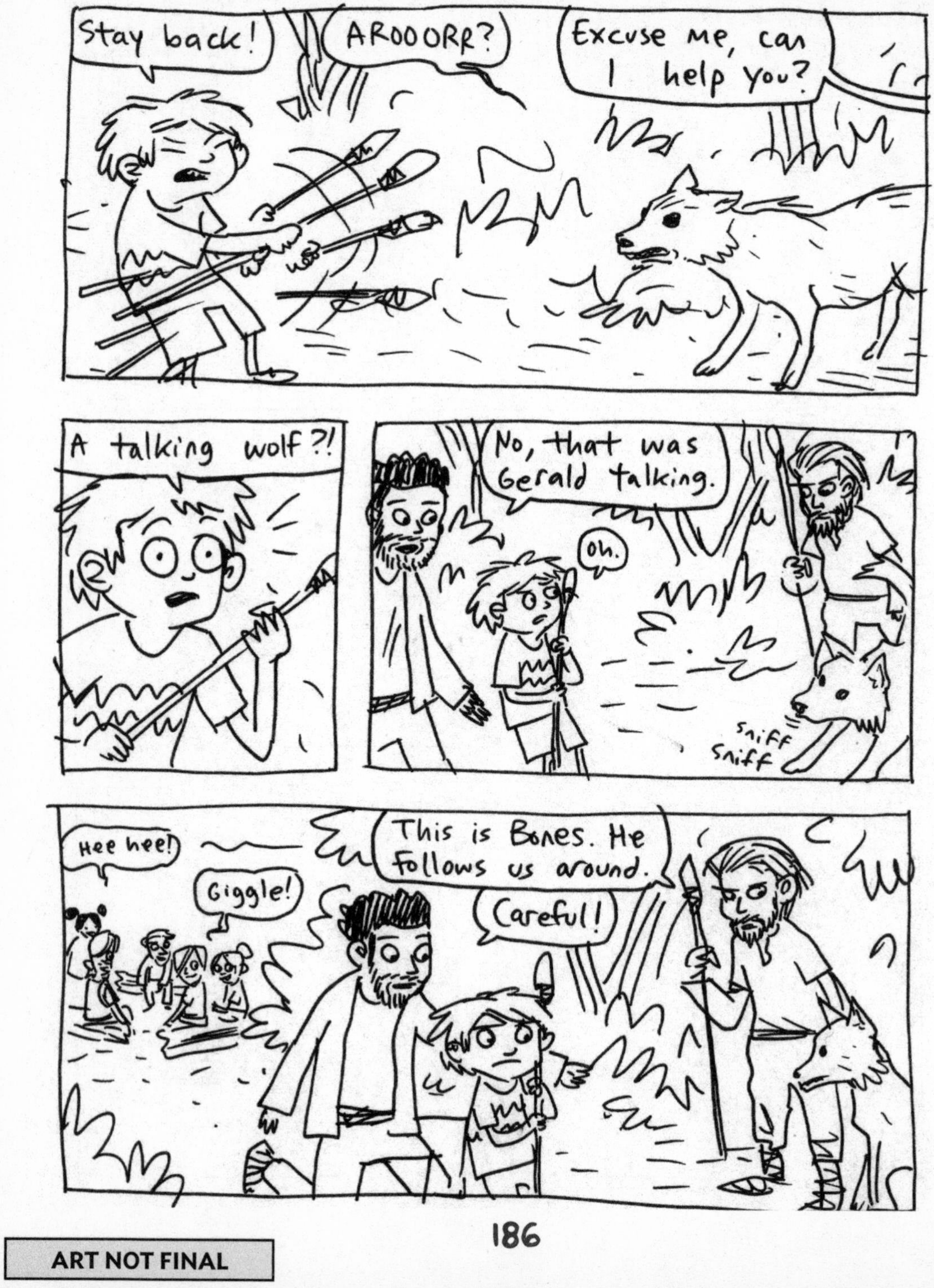
Stay back!
AROOORR?
Excuse me, can I help you?
A talking wolf?!
No, that was Gerald talking.
Oh.
sniff sniff
Hee hee!
Giggle!
This is Bones. He follows us around.
Careful!

ART NOT FINAL

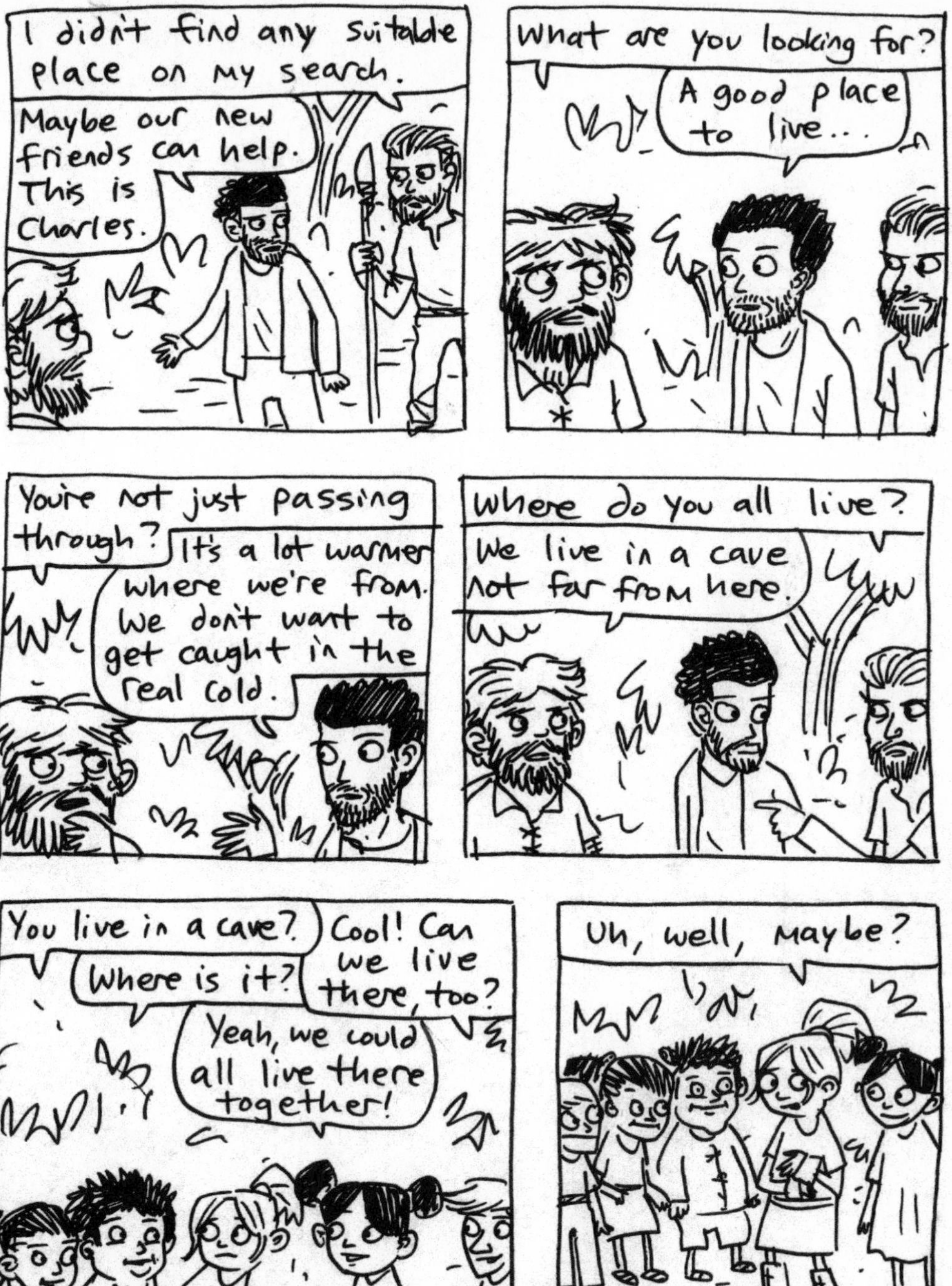
I didn't find any suitable place on my search.
Maybe our new friends can help. This is Charles.
What are you looking for?
A good place to live...
You're not just passing through?
It's a lot warmer where we're from. We don't want to get caught in the real cold.
Where do you all live?
We live in a cave not far from here.
You live in a cave?
Where is it?
Cool! Can we live there, too?
Yeah, we could all live there together!
Uh, well, maybe?

ART NOT FINAL

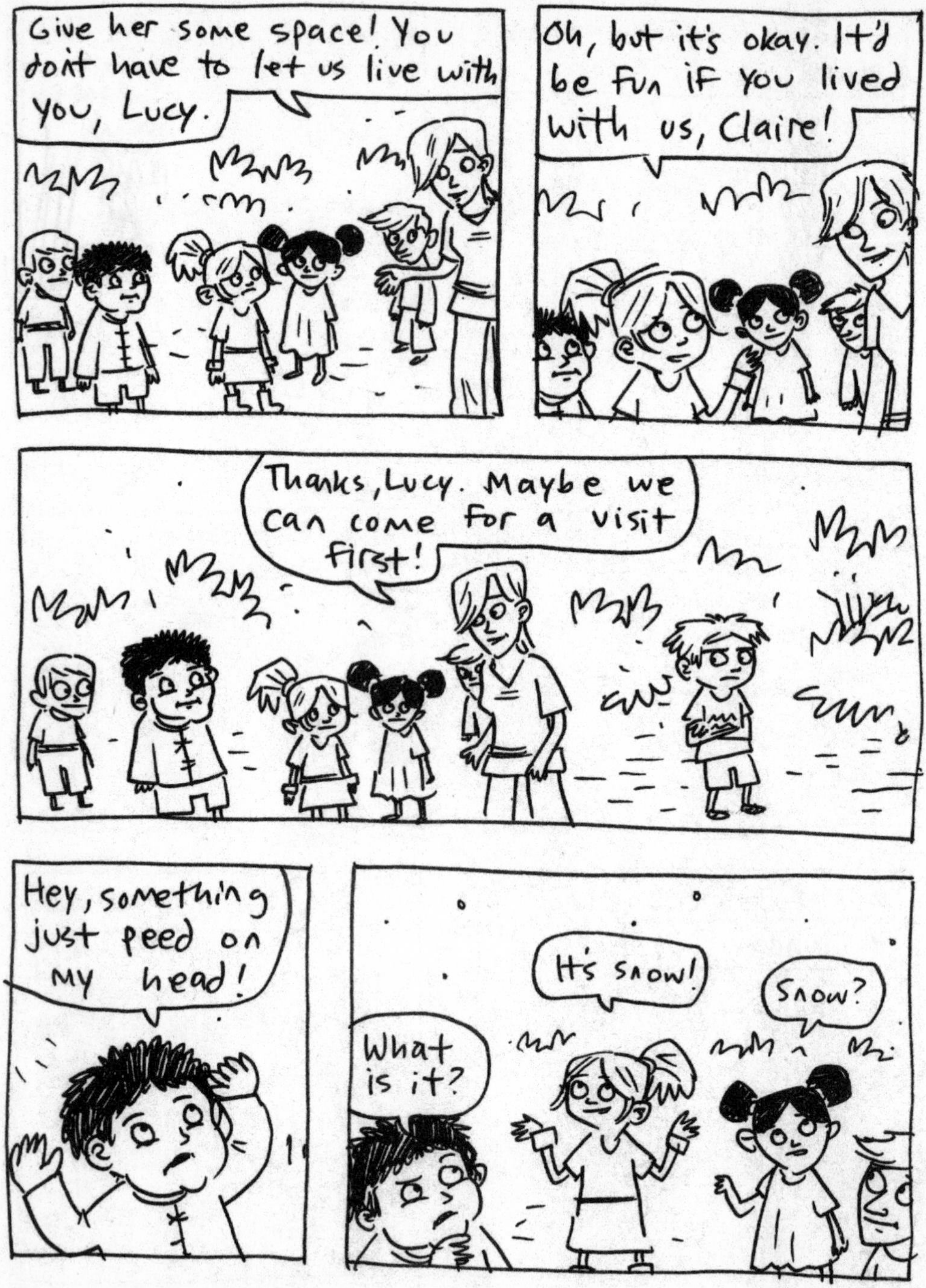
Give her some space! You don't have to let us live with you, Lucy.
Oh, but it's okay. It'd be fun if you lived with us, Claire!
Thanks, Lucy. Maybe we can come for a visit first!
Hey, something just peed on my head!
It's snow!
Snow?
What is it?

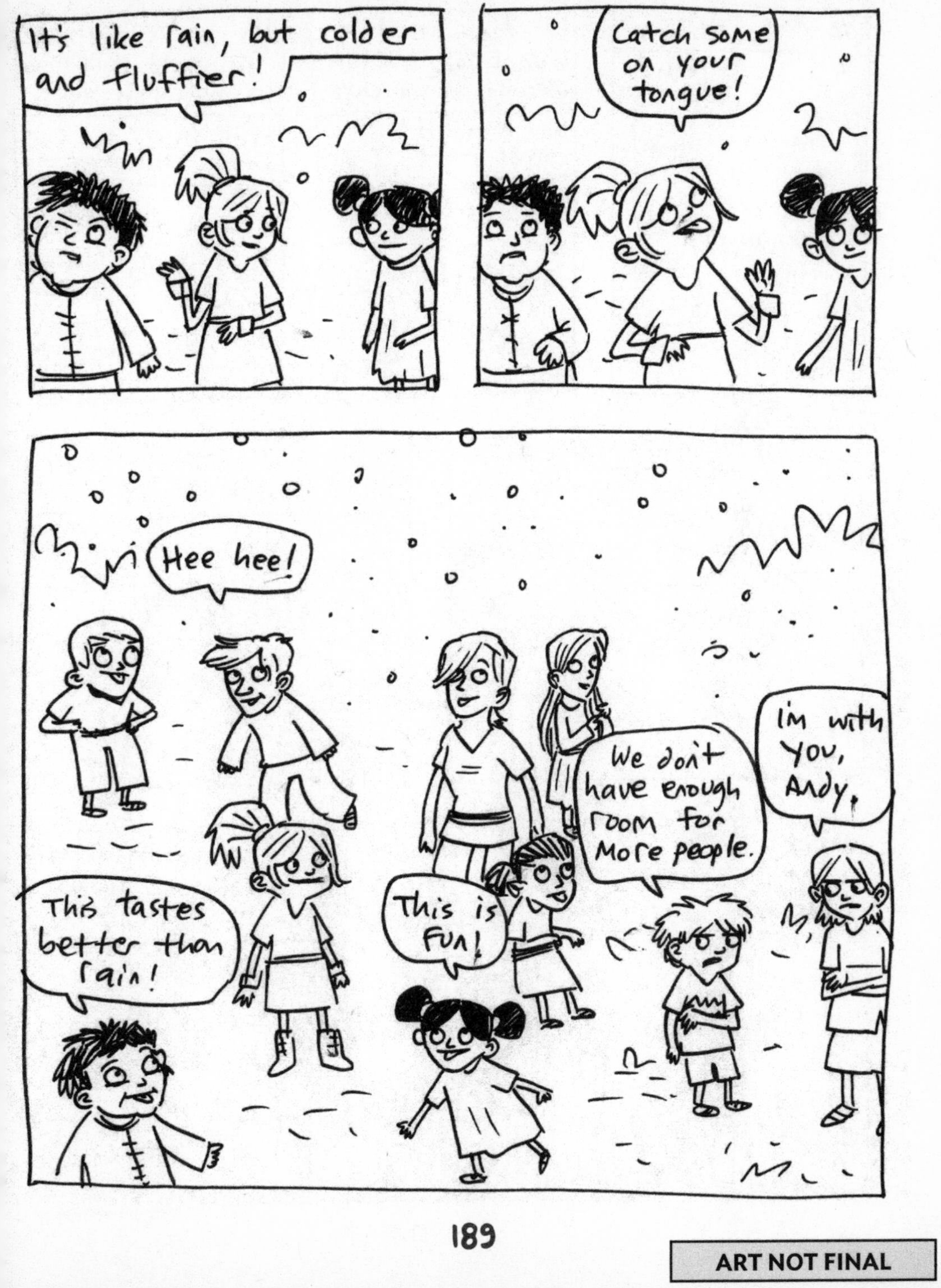
It's like rain, but colder and fluffier!
Catch some on your tongue!
Hee hee!
I'm with you, Andy.
We don't have enough room for more people.
This tastes better than rain!
This is fun!

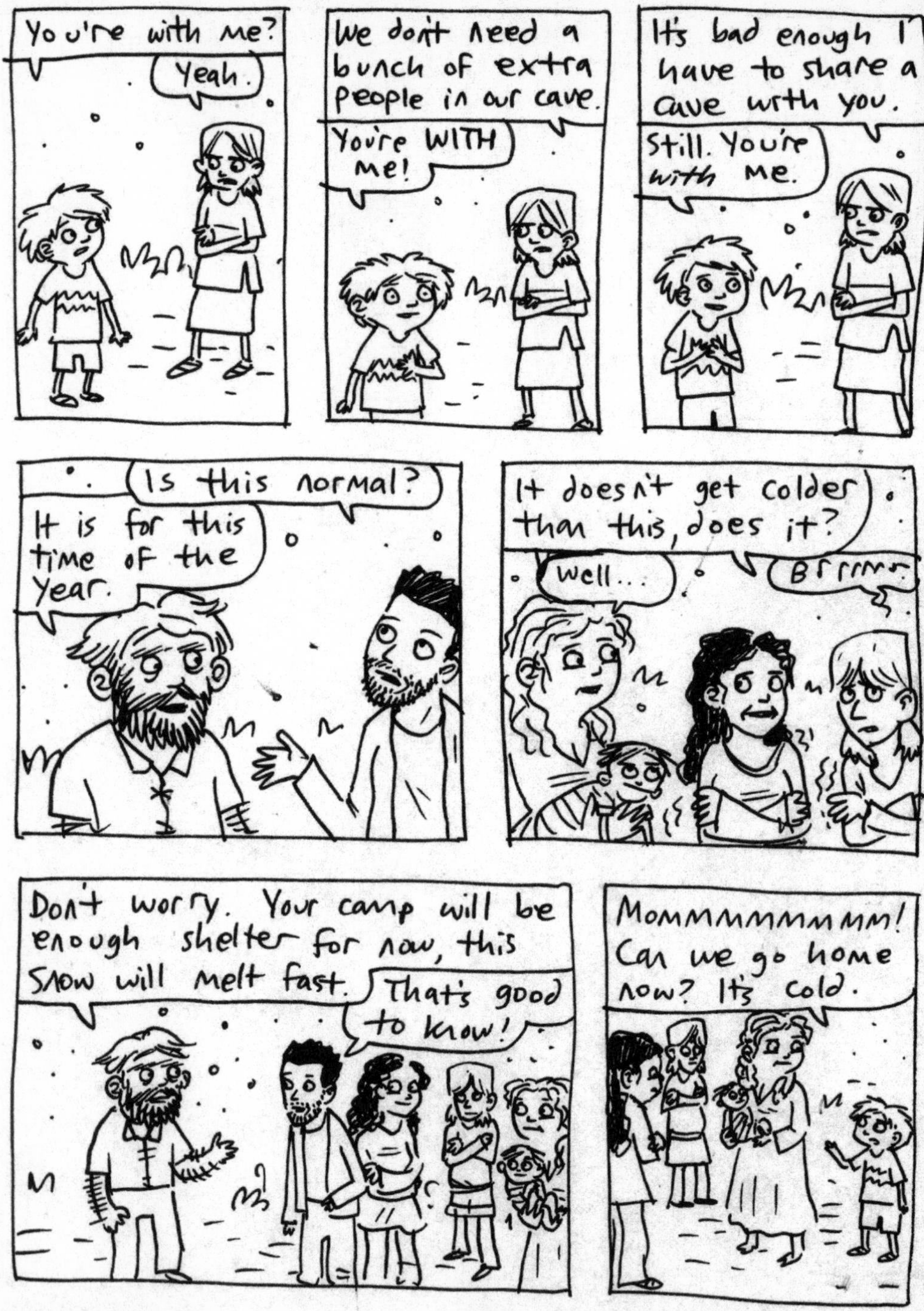
You're with me?
Yeah.
We don't need a bunch of extra people in our cave.
You're WITH me!
It's bad enough I have to share a cave with you.
Still. You're with me.
Is this normal?
It is for this time of the year.
It doesn't get colder than this, does it?
Well...
Brrrrr.
Don't worry. Your camp will be enough shelter for now, this snow will melt fast.
That's good to know!
MOMMMMMMMM! Can we go home now? It's cold.

ART NOT FINAL

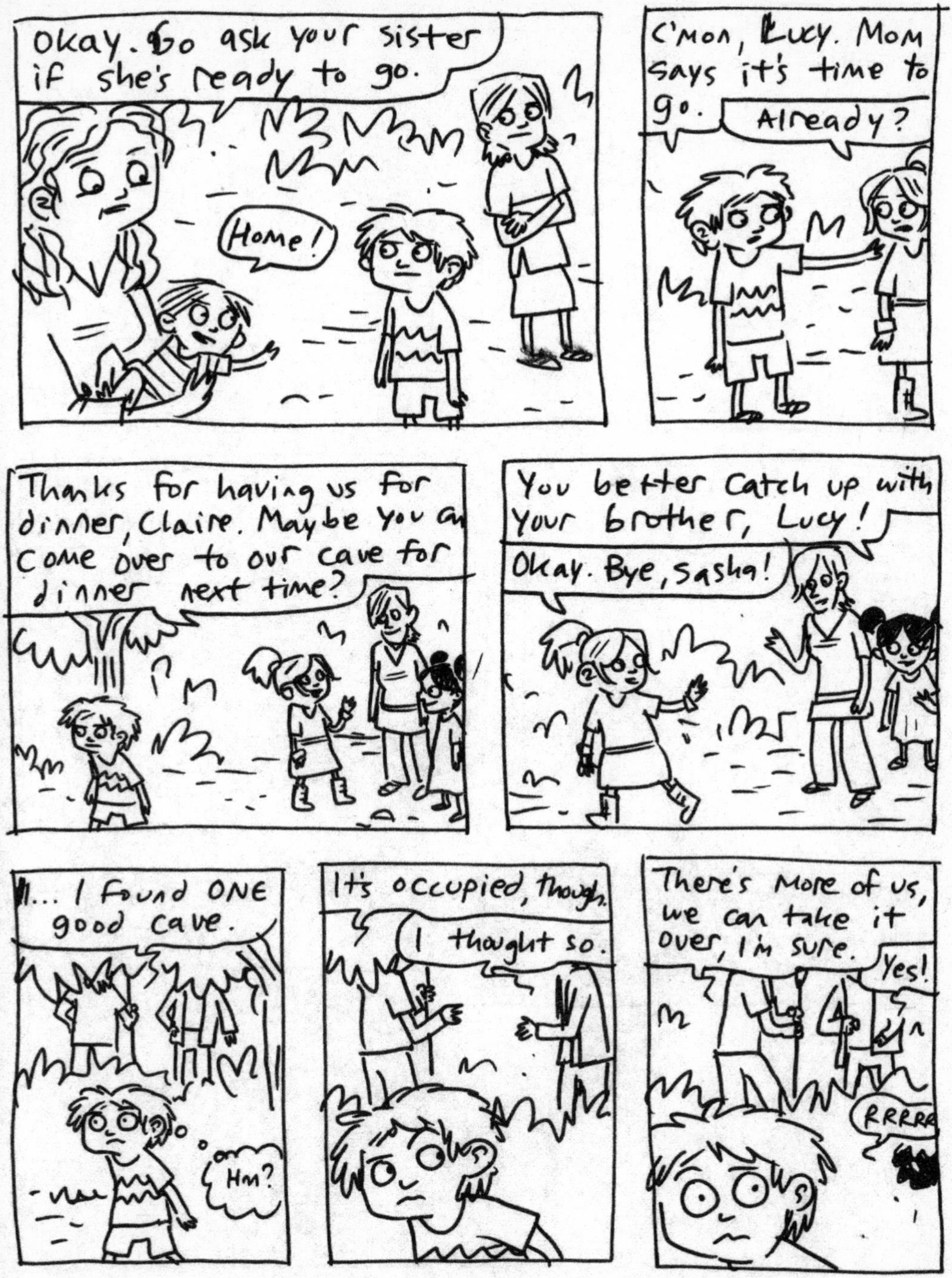
Okay. Go ask your sister if she's ready to go.
Home!
C'mon, Lucy. Mom says it's time to go.
Already?
Thanks for having us for dinner, Claire. Maybe you ca come over to our cave for dinner next time?
You better catch up with your brother, Lucy!
Okay. Bye, Sasha!
... I found ONE good cave.
Hm?
It's occupied, though.
I thought so.
There's more of us, we can take it over, I'm sure.
Yes!
RRRRR

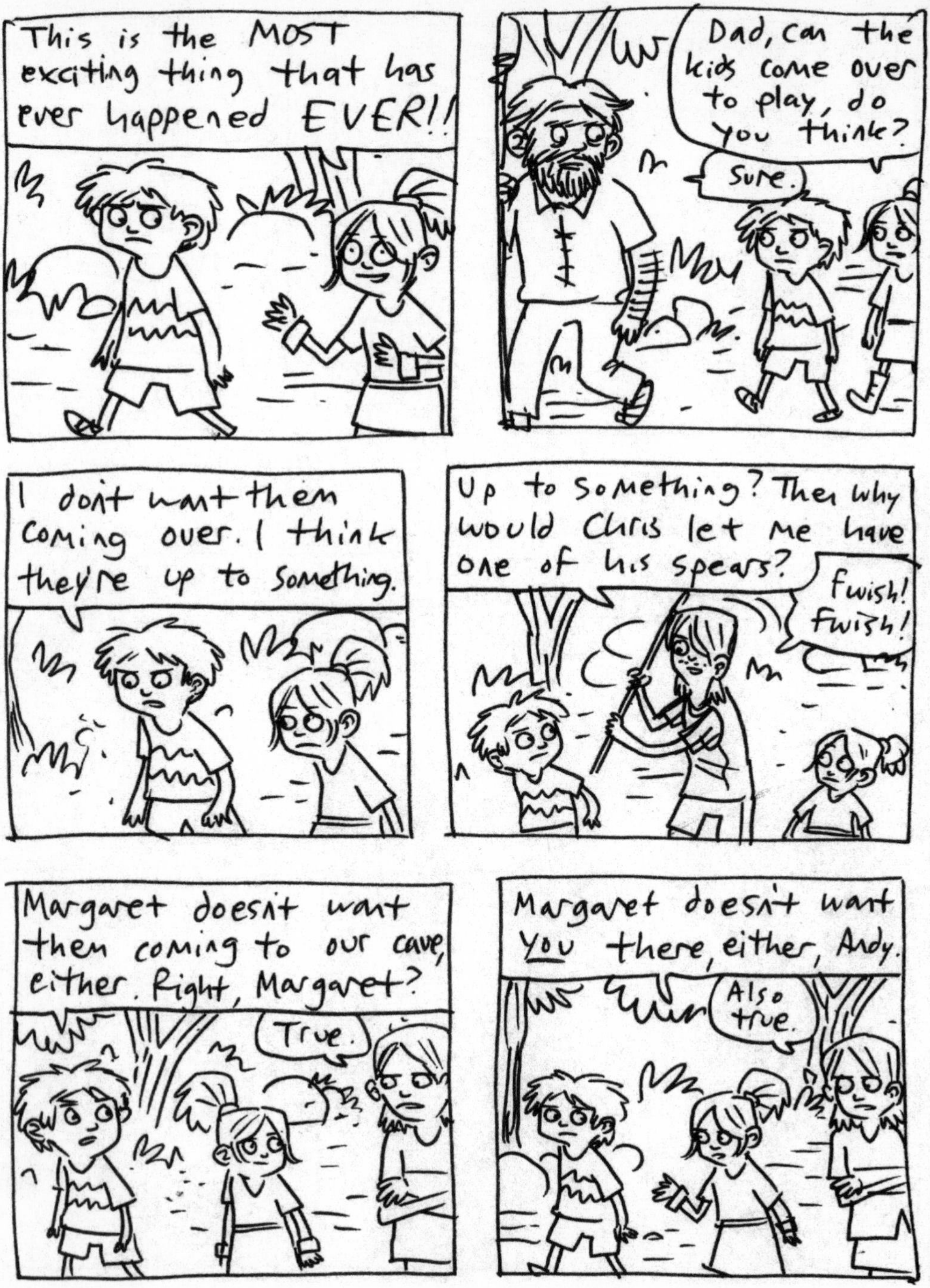
This is the MOST exciting thing that has ever happened EVER!!
Dad, can the kids come over to play, do you think?
Sure.
I don't want them coming over. I think they're up to something.
Up to something? Then why would Chris let me have one of his spears?
Fwish! Fwish!
Margaret doesn't want them coming to our cave, either. Right, Margaret?
True.
Margaret doesn't want YOU there, either, Andy.
Also true.

ART NOT FINAL

I think they're really nice, Andy. You just need to get to know them!
Peepul!
Meeting new people could be great for us, Andy. With a bigger group, it'll be easier to hunt!
Yeah, and now I'll never get to go.
Maybe we'll have more babysitting help, too.
I wonder if they can show us how to make some new tools.
I wonder if they'll kick us out of our own cave.
I can't wait for tomorrow, Mom!
Time for bed, Andy.
You won't like them either, Tiny.
Mreow?

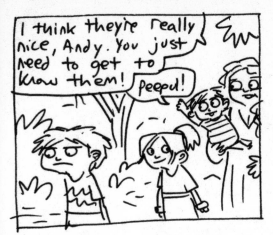

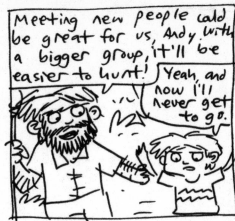

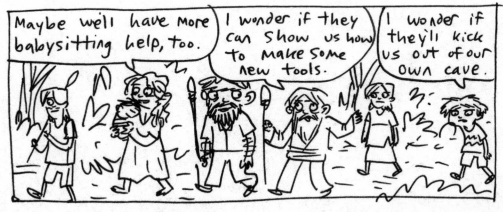

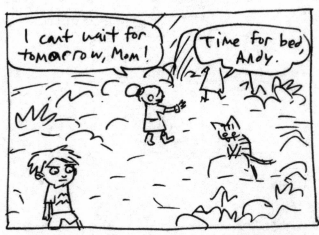

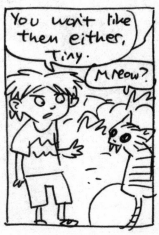

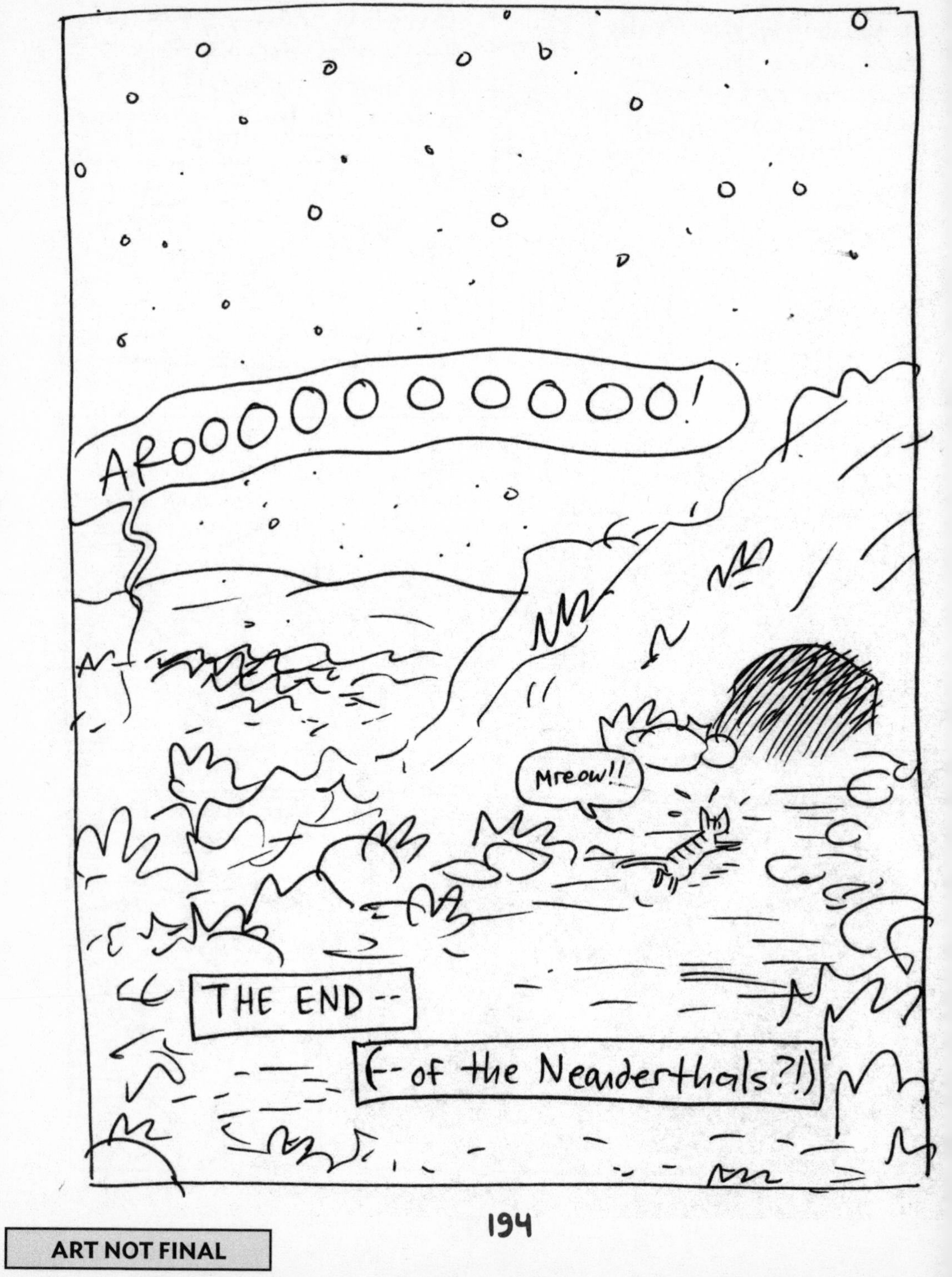
AROOOOOOOOOOOO!
Mreow!!
THE END--
(--of the Neanderthals?!)

ART NOT FINAL

FORTY THOUSAND YEARS LATER...
(TODAY)

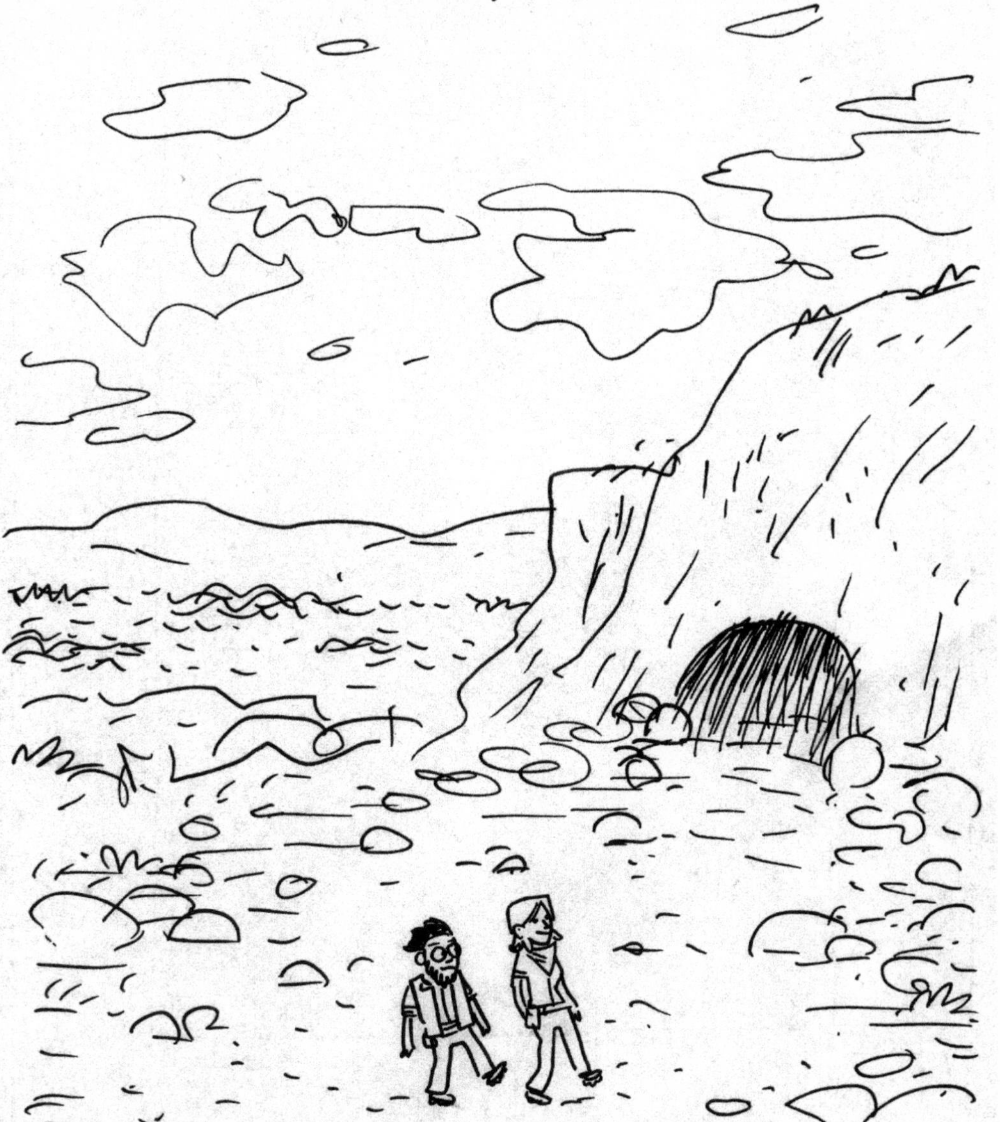

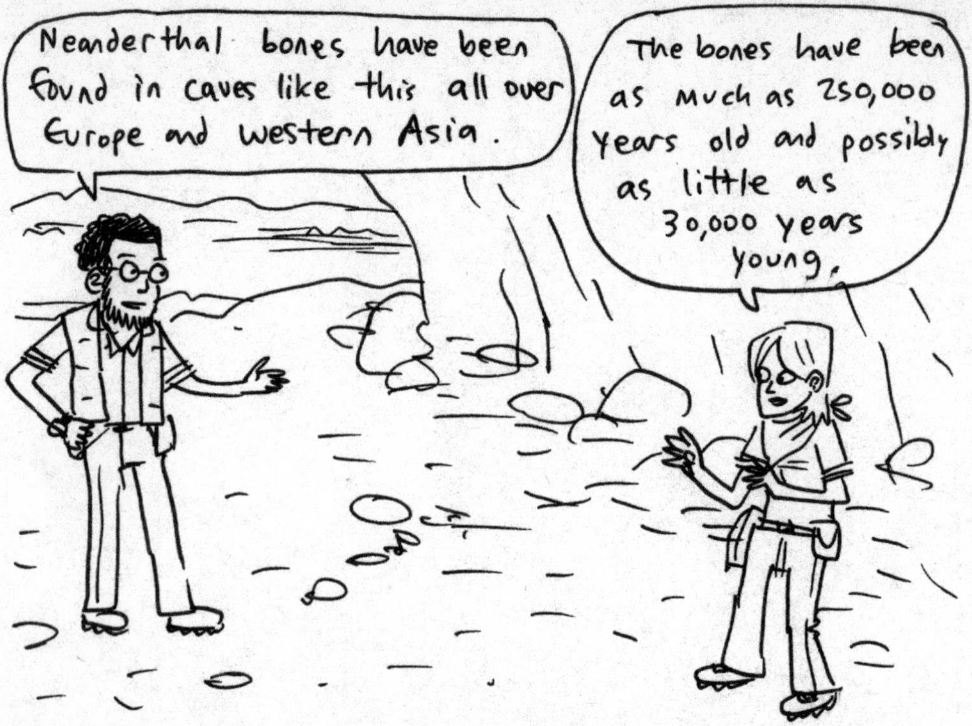
Neanderthal bones have been found in caves like this all over Europe and western Asia.
The bones have been as much as 250,000 years old and possibly as little as 30,000 years young.

Some of the first Neanderthal fossils were found in Germany in 1856.

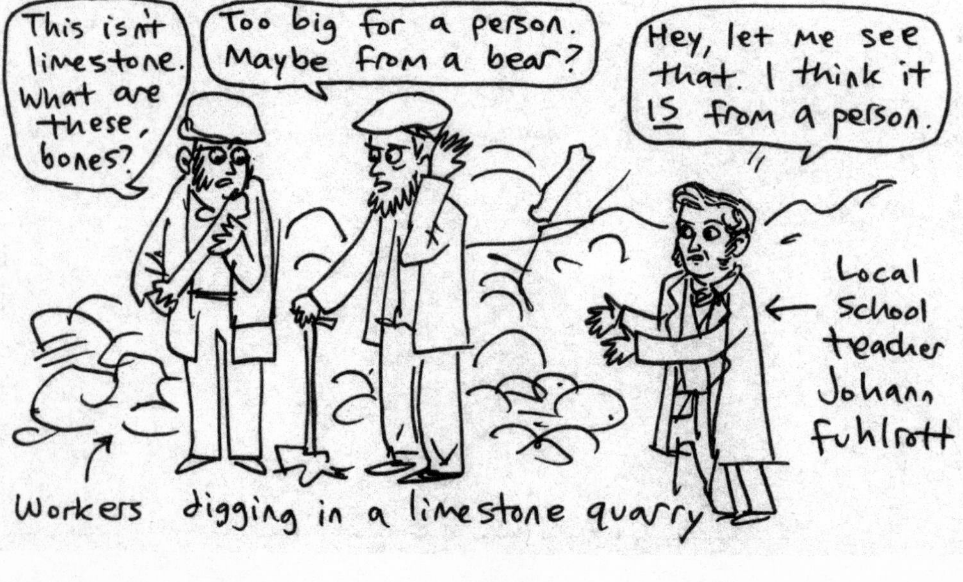
This isn't limestone. What are these, bones?
Too big for a person. Maybe from a bear?
Hey, let me see that. I think it IS from a person.
Local School teacher Johann Fuhlrott
Workers digging in a limestone quarry

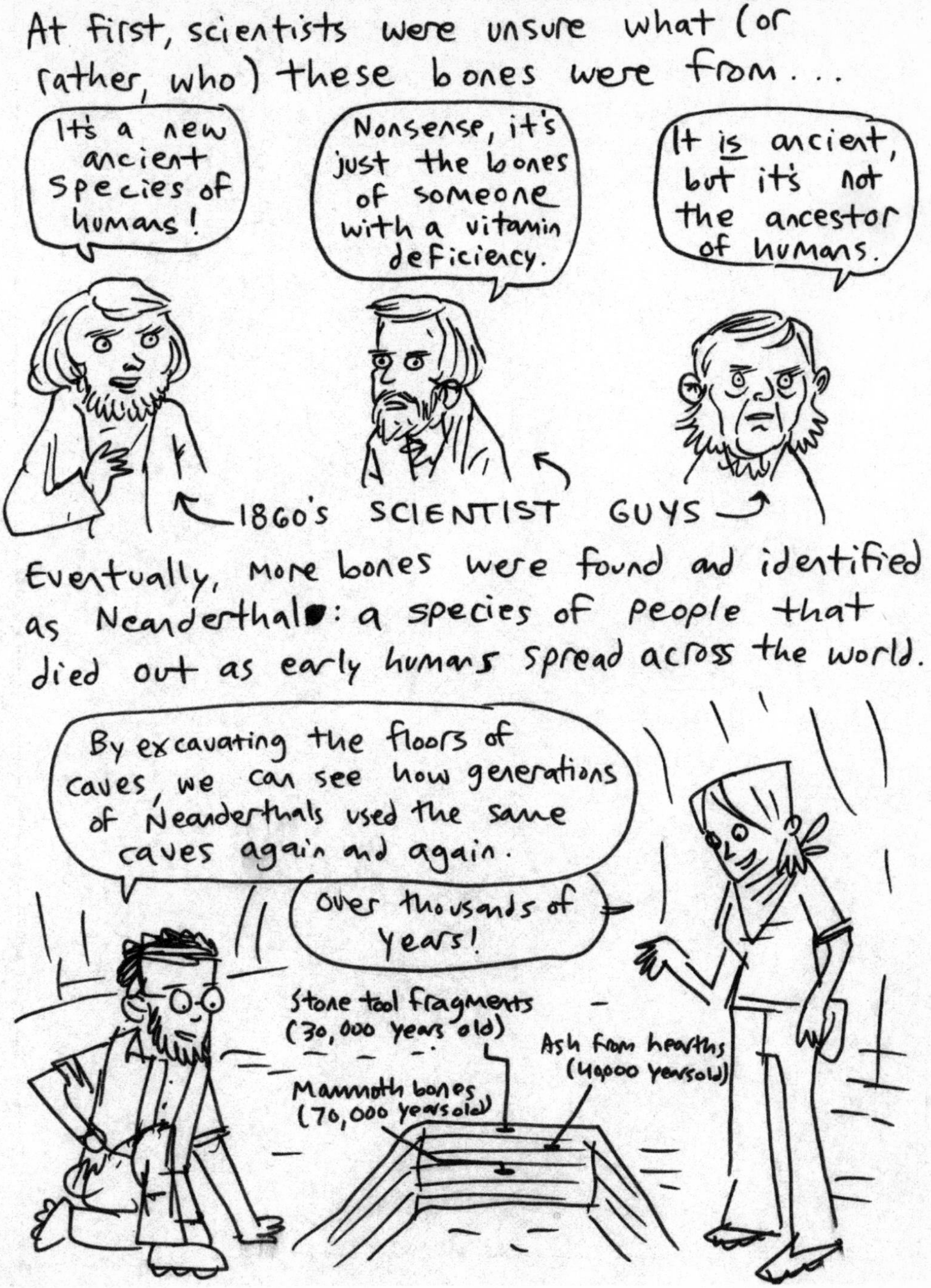
At first, scientists were unsure what (or rather, who) these bones were from...
It's a new ancient species of humans!
Nonsense, it's just the bones of someone with a vitamin deficiency.
It is ancient, but it's not the ancestor of humans.
1860's SCIENTIST GUYS
Eventually, more bones were found and identified as Neanderthals: a species of people that died out as early humans spread across the world.
By excavating the floors of caves, we can see how generations of Neanderthals used the same caves again and again.
Over thousands of years!
Stone tool fragments (30,000 years old)
Ash from hearths (40,000 years old)
Mammoth bones (70,000 years old)

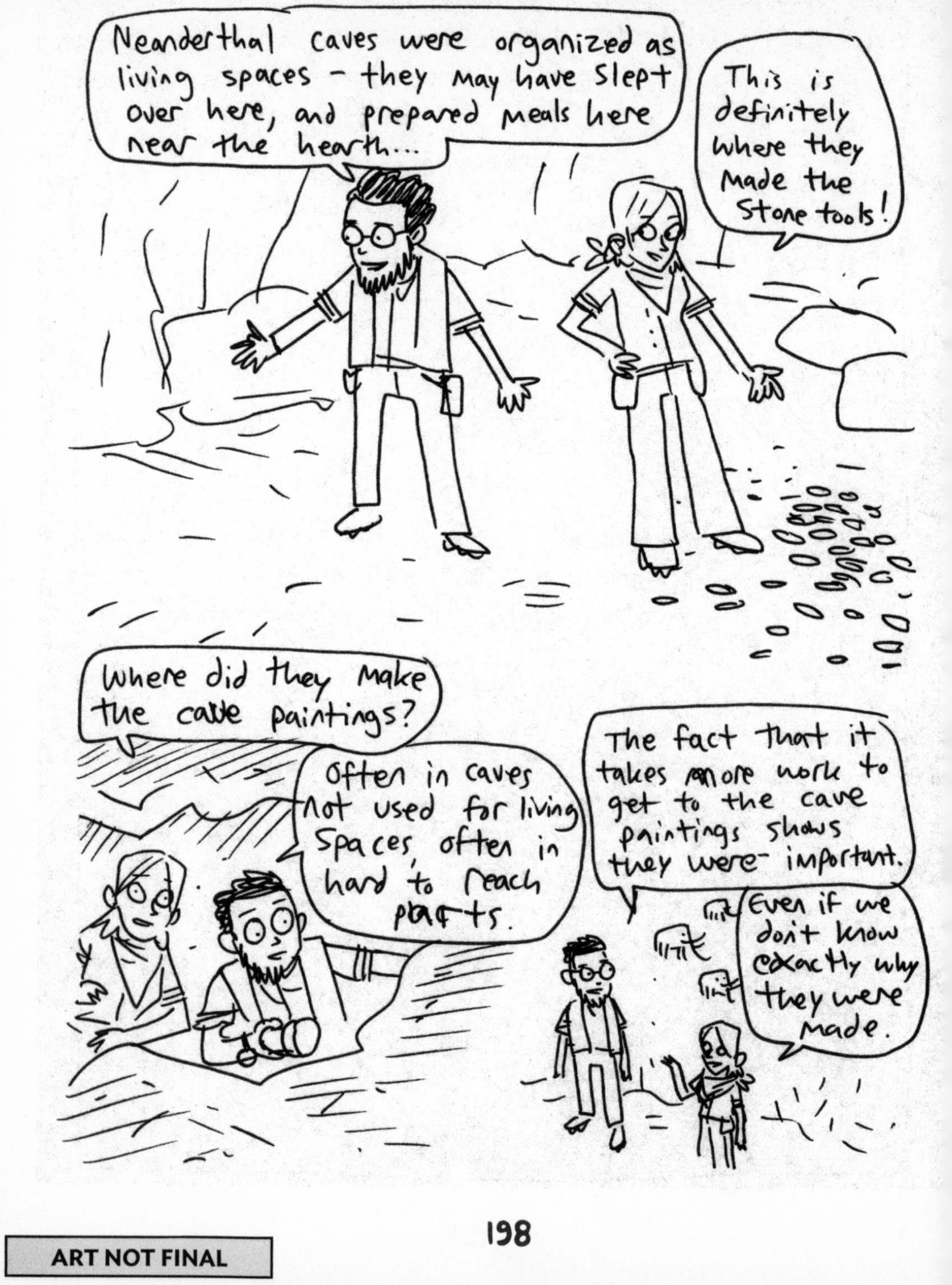
Neanderthal caves were organized as living spaces - they may have slept over here, and prepared meals here near the hearth...
This is definitely where they made the stone tools!
Where did they make the cave paintings?
Often in caves not used for living spaces, often in hard to reach parts.
The fact that it takes more work to get to the cave paintings shows they were important.
Even if we don't know exactly why they were made.

ART NOT FINAL

Caves were chosen based on a number of factors...

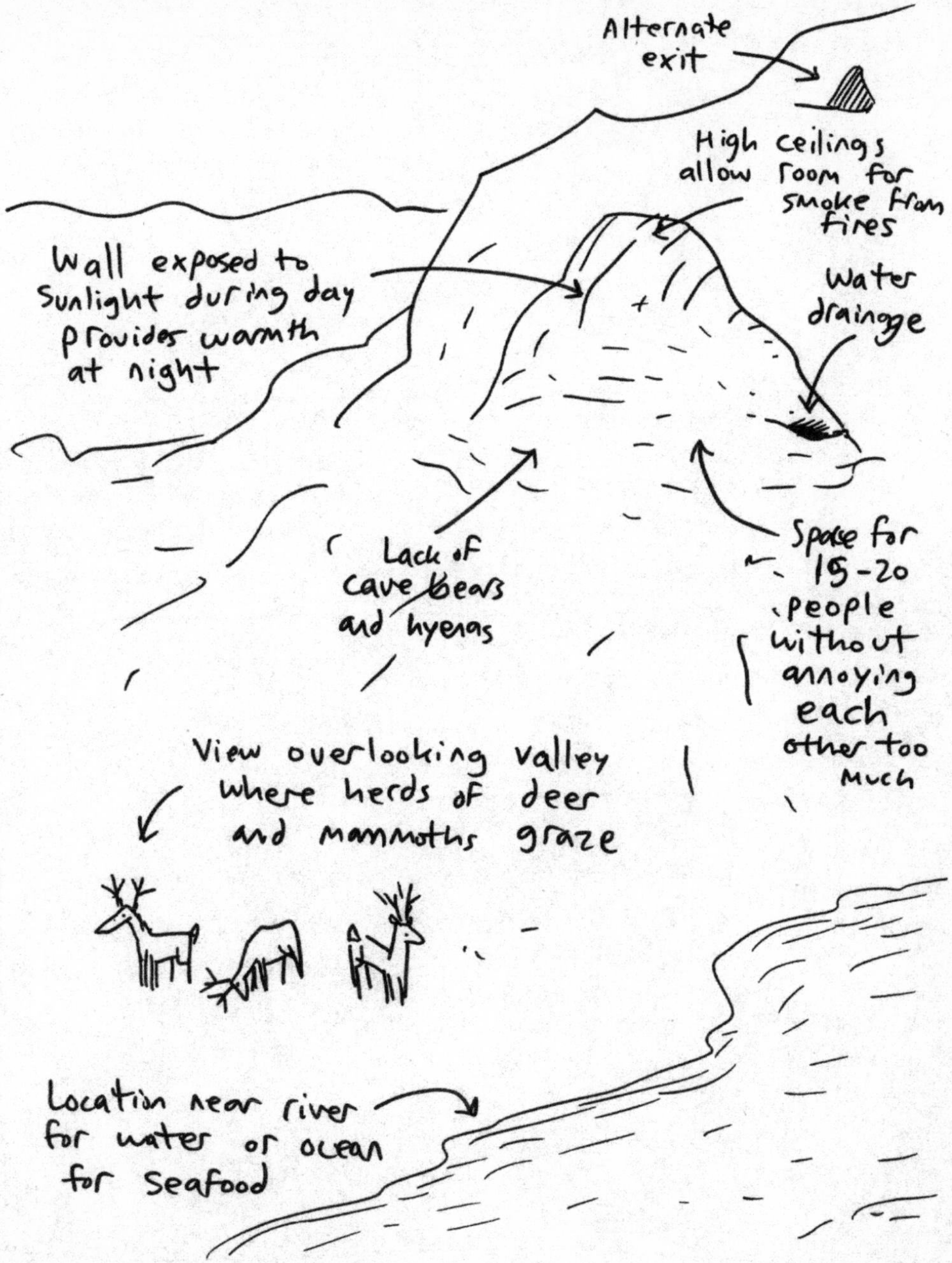
Alternate exit
High ceilings allow room for smoke from fires
Wall exposed to sunlight during day provides warmth at night
Water drainage
Lack of cave bears and hyenas
Space for 15-20 people without annoying each other too much
View overlooking valley where herds of deer and mammoths graze
Location near river for water or ocean for seafood

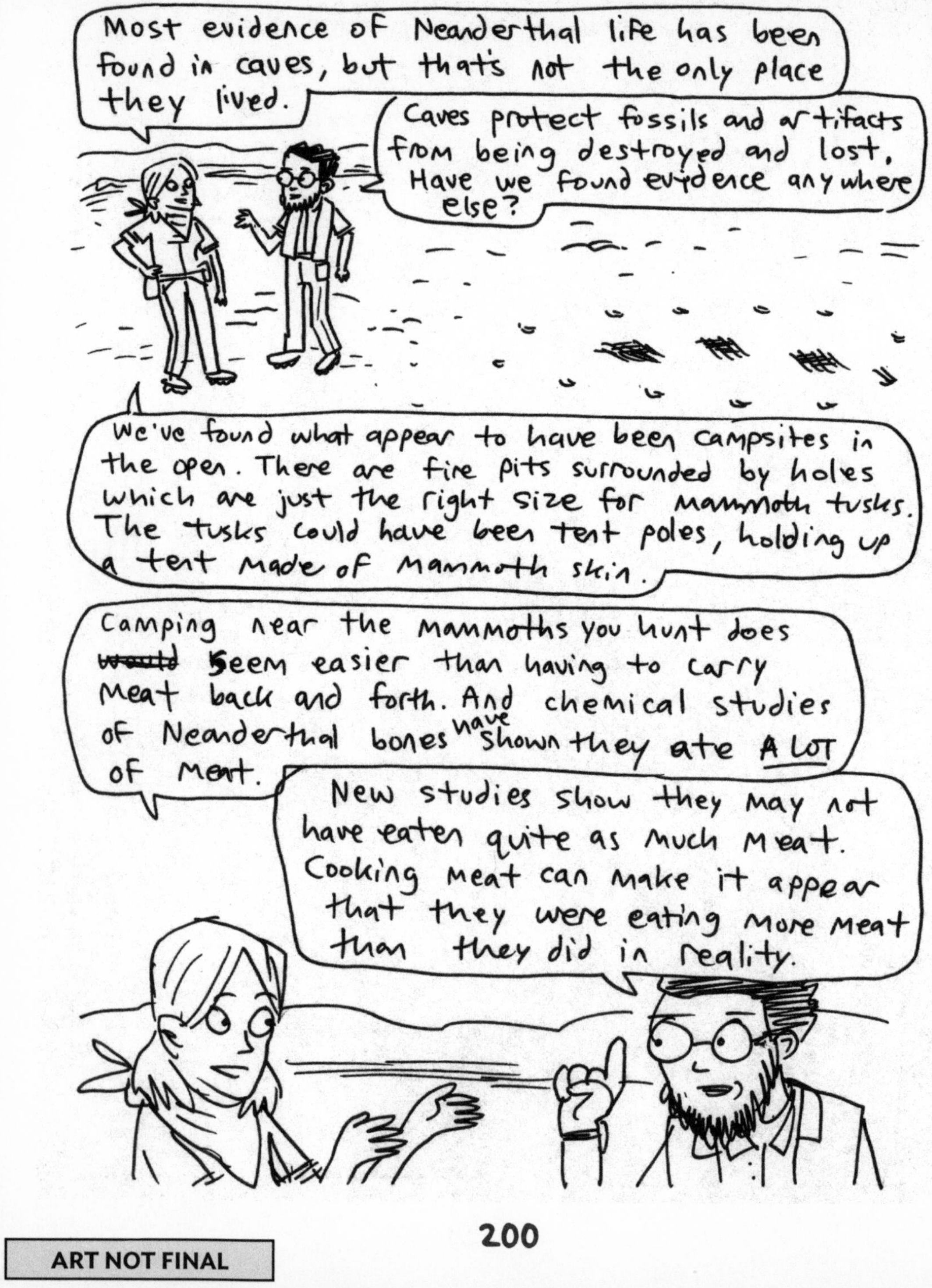
Most evidence of Neanderthal life has been found in caves, but that's not the only place they lived.
Caves protect fossils and artifacts from being destroyed and lost. Have we found evidence anywhere else?
We've found what appear to have been campsites in the open. There are fire pits surrounded by holes which are just the right size for mammoth tusks. The tusks could have been tent poles, holding up a tent made of mammoth skin.
Camping near the mammoths you hunt does ~~would~~ seem easier than having to carry meat back and forth. And chemical studies of Neanderthal bones have shown they ate A LOT of meat.
New studies show they may not have eaten quite as much meat. Cooking meat can make it appear that they were eating more meat than they did in reality.

ART NOT FINAL

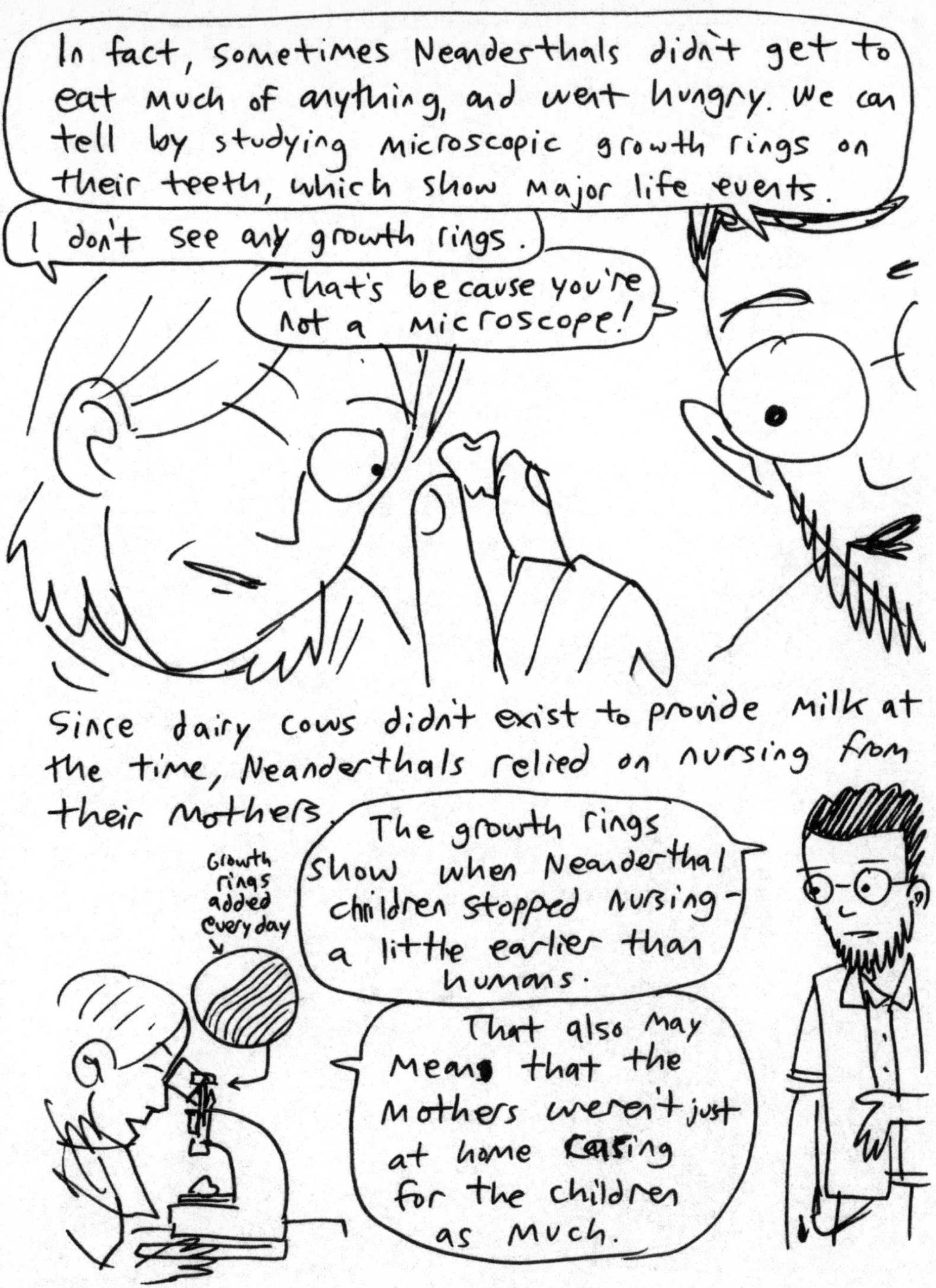

In fact, sometimes Neanderthals didn't get to eat much of anything, and went hungry. We can tell by studying microscopic growth rings on their teeth, which show major life events.
I don't see any growth rings.
That's because you're not a microscope!
Since dairy cows didn't exist to provide milk at the time, Neanderthals relied on nursing from their mothers.
The growth rings show when Neanderthal children stopped nursing—a little earlier than humans.
Growth rings added every day
That also may means that the mothers weren't just at home caring for the children as much.

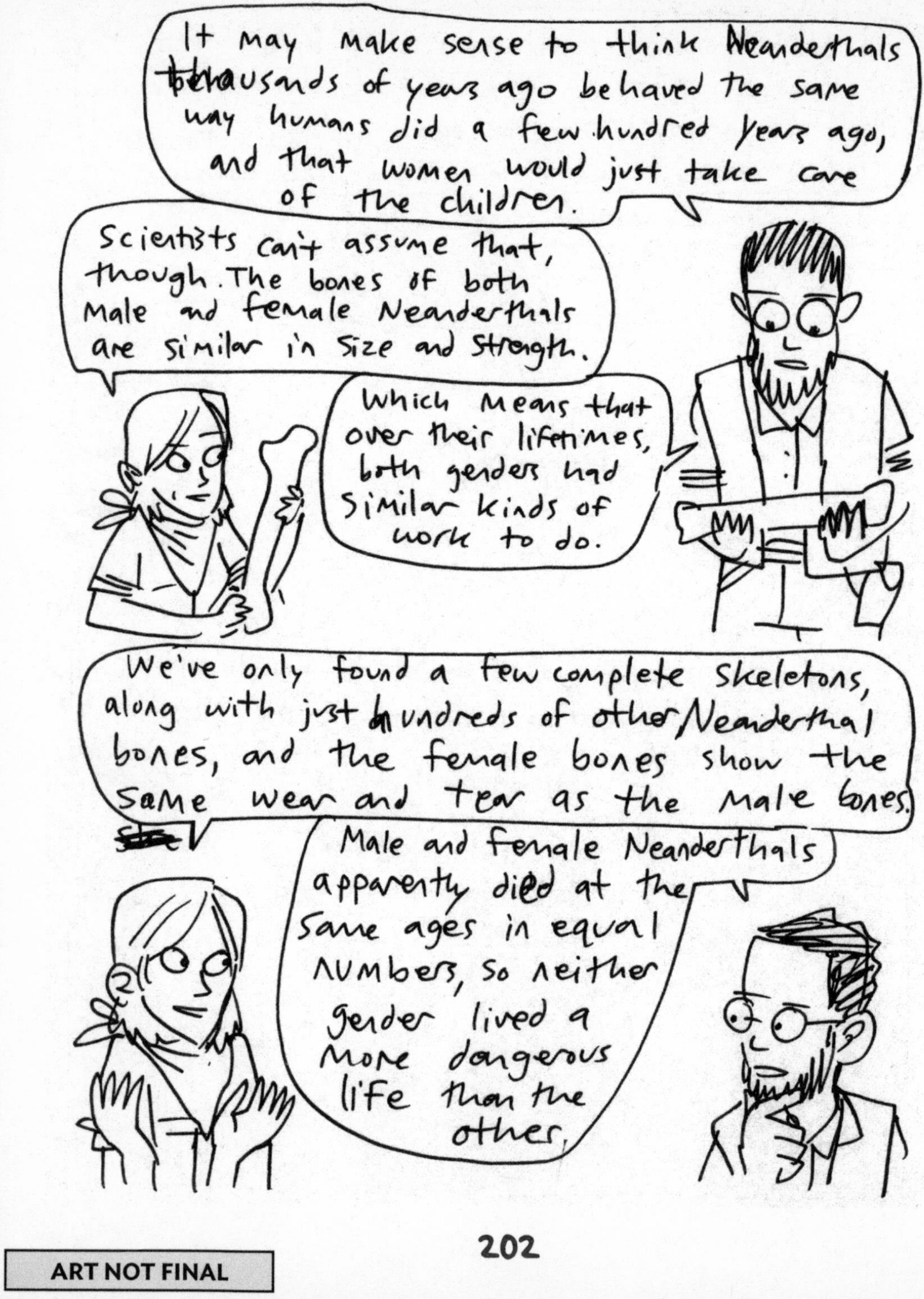
It may make sense to think Neanderthals thousands of years ago behaved the same way humans did a few hundred years ago, and that women would just take care of the children.
Scientists can't assume that, though. The bones of both male and female Neanderthals are similar in size and strength.
Which means that over their lifetimes, both genders had similar kinds of work to do.
We've only found a few complete skeletons, along with just hundreds of other Neanderthal bones, and the female bones show the same wear and tear as the male bones.
Male and female Neanderthals apparently died at the same ages in equal numbers, so neither gender lived a more dangerous life than the other.

ART NOT FINAL

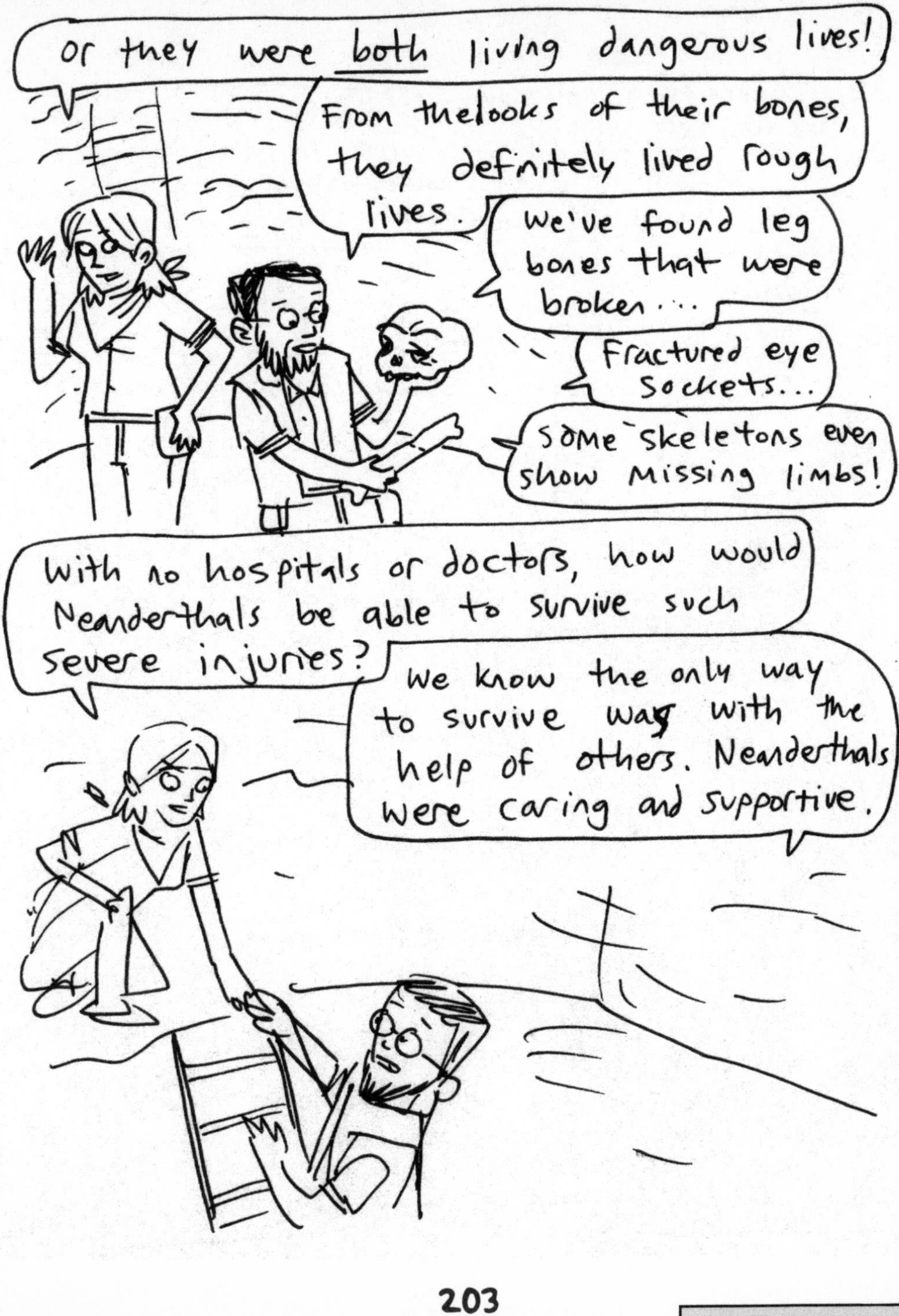
Or they were both living dangerous lives!
From thelooks of their bones, they definitely lived rough lives.
We've found leg bones that were broken....
Fractured eye sockets...
Some skeletons even show missing limbs!
With no hospitals or doctors, how would Neanderthals be able to survive such severe injuries?
We know the only way to survive was with the help of others. Neanderthals were caring and supportive.

ART NOT FINAL

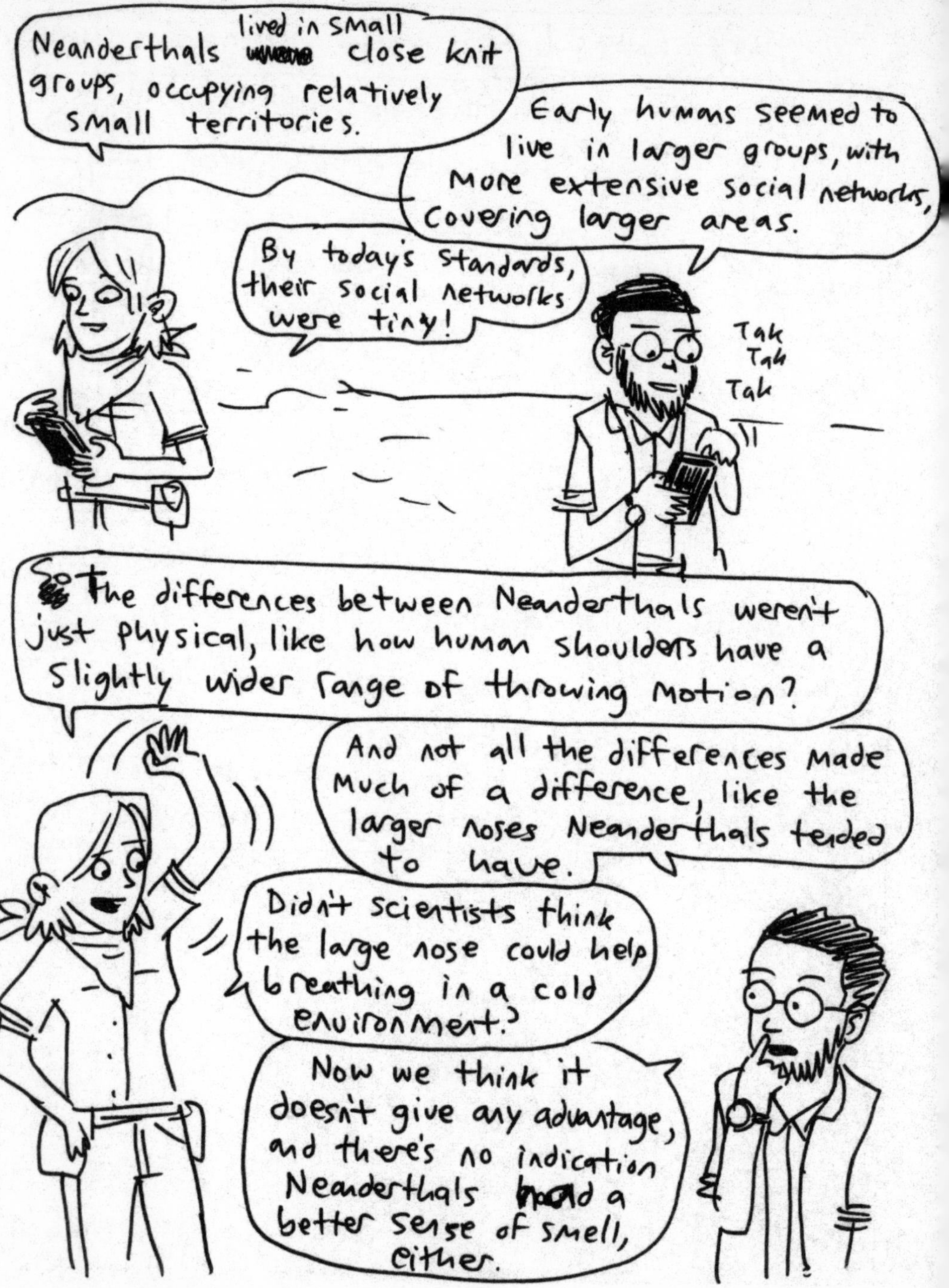
Neanderthals lived in small close knit groups, occupying relatively small territories.
Early humans seemed to live in larger groups, with more extensive social networks, covering larger areas.
By today's standards, their social networks were tiny!
Tak Tak Tak
So the differences between Neanderthals weren't just physical, like how human shoulders have a slightly wider range of throwing motion?
And not all the differences made much of a difference, like the larger noses Neanderthals tended to have.
Didn't scientists think the large nose could help breathing in a cold environment?
Now we think it doesn't give any advantage, and there's no indication Neanderthals had a better sense of smell, either.

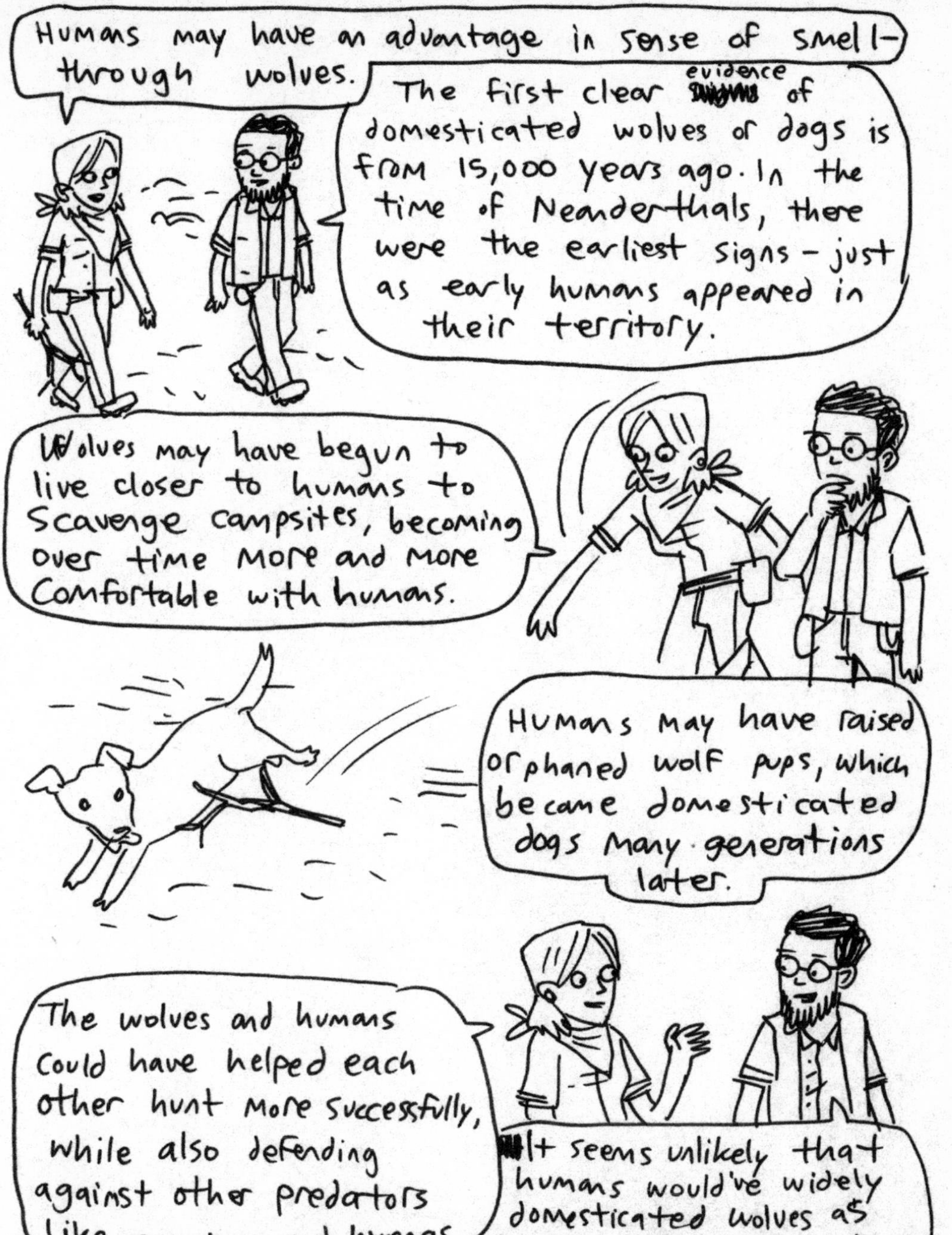
Humans may have an advantage in sense of smell—through wolves.
The first clear evidence of domesticated wolves or dogs is from 15,000 years ago. In the time of Neanderthals, there were the earliest signs—just as early humans appeared in their territory.
Wolves may have begun to live closer to humans to scavenge campsites, becoming over time more and more comfortable with humans.
Humans may have raised orphaned wolf pups, which became domesticated dogs many generations later.
The wolves and humans could have helped each other hunt more successfully, while also defending against other predators like cave lions and hyenas.
It seems unlikely that humans would've widely domesticated wolves as long as 40,000 years ago, though.

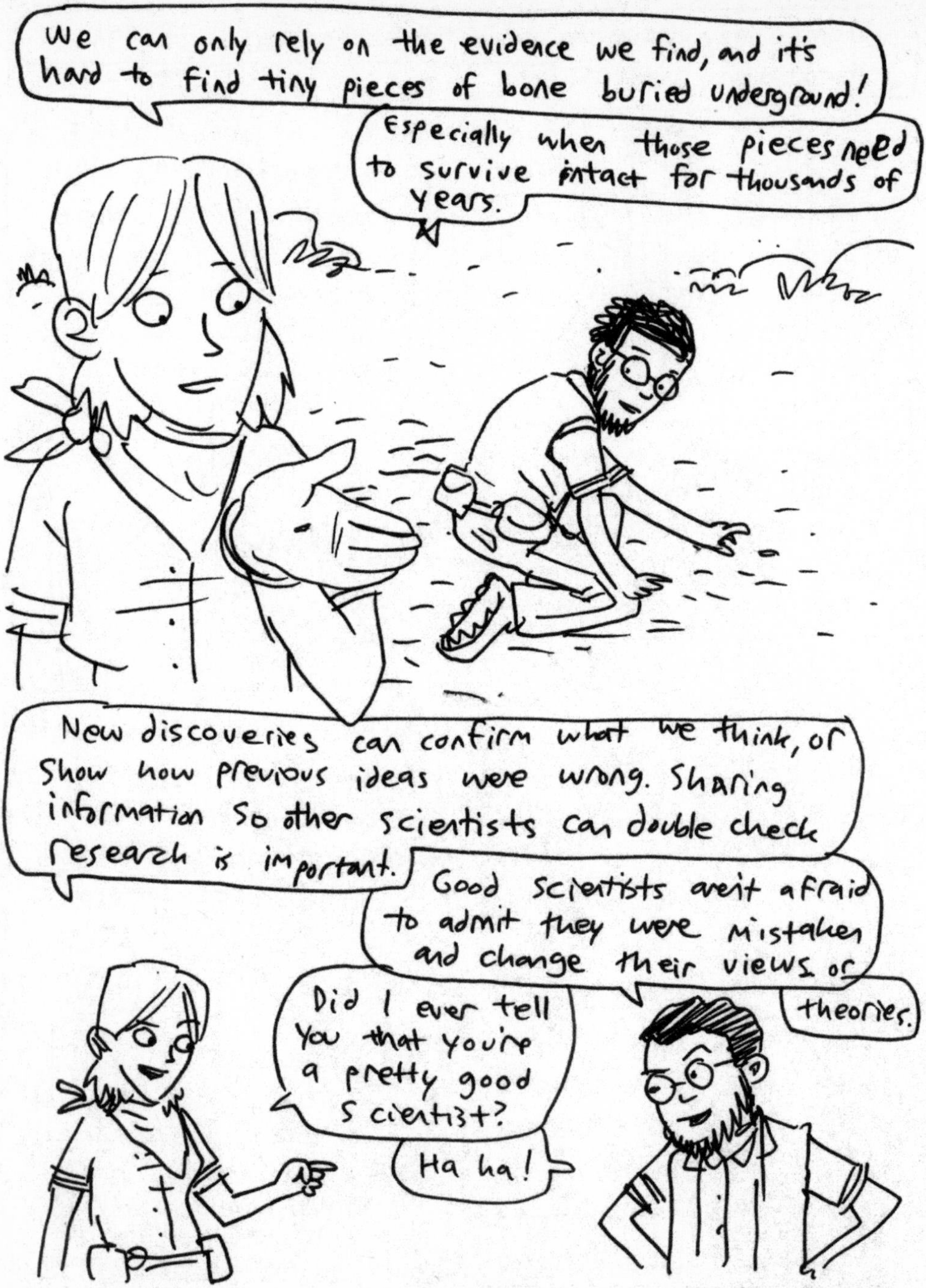
We can only rely on the evidence we find, and it's hard to find tiny pieces of bone buried underground!
Especially when those pieces need to survive intact for thousands of years.
New discoveries can confirm what we think, or show how previous ideas were wrong. Sharing information so other scientists can double check research is important.
Good scientists aren't afraid to admit they were mistaken and change their views or theories.
Did I ever tell you that you're a pretty good scientist?
Ha ha!

A theory is an explanation of some aspect of the world, based on facts that have been confirmed by experiment and observation. As more evidence is gathered, new explanations can be needed.

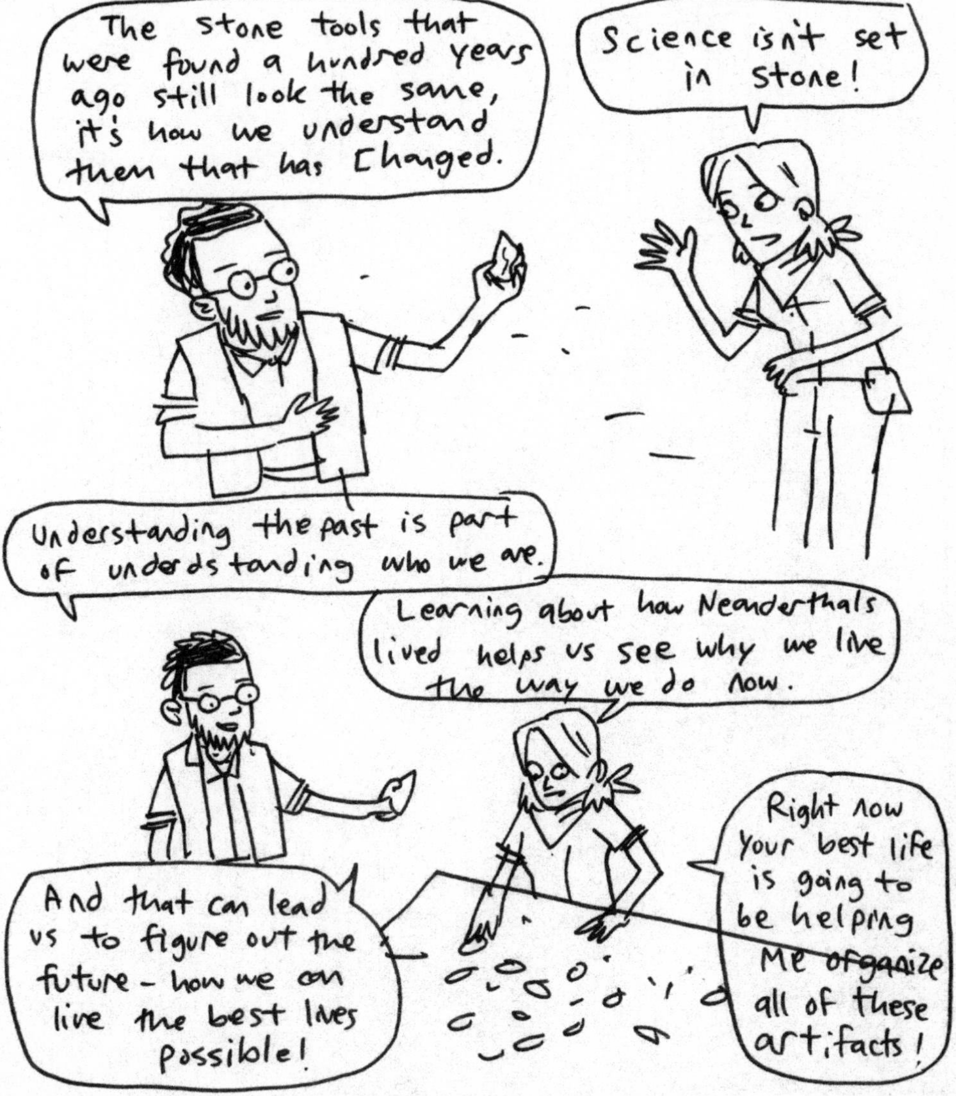

The stone tools that were found a hundred years ago still look the same, it's how we understand them that has changed.
Science isn't set in stone!
Understanding the past is part of underdstanding who we are.
Learning about how Neanderthals lived helps us see why we live the way we do now.
And that can lead us to figure out the future - how we can live the best lives possible!
Right now your best life is going to be helping me organize all of these artifacts!

Some paleontologists work at museums. These are just a few museums you can visit to learn more about Neanderthals and early humans!

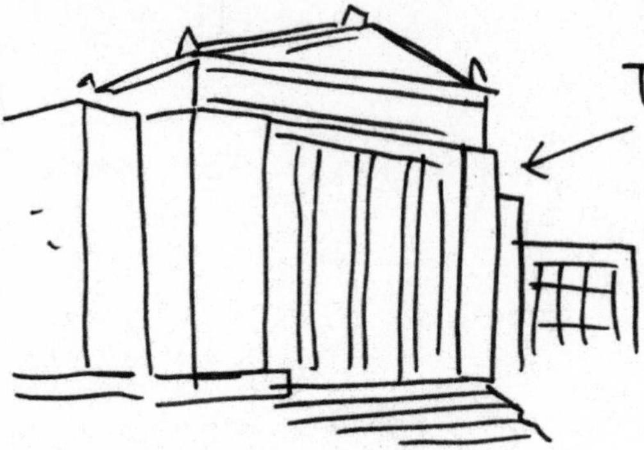

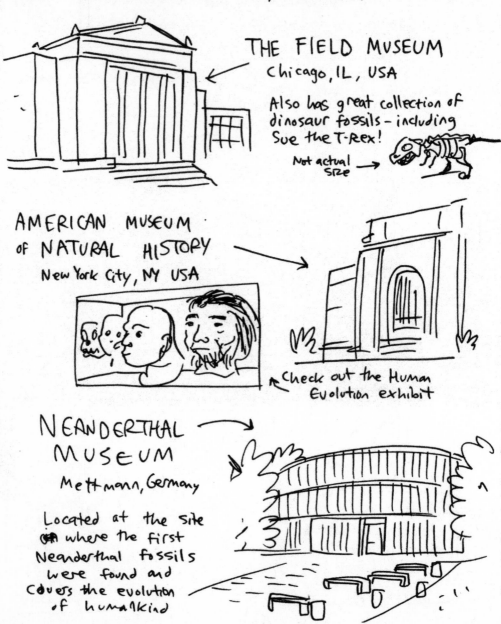

THE FIELD MUSEUM

Chicago, IL, USA

Also has great collection of dinosaur fossils - including Sue the T-Rex!

Not actual size →

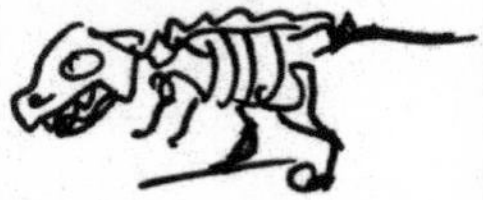

AMERICAN MUSEUM OF NATURAL HISTORY

New York City, NY USA

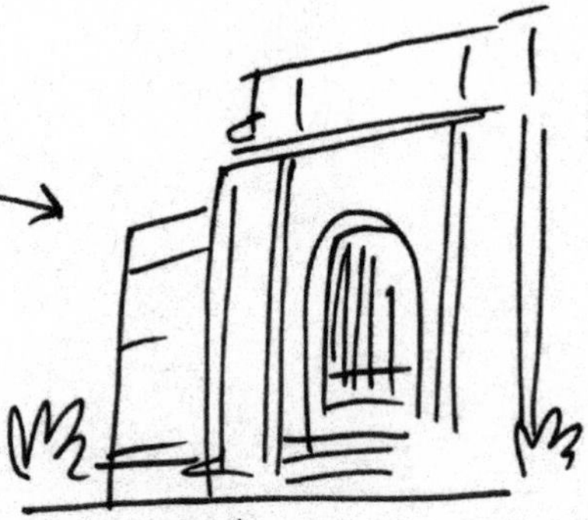

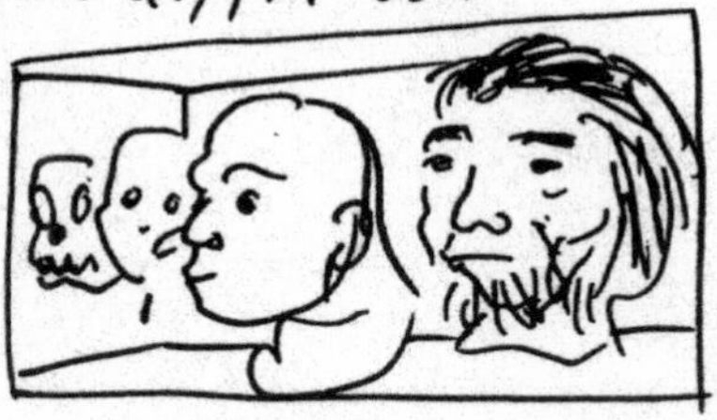

Check out the Human Evolution exhibit

NEANDERTHAL MUSEUM

Mettmann, Germany

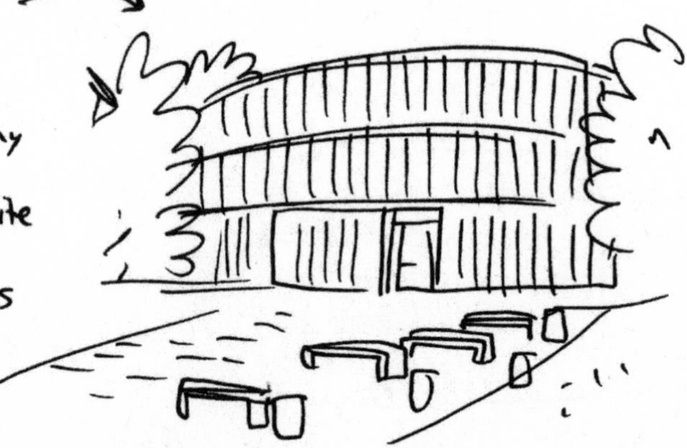

Located at the site where the first Neanderthal fossils were found and covers the evolution of humankind

A NEANDERTHAL TIMELINE*

* Dates subject to change, as new discoveries are made...

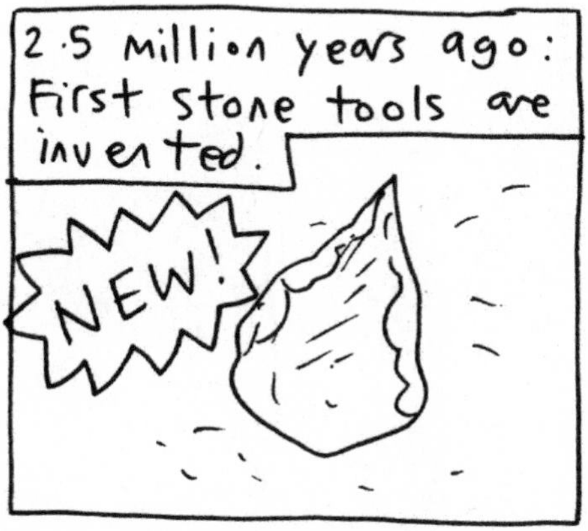
2.5 Million years ago: First stone tools are invented.
NEW!

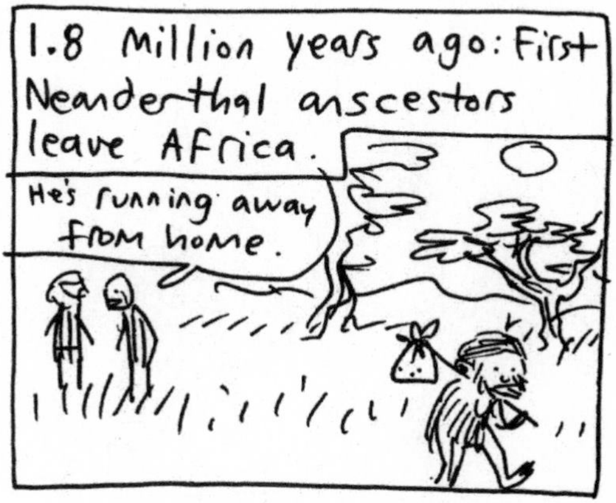
1.8 Million years ago: First Neanderthal anscestors leave Africa.
He's running away from home.

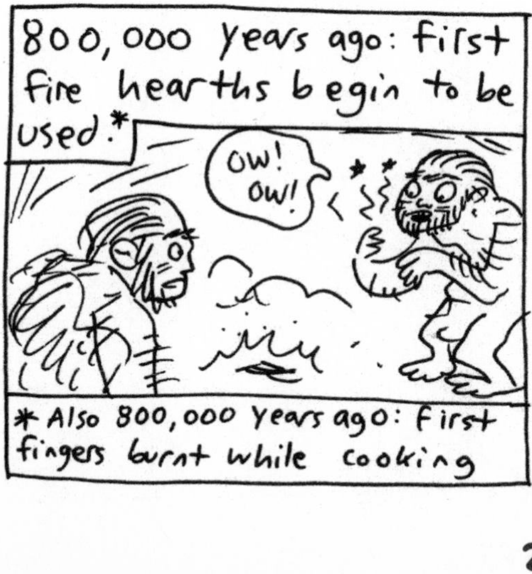
800,000 years ago: first fire hearths begin to be used.*
OW! OW!
* Also 800,000 years ago: first fingers burnt while cooking

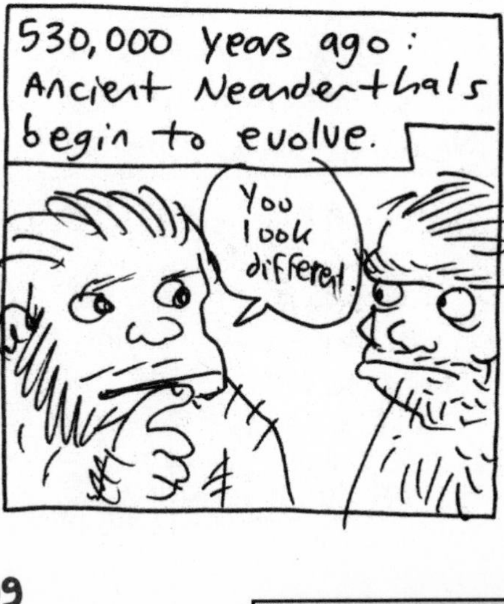
530,000 years ago: Ancient Neanderthals begin to evolve.
You look different!

500,000 years ago: First constructed shelters are built.

400,000 years ago: Hafted tools, wooden spears, and pigments are manufactured.

How do I look?

Great!

180,000 years ago: Neanderthals become a distinct species.

170,000 years ago: The earliest clothes are made.

40,-50,000 years ago: Early humans arrive in Neanderthal territory.

30-40,000 years ago: Neanderthals become extinct.

210

FACT VS. FICTION

While most of Lucy and Andy's story is based on the best of our knowledge, there are some parts that might be stretching the truth...

DID NEANDERTHALS HAVE PET CATS? No, unfortunately not. Cats weren't pets until about 5,000 years ago. But cats are fun to draw and make funny characters!

DID NEANDERTHALS LIVE IN SUCH SMALL GROUPS? Yes, but maybe not quite as small as Lucy and Andy's group. Neanderthals probably live in groups of 10-15, while early humans lived in groups of 25-30.

DID SOME NEANDERTHALS GET BAD ROCKS FOR TOOL MAKING? Yes, sometimes tool debris from poor quality stones is found near debris from good stones. Neanderthals who were just learning probably practiced on the stones of lesser quality.

211

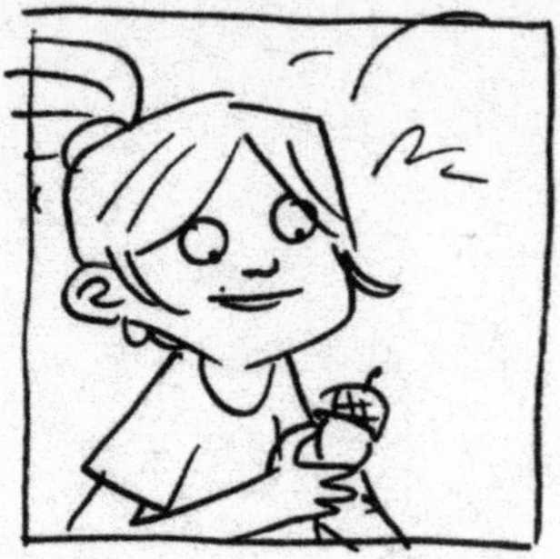

DID NEANDERTHALS EAT ACORNS? Remains found at cooking sites indicate they did. Humans have a long history of eating acorns, and you can still eat them today, with the right recipe!

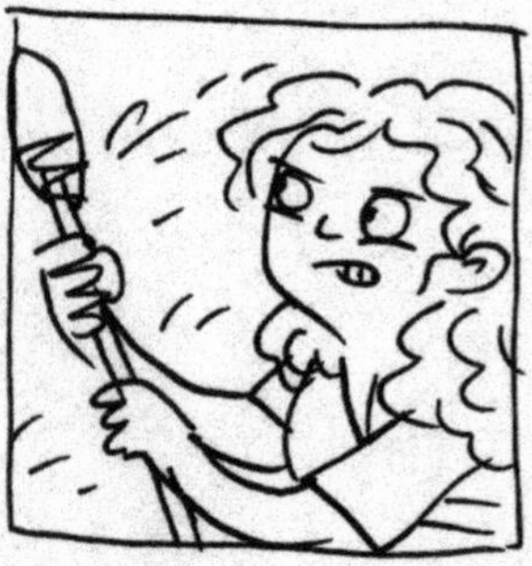

DID NEANDERTHAL WOMEN HUNT? Almost certainly. Scientists still debate on whether men hunted more, but Neanderthal women at least participated in some, if not all, hunting.

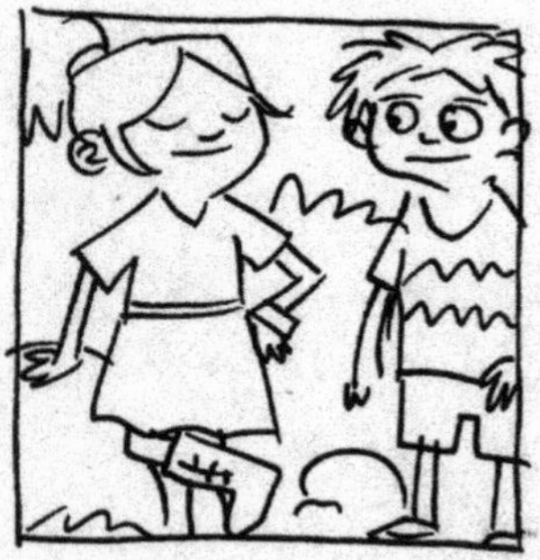

DID NEANDERTHALS HAVE GOOD FASHION SENSE? Neanderthals didn't have time to worry about style, and their clothes were simple and useful, although they may have decorated them with pigment.

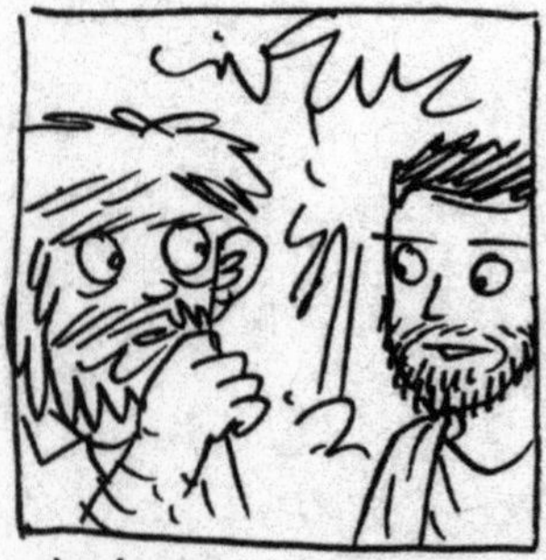

COULD NEANDERTHALS AND HUMANS TALK TO EACH OTHER? They didn't have the same language, but that wouldn't stop them from communicating. After all, people from different countries today still find ways to communicate with each other, ~~when~~ even without knowing each other's words.

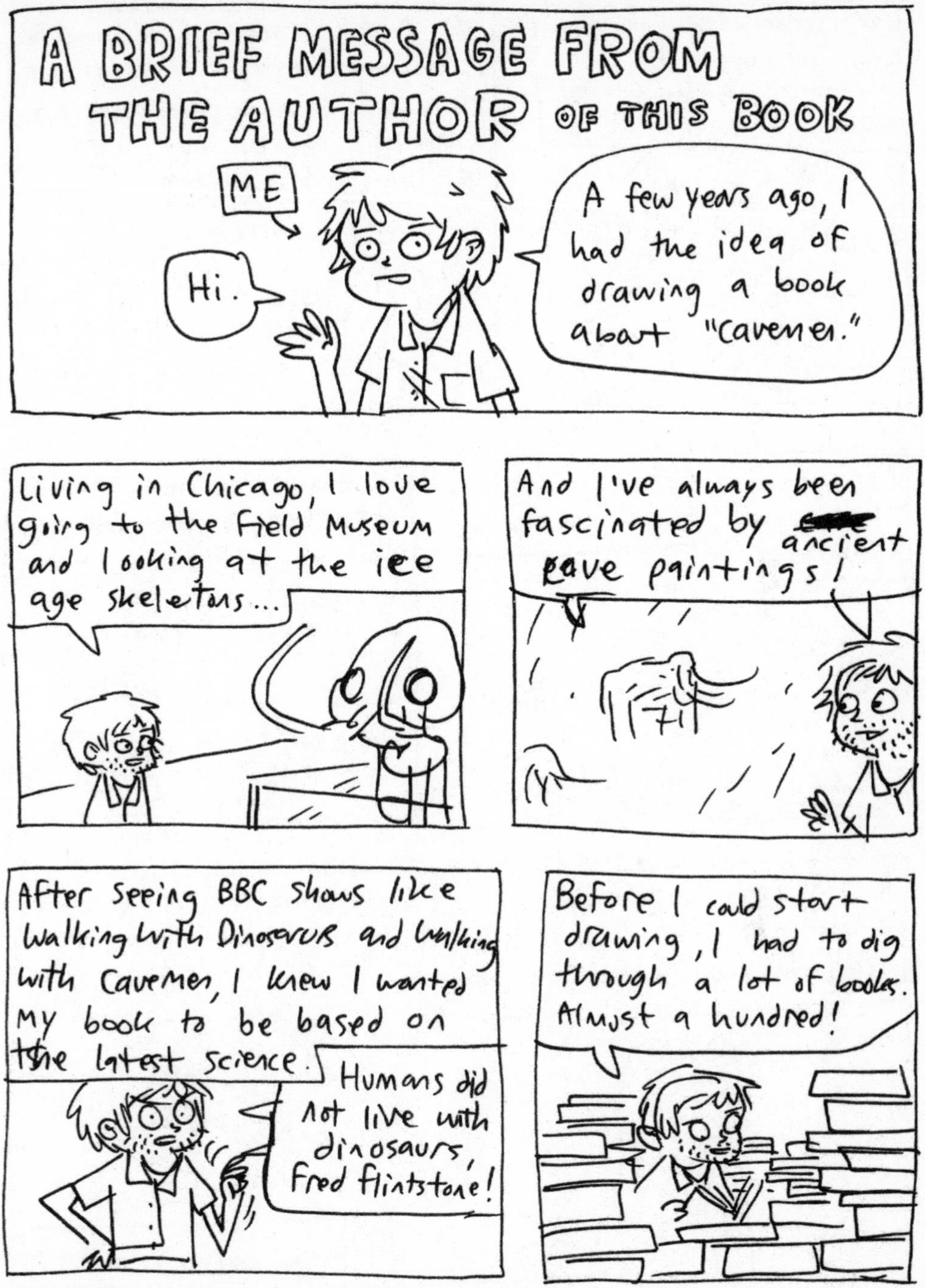
A BRIEF MESSAGE FROM THE AUTHOR OF THIS BOOK
ME
Hi.
A few years ago, I had the idea of drawing a book about "cavemen."
Living in Chicago, I love going to the Field Museum and looking at the ice age skeletons...
And I've always been fascinated by ancient cave paintings!
After seeing BBC shows like Walking With Dinosaurs and Walking with Cavemen, I knew I wanted my book to be based on the latest science.
Humans did not live with dinosaurs, Fred Flintstone!
Before I could start drawing, I had to dig through a lot of books. Almost a hundred!

ART NOT FINAL

It's interesting to see how our view of Neanderthals has changed over the years...

1941

2015

B UP The Neaversi

Neandertha

Of course, since new information is alway being gathered, our view of Neanderthals has even changed while I've been writing this book!

Another new discovery!

NEW DISCOVER

Now I have to re-draw this page that I already re-wrote?!

Someday, this book may be outdated, too, but with the help of scientists, I've tried to make it as accurate as possible.

But since this book is a made-up story, I still get to use my imagination!

Accurate? That doesn't even look like me.

Giggle

Thanks for reading!

A Brief History Of Cavemen in Books and Movies

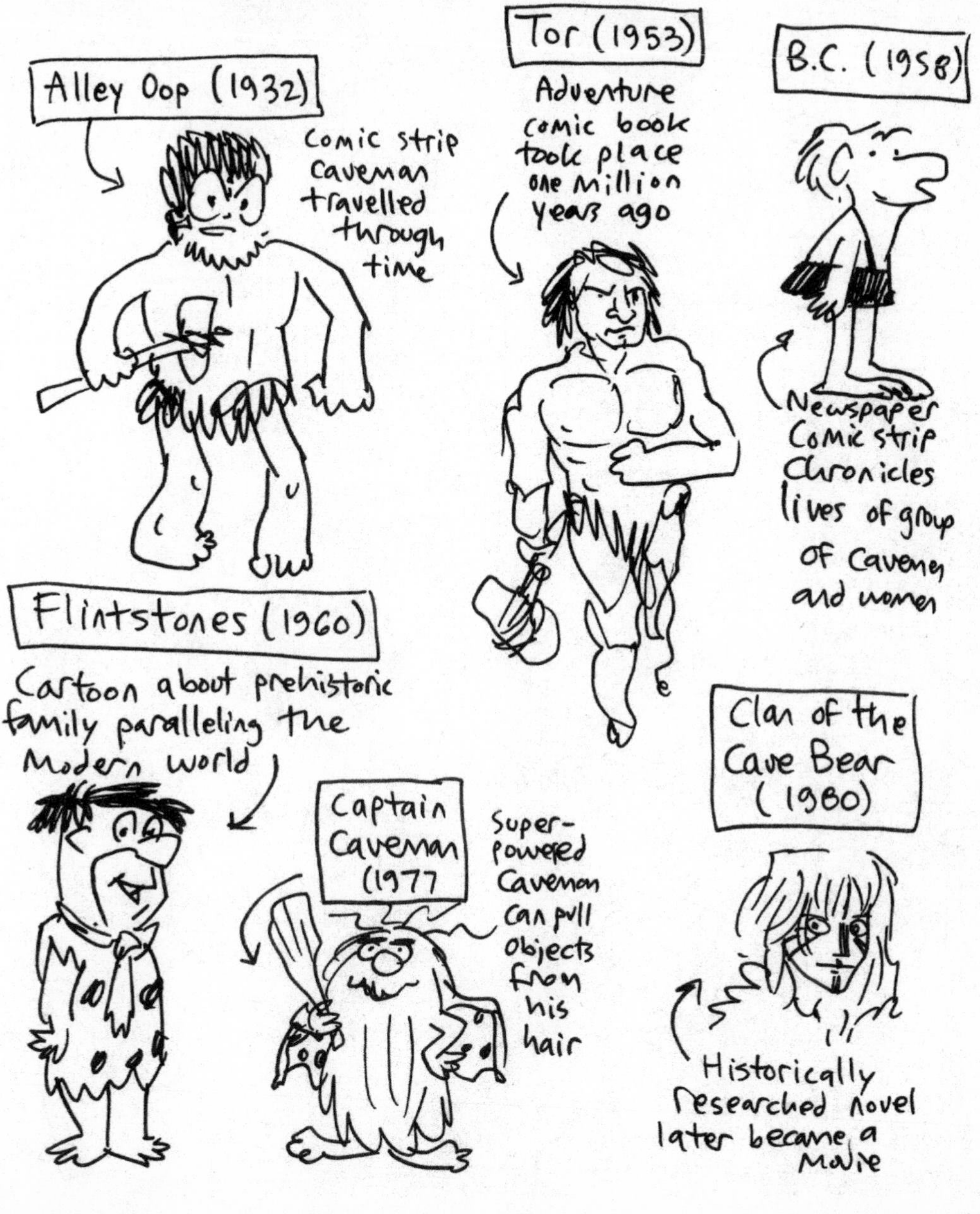

Alley Oop (1932)
Comic strip caveman travelled through time
Tor (1953)
Adventure comic book took place one Million years ago
B.C. (1958)
Newspaper Comic strip Chronicles lives of group of cavemen and women
Flintstones (1960)
Cartoon about prehistoric family paralleling the Modern world
Captain Caveman (1977
Super-powered Caveman can pull objects from his hair
Clan of the Cave Bear (1980)
Historically researched novel later became a Movie

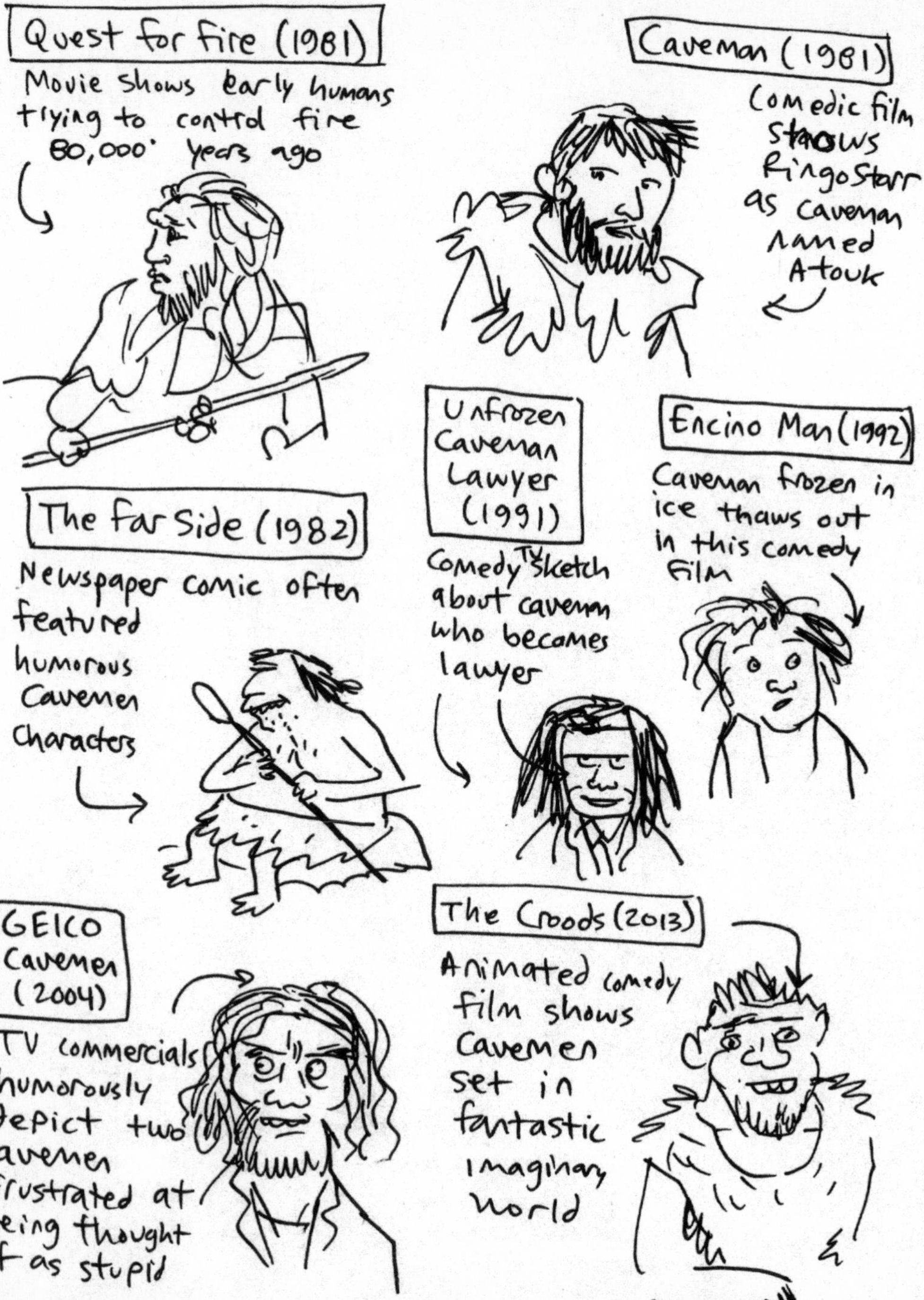
Quest for Fire (1981)
Movie shows early humans trying to control fire 80,000 years ago
Caveman (1981)
Comedic film stars Ringo Starr as caveman named Atouk
Unfrozen Caveman Lawyer (1991)
Comedy TV sketch about caveman who becomes lawyer
Encino Man (1992)
Caveman frozen in ice thaws out in this comedy film
The Far Side (1982)
Newspaper comic often featured humorous cavemen characters
GEICO Cavemen (2004)
TV commercials humorously depict two cavemen frustrated at being thought of as stupid
The Croods (2013)
Animated comedy film shows cavemen set in fantastic imaginary world

ART NOT FINAL

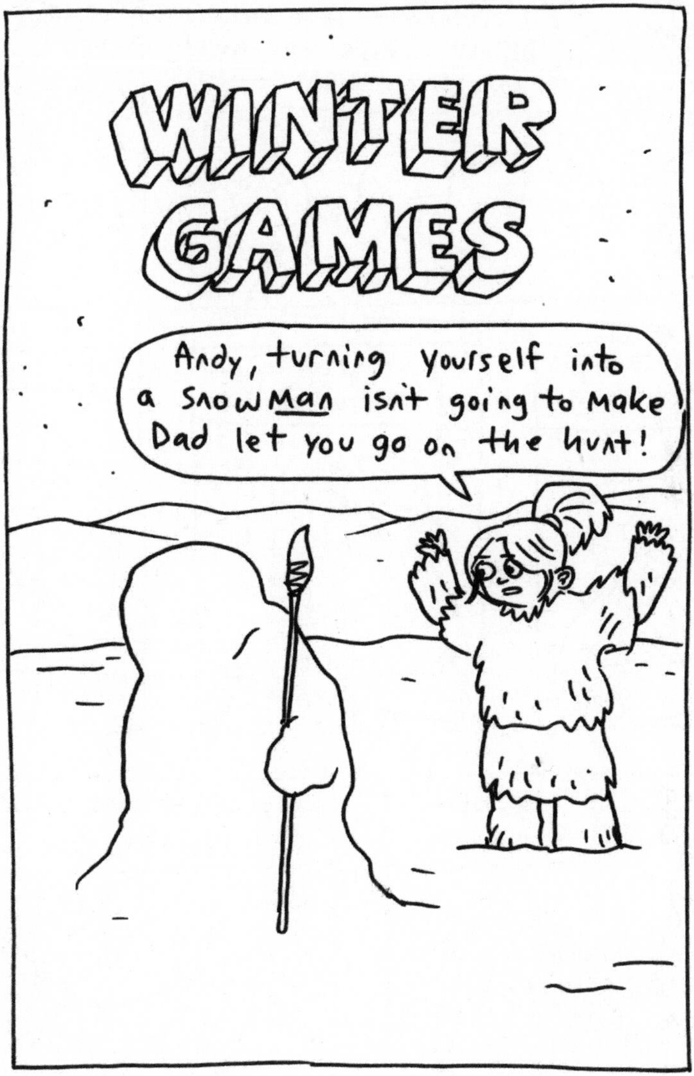
WINTER GAMES
Andy, turning yourself into a SNOWMAN isn't going to make Dad let you go on the hunt!

ART NOT FINAL

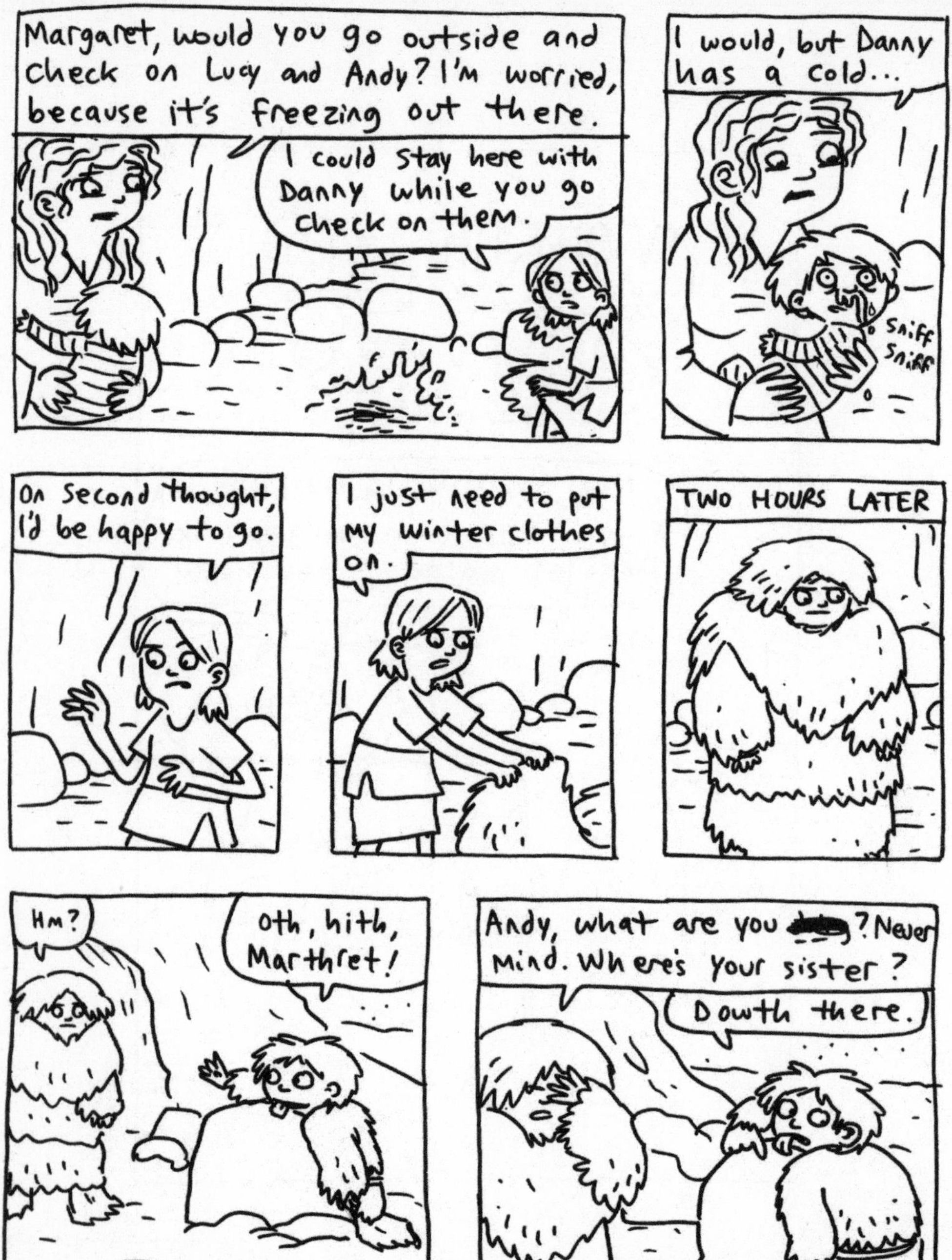

Margaret, would you go outside and check on Lucy and Andy? I'm worried, because it's freezing out there.
I could stay here with Danny while you go check on them.
I would, but Danny has a cold...
Sniff
Sniff
On second thought, I'd be happy to go.
I just need to put my winter clothes on.
TWO HOURS LATER
Hm?
Oth, hith, Marthret!
Andy, what are you [redacted]? Never mind. Where's your sister?
Dowth there.

Cath you help me? My thung ith thuck.

Are they okay?

By their standards, everything is perfectly normal.

Margaret is right. You _are_ strange.

Heh.

Winter continues in Lucy & Andy Book 2! Coming in 2017!

Jeffrey Brown is the author of numerous bestselling Star Wars books, including Darth Vader and Son and the middle grade Jedi Academy series. He is not as old as ancient fossils yet, but he does have 2.2% Neanderthal DNA. He lives in chicago with his wife, and sons, who are not actually allowed to draw on the walls. Most of the time.

www.jeffreybrowncomics.com
P.O. Box 120 Deerfield IL 60015-0120 USA

ART NOT FINAL